SECOND SHOT
Charlie Fox book six

Zoë Sharp

Murderati Ink [ZACE Ltd]

Murderati Ink [ZACE Ltd]
Registered UK Office:
Kent Cottage, Bridge Lane, Kendal, Cumbria LA9 7DD

First published in Great Britain 2007
Allison & Busby Ltd

This edition published 2013
Murderati Ink [ZACE Ltd]

ISBN-13: 978-1-909344-19-8

ISBN-10: 1-909344-19-2

*All characters and events in this novel, other than those clearly in the
public domain, are fictitious and any resemblance to actual persons,
living or dead, is purely coincidental.*

Typeset in 11/14pt Century Schoolbook

For Jane Hudson, cover designer extraordinaire
who has more talent than she knows that to do with ...

ONE

Take it from me, getting yourself shot hurts like hell. Not like absorbing a punch, or breaking a bone, but that full-blown, relentless, ripped-inside kind of pain. The kind where I prayed for oblivion and yet feared the darkness more than anything I'd ever known.

I'd taken one 9mm round through the fleshy part of my left thigh and another through the back of my right shoulder. The first shot was nasty, but it was a through-and-through, passing clean in and out of the muscle without apparently hitting anything vital. Yes, I was bleeding and it burned like a bastard. But under normal circumstances—like reasonably prompt medical assistance—it was not liable to be a life threatener.

The second shot was the one that worried me. The bullet had ploughed into my scapula, twelve grams of lead and copper travelling at roughly 280 metres a second. It had hit plenty hard enough to put me on the ground and deflected off to God knows where inside my body.

The whole of my torso was screaming. When I coughed I tasted blood in my mouth and knew that, whatever other damage it had done, the round had penetrated my lung. I had a vivid mental picture of it still progressing, maybe in a slow-motion tumble, contaminating whatever soft tissue it passed through, like a cancer.

The good news was that I was still conscious, my heart still pumping, my brain still functioning, more or less. But that didn't mean it wasn't still going to kill me, given time.

And, one way or another, time was not on my side.

Right now I was lying on my belly in the bottom of a snow-crusted shallow ditch, bleeding into the dirty trickle of icy water that had collected there, and trying to decide if I really was prepared to die here or not.

"I know you're out there!" shouted a distant voice in the trees further up the mountain. "I know you can hear me!"

I recognised the voice, but more than that I recognised the tone. Hatred and lust. Not a good combination.

Simone's voice. My principal. Seven days ago I'd been sent to New England with the express purpose of protecting her against possible threat. Now she was out there somewhere in the woods with a SIG semiautomatic, while I lay here incapable of protecting anyone, least of all myself.

What a difference a week makes.

I lay quite still. Not moving was the easy part. I felt horribly vulnerable in that position, but turning over didn't seem like a good plan. Even the thought of attempting it made me break out into a cold sweat.

'Cold' was the word. The temperature was four degrees below and the wet blood round the entry wounds in my shoulder blade and leg had already started to crystallise on my clothing. My face was turned to the side so one cheek was scorched by the freezing earth and the other by the freezing air. All I could smell was blood and pine needles and ice. I think I might have been crying.

But, I decided sluggishly, cold was good. It would slow my system down, delay my bleed-out—right up to the point where hypothermia got me. I tried not to shiver. Shivering hurt. I tried not to breathe too deeply. That hurt, too.

The pain was extraordinary. A biting, seething, swirling mass of it that sheathed my entire body but had pooled in my chest. My leg was pulsing like I was being rhythmically and repeatedly stabbed by a red-hot blade. I didn't seem able to feel my right arm at all.

A scatter of small stones cascaded down the side of the ditch and rolled towards my face. I opened one eye and watched them approaching in the light from a clear hunter's moon reflected on the stark ground.

There was a shadow above me, I realised. Someone was standing a little way up from the ditch and staring down at me sprawled below them. They were too far back among the trees for me to see a face, but instinct told me it wasn't Simone. This observer was too quiet and too controlled. *Friend or foe?*

Better to assume foe.

I closed my eye again and played dead. It wasn't a stretch.

In the near distance, higher up the slope, I could hear Simone crashing through the trees, sobbing out little grunting cries as the thin branches whipped back at her. It was like listening to an animal that had been frightened beyond reason and would kill anything within reach just through that fear. And she was heading my way.

I risked another look. The shadow had gone, making the light over me seem brighter now. Or maybe that was just my own shifting perception. Even the pain had receded slightly, dropping back to a leaden throb. But I was achingly aware of every sodden breath, of the urge to just let go of it all and sleep. I fought it with everything I'd got left. Something told me that if I succumbed to this bone-numbing weariness, the game was going to be over.

I'm sorry.

I formed the apology soundlessly, quickly, like I needed to go through this final absolution while I still had the chance. I pictured my parents and wondered if they'd be as disappointed by my death as they had been by my life.

And Sean, who had once *been* my life and had become so again. Sean, who'd sent me out here not expecting me to be careless enough to die on the job. Suddenly I wished I'd told him that I loved him on the day I'd left.

The light gleamed stronger all the time and had begun to flicker. It took a moment for me to realise it wasn't my vision starting to fail, but flashlights being carried up the icy incline at a jerky run. There were voices, too. Loud, and so harsh I failed to make out the words.

A thumping rumble swooped down low over the tips of the trees, making the ground quiver under me, spinning up the loose powder snow. The beam of a high-watt searchlight stabbed downwards, intense and blinding. I knew I should make some signal, offer some sign of life, but I couldn't summon the energy.

"Charlie!"

Close now.

Simone was gasping for air and weeping like her heart was broken. I heard her before I saw her, lunging across the final few metres that separated us, and offered a silent curse that the helicopter should have drawn her to me in this way. I tried to form words but could barely whisper.

My gaze swivelled upwards as she staggered over the rim of the ditch, bleeding from a dozen scratches, wild-eyed, her hair a disordered mass around her face. Her left arm was rigidly outstretched. The barrel of the gun seemed to be pointing nowhere but towards me.

She lurched to a stop. I looked into her eyes and saw the pure intensity of her grief and anger and shock. Any one of those emotions in such quantity and weight would have been good enough to kill for. A mix of all three made it a certainty.

She never got the chance.

In the instant before Simone could act, the shots slammed into her. I didn't hear the shouted warning from the police officers who fired them. My senses were winding down by this time, fading to black.

I vaguely remember seeing her fall, sliding down to come to a crumpled rest only a metre or so away from me. The gun dropped and landed between us, like an offering.

Simone's face was turned towards mine so that our eyes met and held as her blood pulsed out to mingle with my own in the bottom of the ditch. The police were using hollowpoint Hydra-Shok rounds and she'd taken four to the

4

neck and upper body. She never stood a chance. I watched her die feeling only a kind of petty determination not to be the one who gave in first.

And I knew then that I'd just broken the cardinal rule of close protection work—never outlive your principal.

But it was a close-run thing.

TWO

"A bodyguard?" Simone Kerse said blankly to the man sitting next to me. "Rupert, have you gone totally crazy? I absolutely do *not* need a bodyguard." She raked me with a fierce gaze. "Of any description."

My first meeting with Simone, just ten days before I was shot, over a wickedly expensive lunch at a very upmarket restaurant just off Grosvenor Square in the embassy district of London. Not exactly an auspicious start.

Simone had a very slight American accent, more an inflection than anything stronger. She was also young and strikingly good-looking, and nothing at all like my preconception of an engineer.

Just as, it seemed, I was nothing like her preconception of a bodyguard.

Rupert Harrington, on the other hand, could only have been a banker. In his early fifties, tall and thin and bespectacled, he had very little hair and a permanently anxious expression. It crossed my mind after meeting him for the first time that those two facts could easily have been connected.

"I can assure you, my dear," he said to Simone now, with a touch of asperity, "that a number of the bank's clients have had cause to require the services of Mr Meyer's people and he comes with the highest recommendations. And even you must admit that this has all gone rather beyond a joke, hm?"

He sat back in his chair, careful not to spoil the impeccable line of his conservative dark blue pinstripe suit, and flicked a pained glance in my boss's direction as if to say, *Help me out here, would you?*

"I agree," Sean Meyer said obligingly, his voice bland but with an almost imperceptible underlying thread of amusement. Not at the situation but at the banker's discomfort because of it. "The threats have been escalating. If you won't go to the police, you're going to have to take your own measures."

He leaned forwards slightly, resting his forearms on the starched white tablecloth and looking directly into Simone's eyes. There was something utterly compelling about Sean when he pinned you down with that dark gaze, and Simone was no more immune than anyone else.

"I'm not suggesting we surround you with a bunch of heavies," he went on, "but if you won't accept a full team then you should at least consider the kind of discreet, low-profile security we can offer. That's why I brought Charlie along for you to meet."

He nodded in my direction as he spoke, and both Simone and Harrington swung sceptical eyes towards me.

In between them, although somewhat closer to tabletop height, another pair of eyes regarded me unwaveringly. And, I don't mind admitting, that was the gaze I found the most unnerving.

Simone's young daughter, Ella, sat on a booster cushion alongside her mother and carefully speared a dessert fork into the pieces of yellow smoked haddock that had been cut up into child-friendly pieces on her plate. It wasn't the kind of food I would have expected a four-year-old to enjoy, but she was shovelling it in with apparent enthusiasm and chewing largely with her mouth open. I tried not to watch.

Simone's gaze drifted to her daughter and lingered there for a moment with no apparent sign of displeasure. I suppose, if you were maternally minded, Ella was the sort of child who would induce instant broodiness. She was petite, with a miniature version of her mother's dark ringletted curls framing a heart-shaped face. Couple that to big violet-coloured eyes and she had spoiled little brat written all over her. I wasn't too disappointed that her mother seemed so set against my being assigned to protect the pair of them.

Suddenly, Simone let out an annoyed breath through her nose, as though gathering her internal resources.

"OK, so Matt's having a hard time accepting our break-up—and lately I suppose he has gotten to be something of a pain in the butt," she allowed, her eyes still fixed on Ella. She smiled at the little girl, wiped a rogue piece of fish from her chin, and turned away with clear reluctance. Her focus landed squarely on me. "But that doesn't mean I need some kind of nanny."

Much as I didn't particularly want the job, I thought the nanny gibe was a bit below the belt. I'd made an effort to look smart and businesslike for this meeting. Dark brown trouser suit, cream blouse. Under protest, I'd even gunked on some lipstick.

Sean was wearing a charcoal grey made-to-measure that subtly disguised the height and the breadth of him but, to my eyes, did little to hide the deadly grace that was an innate part of his make-up.

I'd caught a glimpse of our reflections in the mirror above the bar when we'd arrived at the restaurant and I reckoned, to the casual observer at least, we probably looked like accountants. That was certainly the effect we'd been aiming for.

Harrington opened his mouth to protest at his client's comments, but before he could speak Sean cut in again. "As I understand it, you've had constant phone calls and you've been forced to change your mobile number—twice," he said calmly. "Your ex-boyfriend has been hanging around outside both your home and your daughter's nursery school. You've had notes left on your car. Unwanted deliveries. I think you need a little more than some kind of nanny, don't you?"

Simone switched her attention from me back to Sean. In contrast to the rest of us, she was wearing battleship grey cargo trousers and a dark red chenille sweater with sleeves that came down almost to her fingertips. Her curly dark hair was pulled loosely back into a ponytail. Harrington had told us she was twenty-eight, a year older than I was. She looked about eighteen.

"You make it sound so much worse than it is, Mr Meyer," she said, folding her arms defensively. "Notes on my car? OK, they're love letters. Unwanted deliveries? Sure, bouquets of flowers. Matt and I were together five years, for heaven's sake! We share a child." She swallowed, lowered her voice. "You're making him out to be some kind of stalker."

"Isn't he?" Sean asked, head tilted slightly on one side. His voice had taken on the same cool note and his face the same impassive watchfulness that had always unnerved me so badly, back when he had been one of my army training instructors, and had always seen entirely too much.

Simone flushed and avoided his gaze. Instead, she spoke to Harrington directly. "I'll talk to Matt again," she said, her tone placatory now. "He'll see sense eventually." She smiled at the banker with a lot more affection than she'd shown to either Sean or me. "I'm sorry you felt you had to take such drastic action on my behalf, Rupert, but there wasn't any need, really."

Harrington looked about to protest further, but he correctly read the stubborn expression on Simone's face and raised both palms in an admission of defeat.

"All right, my dear," he said, rueful. "If you're quite sure."

"Yes," Simone said firmly. "I am."

"Mummy, I need to go wee-wee," Ella piped up in a loud whisper. The smartly dressed elderly couple at the next table clearly subscribed to the unseen-and-unheard school of child raising. They were too British to actually turn around and glare, but I saw their outraged spines stiffen nevertheless.

If Simone noticed their disapproval, she ignored it and smiled at her daughter. "OK, sweetie," she said, sliding her own chair back so she could lift Ella down and take her by the hand as she got to her feet. "If you'll excuse us?"

"Of course," Harrington said, good manners compelling him to stand also.

Sean had already risen, I noted, and for a second I was struck by the air of urbane sophistication he presented. This from a man who had left behind his roots on a run-down housing estate in a small northern city, but who still knew how to slide right back into that rough-diamond skin when the occasion demanded. The banker would not recognise Sean on his home ground.

My eyes followed mother and child as they weaved their way between the busy tables. Although Simone was not my principal—and at that stage I didn't expect she would become so—watching people was beginning to become a habit, all part of the career I'd chosen. Or maybe the job had ultimately chosen me. I was never too sure about that.

Sean didn't need to learn to watch anyone. For him it was an instinct ingrained deep as an old tattoo, indelible and permanent. He was just too driven, too focused, to ever let himself begin to blur.

"I'm awfully sorry about this," Harrington said as the men sat down again and rearranged their napkins across their knees. "She just won't listen to reason and, quite frankly, her refusal to admit there might be any kind of danger, either to herself or to little Ella, terrifies us, as I'm sure you can appreciate."

"How much did she win?" Sean asked, reaching for his glass of Perrier.

"Thirteen million, four hundred thousand, and change," the banker said with the casual tone of someone used to working with those kind of figures on a daily basis, but I still heard the trace of a sneer in his voice as he added, "It was, if I understand it correctly, what they term a double rollover."

"Money's still money," Sean said. "Just because her ancestors didn't steal it doesn't make her any less rich."

Harrington had the grace to colour. "Oh, quite so, old chap," he murmured. "But Simone is having some difficulty adjusting to the fact that, from the day she bought that winning ticket, her life was never going to be quite the same again. Do you know, she arrived at our office this morning having actually come into town, with the child, on the Tube? Didn't want to have to try to park in the middle of London, she said." He shook his head, as though Simone had suggested walking naked through Trafalgar Square.

"I told her she should have hired a car and driver to take her door-to-door and she looked absolutely baffled," the banker went on. "It simply doesn't cross her mind that she can afford to do these things. Nor does it occur to her that, by *not* doing them, she's putting both herself and her daughter at risk from every crackpot and kidnapper out there—quite apart from the situation with her former, er, boyfriend."

"It does, as you so rightly point out, make them a prime target—Ella especially," Sean agreed. "How serious a threat do *you* consider her ex?"

"Well, if you'd asked me that a few weeks ago, I would have said he was a minor irritation, but now ..." The banker broke off with an eloquent shrug. "One of the first things Simone did with her money was hire various private investigation agencies to try and trace her estranged father. One of them now believes they have a promising lead, and ever since that report came in, this Matt chap just seems to have become completely unreasonable." Harrington paused, frowning. "Perhaps he believes a reunion between Simone and her father will spoil his own chances of a reconciliation with her," he added with an almost imperceptible curl of his lip. "She'd have to be quite mad to take him back, of course."

11

"What's the story with Simone's father?" I asked.

Harrington's head came up in surprise. Not at the question, but that I'd been the one who'd put it. Even on such short acquaintance, I'd realised that Harrington didn't speak to anyone he considered at servant level unless he had to, and even then he avoided eye contact. With that in mind I'd let Sean do most of the talking so far. From the expression on the banker's face, he clearly hadn't expected me to wade in at this late stage. His eyes swivelled warily in my direction.

Sean flashed me a lazy smile, one that would have made my knees buckle if I hadn't already been sitting down, and raised an eyebrow to Harrington, as if to repeat the question.

Harrington coughed. "Naturally, one doesn't wish to be indiscreet, but ... well, as I understand it, Simone's mother was an American, who came over here and married an Englishman, Greg Lucas—an army chap, so I understand. They divorced when Simone was not much more than a baby and mother and child went back to the States— Chicago, I believe it was—but her father rather dropped off the map, as it were."

He broke off as the wine waiter glided up to the table and smoothly topped up his glass, finishing the bottle. Harrington ignored him and I wondered briefly what kind of pivotal decisions were made in the afternoons in the world of high finance after boozy lunches just like this one.

"I assume Kerse is Simone's mother's name?" I said when the waiter had departed.

Harrington nodded. "She went back to it after the divorce. Anyway, Simone's mother died a few years ago. There were no siblings, her grandparents on both sides are long gone, and Simone herself is currently expending considerable effort—not to mention her now not insubstantial resources—on attempting to locate this Lucas chap." He stopped to take a sip of his wine.

"Unsuccessfully?"

"Hm." Harrington dabbed fastidiously at his mouth with his napkin. "So far, but then, as I mentioned, a couple of weeks ago one of the firms she's using in Boston thought they'd made some progress and she's been talking about going over there ever since."

"Boston," I repeated blankly, glancing at Sean and finding no reassurance there. "As in Massachusetts, not Lincolnshire?"

Harrington frowned. "Naturally," he said with a flicker of irritation. "The rumour was that Simone's father had followed his ex-wife to the USA, so of course that's where she started looking." He paused, eyes darting from one of us to the other and registering the sudden undercurrents. "Um, one knows America is supposed to be a civilised country and all that, but bearing in mind Simone's somewhat unique circumstances, and given the trouble with her ex, we'd be happier if she had some kind of security consultant along with her when she goes over there." He nodded to Sean but didn't shift his gaze away from me. "Mr Meyer suggested you'd be just the lady for the job, as it were," he finished with a hearty cheerfulness that didn't quite succeed in masking his natural aversion to female equality in the workplace.

Sean had no such prejudices. During the seven months that had passed since I'd started working full-time for his exclusive close protection agency, he'd sent me on jobs all over Europe, South Africa, Asia, and the Middle East, and I hadn't turned a hair.

Things didn't always go smoothly, of course, and sometimes that had nothing to do with dangers from outside sources.

I'd just returned from a month in Prague as part of a four-man detail. The otherwise all-male team had started out trying to treat me as a cross between their own personal maid and private secretary. Three days in, one of them had made what turned out to be, for him, a very unfortunate remark about the sexual proclivities of the

Women's Royal Army Corps, of which I'd once been a member, and my temper had finally got the better of me. Still, they reckoned he should be out of his cast inside six weeks. His colleagues—and his forewarned replacement— had treated me with the utmost respect after that, and the job went off without further unpleasantness.

I'd proved, or so I'd thought, that I was capable of doing the job. It was just the question of where that was still causing me some qualms.

America.

There was no logic to it, but when I glanced at Sean I felt a dull anxiety almost akin to panic. *I'm not ready to go back.*

His face carried no expression beyond a cold determination I barely recognised. *If not now, then when?*

"Um, is there some problem?" Harrington finished, as the atmosphere finally negotiated its way past the Merlot that had formed a constituent part of his lunch. "If it's a question of timing, this trip probably wouldn't be for a month or so, if then. The investigation is still in its early stages at the moment, from what one can gather. There would be no point in Simone going out there until they've actually found the man, or at least until they have more information for her, would there?"

"It's not that." I took a deep breath. "It's just—"

"I think you should check on Simone and Ella, Charlie— make sure they're OK," Sean said. He spoke quietly, calmly, but the demand for utter obedience came across loud and clear in the very softness of his voice, nevertheless. I spiked him with a short vicious glare, tempted to outright mutiny. I told myself the only reason I didn't was because such behaviour would be totally unprofessional in front of a client. Part of me even believed that as a viable excuse.

"Of course," I murmured demurely, pushing my chair back and dumping my napkin onto the tabletop. *Later, Sean* ... "If you'll excuse me?"

14

Harrington didn't treat me to the full rise, just lifted himself partly out of his seat. I saw his eyes flicker with curbed curiosity between the two of us, but he didn't ask questions. Or not until I was out of earshot, at least.

I turned my back and stalked through the restaurant away from them, following much the same path between the tables that Simone had taken, trying not to let my anger show as badly on the outside as I felt it raging under the surface.

America.

Sean *knew* how I felt aboutworking there again. We'd practically been living together for six months, so how could he not?

The last time I'd been across the Atlantic was to Florida during the previous March. My first official assignment for Sean, to a holiday destination that had turned out to be anything but.

What should have been a simple baby-sitting job had escalated into a disaster of major proportions. I'd ended up on the run with my teenage charge and, although I'd got through it, the cost had been a high one on every level. I was still coming to terms with what had happened there. It had taken me several months afterwards to make the decision that close protection was where my future career lay.

Since then, I'd never actually asked Sean *not* to send me to the States, and he'd never actually asked me to go back—before today. I tried not to think of the people who'd died in Florida as a result of the unfolding catastrophe I'd found myself caught up in. I'd been personally responsible for three deaths—'personally' being the operative word.

Small wonder, then, that I was in no hurry to return.

Now, I pushed open the door to the ladies' room, where a rake of low-voltage spotlights picked out the sparkle and flash in the black marble and granite that had been used to lavishly line the place.

Simone was leaning against the door jamb of one of the cubicles, holding the door itself closed with one hand on the top of it. She had her back to the exit, but the wall opposite had a row of mirrors above the free-standing washbasins.

Our eyes met in reflection and she smiled briefly before her eyes slid away, as though I hadn't made enough of an impression to hold her attention for any longer.

I didn't want to make it obvious that I'd only come in to keep an eye on her, but I didn't want to go into a cubicle, either, just in case she left before I came out. Instead, I walked past her to the basins, which were frosted green glass bowls with taps that you had to wave at in order to get any water out of them. I wet my hands, more to give me something to do with them rather than through any dire need. The soap smelt of bergamot, which was nice if you liked to carry out your ablutions in Earl Grey tea.

"Are you OK in there, sweetie?" Simone called.

A big sigh emanated from inside the cubicle. "Ye-es, Mummy," came Ella's voice, slightly singsong, humouring her.

I grinned into the mirror at the tone. Simone let her breath out fast down her nose and rolled her eyes, but a sneaky little smile made a bid for freedom across the corners of her lips. Just for a moment we shared the connection before the smile ran its course and faded away. I finished washing my hands and shook off the excess water into the bowl.

As I moved across to the stack of individual hand towels, Simone said, almost abruptly, "Look, I'm sorry if I was rude out there. Rupert kind of sprang this whole thing on me and I don't like surprises."

I shrugged. "Part of my job," I said mildly, "would be to make sure you didn't get any."

She pulled a face, considering, then said, "You don't look like a bodyguard."

Not the first time I'd heard comments like that. I glanced into the mirror one last time and saw an ordinary face—to me, nothing special—surrounded by a short bob of red-blonde hair. Neat, businesslike. Together with the suit, the surface look said quiet, competent, maybe even a little wary, but the last thing I'd been aiming for was to stand out in a crowd.

I dropped the used towel into the laundry bin provided and returned Simone's cool appraisal, probably still too unsettled to be as diplomatic as I might otherwise have been. "And you don't look like a millionairess."

She froze, her eyes widening. But just when I'd braced myself for an outburst, she smiled, a genuine show of amusement.

"Oh, I'm sorry, Charlie, but everybody's been acting so timid around me lately," she said with a bubble of laughter rising through her voice. "They all want to tell me how to live my life, but you're a breath of fresh air after all these stuffed shirts."

If that's how you think of Sean, lady, then you're not looking nearly deep enough …

"I'm sure they only have your best interests at heart," I said neutrally.

She gave a snort of derision. "Oh, sure," she said, cynicism making her face suddenly hard. "Either that or *their* best interest *rates*—one or the other. Everybody seems to want a piece of me."

"Including Matt."

She shot me a quick warning glance, then shrugged. "Matt's trouble was that he's a man," she said, abrupt. "He didn't always think with his head—if you know what I mean." Her eyes slid to the closed cubicle door, but her free hand gestured expressively to the front of her cargo trousers.

"Even after you won the money?"

Simone's smile twisted. "No, he lucked out there," she said with a hint of bitter sadness. "I knew he was fooling around with some of the girls at the place he works. Oh, he always denied it, but sometimes you just know, don't you?

17

Then one night I caught him coming in late with some lame excuse and I-I just totally lost my temper with him. I just went postal," she admitted, flushing. "He didn't say anything, which was as bad as an outright admission, right? He just went upstairs, packed a bag of his stuff, and walked out. I thought he'd come back the next day, but he didn't—how's that for guilty conscience? And then a week later my numbers came up and now everything's a whole lot more complicated."

There was something in her face. I paused, tilted my head on one side in a way I knew I'd picked up from Sean. "You still love him," I said, that part of it a statement. "So why not take him back—forgive and forget?"

She gave a restless twitch. "It's not that simple anymore, is it? Why did he wait until after he found out about my win before he came back? How can I ever be sure …?"

"That he came back for you or for the money," I finished for her.

Simone nodded unhappily. "And as for the way he's behaving over trying to stop me looking for my dad, well, that's just unbalanced," she said in a low voice, breaking off and shaking her head. She gave a slow weary smile. "Sometimes I wish I'd never bought that goddamn ticket."

"Language, Mummy," Ella's voice drifted over the cubicle door, making both of us start. Simone coloured again, as though she'd forgotten her daughter's eavesdropping presence.

"Four going on forty," Simone muttered, and, louder: "Sorry, sweetie."

"*That's* all right, Mummy," Ella said in a patient tone that suggested she knew adults couldn't really be held responsible for their actions. "I'm all finished," she added.

Simone let go of the top of the door and pushed it open for Ella to come out. She'd tucked most of the back of her skirt into her tights, but apart from that she seemed to have managed to re-dress herself just fine. I waited until

18

Simone had helped her daughter to wash and dry her hands, then held the door for them.

It was for that reason I was behind the pair as they made their way back to our table. Harrington and Sean were still deep in conversation, but I saw Sean's head lift as soon as we appeared in his line of sight. Sean's eyes met mine for a moment, then slid across my left shoulder and narrowed.

I saw him tense instantly, start to come out of his seat. Then I was twisting to the side, keeping my knees soft as I started to turn. I had no idea at that point what I was going to see.

A young, bearded man with a gaunt, intense face, wearing jeans and a baggy military-style jacket, had entered the restaurant and stepped into view only a couple of metres behind us. With surprising agility he'd shrugged away the hand of the maître d' who had tried to detain him, and his whole being was now focused on Simone and the child. His jacket was open and he had his right hand inside it, holding something concealed tight against his body.

Behind me, I sensed Sean was already going for the principals. There was no further need for communication between us. I knew instinctively that he'd selected his role based purely on cold logistics, leaving the threat for me because I was nearer, because it made more sense.

I saw the man's arm flex as he began to withdraw his hand and I took a fast stride sideways, moving to intercept. I grabbed his right forearm just below his elbow and dug my left thumb hard into one of the main pressure points located there.

With my right hand I reached for his throat, using my own forward momentum to force him over backwards with that hold, hooking my leg around his calf to unbalance him and take him down. At the last moment I jerked my hand up slightly, enough to protect his head but not enough to stop him winding himself.

19

He landed with a sharp explosive whump of sound, the air gushing out of his lungs. His breath in my face smelt of peppermint. His right hand had drooped where I'd dead-armed him, letting whatever it was he'd been hiding slip to the floor.

I took a fraction of a second to scan it, just in case. It was a pink soft toy, a rabbit with long silky ears. I found myself kneeling partly on the toy animal's body as the man who'd been carrying it struggled against my restraint.

A pink rabbit?

Suddenly, Ella's voice was a piercing wail in my ear, accompanied by the stab of two tiny fists beating at my upper arm. Damn, she had a healthy punch for a four-year-old.

"Don't you hurt my daddy!"

Daddy?

My grip on the man's throat slackened just a fraction and he didn't need a second invitation. In a flash he had levered his body half off the floor, shoving me backwards. I fought for balance and lunged for him again, seizing his jacket at the shoulder. He gave a kind of jerking twitch, as though to jettison the coat. I yanked the back of his collar down and twisted a great handful to form makeshift handcuffs around his lower arms. Then I piled onto his back, forcing him face-first into the carpet.

When I looked up I found the entire restaurant had frozen and were staring down at us. Harrington was on his feet, gaping at the tableau we presented in open-mouthed horror.

Sean had his body between where I had the man pinned and Simone, his eyes scouring the rest of the crowd in case this was a diversion rather than the main event.

Simone had swept a loudly weeping Ella up into her arms. She was cradling the little girl on her hip and glaring ferociously at the man on the floor. His head was turned towards her, his nose mashed into the carpet by the pressure of my knee on the back of his neck. That might have been what had brought the tears to his eyes, or it might not.

"Simone, baby, please listen to me," he managed in a muffled voice, scratchy with stress. "Don't go to America. Don't take Ella away from me. Please—"

"For God's sake, Matt!" Simone snapped, and any trace of affection she'd shown for her ex when she'd spoken of him in the ladies' room only a few minutes before had vanished, flattened out by anger and embarrassment. She leaned down towards him. "Who the hell are you to tell me what I can and can't do?"

"Baby, please, don't go. You don't need him. I love you. I'll do anything to make it up to you. Please." He was almost gabbling, his voice wavering between a whine and a plea. "I'm begging here."

"Well save your goddamn breath," Simone told him in a savage whisper, and this time Ella didn't bother to admonish her mother for swearing. "It's nothing to do with you what I choose to do, or where I choose to go, or who I choose to see anymore. Get used to it!"

She straightened, juggling a tear-streaked Ella to the other hip, and swept her eyes over Harrington's shocked and immobile figure. He was still standing by the table, with his napkin still clutched in his hand. Simone's defiant gaze met mine over the top of Matt's tethered body.

"I think I just changed my mind about needing a bodyguard, Charlie," she said, her voice tired and bitter to the bone. "You're hired."

THREE

By the time we got back to where Sean had parked one of his company Mitsubishi Shoguns, I knew I was in trouble. Even for Sean, he was much too quiet.

Sean Meyer was quiet on many different planes. His hands and body were always quiet unless there was something to engage them. It made his actions all the more intense.

Even back when he'd been one of the most feared sergeants on the Special Forces training course I'd abortively attempted in the army, he'd never had to shout and bawl in order to instil a dread respect in his trainees. The quieter he was, the more scared of him we'd all become. The clever ones, at least.

And now, most people wouldn't have spotted there was anything wrong. He'd been nothing but coolly professional while we'd ejected a still-protesting Matt from the restaurant and evacuated Simone and Ella to the safety of Harrington's office at the bank, where security was tight as a matter of course. For speed we'd used Harrington's waiting car and driver rather than retrieving our own vehicle, and I'd half-expected Sean to order me to stay with them while he went to fetch it. Instead, he ordered me along, and that was my first inkling that something was seriously awry.

He strode along the icy pavements from the bank to the car park with an easy poise, plaiting his way smoothly between the other pedestrians, who were making their hurried assaults on the last remnants of the January sales. He moved without ever missing a step, but under the surface I could sense something simmering. It was there in the slight angle of his head, the way his arms swung fractionally tense from his shoulders.

I held out, waiting for him to make the first move, until we'd actually reached the multi-storey parking structure and were on the right level, almost at the car. Then I sighed and stopped walking.

"OK, Sean," I said, short. "Spit it out. Don't give me this silent treatment."

He deliberately kept moving so there were half a dozen paces between us before he stopped and turned. For a few moments he just stood there, staring at me, hands loose by his sides, his face that of a stranger.

A sullen, sneaky wind whipped into the open concrete building, causing his long overcoat to flap lazily round his legs like that of a western gunslinger. It was only three in the afternoon but already the sky was darkening and the sodium lights strung across the concrete ceiling lit us both with an unearthly orange glow. The whole place smelt of diesel and burnt clutches.

Just when I thought he wasn't going to speak at all, when an unnamed fear had reached into my chest and squeezed my heart tight shut with it, he said:

"You hesitated."

It was said flat, without inflection, but I heard the accusation as an underlying harmonic, even so.

"I took him down," I said, defensive. "And kept him there. What more do you want?"

"It was messy. He nearly got away from you, and he wasn't even a professional."

I felt my exasperation rise, partly at the harsh criticism and partly annoyance that I knew he was right. "Don't you think you're being overly critical? OK, so you feel I made a mistake. But I contained it—nobody else noticed. And come on, Sean—he was the kid's *father,* for heaven's sake!"

Sean cocked his head from one side to the other, slowly, like he was shifting the weight of his thoughts. "So?" he said coolly. "What difference does that make?"

What I'd heard of his own father, I recalled belatedly, sketched the man as a drunken bully, both to his wife and to his children. When Sean spoke, rarely, of his father's premature death in a largely self-induced car accident, it was with a kind of quiet resentment. It had taken me quite a while to realise that was probably because Sean had harboured a secret ambition to kill the man himself.

I sighed. "In this case, it makes all the difference. Simone had just got through telling me how she still loves the guy. If she could be sure he was after her for herself and not just her money, she'd probably take him back in a heartbeat."

"That's only a small part of the story, seen from her perspective." Sean threw me a sceptical glance. "Quite apart from the fact that you gleaned all this from what—a two-minute conversation in the ladies' room?" he said mildly. "Did she have time to show you a photograph while she was about it?"

I knew where this was going but it was like playing chess with a grand master. Defeat was coming, but I didn't begin to have the skill to fend off the inevitable.

"No," I said, and felt my pawns scatter as my knights fell and my queen faltered.

He nodded briefly and went in for the kill. "So how did you know that the guy who came into the restaurant was Matt?" he said. *Check.* "He could have been any psycho stalker you care to name. Just because you've only been told about one threat doesn't mean there won't be others. You should know that, Charlie. You of all people."

His voice was gentle and he hadn't moved, but that very stillness seethed.

"Ella called him Daddy," I said between my teeth, in a last-ditch castling to regroup. "He was carrying a pink rabbit."

24

"You didn't know that until after he'd made his move—and you'd made yours," Sean countered. He took a step towards me, then another. It took conscious effort not to retreat. "You had him under control and you let yourself be distracted. The fact that he was Ella's father shouldn't have made a blind bit of difference. Children are murdered by their fathers and women are murdered by their spouses every day."

Checkmate.

Exasperation curled into anger like smoke into fire.

"So I made a judgement call," I bit out.

"Really? Is that what you think it was?" He paused. "It was an emotional call, certainly."

I felt my chin come up, almost bobbing to the surface. There may as well have been a red flag attached to it for the signals it sent to him. I snapped, "Of course, and that's a failing."

"In this job, yes," he said, closing his eyes in a slow blink, like he was gathering strength. "Carry on making decisions like that in the field, and I can't use you."

My mouth dried. I swallowed in reflex and tried not to make it obvious that's what it was. But I saw him note my body's automatic reaction with cold hard eyes, and something flickered in his face. *Disappointment?*

"I can do the job," I said, keeping my voice even only with willpower. "Haven't I proved that to you already?"

He paused again, just fractionally, then inclined his head in slight acquiescence. Just when I thought he'd given ground, he said, in a voice I wasn't sure I recognised, "Prove it to me again."

My eyebrows arched in surprise. "What? *Now?*"

He nodded, more fully this time. "Here and now."

I glanced around me, took in the dirty, oil-blotched concrete floor, the rows of parked cars. Both of us had shifted our stance, I realised. Sean into offence, me into defence. My elbows were bent and my hands had come up slightly, but I didn't remember raising them.

25

We both tensed as a salt-splashed BMW blipped up the ramp from the lower parking floor, then slowed as it drew level. The driver was a middle-aged woman with aggressively coiffured hair who stared at the pair of us as she crawled past. Not because she had hostile intent or was concerned for my safety, but more likely because she thought there might be a chance we were about to vacate a valuable parking space.

When she was just past us, she braked, the rear lights flaring, and I saw her head angle towards the interior mirror. She must have realised, from our lack of movement, that we were having a stand-off of some kind, that the situation was far from normal. *But, would she intervene on my behalf?*

After only a moment, the car's brake lights snapped off again and the car began to edge forwards, then quickened. *No, she wouldn't.*

My eyes went back to Sean. His body was giving off threat cues in waves, like heat. I could see them rippling outwards from his centre.

"Sean, come on—"

"What?" he threw at me. "Do you want me to make things easy for you, is that it?"

And that's when I saw the knife in his left hand.

In truth, I only saw it because he let me. Because he meant for me to do so. He was holding it concealed, with the blade slanted upwards so it was hidden by the sleeve of his coat. The hilt pointed downwards and as he spoke he'd flexed his fingers slightly to allow it to drop just into view between his forefinger and thumb. He must have palmed it just as he'd turned towards me.

Christ.

I stared at him and the hurt and the surprise must have been clearly visible on my face. *How long have you been planning this?*

I didn't get an answer, vocal or otherwise. As we stood facing each other I was aware of the adrenaline now punching through my system, constricting my breathing and locking my muscles as it tried to override sense and training in a stampede of panic.

A knife. Oh, it would have to be a knife, wouldn't it, Sean?

I swallowed again, shrugged out of the constriction of my jacket and let it drop to the ground, using the time to make my decision.

"OK," I said softly, abandoning all pretence that I might still be able to dissuade him from this course. "If that's the way you want to play it ..."

I just had time to see the gleam form in his eyes.

"Hey, you!" yelled a voice from over to our right. "What's going on? Back off or I'll call the police!

I jumped and half-turned to cover both threats, guilty. Sean barely seemed to move, but he pocketed the knife as slickly as he'd brought it out in the first place. One moment it was there. The next, his hands were simply empty.

A uniformed security guard was standing at the top of the far ramp, body tense. His unease was such that it was causing him to bend slightly forward at the waist, like the possibility of engagement had brought on an actual pain in his stomach. His gaze was on Sean, not me.

"There's nothing for them here," Sean said calmly, raising his voice enough to be heard. Just the fact that he'd turned his focus onto the guard visibly increased the man's anxiety.

The guard stayed thirty metres away, unwilling to advance any further. He had one hand clenched round the large flashlight he carried at his belt—his only weapon—and walkie-talkie in the other. Despite the distance, I could see his Adam's apple bobbing convulsively above the button-down collar of his khaki shirt.

He was wearing dark green trousers with a gold stripe sewn into the side of them and had the polished peak of his cap pulled well down over his forehead, military police style. Even in civilian dress, Sean had him outranked and

27

outclassed in every way possible, and it was clear that both men knew it.

Still, he stood his ground—I'll give him that. "Are you all right, miss?" he called to me. "Is this bloke bothering you?"

I glanced at Sean. There was nothing in his face. No heat, no light, no anger. I wondered if it counted as successfully dealing with the threat he presented if I said yes and had him arrested. I waited a beat but, if I'd been hoping to make him sweat, it didn't work.

"No, everything's fine," I said, consciously injecting some warmth into my voice to drive out any notion that I was under duress. I leaned down and picked up my jacket from where it had fallen, shaking the worst of the dirt off it. "But thank you for checking on me. Actually, we were just leaving."

The guard nodded and remained by the ramp, shifting his feet uncomfortably, until Sean had crossed to the Shogun, unlocked it, and we'd both climbed inside. He finally moved away only as the engine turned over and fired. I followed my would-be protector's progress in my door mirror. He looked back twice before he finally disappeared from my field of view.

When I glanced over I found that Sean had sat back in his seat and was regarding me with those bottomless black eyes.

I had a raw fluttering in my chest as reaction set in, a kind of adrenaline hangover. I knew if I reached out now he'd see that my hands were shaking, and I would not give him that satisfaction. I kept my hands together in my lap and refused to meet his eyes.

He sighed. "I was wrong about you, Charlie," he said evenly. His eyes flicked to the windscreen. "You'll never know how sorry I am that I had to threaten you to find out for certain."

I wanted to ask, *What were you trying to find out?* But what I asked instead was: "So why did you?"

The question came out stark and I knew he'd picked up on what was there between the lines, but he was silent for long enough for me to regret asking. *Did I really want to know the answer?*

"Because I care about you," he said at last, turning his head and looking straight into my eyes with such sincerity that my body lit up in reflexive response, the way a pupil reacts to light.

So, yes, I did want to know, after all.

He had exactly the same concentrated look on his face that he'd had when he'd pulled the knife on me. It was that, more than anything, that shut down my unexpected spike of pleasure.

"Oh, of course," I said with a kind of breathless little laugh that didn't entirely obscure the bitterness in my voice. "In some cultures, coming at me with a blade could be considered almost akin to a proposal of marriage."

He reached out and pushed a few strands of hair back from my face with infinitely gentle fingers. My heart stammered in my chest, then overreached in its effort to catch up.

"In my head, I know how good you are, Charlie," he said. "I've always known. Right from the moment I first started to train you—you had that instinct, that spark. You should have had a brilliant career as a soldier. You burned so bright you were dazzling." He paused, looked away and said quietly, "What happened to you was criminal, in every sense of the word."

I didn't speak. There didn't seem to be anything I could say.

Somewhere below, on another floor, a multi-tone car alarm siren was sounding, muffled by the distance and ignored anyway. London teemed and bubbled around us. We were encircled by millions of people, and utterly isolated from all of them.

"But in my heart," he went on, "I'm so afraid for you every time I send you out on a job, I can hardly function."

Part of me knew what he was saying, but something goaded me into provoking him, even so. "You don't trust me," I said, an accusation rather than a query.

He made an uncommon gesture of frustration. "Christ, you know that's not it. It's not being able to be out there with you." The Shogun's engine note dipped as the cold-start disengaged and it dropped back to slow idle. "It would break every rule in the book if I put us on a team together when we're involved. How could I be sure, if you were in the line of fire, that I'd always cover the principal? And if that happened, well—" he shrugged his shoulders, '—I'd be finished."

"So instead you have to keep reassuring yourself that I'm ready," I said slowly. "Is that why you assigned me to work with Kelso in Prague? Is that why you've sprung this trip to the States on me? Some kind of test."

"Partly," he said, throwing me a tired smile. "Kelso's a useful man but a hopeless misogynist, and you proved—yet again—that you've got what it takes to cope with the Kelsos of this world."

He'd carefully avoided the rest of the question, I noticed, but I wouldn't let it go.

"And what about America?"

"You've got to get over it sooner or later, Charlie," he said gently. "This should be a nice easy job. You've got weeks to get used to the idea. And once you get to Boston, away from Simone's ex, it's just a case of holding her hand while she reacquaints herself with Daddy."

It sounded simple enough when he put it like that. And besides, I knew all about difficult family relationships from firsthand experience.

So why couldn't I shake off the uneasy feeling in the pit of my stomach?

"OK, Sean," I heard myself saying. "If you want me to take this, I'll do it."

He fastened his seatbelt and set the car into gear before regarding me, and his face was suddenly hard again, the way it had been when he'd first shown me the knife.

"Just remember, Charlie, today you let emotion cloud your judgement and you must not let that happen, do you understand me?" he said, so coldly it was almost impossible to imagine that he had ever softened towards me. "It will kill you if you do."

FOUR

I didn't expect to hear from Simone again for a couple of weeks. Not until her tame private investigators had made more progress, at any rate. And because that meant I could put off making a decision about whether I was really ready to go back to the States or not, I put it off.

It was something of a surprise, therefore, to get a call on my mobile just before six-thirty the next morning.

It was still dark outside and I could hear rain slatting against the outside of the window. Disorientated, I rolled over in my bed and groped for the phone. By the time I'd flicked it open and recognised Sean's number as the caller, I was fully awake.

I hadn't gone back with him to Harrington's office the afternoon before. Instead, Sean had taken Simone and Ella home himself and had offered to arrange overnight cover for her. Apparently she'd dug her heels in at the idea of being surrounded by a group of strangers, insisting that Matt was unlikely to try again and she'd be in touch when she needed us.

"Sean," I said now by way of greeting. "What's up?"

He heard the wary note in my voice. He must have done. He'd been cool towards me since our altercation of the day before. For the first time in weeks pride had dictated that I go back to the room I was renting near his base of operations in King's Langley, rather than to his place. But as soon as I'd shut the door behind me and the silence had closed in, I'd regretted it. I knew I was punishing myself as much as Sean, but forgiving him too readily had seemed much worse an option.

"I've just had a call from Simone," he said. "Apparently the press have got wind of what happened yesterday and they're camped out on her doorstep."

"The press?" I repeated, alarmed, my first instinct one of guilt. For a moment I had the irrational fear that somehow the run-in Sean and I had had with the security guard the day before had leaked out and made the headlines.

"Yeah, it would seem that her ex didn't appreciate being slung out on his ear and he must have decided to go very public about the whole thing."

"Oh," I said, hit by relief and then dismay in equal parts. "Shit."

"Yeah, you could say that," he said, his voice wry. "Anyway, she's under siege and she needs some support. I told her to close all the curtains and stay inside, and offered to send a full team, but she just wants you. How soon can you be up there?" He gave me the address, a quiet suburb in north-west London. Not exactly your usual lottery winner neighbourhood.

I sat up in bed and swung my legs out from under the covers. "On the bike? About forty-five minutes," I said, thinking of my Honda FireBlade sitting chained up in the garage below. Nothing sliced through the morning rush quite like a big-power motorcycle.

"No, I think you should swing by the office and pick up a pool vehicle," Sean said. "Then if things get too bad you can always move the pair of them to a more secure location."

"If I do, it could take me another hour to get to her now."

"She's not in any immediate danger. The press are a nuisance, but they're not about to break down her front door for the sake of a story."

"OK," I said, on my feet and heading for the shower. "Tell her I'm on my way and I'll be with her as soon as I can."

"I already did," he said with the ghost of a smile in his voice. There was a pause, almost a hesitation. "Are you OK?"

I stopped moving, heard the tension under the words and knew there was a lot riding on my answer, one way or another.

"Fine," I said at last, and found I had to force myself to breathe. I swallowed, started again, more casually this time. "I'm fine, Sean. Don't worry about it."

"Good," he said, so devoid of emotion that I didn't know if I'd said the right thing or not. "I'll let you get sorted," he added, more businesslike. "Take care, Charlie," and with that he was gone.

"Yeah," I said to a dead connection. "You, too."

***

Simone's house was an ordinary post-war semi-detached, with fake Elizabethan-style timber on the upper storey and crisp red brick below. The front door was solid wood and painted pillar-box red. There was an integral garage to one side, with a tall narrow gate leading to the back garden.

It looked as though the front garden had been on the neglected side, although the booted feet of the journalists and photographers now trampling all over it had reduced it to a soggy brown mush underfoot and made it hard to tell.

I braked to a halt just short of the patchy gravel driveway and called ahead on my mobile before I attempted going in. It rang out at the other end for what seemed like a long time before Simone answered.

I wasn't brave or foolish enough to attempt getting out of the car while I waited for her to pick up. As I eyed the movements of the pack in front of me, it was like watching hyenas bickering among themselves while they waited for the next kill.

It had taken me two and a half hours, all told, from Sean's phone call to my arrival, including the time I'd spent detouring to pick up one of the company Shoguns.

I'd spent a lot of the journey sitting in neutral, looking at the brake lights of the car in front through the sweep of the windscreen wipers, and thinking about Sean. Or, more specifically, thinking about his actions of the day before.

I understood his motives, in a way, but surely he could have found another method of expressing his doubts over my abilities, short of pulling a knife on me. I could just imagine what my father would have to say on the subject, if anybody ever tortured me enough to make me tell him. He and Sean had never exactly been close, and this would hardly have endeared him further.

One of the photographers turned in the driveway, spotted the Shogun, and tried to get his camera up without his fellow paparazzi noticing. When the rest finally cottoned on they all surged towards me, elbowing one another out of the way, their apparent camaraderie vanishing the instant there was the scent of fresh blood in the air.

I put the car into gear and nudged forwards. The press men took one look at the substantial bull bars on the front of the four-by-four and reluctantly parted to let me through. Had they not done so, I was in two minds about whether I was prepared to stop.

I pulled up as close to the front door as I could manage, checked my shirt collar out of habit, and shoved my way through the jostling pack, ignoring the questions and microphones and flashguns that were thrust into my face. Simone must have been watching for me because she opened the front door just as I reached it and I slid through the gap with hardly a pause.

The baying of the press continued outside, muffled by the thickness of the wooden door. Simone leaned back against the timber and closed her eyes momentarily.

The hallway was small and painted pale yellow, with three doorways leading off it and a carpeted staircase to the upper floor. The pictures on the walls were conventional mass market prints in cheap but cheerful frames. I wondered briefly if the fact that Simone could now afford to shop for originals would change her taste in art.

"How long have they been here?" I said, jerking my head towards the driveway.

"It seems like forever," Simone said wearily, opening her eyes. "Since first light, I think. That's when they started ringing the goddamn doorbell, anyway."

"Where's Ella?"

She rolled her eyes upwards. "They were scaring her, banging on the front windows, so I told her to stay upstairs. She has her own TV and stuff in her room."

"Sean said Matt had gone public. What happened?"

Simone glanced briefly towards the stairwell as though to check there were no tiny ears within hearing distance. Then she picked up a folded newspaper from the hall table and thrust it towards me.

"Here. Read it for yourself."

I scanned the front page quickly. It was all laid out under a big bold, if somewhat coy, banner headline:

R!CH B!TCH!

Underneath it was a luridly written story about how Simone had won millions and had then, with casual cruelty, thrown the father of her child out of the house they'd shared for the past five years. I glanced up to find Simone watching me, her face tight with embarrassment and anger. I read the piece again, more fully this time, making her wait.

Even allowing for gutter press exaggeration, Matt had clearly wasted no time airing his grievances. The way he'd told it, the moment Simone had realised the size of her win, she had more or less sent him out to the supermarket and changed the locks while he was gone. Now she was refusing to give him access to the daughter he idolised and, when he'd tried to bring the little girl a simple present in a public

36

restaurant, Simone's "hired thugs'—that was us—had jumped him.

It was the stuff of tabloid editors' dreams. A scorned lover, a tug-of-love child, a whiff of violence, and—best of all—money. Lots of money. They'd wrung every last ounce of salacious indignation out of the story.

Somehow they'd managed to snatch a long-range picture of Simone, cradling Ella, with a caption claiming she was "heartlessly out on a spending spree in London's Knightsbridge' while her rejected suitor was reduced to camping on a distant relation's sofa.

In the picture both Simone and Ella were wearing the same clothes they'd had on the previous day. Some fast-moving paparazzo had obviously snapped them in the street as we'd left the restaurant. The fact that there were clearly no shopping bags to be seen was conveniently overlooked.

When I'd reached the bottom of the page I looked up and caught the sheer disgust on Simone's face.

"How could Matt do this to us?" she demanded, her voice low with rage. "And how the hell can they get away with printing crap like that? It's all pure fabrication."

"People lash out without thinking when they're hurt," I said, suddenly feeling the need to come to her ex's defence. "And what Matt didn't tell them they've probably made up anyway. Once you've let them out of their cage, you can't hope to control them."

She swallowed, pulling a face, and was about to say more when Ella edged into view at the top of the stairs. She'd lost the bounce I remembered from the day before, seeming listless and subdued.

"What is it, sweetie?" Simone said quickly.

"I'm thirsty, Mummy," she complained, her voice whiny. "Is it OK if I come down and get a drink of water?"

Simone's face softened. "Of course you can."

Ella negotiated the stairs with care, holding on with one hand and trailing a comfort blanket and a small rather grubby stuffed Eeyore in the other, its detachable tail obviously long since lost. She clutched the bedraggled toy donkey tight to her chest as she came past us, giving me a wide berth.

Simone's smile for her daughter hardened as she watched her disappear into the kitchen at the end of the hallway. A moment later I caught a glimpse of the little girl dragging a wooden chair across the floor so she could climb onto it and reach the sink under the kitchen window.

"I hate what this is doing to her," Simone said quietly.

"Is there anyone you could go and stay with?" I asked.

She frowned and shook her head. "Nobody I'd want to subject to something like this," she said, jerking her head towards the swarming pack at the front of the house.

"Are you sure—no family or friends?" I pushed. "It might help if you can get away, even just for a few days. The press are vicious while they're after you, but they tend to have a pretty short attention span." As I well knew from personal experience.

"No, there's only me and Ella," Simone said firmly, wrapping her arms around her body as though she was cold. She bit her lip. "Matt was the one with the big family." She spoke of him in the past tense now, I noted, like he was dead.

"What about a hotel?" If nothing else, it would provide an additional layer of security. Without that, I couldn't ignore the possibility that I was going to have to get Sean to send in more people, regardless of how Simone felt about that. Just getting the two of them out of the house was probably going to be a nightmare. *Damn. I hadn't been on the job ten minutes and already I was thinking about calling for back-up.*

Then, in the kitchen, two things happened almost simultaneously.

Ella dropped her drinking glass and let out a piercing shriek of terror. Her cry, and the sound of the glass shattering on the tiled floor, hit us at the same time or so close together that it was impossible to tell which event had caused the other.

Simone and I both sprinted for the kitchen. I was the one who reached it first, elbowing the door wide. Inside, we found Ella standing frozen on the chair, surrounded by a pool of water and shards of broken glass.

She was still screaming at the two-headed apparition that loomed at the kitchen window—two rogue photographers, pressed up against the glass with their flashguns firing like machine pistols. Simone had drawn the blinds, but one was snagged on a pot-plant on the windowledge and there was a big enough gap for a lens to get a perfect view.

I took two strobe-lit strides into the room and snatched Ella off her perch, spinning her out of line of the cameras and yelling at Simone to sort out the blinds and blank off the window as I did so. The press men jeered and hammered on the glass outside.

Ella got a death-grip on my shirt collar and continued to screech in my ear, even after we were safely back in the hallway. Out of my depth, I patted her back and made shushing noises. Simone appeared by my side, white-faced, and tried to take her daughter from me, but Ella held on tighter still and wailed all the louder. I could feel her bony little knees digging into my ribs as she clung on.

We ended up unpeeling her, the way you disentangle a frightened cat that's got its claws firmly hooked up in your sweater. Eventually, she was forced to let go of me and grabbed for her mother's hair instead, still grizzling.

For a moment Simone and I stood and stared at each other over the top of Ella's head.

"Do you think you could find us a hotel for tonight?" Simone asked in a small, shocked voice.

I nodded, pulling out my phone. Sean had a list at the office of places all over the country that had good security and who were prepared to work with us to protect a principal.

Before I could punch in the number she added, "And tomorrow we'll go—get away, like you suggested." The horde outside continued to roar and clamour like a lynch mob, inflamed by their minor success. Simone rocked Ella and listened to them and her face grew stony. "Would America be far enough, do you think?"

***

"She wants to go to the States," I said.

"We know that—," Sean began.

"Not next week, or next month, but now," I cut in. "Today, if Madeleine can get her on a flight. What were her exact words? Oh yes. 'Everybody's telling me how rich I am—I'll buy a goddamn private jet if I have to.' I think that was the gist of it."

"What happened?" he said, clipped.

I went through the events of the last hour, adding, "Now she's getting over being scared, she's pretty angry instead."

"Hardly surprising," he said, and then was silent for a moment at the other end of the line. "And how do *you* feel about it?"

I shrugged. A useless gesture when he wasn't there to see it.

I was in the living room, with the curtains firmly drawn. Simone's house didn't have double glazing and I kept my voice low, only too aware of the movement and raucous chatter going on outside the window. Simone was upstairs, trying to settle a still-tearful Ella in her bedroom. I reckoned she was likely to be there for some time.

"I think getting Simone—and Ella—out from under the media spotlight would be the best thing for them right now," I said carefully. "I'm just not exactly thrilled about the prospect of going along for the ride."

"The circumstances are very different from Florida, Charlie," he said quietly.

I shut my eyes, gripping the phone more tightly and feeling like a coward. "Yes, I know."

He sighed. "OK, I'll call you as soon as we've got Simone's travel arrangements sorted out," he said. "We'll contact the private investigators as well, make sure they're briefed. I'll get Madeleine onto it."

Madeleine ran Sean's office for him and handled the electronic security side of the firm as well as being an organisational genius and general paragon of virtue.

At one point I'd thought she and Sean were more than work colleagues, and that was probably yet another reason she and I had never quite got along as well as we might have done. Somehow it didn't help that, in the last few months, Sean had started talking about making her a partner. With more and more clients coming to Sean to secure their data as much as their personnel, I couldn't argue with his logic, but on some lower level it still rankled.

"Look," he went on now, sounding weary. "If you're really not ready for this, Charlie, tell me and I'll assign someone else." He paused a moment, as though giving me one last chance to change my mind.

"Right now, I don't know," I said, aware of a trickle of nervous tension down my spine at my own vacillation. "I suppose I thought I'd have longer to get my head round the idea."

"I'll call you back in an hour," Sean said, without inflection. "You've got until then to make your mind up."

"OK," I said, chastened. "Would you tell Madeleine if we're *not* on a flight out of here today then we're going to need a hotel for tonight as well?" I glanced at the curtained window. "Simone wants to get out of the house as soon as possible."

"Mm, I can't say I blame her," Sean agreed. "For the moment, though, just sit tight and let's hope the press get fed up with hanging around in the cold. We'll have her out of the country within a couple of days at the outside, in any case."

"I'm sorry," I said. "I know I'm being a pain about this, but—"

"Don't worry about it," he cut in. "If you're not ready, you're not ready. Just make a decision and let me know when I call back."

His tone was nothing but reasonable and I ended the call aware of a deep stab of disappointment that he seemed to have given in to my weakness quite so easily.

***

It was another half an hour before Simone reappeared downstairs. I was in the kitchen by that time, mopping up the spilt water and wrapping the bits of broken glass in newspaper so I could put them into the dustbin later. Strictly speaking, it wasn't my job, but it needed doing and I wasn't about to stand on ceremony. The blinds were still drawn and I had the lights on, making it hard to tell that it was still morning.

"How's Ella?" I asked, getting to my feet.

Simone hovered in the doorway, looking tired and strained. "OK, I guess," she said. She paused, more of a hesitation. "She wants to see you."

"Ella?" I said, surprised.

Simone nodded and stepped back into the hallway, taking it for granted that I'd follow.

I dumped the wrapped-up package of glass onto the kitchen worktop and went after her, aware of a prickle of nerves. I had almost no experience with children of Ella's age. I had no real experience with children of any age, for that matter. She'd been through traumas over the past two days that no four-year-old should have to endure and I had no idea how to counsel or comfort her, if that was what was required. Hell, I couldn't even do that for myself.

I opened my mouth to ask Simone why Ella was demanding an audience, but she was already halfway up the stairs and I had to hurry to catch up. By the time I reached the landing she was waiting for me by one of the bedroom doorways, beckoning me on.

42

My immediate impression of Ella's bedroom was that it was overwhelmingly pink. Pink carpet, pink curtains, pink quilt cover with pink unicorns on it. Even as a small child I remember disliking the colour and my mother would have died rather than decorate so heavy-handedly. She wouldn't even buy anything other than plain-coloured lavatory paper.

Ella was sitting up in bed with the covers banked protectively round her. She was cuddling the battered Eeyore tightly against her chest and absently chewing on one of his ears. From the state of the animal, I gathered this was something of a regular habit. Those violet eyes regarded me, wide and unwavering.

Simone went over to her and perched on the edge of the single bed. Ella tugged on her mother's sleeve until their heads were together, then whispered something into Simone's ear, hiding her lips behind her cupped hand. And all the time, her eyes never left me.

I tried to keep my expression bland, but I never did like being talked about behind my back. Even by a four-year-old.

Now Simone was looking at me, too, her cheeks flared pink to match the bedroom décor.

"Um, she wants to know what happened to your neck," Simone said.

"My neck?" I repeated, dumbly. Automatically, my hand went up to my shirt collar, checking it was in place. It was. For a moment I couldn't work out when Ella might have caught a glimpse of my scar, but then I realised she must have done so when her mother was wrestling her away from me in the hallway.

Simone's gaze met mine and I saw shock in her eyes. I think for the first time it really came home to her what it meant to be a bodyguard. And what it might mean to need one.

The scar was a thin line that ran round the base of my throat from my voice-box to just below my right ear, crossed

43

by fading stitch lines like something from a horror flick. Too uneven to be surgical, too precise to be accidental, it looked what it was. An attempt to murder me that had very nearly succeeded.

Simone nodded, just a single jerk of her head, still looking embarrassed. "And she wants to know if it hurts," she said, speaking like her lips were numb.

I shook my head. "Not really," I said. "It happened a long time ago." *Not quite two years, but to Ella that would be half a lifetime.*

Ella whispered again. Simone's discomfort deepened. Ella tugged more insistently. She was hiding her face behind her hair now, peeping out at me from underneath it.

"She wants to know if she can kiss it better," Simone said, flushing. There was a pleading message in her eyes, but I couldn't tell if she was desperate for me to refuse or comply.

Ella snuck another coy glance through her lashes and suddenly I found myself saying, "Of course she can," in a disconnected voice I didn't entirely recognise.

The right choice, obviously. Simone's answering look was one of relief. She half picked Ella up so she could lean up towards me across her mother's lap.

I found my feet moving me forwards. I bent and dragged the collar down and felt the lightest touch of Ella's lips on the side of my neck before I stepped back quickly, yanking my shirt into place.

"There," Ella said with satisfaction, pulling back, smiling. "All better now?"

I dredged a smile from somewhere even though my mouth tasted of ashes. "Yes, Ella," I said, my voice hollow. "All better now."

I waited by the doorway while Simone settled Ella down and switched on the portable TV on the shelf at the foot of her bed, tuning it to the cartoons. On the screen a pair of pink hippos in what appeared to be ballet dancing outfits were hitting each other over the head with frying pans, each blow accompanied by the sound effect of a hammer hitting a cast-iron rivet.

I wondered at the wisdom of letting Ella watch something like that, all things considered. I had visions of wild and uncontrollable nightmares. But, after her eyes had blankly followed the action for a few moments, she began to giggle. Good job I'm not a parent.

Simone ushered me out of the room and pulled the door almost closed behind her.

"Don't shut it, Mummy," Ella called.

"Don't worry, sweetie. I won't."

I led the way back downstairs. Simone followed me into the kitchen and I offered to make coffee just so I had something to do with my hands. I noted the way Simone's shoulders came down a fraction, seemingly thankful for the distraction.

"Actually, I'd rather have tea," she said with a hesitant smile. "My English half coming out, I guess."

I filled the kettle from the kitchen tap and plugged it in, half-waiting for Simone to start asking questions about the scar. When I glanced at her she seemed to be waiting for me to offer an explanation without prompting. *No way.*

"I've spoken to Sean," I said instead. "He's arranging flights to Boston for you as soon as possible."

"Oh. Great." She looked so relieved I shied away from telling her that there was a possibility I might not be going with them. "Thank you for doing that before—for Ella, I mean."

"It's no big deal," I lied, then switched to the truth. "She's a nice kid."

Simone smiled. "She is," she agreed softly. Her eyes slid to the blind that still covered the kitchen window and her next words seemed almost to be to herself. "I'd do anything to protect her."

I said nothing. The kettle clicked off and I poured the boiling water onto teabags and mashed them with a spoon.

I was more of a coffee drinker myself but Simone only had cheap instant, so tea seemed the lesser evil.

"Do you think it's wrong to take a child away from its father?" she asked abruptly, as I was opening the fridge door.

I paused, milk bottle in hand. "That depends on why you're taking them away," I said. I shut the door and poured milk into the tea until it seemed about the right colour, then put one cup on the worktop in front of her. She hardly seemed to notice it.

"I don't really remember my father," she said abruptly. "He left when I was about the same age as Ella is now. My mother went back to her maiden name—Kerse. God, I've always hated that name." She glanced at me and managed a tired smile. "The other kids at school always used to call me Curse. Can you imagine?"

"Children can be very cruel," I said.

She nodded, distracted. "Mom would never talk about him. I suppose, the less she'd say, the more I wanted to know—just awkward, I guess."

"I think that's a natural reaction."

"Not knowing why their marriage broke up—that's the worst thing. Wondering if, somehow, I might have been to blame, you know? Matt and I went over to Chicago just before my mom died, I hoped she'd tell me then, but she never did. She must have had her reasons, but she took them with her."

"And you're hoping—if you do find your father—that he might be able to give you his side of it?"

She nodded again, then gave a nervous laugh. "Maybe Matt's right, and I should leave things as they are, but I've reached a stage in my life where I can't move forwards without knowing who and what he is. And if he's a monster, well—" She shrugged, with more bravado than nonchalance. "I'll just have to deal with that one when I get to it. At least I'll have you to protect me, won't I?"

46

She lifted her cup, drank absently, oblivious to the way my face must have frozen. "It's made me decide that I won't ever try and keep Ella away from Matt," she went on. "Not unless he does something really awful. If I thought for a moment he'd ever try to hurt her—"

My mobile started shrilling at that moment. I put my drink down and flipped the phone open. I hardly needed to glance at the display to know who was on the other end of the line.

"Hi, Sean."

"Madeleine's got seats reserved for Simone and Ella on tomorrow's Virgin Atlantic flight to Boston out of Heathrow," he said without preamble. "Whose name do you want me to give her for the third ticket?"

I remembered the look of stark terror on Ella's face in the kitchen and then the delicate touch of her lips on the side of my throat.

I glanced across the room to where Simone stood now, wrapped in turmoil and memories, clutching her cup with both hands like it was some kind of lifeline.

What were my own fears compared to theirs?

"Mine," I said.

FIVE

The private investigator's dead," Sean said.

Whatever else he added to that was drowned out by the PA system above me, announcing a final boarding call for all passengers for some charter flight to Malaga.

With scant regard for the possibility of brain tumours, I jammed my mobile phone hard up against the side of my head and stuck my finger into the other ear. It was only partially successful at damping down the outside noise.

"What?"

"The private investigator Simone hired to trace her father—guy called O'Halloran," Sean explained, raising his voice beyond the tolerances of the phone's tinny speaker, which buzzed painfully in my ear. "He died in a car accident last week."

"When you say 'accident', I assume that's what it was?"

"As far as we know, yes," Sean said. "I've spoken to his partner. They're arranging for someone to collect the guy's files and brief you. They'll meet you when you land."

"Great," I muttered, unable to shake the uneasy feeling this latest news provoked.

It was just after nine the following morning and Simone, Ella, and I were waiting at Heathrow for our flight to Boston. Madeleine was nothing if not efficient.

We'd spent the previous night in one of the big hotels near the airport, having braved the press pack to escape from the house around lunchtime. The hotel was part of a major chain that was used to celebrity guests and took a

48

very dim view of letting journalists and photographers harass them unduly. The hotel also employed a number of rather large door staff who wouldn't have looked out of place outside a town centre nightclub and who had a definite no-nonsense reputation.

I'd made a point of going and chatting to them briefly once I had Simone and Ella safely tucked away in their room. I was polite and respectful and gave them as much information as I could about the situation.

In return for this professional courtesy, they'd promised to be extra vigilant, and proved it by firmly repelling the first paparazzi incursion shortly afterwards. The reporters had made a few more experimental forays, then retreated to lurk sulkily in the car park. I was pleased to note the rain had hardened into sleet as the light began to fade.

Madeleine, meanwhile, had been doing some furious coordination behind the scenes, setting up all our travel arrangements.

She had automatically assumed that Simone could afford—and would want—the best of everything. She'd reserved us seats in Virgin Upper Class for the transatlantic and rooms in the best hotel, overlooking Boston Harbor, for the open-ended duration of our stay. Simone had flipped when she'd seen the cost.

Privately, I thought she was making a fuss about nothing, but I recognised it would be all too easy to develop a money-doesn't-matter attitude that lasted right until it was all frittered away. Eventually, Madeleine had talked her into sticking with the plans on the grounds that there wasn't time to change them. Madeleine had also sneakily sent her an e-mail link to the hotel she'd selected. One look at the sumptuous rooms and the in-house health spa had Simone's objections crumbling.

"One more thing," Sean said now. "You might be interested to hear that I went and paid a visit to Matt yesterday afternoon."

"Why?"

"I wanted to pre-empt any problems. There was a chance he could have kicked up a fuss about Simone taking his daughter out of the country without his agreement, and the law would have been on his side," Sean said, his voice grim.

"Hell," I said. "I never even considered that."

"Mm, well, the guy's seriously paranoid about Simone getting in contact with her father, let me put it that way."

"So, is he going to make trouble?"

"No, he saw sense eventually," Sean said, his tone dry. I had a pretty good idea of the form Sean's persuasion would have taken. I could almost feel sorry for Matt. Then I remembered Simone's anger, and Ella's fright, and my sympathy faded somewhat. "He's denying he had anything to do with the press invasion, by the way," Sean went on, "and I think I might even believe him."

My eyebrows went up. "Really?"

"He's been borrowing a bed at his cousin's place since he and Simone split, and the cousin turned up while I was there. I wouldn't actually be surprised if he was the one, rather than Matt, who went to the papers."

"Based on ... what, exactly?"

"A feeling," he said, and I heard the smile in his voice. "That and the fact that his cousin is possessor of a lot of nervous twitches, a permanent sniff, and a glass-topped coffee table with an interesting set of scratches on it. I get the impression he's the type who might well have been tempted by the offer of some easy cash to dish the dirt."

"He could just have a head cold and be particularly careless with his furniture," I pointed out.

"True," Sean allowed. "Or he could have an expensive coke habit and need of some extra income. Either way, he'd just been out and spent a fortune on games and DVDs and—when I arrived with a rake of tabloids—I think even Matt figured it out. To be fair to Matt, he did seem to be pretty upset by what happened to Ella."

"He's going to be even more upset when he gets the papers today, then," I said, thinking of the two photographers jammed up against the kitchen window. Madeleine was already taking the breach of privacy up with the Press Complaints Authority, even though I felt it was too late for an apology. "But he's definitely agreed to let them go?"

"Relax, Charlie. If it means they're out of harm's way for a while, yes," Sean said. "I don't think we'll have any trouble providing it doesn't take these private eyes months to find this guy."

"What happens if it does—?" I began, just as the PA issued another raucous reminder to reduce the number of security alerts by not leaving baggage unattended.

"Bloody hell, Charlie, where are you?" Sean asked. "I thought you were all supposed to be tucked away in the VIP lounge?"

"We are. At least, I've left the pair of them up there—security's pretty tight, so I thought they'd be quite safe," I said hurriedly, in case he thought I was being unforgivably lax. "I'm just raiding the concourse shops to try and find enough puzzle books to keep Ella occupied across the Atlantic. She may be cute, but she's also four years old and hyperactive—and it's a seven-hour flight."

"Good luck," Sean said, amused. "You can always get the cabin crew to slip her a Mickey Finn."

"It might come to that."

"Look, something's come up and I'm going to have to go. Call me if you have any problems, but we're just going to have to play things by ear on the time front," he said. His voice softened. "And you take care of yourself, Charlie, OK?"

"Don't worry," I said, with way too much confidence. "We'll be fine."

***

The flight itself was uneventful. One of the things that had most surprised me when I first started working for Sean's agency was the way the rich travel. The kind of people who need to surround themselves with close protection personnel don't go anywhere on the cheap. In the six months since I'd got stuck into the job I'd never flown anything less than Business Class when actually accompanying a client, and I'd gone twice by private jet.

Even Simone, after she'd boarded the plane and accepted a glass of champagne from the cabin crew who greeted her like an old friend, had seemed to forget her initial reservations. I'd glanced across from my seat in the centre of the aircraft and caught the little smile on her face, like it was suddenly dawning on her that from now on she could afford to always fly this way.

Despite my worries, Ella played with her food, watched some TV, crayoned in a couple of pages of one of the books I'd bought for her, then we folded her seat into a bed and she fell asleep like a seasoned traveller. She looked tiny, snuggled down amid the mussed-up blankets and pillows. The cabin crew stopped by regularly to cluck and coo over her.

Things didn't go quite so smoothly once we'd landed, though. Nobody from the private investigation firm who'd been tracing Simone's father met us at Boston's Logan International, and I didn't want to hang around long waiting for them.

Madeleine had arranged for a limo service to be available on our arrival. Once we'd cleared US Immigration and reclaimed our luggage, I called to make use of it. Whatever spiel Madeleine had given them, they answered their phone with excessive courtesy that only deepened when I identified myself. They were already aware of the arrival time of our flight and had the driver circling the airport waiting for us as we spoke, they said. They would call the man, who would be with us in minutes. Madeleine was very good at clearing a path, too.

The limo was a new Lincoln Town Car with a mild stretch, in discreet black rather than the gaudy white I'd been fearing. The driver was a big black guy in uniform, whose company badge said his name was Charlie. I resisted the urge to say, "Hey - twin!"

We crossed underneath Boston Harbor using the Ted Williams Tunnel, which seemed to go on forever. As we drove into Boston there were several feet of snow blanketing the city, much to Ella's obvious pleasure. She pressed herself eagerly against the car's tinted window, occasionally giving out little squeaks of delight as though someone had laid on this special weather just for her.

"It's just like Christmas, Mummy," she said.

"Yes, it is," Simone said, craning forwards to stare at the outside landscape herself. "But that doesn't mean you're getting any presents."

Ella's brow wrinkled as she gave this considerable thought. "Well, as it's *so* like Christmas," she said thoughtfully, "perhaps I ought to just have *one* present ..." She could have charmed gifts out of Scrooge.

"We'll see," was all Simone said, but when she sat back she was smiling.

I'd studied the city maps before we'd left and it seemed that the limo took us into the city by a very roundabout route. Charlie the driver blamed what he called the Big Dig which, he told us over his shoulder, had been going on in Boston for more than ten years. "By the time they're all done, they'll be tearing it all up again and starting over, yes, ma'am," he said as we drove past yet another construction crew attacking the frozen earth.

I watched two barge-like white Ford Crown Victoria cabs jostling for position in traffic alongside us, and craned my neck up at the sombre brown stone and brick buildings. The snow flurries that were still falling made it all seem alien and slightly distant.

I tried not to think about the last time I'd been in America, sweating in the Florida heat. I couldn't even prevent a tiny jerk of alarm when a pair of full-dress police cruisers came flashing across an intersection in front of us, their sirens yelping in and out of sync with each other.

Relax. They're not after you, I told myself. *Not this time.*

***

The Boston Harbor Hotel, when we reached Rowe's Wharf, was a magnificent building with an impressive arched rotunda next to the discreet entrance.

The hotel lobby was as grand and tactfully opulent as the outside led me to expect, all marble archways and huge paintings of harbour scenes from days gone by. Even the wallpaper was padded. Again, Madeleine had made the arrangements so that the bags were whisked up to our rooms with the minimum of fuss. Simone herself grew more quiet and tense with every passing minute, clearly overwhelmed by the sudden elevation in luxury.

I had the room next to the one Simone was sharing with her daughter. By dint of closing the outer doors onto the corridor and leaving the inner doors open the two rooms could be connected together, but still leave both Simone and me some privacy.

Once the staff had finished unsettling Simone still further in their efforts to put us at our ease, I left her flicking through the hundreds of TV channels, searching for cartoons for Ella. I went into my own side and shut the door behind me. The room had a picture window that offered a breathtaking panorama across the snow-speckled harbour below, and a double bed the size of Canada. Suddenly I missed Sean.

For once, I wished Madeleine had given our accommodation a bit more thought. Finding something at the top of the tree is easy. Finding somewhere a bit less majestic, a bit more in keeping with Simone's current lifestyle, would have been more time-consuming but might have been a better move. She might be a millionairess on paper, but she had a long way to go before she got her head round the idea. It seemed ironic that I was probably more used to staying in places of this calibre than she was.

54

I dug my briefing pack out of my bag, turning my back on the view, and dialled the number for the private investigators' office first. Their answering service clicked in. I left a message asking them to call me and gave my UK mobile number, including the full international code. It seemed easier than relaying messages via the hotel switchboard.

I checked in with Sean, too, thankful to be able to reach him right away on his mobile, even though it was late evening at home.

"I don't like it that they didn't turn up," he said. "We'll chase it at this end, but it's well past close of play over there, so there's probably nothing you can do other than sit it out until the morning. How's Simone doing?"

"Nervous," I said. "I think perhaps we should have stayed somewhere a bit less plush."

"Mm. Well, you could always try retail therapy," Sean suggested. "If she doesn't fancy the haute couture of Copley Place, take her bargain hunting at Filene's Basement instead."

"Since when did you get to know your way around Boston so well?" I asked, aware of a tinge of jealousy at the image of Sean buying gifts for some shadowy previous lover. Someone who came both before and after me. There had been a break that had lasted over four years in the middle of our relationship. In the intervening period I knew full well there'd been other people, for both of us. But that didn't mean I had to like thinking about it.

He must have read my mind because he laughed. "Work, Charlie, all work," he said, gently mocking. "Come on, you've looked after enough clients' wives now to know the first thing they ever want to do in a strange city is shop 'til one of you drops—and it's usually me."

"Really?" I said, allowing my voice to drawl. "I'd never have thought of you as being short on stamina ..."

***

55

It was breakfast the following morning before the dead private investigator's partner turned up.

We were in the Intrigue Café at the hotel, sitting at one of the tables overlooking the corrugated waters of the harbour itself. A fast cat ferry was moored just over to one side, and further out were a group of sleek-lined little yachts, built for fast summer cruising and which, at this time of year, now looked like a group of racehorses shivering together in a muddy field.

I noted the woman from the moment she stepped into the room and started heading our way. There was something about the flat professional way she surveyed the room, like she was used to summing people up fast, assessing them. She was medium height and trim in the way people are when it's their job to be fit, rather than through vanity. Her hair was short and dark and cut in a neat bob, parted in the centre, a style chosen to survive being under a hat all day as part of the job. There was cop, or ex-cop, written all over her.

As she approached I put my napkin aside and casually pushed my chair back a little, giving myself some space. Her eyes narrowed as she caught the action and she nodded, as though acknowledging my status, before she spoke to Simone.

"Excuse me. Would you be Miss Kerse?" She rhymed the name with *furze*.

Simone looked startled. Her eyes flew to me as though asking for permission to confirm the question.

"Er, yes, I am," she said, not correcting the woman's pronunciation. "And you are?"

"Oh, I'm sorry. I'm Frances L Neagley," the woman said, and I recognised the name from the file Sean had given me on the private investigators, although Simone still looked a little blank. "I'm sorry I wasn't at the airport to meet you yesterday. I was dealing with the arrangements for the funeral and I guess I must have gotten kind of hung up."

"Oh yes. Don't worry about it," Simone said, shaking her hand. I'd told her all about the private investigator's accident before we'd left Heathrow, just in case she decided to change her mind about coming. She hadn't. "I realise this must be a difficult time for you. I really appreciate your making time to see me."

Neagley's shoulders came down a fraction, as though she'd been expecting a chewing out. We were sitting at a table for four, with Ella on a booster seat next to her mother. Simone gestured to the spare seat and the private investigator slid into it gratefully. Close up, she looked tired, strained.

I caught the eye of a passing waiter. "Can we offer you something to drink, Ms Neagley?"

"Thank you, ma'am," she said. "I don't suppose they serve Tab here, do they?"

The waiter shook his head and Neagley reluctantly accepted Diet Pepsi as second-best. A glass appeared in front of her almost immediately. The service throughout the hotel was slick and unobtrusive.

Frances Neagley smiled vaguely at Ella, who was mutely watching her every move while dunking toast and grape jelly into the yolk of her poached egg. She was occasionally washing this concoction down with great gulps of fresh orange juice, picking up the glass in both hands as she drank. I expected her to throw up at any moment and, from Neagley's expression, I wasn't the only one.

"So, do you have any news for me?" Simone asked when the waiter had departed. The question burst out of her, like she'd been doing her best to wait a decent length of time, but she couldn't contain it any longer.

Neagley had just lifted her glass towards her mouth with the reverence of someone who has been too long deprived of caffeine. When Simone spoke she hesitated a moment, then put the drink down again, untasted, with the barest hint of a sigh.

"Not at the moment. We're assuming Barry—that's my partner, Barry O'Halloran—well, that he had his case notes with him when he went into the river," she said, with a sideways glance at Ella to check how much she was taking in. Neagley didn't sound Bostonian to my ears, but I wasn't familiar enough with American accents to place her beyond that. "Lotta the stuff inside his car was washed away. They haven't found his briefcase."

"He went into the water?" I asked.

Neagley turned and regarded me fully for a moment without speaking, as though trying to gauge whether I warranted the information or not. Then she saw Simone's expectant air and said, reluctantly, "Yeah. He was driving back down from Maine. It was late at night and the last fall of snow was just getting started. The cops reckon he most likely hit some ice on a bridge and just went off the road."

There was doubt in her voice, though, or maybe it was just a little disbelief. Everybody thinks they're a good driver until an accident happens to them.

"Surely he would have kept copies—duplicates, back-ups—of his files?" Simone said.

Neagley took a hurried swig of her Pepsi and her face pinched.

"Look, I'm sorry, Ms Neagley," I said quickly. "I know this must seem heartless to you, but you have to understand how important this is to Miss Kerse."

Neagley now included me in her distaste, but after a moment she nodded slowly and let her unconscious bristling subside.

"Barry had been away for a few days," she said, almost grudgingly. "Last time I heard from him he was in Freeport, Maine. Said he'd gotten a promising lead but it had led nowhere. I would have expected him to file a full report when he came back. *If* he'd come back," she added quietly.

"So we're back to square one," Simone said, trying not to sound too disappointed and not succeeding.

"I'm sorry, ma'am," Neagley said stiffly. "I'll do what I can to find out where Barry went and who he saw, but it could take a little while. How long do you plan to stay?"

Simone met my eye, steely. "As long as it takes," she said.

SIX

At the concierge's suggestion, later that morning we went to the Aquarium to fill in some time. We'd left Frances Neagley my mobile number in case of developments and, besides, Simone was going stir-crazy sitting around waiting in her suite, however sumptuous.

The New England Aquarium was not far from the hotel, just a short walk along the harbourside. The sun was out, giving a pale penetrating winter light, and the air was still cold enough to see your breath. The snow that had fallen overnight was lying thick across the whole city, muffling both the sight and the sound of it. It had snowed just before we left London, little more than a mean dusting that was nevertheless causing havoc with the transport system. Over here it seemed to be expected and embraced.

Ella was eager to be out scuffing her booted feet in the white stuff and had to be forcibly restrained from running off to investigate the seagulls loitering at the edge of the brick-lined wharf. There only seemed to be a length of heavy chain strung on bollards between her curiosity and the frigid water.

She was boisterous and demanding of Simone's complete attention, but at least Ella obeyed the instruction to hold her mother's hand, even if she pulled and dragged at her most of the time. I thought one of those retractable dog leads would have been a good idea, and she was certainly small enough. Let her get so far away, then just reel her in. But I didn't voice the suggestion.

I walked a few paces behind them and to the right, keeping my eyes roving over the people who approached us. It was bright enough to make sunglasses unobtrusive, and I slipped mine on. It made it easier and less obvious that I was watching hands and eyes. Every now and again I glanced behind me with what I hoped was the casual air of a tourist, just taking it all in. The whole of the waterfront seemed to be lined with renovated offices and brand-new condominiums valued, so we'd been told, well into seven figures. And sometimes into eight.

Nobody appeared to be paying our little group any undue attention. I spotted a couple of guys who seemed a little out of place. Nothing specific, just a subtle sense of awareness about them, something that didn't quite gel. Both of them passed us by without a second look.

At one point I found Ella watching me covertly over her shoulder. I would have thought she would have been more curious about why this complete stranger was suddenly shadowing their every move, but Ella had seemed to accept me without comment. Every now and then, though, I'd find her watching me and frowning, like she was remembering me knocking her daddy flat on his back in the restaurant, or the way the photographers had lunged at her outside her kitchen window. Like none of this had happened before I came into her life and I was somehow to blame. I thought kids that age were supposed to have the memory span of a goldfish.

Unfortunately, it seemed Ella was the exception to the rule.

***

The Aquarium was housed on the edge of Central Wharf, a starkly modern, almost thrown-together building, all sharp angles of steel and glass. As soon as we got inside, the first thing that hit me was the smell of fried food from the café upstairs, particularly of what seemed to be fish, which I thought had a somewhat cruel irony in the circumstances.

61

Inside, the building was dimly lit and the bare concrete walls reminded me of a multi-storey car park with a major damp problem. In the centre was a huge pool for the penguins. Ella was captivated by them—Africans and rockhoppers and little blues that didn't look fully grown. I would have liked to spend time reading the information, but I wasn't here for my own amusement.

Ella asked constant questions, which Simone did her best to answer as though she were talking to an adult. It was often a pleasure to watch the two of them interacting.

I couldn't believe how busy the place was. Everybody seemed to be taking pictures with little digital cameras no bigger than a credit card, which nevertheless had built-in flash that would have put a lighthouse to shame.

And the place seemed to be heaving with small children, which had Ella pulled in all different directions at once and made me nervous. She was naturally gregarious and keeping her at Simone's side became more and more difficult.

At various times during the day the Aquarium held demonstrations and events. Our arrival coincided with a training session at the sea lion enclosure just outside the rear door. The enclosure had glass walls onto the viewing gallery on two sides, and by the time we arrived people were already six deep at every available vantage point. Ella instantly slipped Simone's hand and squirmed her way through the press of legs to the front of the crowd, where it was impossible to follow.

"We need to keep tabs on her," I warned.

Simone threw me an almost amused glance that clearly said I wasn't used to dealing with small children, who couldn't be kept tethered all the time. Then her eyes were on the first of the sea lions, which had waddled out onto the artificial rocks like a fat man with his trousers round his ankles.

"She'll be fine, Charlie," Simone said, distracted. "Don't worry."

"Yeah, right, 'cause that's just my job," I muttered under my breath.

Just before the trainers appeared, what I took to be a generator plant just behind us cranked up, making the commentary all but inaudible from our position. The sea lions slipped off dry land and became instantly graceful, twisting and diving smoothly through the murky water of the enclosure. I caught a glimpse of Ella, pressed up against the glass wall, entranced.

The trainers came bouncing out, complete with audience volunteers. The sea lions bounded out of the water onto the wooden dock in one corner of the enclosure and did some messing around with paintbrushes in their mouths, which—if the snatch of commentary I managed to decipher was correct—was apparently just an extrapolation of natural sea lion behaviour in the wild. I mean, who hasn't seen a sea lion doing a little watercolour number out there on the rocks?

I ducked and peered between the people in front of me, checking on Ella. A few moments before, she'd been right there, jiggling with excitement against the glass. Now she was gone.

Uncaring of the glares from the adults, I shouldered my way through, but she definitely wasn't there.

"Simone," I said over my shoulder. "Stay there while I find Ella." The noise level was such that I don't know if she heard me.

I plunged further down the sloping walkway, madly looking for Ella and cursing under my breath at Simone's too laid-back attitude to parenting.

"Sorry, sorry," I said as I muscled my way in, scanning the rows of tiny bobble hats in front of me. "I'm looking for a child."

One harassed father looked over at me, laconic. "See anything you like?"

Any other time, I would have laughed. Now I didn't have time for a second glance as I worked my way further down.

And then, just when I'd begun to panic, I spotted her.

"Ella!" I called sharply. "Come here!"

She gave me a look that, regardless of her age, clearly said, Get real! and squirreled her way deeper into the crush as the sea lions dived back into the tank to a spattering of applause.

I glanced back behind me. A moment ago Simone had been standing by the double doors leading back into the Aquarium proper, apparently enthralled by the show.

Now she was gone, too.

Oh shit.

I hesitated just for a second, then went after Ella. The walkways were packed now, to the point where several people had hoisted their kids onto the fence surrounding the enclosure. I was a clear front-runner in the Miss Popular contest as I shoved my way through.

At last, I managed to snag Ella's sleeve before she could escape again and had her pinned. She squealed in mock outrage, giggling at the same time. Thoroughly embarrassed by the glares I was getting from just about everybody, I scooped her up into my arms. She kicked at me briefly, still laughing.

"Ella, it's not funny," I said as I hurried against the crush of bodies back towards where I'd last seen Simone.

"'Tis," Ella said, still sniggering.

"No, it isn't," I said, frustration putting a bit of snap into my voice. "What if your mummy's lost? What will you do then?"

I reached the top of the ramp. To my left was a small deck area that looked out over a low fence to the harbour. It had the look of an exit about it, even though it wasn't signed. I made a fast decision and darted down the short flight of steps, past a row of vending machines and the back of the fence round the sea lion enclosure. I could see the backs of the kids sitting precariously on the fence and hear the muffled commentary.

I knew there was no logical reason for Simone to have come this way and I almost turned back. Surely she wouldn't willingly leave her child behind, unless there was something amiss. I hefted Ella onto my hip and started to run.

Round the corner was an open dock area filled with disused benches. By the time I'd reached it, something of my alarm had communicated itself to Ella, who was clinging on tight to my shoulder and chewing her hair.

Then I rounded another corner to find Simone standing by the railing looking out over the choppy harbour. There was a man in a long tweed coat standing next to her. They were shoulder to shoulder, like they were admiring the view. He was pointing out one of the buildings on the skyline, his hand resting lightly on the small of her back. Both their heads snapped up when I hove into view.

"Simone!" I said, annoyed and relieved at the same time.

"Mummy!" cried Ella, and promptly burst into tears.

Simone turned away from the man and immediately swept Ella out of my grasp. Shame she hadn't been so bothered about her child when she'd walked away from the sea lions, leaving us both high and dry.

"She said you were l-lost," Ella sobbed, bottom lip wobbling.

Simone gathered her close and shot me a daggered look.

I didn't bother trying to explain, just eyed the guy next to her with no small measure of distrust. He was possibly in his early thirties, blond haired and good-looking.

"Hey, I'm real sorry," he said easily, stepping forward and smiling. "We didn't mean to scare you."

I noted the "we'. *Fast mover*. He had what I was coming to recognise as a Boston accent, a slight drawing out of particular vowels. He sounded genuinely contrite but I didn't care.

I glared at Simone. "You gave your daughter a fright, disappearing like that," I said, and heard the accusing note.

Simone heard it, too, and bristled. "I'm sure she wasn't worried until *you* frightened her," she said, glaring back. "I don't need your permission to talk to people."

"That's just it, Simone. Yes, actually, you do."

The guy's smile had faded by this time. Ella, realising that attention had shifted away from her, began to wail louder.

He edged back a step. "OK, I didn't realise I was getting in the way of anything here," he said, and I could have sworn he sounded amused more than insulted. "I think I'd better give you two a few moments alone."

"Yes," I said, without taking my eyes off Simone. "I think you better had."

He inclined his head to Simone, a "nice meeting you— but not that nice' kind of a gesture, and sauntered away. Simone made soothing noises to Ella, who—once she'd reclaimed her star status—quickly allowed herself to be quietened. Simone shifted her onto her other hip and moved in close to me, her face tight.

"Embarrass me like that in public again, Charlie," she bit out with quiet ferocity, "and *you're* the one who's going to need a bodyguard ..."

***

I took the pair of them up to the café on the second level and we sat looking out across the bright water drinking hot chocolate while Ella continued to sulk over a milk shake. The walls in the café were decorated with more sea lion art. The carefree brushwork was starting to grow on me. Certainly, I'd seen less impressive canvases in London galleries with four- and five-figure price tags.

"We've got to have some ground rules here, Simone," I said, speaking low and trying to keep the temper out of my voice. "I can't be in two places at once. I can't protect both of you if you don't stick together. If you're not prepared to do that, I'll have to call Sean and get him to send over more people." I was doing my best for cool professionalism but it

66

sounded childish, even to my own ears. *Do as I say or I'm telling on you!*

"I don't *want* more people," Simone said through her teeth. "One's bad enough!" She shut up abruptly and looked away, staring at a ferry chugging across the harbour towards the airport.

"So, who was that guy?" I asked quietly. It took Simone a long time to answer. Stubbornness or embarrassment, I wasn't sure which.

"Just a guy," she said at last. "A nice, *normal* guy. Not someone who knows anything about—" She broke off, checked about her, guilty. "About us," she muttered.

"A nice normal guy," I echoed flatly. "You know that for certain, do you?"

She sighed heavily, like a teenager told off for her choice of unsuitable boyfriend. I suddenly felt very old.

"OK, he *seemed* very nice. Friendly. So, he flirted with me? So what?"

"Simone, he could have been anyone," I said tiredly. "His sole purpose could have been to lure you out of there and I can't believe he succeeded so easily."

"Oh yeah, sure, because of course I'm so ugly that no *normal* guy could possibly like me just for myself!" she shot back, bitter. "I liked him," she added, lower now.

"Enough to leave Ella on her own to go for a quiet stroll with him?" I said, and couldn't quite keep the bite out of my voice.

Simone's eyes flashed a warning. *Don't criticise the way I bring up my daughter.* "Ella was fine. She wouldn't have moved from the sea lion enclosure until I came back for her."

And you know this because ... you've left her alone like that before?

I knew I was staring. I could see Simone gathering herself for a full-blown argument, and that was going to do us no good at all. However much I disapproved of Simone's parental style, it had worked for her this far and there

67

wasn't much I could do about the past. The immediate future, however, was my responsibility.

"Look, I know this is difficult for you—both of you," I said, as gently as I could, trying a smile. It crashed and burned on both of them. I sighed. "I know you don't like it, Simone, but you just have to accept that things are very different now. You may have thought that this money wasn't going to change you, and maybe it won't, but everything around you has changed instead. It's just up to you to make it a pleasure, not a burden."

She let her breath out fast down her nose, a habit I was getting used to. "OK," she said at last with the barest hint of a smile. "But now we're away from ... England," she added, checking Ella's reaction, "surely there's no real danger, is there? Nobody knows us here."

"Probably not, but I'm paid not to take chances."

She paused, seemed to consider that for a moment. "OK," she said again. "I'll try not to make your life difficult."

"Thank you."

"And in return," she murmured, "you have to promise not to play gooseberry in the future, OK?"

Ella stopped trying to noisily suck the bottom of her glass up through her bendy straw.

"What's a goo'berry, Mummy?"

Simone switched the smile over to her daughter and for a moment I wondered how she was going to explain the concept of an unwanted third party on a hot date.

"It's a very sticky kind of fruit, sweetie," she said with a sly glance at me. "One that's really difficult to get out of your hair."

***

We managed to get round the rest of the Aquarium without further incident. In the afternoon I followed Sean's advice and directions from the concierge and took Simone shopping at the exclusive stores on Newbury Street, which proved an interesting experience.

I'd shopped with millionaires before. One of the early jobs I'd done for Sean, back in the summer, involved several days accompanying the wives of an Arab sheikh round London watching them spend more in a few hours on jewellery and fashions than they could ever wear in a year—and more than I would ever find use for in a lifetime.

Simone shopped in fits and starts. She blew hundreds of dollars in a very upmarket home furnishings place, almost on a whim, on a set of hideous glass vases that seemed totally out of place with what I could remember of her home décor and were going to be a pain to ship. Then later she dithered so much between two pairs of moderately priced shoes in one of the big department stores that she even taxed the patience of the professionally cheerful sales assistant, and ended up buying neither of them.

The more the afternoon wore on, the more bad-tempered Simone became, snapping at Ella when she pestered for toys or sweets or clothes, then giving in to her on a giant stuffed teddy bear with a somewhat sinister expression, that I thought privately would give Ella serious nightmares if she woke in the dark and found it looming over her.

And when I suggested calling for Charlie the limo driver to come and pick us up and take us back to the hotel, Simone turned on me, too.

"How much is that gonna cost me?" she demanded in a savage whisper. "More than a cab, huh? Just because you want to show off and ride in style doesn't mean *I* should have to pay for it."

I waited a moment before I spoke, holding the eye contact until she let her end drop, flushing.

"I don't give a rat's how I travel, Simone," I said when my silent count had reached double figures and I could speak in level tones. "But I do care about getting into a vehicle with you where I have some idea of who the driver is. Yes, I should imagine there will be a charge for using the limo service. No, off the top of my head I don't know how much it will be. But even if it's twice the cost of a cab, it's worth it for the security it offers."

Ella, already fractious from her earlier power struggles with her mother, dragged at her sleeve and tried loudly to attract her attention. Not that the three of us weren't getting plenty. And none of it good.

I stepped in closer, lowered my voice. "Don't give me a hard time on this, Simone. I will only spend as much of your money as I need to, to keep you both safe. Apart from that, I don't give a damn how much you've got. I thought we'd been through all this once today, but if you really don't want me to do my job, tell me now and I'll be on the next flight out of here."

There were times afterwards when I wondered what might have happened if she'd agreed to that. As it was, we stood and faced each other with the soothing music of the store playing gratingly over our heads.

"I apologise," she said, stiffly, at last. "Call the limo. I think I've about had enough for today."

I nodded without further comment and pulled out my mobile phone. It wasn't until we were in the limo's voluminous back seat, with Ella lying curled up on the thick leather upholstery next to her, and the giant bear glowering opposite, that Simone spoke to me again.

"I'm sorry," she said, still sounding as stiff and awkward as she had done in the department store. She stroked Ella's curls, not looking at me. "You weren't serious, were you?" Simone asked in a small voice. "About leaving, I mean— about going home?"

"I'll stay as long as you want me to," I said. "On the condition that you understand I'm not trying to ruin your personal life, or part you from your money—for my own benefit or anyone else's—OK?"

She nodded again, letting her hair swing in front of her face. We rode in silence for a little while before she said, diffidently, "Do you think they'll let me change my mind about those vases?"

"I expect so," I said, and she sounded so forlorn I felt suddenly sorry for her. "I'll call them for you, if you like, explain that your interior designer has gone into a fit of hysterics about your terrible taste."

That won me a tired smile. "I always thought that having a lot of money would make things easier, somehow."

"It doesn't," I said. "It just makes the problems different. And some of them it just seems to make worse."

She nodded, sober. After a few minutes she said, "And they were pretty awful, weren't they?"

"The vases?" I said, smiling. "Yes, they were."

***

Later, we ate in a small, Italian family diner in the historic North End. The restaurant—serving pizza and pasta, as you would expect—was recommended by Charlie the limo driver, who took us there and collected us again afterwards. It was small and cosy and both Simone and Ella looked a lot more at home there than in the grander surroundings of the hotel.

It was still fairly early when we finished eating, but our stomachs were still working on UK time, running five hours ahead, which made a normal evening meal far too late for any of us to manage, least of all a four-year-old. As it was, Ella had fallen asleep again on the short ride from the restaurant back to the hotel, and Simone had to carry her.

It bugged Simone, I could tell, that I didn't offer to help cart Ella inside. Even after I'd explained that it would completely hamper my ability to do my job, I'm sure Simone suspected I was merely shirking.

I did a casual sweep of the marble-clad lobby as we went through and noticed a woman hovering by the entrance to the gift shop. She was wearing a dark blue blazer over a polo-necked sweater and jeans, and it only took me a moment to recognise her as Frances Neagley.

My stride faltered and I got as far as opening my mouth to call back Simone, who was hurrying towards the bank of elevators ahead of us, but the private investigator shook her head quickly and pointed just at me, then made the universal gesture for drinking. I raised my eyebrows in question and she nodded. I held my hand up, fingers spread, to indicate I'd be back down to meet her in the bar in five minutes, and kept walking.

In fact, by the time I'd settled mother and daughter in for the night it was more like half an hour before I could get back down to the lobby. Neagley had gone from her loitering position by that time, but I soon found her in the long, narrow bar, nursing a glass of Scotch and intently people watching. When she noticed my approach she stood and indicated the empty seat opposite. She still hadn't quite lost that wary air as she regarded me.

"You wanted to see me?" I said, neutral, returning the favour.

"Yeah," she said shortly. "Sit down, Charlie. Drink?"

"Coffee would be good," I said carefully. A waiter came, took my order, and departed again. Silence fell, lying heavy.

The bar was moderately busy, mainly with hotel guests having drinks before going out for their more conventionally timed dinners. I let my gaze trail over them while I waited for my drink to arrive. There was one big guy in a green sports jacket sitting alone at the bar who caught my eye. He had a watchful air about him, like he might be hotel security. Nobody else rang any alarm bells.

"So," I said at last, turning back to Neagley, who had yet to speak, "are you going to tell me what the secrecy was all about? Have you found any trace of where your partner went? Who he might have spoken to?"

"What do you know about this missing father of Simone's?" she asked abruptly instead.

I paused, considering. "Not much," I admitted. "Simone claims she doesn't remember him, so she hasn't said much, and my job is just to ... keep her company," I finished, suddenly not sure how much I wanted to reveal.

Neagley made a small gesture of impatience. "Don't mess with me, Charlie. You're a bodyguard, not some kind of nanny."

The waiter returned at that moment with my cup of coffee. I didn't speak until he'd gone again.

"You've been doing some digging," I said then.

"Yeah, well, it's kind of in my job description," she agreed, sitting back and crossing her legs. She regarded me with slightly narrowed eyes, head tilted to one side. "As is finding out that Greg Lucas spent years in the SAS and had a rep as a real hard man."

I stilled, trying to work out if I'd known that information. *Army chap,* Harrington had said, implying some chinless wonder in the Guards. Neagley's information changed things, but I still didn't see what real significance it had. "So?"

"So he's the kind of guy who would know when someone was asking questions about him—and possibly have the abilities to get rid of that someone, if he did not want to be found."

I didn't think it was good politics to let Neagley know that questioning the accidental nature of that accident had been my first thought. So I allowed my eyebrows to come up and asked, neutral, "You think he might have arranged for your partner's crash? Run him off the road? Why?"

Neagley shifted uncomfortably. "I don't know, but I've been in this business long enough to know that normal people—with nothing to hide—don't go to the trouble to disappear that this guy did. He must have had a reason for not wanting to be found. And besides, Barry was a good driver," she added, defensive now. "Me, I'm from California. I'd never seen ice until I moved east five years ago. If it had been me who went off that bridge—" she shrugged, '—that

73

woulda been understandable. But Barry lived here all his life. He was careful, knew what he was doing."

"Have you talked to the police about this?"

Her face tightened. "Uh-huh. They're not going to be swayed from driver error unless I find them some real good evidence of sabotage or interference. And, like I say, your boy's too good to have left anything obvious behind."

I didn't like the way she said "your boy' any more than I liked the way she seemed convinced Simone's father had in some way caused O'Halloran's accident, but I let it slide. She took a breath.

"And I think I'm under surveillance."

"You think, or you know?"

Her eyes flashed a warning. "It's nothing obvious, just a feeling, but you get to trust your instincts in this job."

"When did you first notice this tail?" I asked.

"Since just after Barry's accident. It could be coincidence, but I'm not working on anything at the moment that would warrant it, so I can only conclude it's because of Barry." She stared at her drink, her face pinched. "I don't mind admitting, it's got me a little spooked."

"Are you saying you want to quit?"

"No," she said carefully, not rising to the challenge in my voice, "but we should have been told up front if this assignment was likely to be risky."

Hey, I'm just another employee, not management. Don't give me a hard time about it. Not an attitude likely to win me Neagley's cooperation, so I left the words unspoken.

"I don't believe anyone thought it was," I said instead, "or they would have done."

"Yeah?" Her voice held a disbelieving note. "So why are you on the job, Charlie? You're ex-SAS as well, aren't you?"

I glanced at her sharply. She was almost right, but not quite. Special Forces in the UK covers a lot more than just 22nd Regiment, but that's who everybody automatically thinks of. And anyway, I hadn't made it past the training stage, but I wasn't about to volunteer that little titbit.

"Well, well," I murmured. "You *have* been doing some digging, haven't you?"

"Like I said, it's part of the job," she threw back at me. "So, why would someone like you be assigned if this is just a simple hand-holding exercise?"

I knew explaining about Simone's money would clarify my position, but I couldn't do so without clearing it with Simone first. Neagley saw my hesitation and read all manner of things into it—most of which weren't there. She got to her feet, leaving what remained of her drink on the table.

"No, I'm not a quitter," she said with quiet vehemence, leaning in. "But if I'm going to continue I want someone watching my back. I've called in some people I know—an executive protection firm outta New York who owe me a favour. When I've used up their goodwill I'll be putting their fee onto Miss Kerse's account. If she doesn't like it, she can fire me, OK?"

I nodded. She was within her rights to be angry and I knew my silence hadn't helped.

Neagley pulled a business card out of her pocket. "When you decide to level with me, here's my cell number," she said, tossing the card onto the table as she straightened. "And a piece of advice for you, Charlie—watch your back." And with that she turned and strode out of the bar.

I wasn't overly surprised when the big guy in the green sports jacket abandoned his drink and strolled out after her. As he went past he inclined his head a fraction, the friendly nod of one professional to another.

SEVEN

Y ou're the one on the ground, Charlie," Sean said. "If
you feel you need more people, say the word."

"It's not a question of that," I said. "I talked it
over with Simone again last night and she won't *have* any
more people. I spoke to the police here this morning—and
getting anything out of them was a bit of a saga—but
they're still adamant that O'Halloran's accident wasn't
suspicious. In fact, the guy in charge reckoned he'd had a
drink or two, which doesn't help convince them he was
bumped off."

"So you think Neagley's overreacting?"

I paused a moment before replying. I was in my room
overlooking the harbour again, watching the commercial
jets angle out of Logan. We'd just had an early breakfast
and Simone was getting Ella wrapped up and ready for a
trolley bus tour of the city. The concierge, no doubt trying
to be helpful, had given Simone all the details. Ella was
excited about it and I could hear her high-pitched voice
giggling and asking questions through the open doorways
to the next room. I shifted the phone to my other ear.

"I don't know," I said then. "She's certainly taken it
seriously enough to call in close protection of her own, and
Neagley didn't strike me as the kind of woman who would
panic over nothing. This has got her rattled, that's for
sure."

"Mm," Sean said. "Armstrong's are a good firm—head
office in New York and very switched on. I've worked with
the boss, Parker Armstrong, a few times myself. And

they're fair. They wouldn't take her money unless they thought she needed their services."

"Which brings us back to Greg Lucas," I said. "Why didn't anybody warn me he might react badly to being confronted with his long-lost daughter?"

"At this stage we don't know how he'll react. Nothing in the information we were given suggested he would go to those kinds of lengths to avoid being found."

"Well then," I said, "I suggest you dig a little deeper. Simone's determined not to give up looking and, if he's going to become a threat, I think it would be a good idea if I knew about it sooner rather than later, don't you?"

After my conversation with Neagley in the bar the night before, I'd gone back up to our rooms to find Simone curled up watching TV on my side, Ella already in bed and dead to the world, poor kid.

Without much of a preamble, I'd given Simone the gist of Neagley's grievances. For a few moments Simone had sat in silence, feet tucked up underneath her, apparently lost in her thoughts. It was only when she finally spoke that I heard the anger vibrating in her voice and realised she'd been bringing herself up to the boil.

"OK, so my father was in the army—so were you," she threw at me. "Does that make you both killers?"

I stilled. *Don't go there, Simone …*

When I didn't answer immediately she took a deep breath and said, quietly but with more bitterness. "Why are you telling me this, Charlie? You want me to give up and go home, is that it?"

"Of course not," I said, too patiently. It had only inflamed her.

"Tell me something. When did you last see your father, huh?"

"Six months ago," I said shortly.

She'd already opened her mouth to snap back at me before she registered what I'd said and closed it again. "OK, but that's your choice, right?" she said, slightly mollified. "You know who and where he is, right?"

"Yes," I agreed. But that didn't mean I knew him—not really. My father was one of the top orthopaedic surgeons in the UK, and while he might be my biological parent, most of the time I found him a cold aloof stranger. So much so, in fact, that when my short-lived army career had ended in scandal and disgrace I'd shortened my name from Foxcroft to Fox in an attempt to distance myself from him still further. It had been only partially successful.

Sean had never met with my parents' approval, either. One more thing we had in common. When I'd made the decision to take him up on his job offer and moved down from my home in the north permanently, they'd made a somewhat disappointingly brief bid to talk me out of it, then retreated into a martyred silence that I had not yet felt inclined to break.

I hadn't even told them I was going back to the States. Partly because I didn't want to face another argument when I had enough reservations of my own about the trip. But mainly just in case they made no comment on the subject at all. I'm not sure which would have been worse.

Simone's eyes slid back to the TV screen, but I knew she didn't see the picture. "I only remember odd fragments of my father," she said abruptly. "A lullaby, a deep voice sitting by my bed reading Beatrix Potter stories. But I can't see his face at all." She looked up, her face defiant, as though I would contradict her. "It's one of the things that's been bothering me, since we came out here. Will I recognise him when I finally meet him? My mother never kept any pictures. It's all this huge blank."

She shook her head and for a moment I thought she was going to cry, but she swallowed the tears back down again. "And now," she continued in a low voice, "you tell me he might have somehow caused the death of this investigator? What kind of monster would that make him?"

"That's Neagley's theory, not mine," I said quickly. "She's worried enough to have hired in some additional security. I think perhaps it might be a good idea if you considered doing the same."

"No," Simone said without pause for thought.

I took a breath. "I'm not armed, Simone," I said quietly. "I can't legally carry a gun over here. Maybe, if Neagley's right, you should think about bringing in someone who can."

"No. I won't have guns around Ella." Simone met my eyes, determined, stubborn. "Looks like you'll have to do the best you can, Charlie."

***

We picked up the trolley bus for our tour of Boston at the stop just outside the Aquarium, retracing our steps along the harbour front to get there. No more snow had fallen since our arrival, but despite the pale sunshine, what was on the ground was showing no signs of melting. Ella still seemed enthralled by it, dragging her mother on a meandering course to inspect the larger piles of the stuff.

As usual, I walked a pace or so behind Simone and to the side, keeping my eyes open. After her confession of the night before, she didn't seem much inclined to talk to me, in any case.

There were around twenty stops on the tour and—with buses running every twenty-five minutes—you could get off and get back on again more or less at will. Simone sat next to Ella in the seats directly in front of mine. It was below freezing outside and the little girl was dressed up warmly against the bitter chill in the air, with fake-fur ear warmers and some new sheepskin mittens that were actually on strings from her coat sleeves. Just because Simone was rolling in it didn't mean she was going to be happy if her daughter lost a brand-new glove.

The trolley took us on a set route, the driver giving an informal and joke-laden commentary that mainly seemed to centre on how badly the British army had got its arse whupped during the War of Independence. I tried not to take it personally. We passed the house where Paul Revere lived with his fourteen children and the obelisk-like memorial to the battle of Bunker Hill.

Stop number six on the tour was Boston Common, an open area that presented a startlingly white blanket. The sun had put in an appearance and the reflection off the crystallised surface was almost too bright to look at directly.

Ella jiggled in her seat at the sight of it, tugging on her mother's sleeve, and when Simone bent towards her, whispered in her ear.

"I promised, didn't I, sweetie?" Simone said as the bus came to a stop. She twisted in her seat as the bus slowed, and said casually over her shoulder, "We'll get off here, Charlie. Ella wants a walk in the park." And before I had a chance to object, they were on their feet and moving towards the doorway.

I hurried after them, trying to clamp down on my irritation. I had time briefly to wonder what part of the possibility of the increased danger Simone and I had discussed the night before she was having difficulty taking on board.

Boston Common was surprisingly quiet. Apart from the skaters on the frozen Frog Pond, who were all progressing in a slow clockwise crawl, I think the squirrels outnumbered the people. Ella quickly wore the novelty out of the huge white carpet that covered the grass, and it wasn't until her mother suggested building a snowman that she perked up.

Ella was an enthusiastic but not very scientific snowman builder. Simone ended up being the one who scooped together enough snow to make a rounded body, while Ella ran round chucking wild fistfuls of the stuff at both of us and shrieking whenever she thought we were going to retaliate.

Simone just grinned at her and flicked me a reproachful little sideways look, as if to say, *How could you want to deprive her of this?*

I picked up a handful of snow myself and moulded it absently into a ball, but apart from dodging Ella's less inaccurate throws, I didn't join in the fun and games. Boston Common was open enough for nobody to be able to creep up on us without my being aware of it, but we seemed a long way from the surrounding streets and any passers-by who might help to deter any attempt as well. Neagley's warning went round and round in my head. Why hadn't anyone asked more questions right from the start about Simone's mystery father?

Without any activity to keep my circulation going, it was bitterly cold. I was glad I had a hat pulled down over my ears, but my cheeks were going numb. I huddled down further inside my coat and tried not to shiver as I did yet another sweep of the area surrounding us, as I'd been doing every minute or so since we'd got off the trolley bus, without spotting anything that set any alarm bells ringing.

This time, though, there was a man walking along one of the pathways towards us. A big guy in a tweed flat hat and a three-quarter-length tweed coat, unbuttoned. It was too cold to be wearing a coat that way and I didn't like the way his eyes never shifted away from Simone and Ella as he moved. Surely Tweed had seen a kid and her mother building a snowman before? I checked around me, looking for a second prong before I edged sideways so I was directly in his line of sight, blocking his view of my principals.

Not for the first time, I missed the weight of a nine-millimetre SIG SAUER P226 on my hip. There were a lot of countries around the world where accredited UK bodyguards were allowed to carry a concealed weapon while they were on the job. The US, sadly, wasn't one of them.

Tweed flicked his gaze onto me. Our eyes held for a second, and it was only then that I realised where I'd seen him before. It was the man from the Aquarium who'd lured

Simone away from her daughter and me by the sea lion enclosure. *A nice, normal guy, huh?* I wheeled away and scooped up Ella, ignoring her wail of protest.

"We're leaving," I said sharply to Simone. She had just finished rolling a snowball the size of a watermelon for the snowman's head and was halfway through lifting it onto the larger sphere of his body. She gave me a startled look but must have caught enough of what was in my face to quell any arguments she'd been about to make. She dropped the snowman's head, which broke in two on the frozen earth. I thrust Ella into her arms and hurried the pair of them back towards Beacon Hill, which ran along the north side of the Common.

"What?" Simone demanded, breathless, as I hustled her along. "What is it?"

"Just keep moving," I muttered, resisting the urge to glance round until we reached the edge of the park and scrambled up the steps by the Shaw Memorial. Tweed— Aquarium man—was still fifty metres behind us but closing in a leisurely kind of way. Like he knew we didn't have to hurry because he knew we had nowhere to go.

But luck was on our side for once. A lone cab was cruising towards us up the hill with its "for hire' light on. I stepped off the kerb and stuck my arm out, abandoning my usual reluctance for transport I didn't know. The driver swerved slightly towards me and pulled up right alongside, so all I had to do was lower my arm and my fingertips touched the rear handle. I yanked the door open and piled a baffled Simone and Ella inside, climbing in after them and slamming the door behind me.

I gave the driver the address of the hotel and he set off with commendable haste, setting up a wallow in the suspension like an ocean liner.

I looked back through the rear window as we made the first corner by the gold-domed State House building, to find Aquarium man standing by the kerb, staring after us. I couldn't see his face clearly, but it wasn't difficult to read

his body language, even at that distance, and I know anger
when   I   see   it.

It took Simone just about until we were back at Rowe's
Wharf before she'd got Ella quietened down enough to turn
her attention to me. I greeted Simone's shocked questions
with a meaningful nod towards the back of the cabdriver's
head. For a moment Simone seemed set to protest, but then
she looked away, concentrating on distracting Ella instead,
and we didn't speak at all until we were back at the hotel.

But as soon as we'd paid off the cab and headed for the
hotel entrance, she grabbed my arm.

"What the hell was all that about, Charlie?" she
demanded, keeping her voice low. I don't know why. She
was holding Ella balanced on her hip. The little girl was
watching the pair of us intently and looked like she was
picking up on every nuance.

"Remember the guy from the Aquarium?" I said. "Well
he turned up again at the park, heading right for us. I don't
know if you believe in coincidence, Simone, but I—"

"The guy from the Aquarium," she repeated flatly, and I
didn't like the dull flush that crept up her cheeks any more
than I liked the glitter in her eyes. "And that's what you
were panicking about, was it?"

"I did not panic, Simone," I said, struggling against a
rising temper. "I got the pair of you away from what I
considered was a possible source of danger. That's my job."

"I don't suppose it occurred to you to tell me what you
were up to before you hustled us away from there, huh?"

I stopped and turned round. We were halfway across the
lobby, which was almost deserted. Just a grey-haired guy
with a short beard talking to the concierge and a middle-
aged couple sitting reading guidebooks at the far side. I
moved in, getting right in Simone's face and not caring
about the way she flinched back from me.

"I can't run this as a democracy," I said through gritted
teeth. "If I feel there's a threat, I can't stand around and

ask your opinion on it. I have to use my judgement and act."

"Uh-huh," Simone said, ominous. "And I also don't suppose it occurred to you that I might have *wanted* to see that guy again. That he just might have been interested enough in me to have given me his phone number and I *just might* have given him a call ...?"

"You did what?" I said, and even though I spoke hardly louder than a whisper I heard the cold anger and the disbelief in my own voice. "No," I said blankly. "You couldn't have been so stupid."

Simone flushed fully then and opened her mouth to snap back at me when I suddenly realised by the shift in Ella's gaze that someone was approaching us across the lobby's polished floor.

The grey-haired man who'd been talking to the concierge stopped a few metres away and looked uncertainly from one of us to the other. He was in his late fifties, the neatly trimmed beard giving him a distinguished air. He wore a good coat and expensive shoes. His eyes were darting from one of us to the other, as though waiting for his opportunity to break in without getting clawed.

"Pardon me," he said politely to Simone, "but you *are* Simone, er, Kerse, aren't you?"

"Yes," Simone said immediately, shooting me a defiant glare. "Yes, I am!"

"Ah," the man said. He smiled, a little uncertain at the vehemence of her response. "Well, in that case ... I understand you've been looking for me. I believe I'm your father."

EIGHT

You OK back there, Charlie?" Greg Lucas asked. "Comfortable? Warm enough? Shout out if Ella needs to stop to go to the bathroom or anything."

"We're fine at the moment, thanks," I said. It took an effort to keep my voice pleasant. I didn't think Lucas was being deliberately patronising, but Simone had presented me more as the hired help than anything else and, so far, I hadn't found a reason other than pride to contradict the opinion he'd formed. Now, his eyes flicked to meet mine in the rear-view mirror and I saw the crow's-feet at the sides of them crinkle as he smiled at me. I couldn't see the rest of his face but so far he'd behaved without apparent guile, however hard I'd looked for signs of treachery.

We were in a new-model Range Rover Vogue SE, barrelling north out of Massachusetts and into New Hampshire on Interstate 95. Simone up front with Lucas, and me and Ella in the rear seats. Our luggage—including the giant bear with the scowl—was piled up behind us.

It was the day after Greg Lucas had introduced himself to Simone in the lobby of the Boston Harbor Hotel, and, to my mind at least, it was much too soon to be going anywhere with him. Convincing Simone of that, however, had caused major ructions.

From the outset, she hadn't liked the fact that I'd headed her off from inviting Lucas up to the suite to talk but had instead suggested more neutral territory in the restaurant. He'd looked momentarily a little surprised at my cool reception, but had agreed equably enough. We'd left him to secure us a table in the Intrigue Café while I took Simone back upstairs, ostensibly to drop off our coats and change Ella out of her boots, but mainly so I could get her on her own long enough to advise caution.

Not exactly what Simone wanted to hear.

"Oh for heaven's sake, Charlie!" she snapped, and there was a glitter in her eye I didn't quite like. She was almost feverish with a kind of scared excitement. "Why would he pretend to be my father if he isn't?"

I could think of over 13,400,000 good reasons, but didn't voice them. Maybe Simone had realised that as she'd spoken, because she sighed without waiting for an answer and said, "OK, I'll be careful, but you don't know how long I've waited and wished for this."

"I know," I said, gently, "but that's exactly why you shouldn't rush into anything now. It's been twenty-five years since you last saw him. You admitted yourself that you couldn't remember much about him, and he wouldn't have had that beard while he was in the army. So, he must expect that you're going to ask questions, that you're going to be suspicious. Anybody would be. And that's quite apart from telling him about your win. I certainly would not mention anything about that for a while—at least until you're sure."

She was quiet for a moment, then nodded.

"OK Charlie," she said, more subdued now but with a stubborn set to her jaw. "But he doesn't exactly look as though he's living out of soup kitchens, does he? And this is what we're here for, isn't it? So I could find and meet with him? And now I have found him—or might have," she allowed when I opened my mouth to interrupt. "Look, either I get to know him a little and find out for sure, or we may as well go home now."

I shrugged. "OK, Simone," I said. "Just be careful, all right?"

She smiled, too fast, too bright. "I am being careful," she said. "I have you with me, don't I?"

Back down in the dining room, Lucas rose as we approached the table he'd selected near the fireplace at the far end, reminding me of the old-fashioned manners of Harrington, the banker. Lucas had shed his coat and was wearing a polo-necked sweater in some fine-knit wool that could well have been cashmere. He was quite slim apart from a barrel chest that enabled him to carry off a little excess weight around the centre of an upright frame, and he looked confident and successful.

Simone hesitated when she reached him, as though not sure whether to kiss his cheek or shake hands. Lucas took over, putting both hands on her upper arms and leaning back slightly, head on one side as though he was surveying a work of art.

"So, it's really my little princess, all grown up," he murmured with a smile. His accent was a strange mixture of American inflection laid over something British and regional. Possibly Liverpudlian, but with all the rough corners knocked off it like a rounded pebble on a beach.

Simone's answering smile was a little tremulous, her eyes bright with unshed tears. For a moment her throat was too constricted to speak, and Lucas just gave her arms a reassuring squeeze before turning to me.

"And who's this?" he asked, friendly, casual.

"I'm Charlie Fox," I said, holding out my hand to avoid the arm squeezing. "I'm here to look after—"

"Ella," Simone supplied quickly. "Charlie's here to look after Ella, my daughter."

His check was so slight as to be almost imagined, but there was a certain reserve when he nodded to me that disappeared as he crouched to Ella's eye level.

"Hello Ella," he said softly. "You know, you're the spitting image of your mother when she was a little girl. She was beautiful, too."

Watching his face as he regarded Ella, I was more inclined to trust him then than at any point previously. Either that or he should have been working in Hollywood, because the way his expression softened was utterly convincing. Ella suddenly went all bashful, ducking her face under her curls and sidling behind my leg. He grinned at her, a flash of a younger, almost roguish smile, and straightened.

The waiter ushered us into seats and took our drink order before departing. There was a short awkward silence before both Simone and Lucas launched in at once.

"So, how long have you—?"

"How did you—?"

They both stopped, smiled, and both tried to say, "You first," at the same time, ending up laughing together a little too hard. Simone shot me a hard little look that clearly said, *How can you have any doubts about this man when we're so clearly in tune?*

"Ladies first—I insist," Lucas said, linking his hands together, fingers relaxed, on the tablecloth.

"I was just going to ask how you found me."

He looked surprised. "But surely *you* found *me*," he said, frowning. "That guy you hired—Barry O'Halloran. He came to visit me about a week or so ago, telling me my daughter wanted to make contact." He said the word "daughter' with a certain wonder, as if he thought he'd lost the knack and had suddenly discovered it again. "Well, that came as quite a shock after all this time, let me tell you, but I told him, sure, why not?"

It was my turn for surprise. "You agreed?"

"Sure," he said again, with a shrug. "I got no reason not to. She was a terrific kid." He smiled at Simone again, rueful. "It wasn't her fault that things didn't work out between her mother and me. And, well, I've changed a lot since those days."

At the soft sincerity in his voice, Simone went a little pink, suddenly fussing with the collar of Ella's dress. It was left to me to ask, "So, how did you find us here?"

"Well, Barry said he was going to call Simone as soon as he got back to the office and she'd probably fly right over. Then he left and I waited to hear."

"When was this?"

He raised his eyes, remembering. "Oh, a week or ten days ago, I guess."

"A week or ten days," I repeated blandly.

"That's not long, Charlie," Simone said, defensive, even though she'd been the one in the all-fired hurry.

Lucas nodded and smiled at her. "Well, I've been kind of busy lately, I admit, but yesterday I started to wonder what had happened and I tried to call Barry, and that's when I found out about his accident." He broke off and shook his head. "Poor guy, ending up in a river like that, huh? The winters can be brutal out here. Not like England. You gotta be prepared for the weather."

"How?" I said.

"Excuse me?"

Simone stabbed me with a meaningful look and I moderated my tone with a smile. "Sorry. I meant how did you find out about the accident?"

"Oh, one of the local cops happened to stop by and I guess he must have mentioned something—or I brought it up—and that's when I thought I'd better do some checking, just in case you'd flown right over, like Barry said, and were sitting here waiting for me to call."

Even I had to admit that he had a disarming quality about him, but, I reminded myself, all the best con men do. Besides, that didn't explain how he'd tracked us down so quickly.

"So how," I began, ignoring Simone's furious glance, "did you know we were staying here—at this hotel?"

"Process of elimination," he said, the first hairline fractures beginning to appear in his cheerful demeanour now. "I couldn't leave my little girl waiting for me, could I? I started calling the hotels."

My eyebrows went up. "All of them?"

He nodded. "I started at the top, which was lucky, because this is one of the best in town. As soon as I found out Simone was here, I hightailed it down."

"But—"

"That's enough, Charlie," Simone said, her voice quiet but no less commanding for all that. "Poor ... " Her voice tailed off and I realised that despite her earlier confidence, she was struggling to find the right word to use.

Greg Lucas treated her to his brightest, warmest smile. "Just call me Greg," he said gently. "For the moment, anyways. Let's take this one step at a time, honey, hm? I know how hard this is for you and I know I haven't been much of a father to you," he went on, reaching out and covering Simone's hand on the tabletop with his own. Ella, I noticed, couldn't take her eyes off the gesture. "But now we have a second shot at it, and I'll do anything I can to make it work."

Simone nodded, her lips pressed together for a moment. Next thing, she'd jumped up out of her chair and hugged him, fiercely. I heard her muffled voice saying, "I've missed you, Daddy. I've missed you."

After only a moment's hesitation, Lucas's arms went round her shoulders and his hands drew soothing circles on her back. "I know, honey," he said softly, but his face, visible over Simone's embrace, was curiously stiff and cold. "You don't know how much I've missed you, too."

**

The following day, riding north into a sky heavy with the promise of more snow, I had to admit that Greg Lucas wasn't behaving like a man who was after Simone's money—if he knew anything about it. The Range Rover we were riding in was the latest model and so new it hadn't had time to lose the smell of fresh leather inside. Besides, Range Rovers were expensive enough in the UK, but over here they carried even more cachet. And despite the fact that we were staying in a fancy hotel, Simone still didn't look or dress or talk like she had money.

She'd admitted to Lucas that she was an engineer by training and told him about her split-up with Matt. She carefully blamed Matt's wandering eye for their estrangement and made it sound like he was little more than a distant memory. Ella nearly dropped her in it at that point by saying, loudly, "But Mummy, you and Daddy were arguing about the money, too, weren't you?"

Simone had flushed pink right to the roots of her hair and come up with a hasty excuse that Matt earned less than she did and it had caused some friction.

Lucas had swung his eyes towards me and said, "Well, you must be doing pretty well for yourself if you can afford full-time help for little Ella here." Simone heard only the paternal pride in his voice, but I heard the trace of suspicion underlying it, and I'm not sure which one of us was picking up the right vibes.

Still, I tried to keep an open mind about Simone's father. He certainly made every effort to be amenable, taking us on his own guided tour of Boston and for an early evening meal at the Top of the Hub restaurant on the 52nd floor of the Prudential Center, where we could enjoy a stunning view of the Boston skyline. But I still couldn't shake the feeling that I didn't quite trust him.

And when he invited the three of us to stay at his home in New Hampshire, Simone had accepted practically before the words were out of his mouth. Partly, I suspected, to stop me sticking my oar in. She waited until Lucas had gone to the restroom before she quietly tore into me for my intransigence.

"The whole idea of this trip was for me to find my father, and I did not go to all this time and trouble only for *you* to scare him off again!" she said in a savage whisper. "For God's sake, Charlie, lighten up!"

"All I'm trying to do is ensure your safety," I said, trying to keep hold of my own temper.

"Well, that's fine and dandy," she said, glaring. "Just don't stop me doing what I want to do or I'll damned well go on my own."

I'd called Neagley to see what her impression had been of Lucas, but got her answering service. I left a message asking her to call me urgently. I also rang Sean for advice, but he wasn't helpful.

"You've got first class instincts, Charlie," he said drily, "but you can't stop Simone from seeing this guy unless you can give her a better reason than you don't really like him."

"I know," I said. "But there's something about this whole situation that makes me uneasy. I just can't quite put my finger on it."

"Well, until you can, you're just going to have to go along for the ride. I'll hurry Madeleine along with the background on Lucas at this end and we'll see what pops up, but don't hold your breath."

"Neagley seemed to have managed to find out a fair amount," I said, ruffled.

"I know, but what she'd got was public record. Yes, Lucas was SAS and by all accounts he had a bit of a hair trigger, but we need more than that. Trying to get information out of the Ministry of Defence is a nightmare, and they get especially awkward when it's someone who's been in the Regiment. Just stay sharp and you'll be OK."

I ended the call with a sense of nagging foreboding. The army hadn't been quite so reticent when it came to leaking the story of my own downfall, so why were they being so difficult about spilling the beans on Greg Lucas when he'd been out for close to twenty-five years?

Mind you, even I had to admit that my case was different. The army brass hadn't wanted me to get through the selection process to begin with. There'd been dismay in some quarters when I and two other girls had stayed the course and made it into training.

A woman wasn't physically up to the job; a woman would compromise an operation if she was killed, wounded, or captured; a woman wasn't psychologically equipped to kill, up close and personal. I heard every argument in the book—and quite a few that weren't.

And I suppose, back then, they were right. When four of my fellow trainees decided to prove, in a drunken outburst of testosterone, that women really were the weaker sex, I hadn't been able to dig deep enough into my own psyche to find the vital killer instinct.

That had come much later.

**

Keeping Ella amused was one of the trickiest parts of the journey north. She was bright and inquisitive, which meant you had to be on your toes all the time. She seemed to cotton on straight away if you made an automatic response to any of her constant questions, and after half an hour in her company I was mentally exhausted.

I wondered how on earth Simone coped with her, day after day, but then remembered that up until Simone's lottery win Ella had normally spent working hours in day care. That gave me another topic of conversation, at least, and over the next twenty minutes or so I learned all about Ella's favourite teacher and the names of her best friends and that finger painting and making Plasticine animals were what she enjoyed doing most.

I even resorted to a game of I Spy, which would have been easier if Ella didn't have a fairly fluid idea of coming up with objects that actually began with the letter she'd originally chosen. Plus we were passing through great tracts of wooded countryside, which somewhat restricted the options.

At one point we passed a huge billboard carrying the information that the New Hampshire Sweepstake lottery prize was now up to $365 million. I saw Simone's head turn to look and caught the merest suggestion of a smile on her face.

She and Lucas talked in the front seats as we drove, their voices too quiet for me to be able to easily follow the conversation without craning forwards, at which point Ella, realising she was being ignored by all the adults, became even more vocal. Eventually, I abandoned all my efforts at eavesdropping and gave her my full attention, which she liked much better.

After about an hour and a half, Lucas suggested a rest stop at the New Hampshire border, at which point I could cheerfully have kissed him. That changed with the sudden fear that I was going to be the one who was expected to take Ella to the toilet. Fortunately, it was Ella herself who insisted that she wanted her mummy to take her.

I went with them, as a matter of course. In front of Ella, Simone didn't say much other than to tell me that she was genuinely enjoying Lucas's company. I bit back the comment that it was in his interests to make sure she did and just nodded. By the look on Simone's face, it was not a satisfactory response.

We were halfway back across the snow-strewn parking area when my mobile rang. I stopped in order to dig it out of my inside pocket, watching while Simone and Ella carried on back towards the Range Rover. It was too cold for them to linger, even if they'd wanted to.

"Charlie? It's Frances Neagley. You wanted to talk with me?"

"Yeah, thanks for getting back to me." I said. I paused, partly to let the two of them get further ahead of me, so they were out of earshot, and partly because I wasn't sure where to launch in. "So, you've dispensed with your bodyguard?"

She was quiet for a moment and I could almost imagine her looking round, as though to check the man from Armstrong's was still with her. "I haven't," she said.

"Oh." My turn to pause. "But you spoke to Greg Lucas about your partner? He rang you, right? Before he made contact with Simone?"

94

"He's made contact?" she said and her voice came out both tense and baffled. "When?"

"Yesterday." Out of the corner of my eye I saw Simone open the rear door of the Range Rover and lift Ella onto her booster cushion on the back seat. "He showed up at the hotel." I tried to remember the exact wording. Had Lucas actually said he'd spoken to Neagley? I scanned my memory. Maybe not, but he'd certainly given that impression.

Simone had finished buckling Ella into her seat now and I started walking towards the car. She had already climbed into the passenger seat as I did so, and I saw the brake lights flare as Lucas shifted the transmission out of park.

"Lucas said that when O'Halloran didn't get back in touch with him after their meeting, he'd tried to call him," I said quickly, breaking into a jog. "I assumed you thought he was on the level or you wouldn't have passed on the details."

"Charlie, I didn't pass on anything," Neagley said, sounding anguished now. "I haven't spoken to the guy. Not a word. I don't know how he found your client, but it wasn't through me."

Suddenly, the Range Rover swung out of its parking space. I abandoned the call, slamming the phone shut as I slipped and slithered across the icy surface that separated me from my principals. I didn't even have the breath to curse. I could only watch as the big car picked up speed away from me between the rows of other vehicles. I made a mental note of the plate, the call I was going to have to make to the police already formulating in my head.

At the end of the row, the Range Rover's brake lights came on and I put on a burst of speed in the vain hope I might still catch them, skidding on the icy ground. A moment later, they had pulled away again and for a second it looked like Lucas was heading straight for the exit. Then he swung round in a big lazy semicircle and headed back down the next row, towards me. I cut through the line of cars and practically threw myself in front of him. As it was, he had to hit the brakes hard enough for Simone's head to snap forwards in the passenger seat. She looked startled, with the first beginnings of annoyance on her features.

My gaze swapped across to Greg Lucas but the way the light reflected on the glass meant I couldn't see his features clearly.

I waited a beat, then walked down the side of the car and snatched the rear door open, scrambling in through the gap. By the time Simone and Lucas looked round, I'd already half-launched myself between the front seats, fist clenched ready to strike at the man's throat. I knew I could take out his voicebox with my left hand and yank the gear lever back into neutral with my right before he had a chance to pick up enough speed for the resulting accident to do us any damage. He would make very little noise as he died, and Ella—seated directly behind him—wouldn't see enough to traumatise her too badly. Simone I'd worry about later.

Then Lucas swivelled in his seat and smiled at me.

"Sorry, Charlie, I didn't mean to scare ya," he said, sounding almost genuinely penitent. "I was just coming around to pick you up there."

I pushed myself back into my seat slowly, uncurling my stiffened fingers and taking a deep breath to dilute the adrenaline that was coursing through my system. I checked his face carefully. Was it my imagination, or did the smile not quite reach his eyes.

"Of course you were," I said softly, letting the double answer play out. "I never thought you were doing anything different."

NINE

I didn't get the opportunity to tell Simone about my conversation with Frances Neagley before we arrived at our destination, by which time I felt it was already too late. The only good thing was that Ella had nodded off soon after our last rest-stop and so I could give my full attention to our current situation.

Greg Lucas lived in a small town called North Conway in the White Mountains, about three hours north of Boston, and the contrast from the dark and serious city was marked. North Conway was picture-postcard pretty, for the most part, with clapboard houses painted a variety of pastel shades. Very few had garden fences separating them, adding to the friendly feel, like there was no need to keep out strangers. Like nothing bad could happen here.

Christmas fairy lights still decorated the shop fronts, even in early February. And there did seem to be a lot of shopping available, outlets mostly, boasting just about every famous name designer brand I'd ever heard of. When I remarked on this, Lucas smiled and explained there was no state sales tax in New Hampshire.

"This time of year, people come to North Conway mainly to ski, but when they're done on the slopes there's plenty for them to spend their dollars on," he said, flashing a quick smile. "Keeps the wheels turning."

He'd already told us, in broad terms, that he had a business dealing in military surplus supplies in the neighbouring town of Intervale. For once I didn't have to probe further into that. Simone was curious enough about what the man who claimed to be her father did for a living to ask him enough questions of her own. She seemed calmer than she had done when we'd left Boston, but as she listened to Lucas's explanations there was still a certain eagerness about her that concerned me.

He was, to my mind, still pretty vague about it. The way Lucas talked, you'd think all he handled was army boots and camouflage-coloured tents. But given his military background I couldn't help but wonder what else he might be involved in. I was just wondering how to phrase a question when Simone beat me to it.

"So, does that mean you sell guns?" she asked. I glanced at her in surprise. Maybe she wasn't quite as taken in by Lucas as I'd feared.

He frowned, slowing for a stoplight. "Not really," he answered, which was no answer at all. "I have them, of course." In the mirror I saw him flick his eyes sideways at her, as if to gauge her reaction. "It's kind of a natural thing out here."

Simone shook her head. "Not to me it isn't," she said sharply. "I can't stand them, and I won't have them around Ella."

Lucas nodded seriously. "They're all safely under lock and key, honey," he said mildly. "Don't you worry about it."

Simone didn't reply to that, but I could tell by the way she'd turned her head away and was staring fixedly out of the window that his answer hadn't entirely reassured her.

It was nearly one in the afternoon and the landscape was blisteringly white in the stark bright sunshine. We'd drive through enclosed forest sections, then suddenly there'd be a gap in the trees and you'd see distant snow-covered mountains. The scale of the place was overwhelming.

Lucas pointed out the local ski resort over to our right as we trundled down the seemingly never-ending main street. Mount Cranmore, he told us, adding that they had some nice easy nursery slopes there, for when Simone was thinking of getting Ella out on skis.

"Oh, she's much too young for that," Simone protested, glancing back at where her daughter lay sleeping alongside me.

"You never can start them too early," he said. "You'll be amazed how soon she picks it up." There was something a little earnest about the way he spoke, as though he was looking for reassurance that they would be staying long enough for something like skiing lessons to be a possibility.

For some reason the thought unsettled me. We were passing a variety of restaurants and I grasped at the idea of getting Simone away from Lucas long enough to speak to her, especially somewhere safely public.

"What about stopping for a bite of lunch?" I suggested brightly.

"I have lunch all set once we get to the house," Lucas said, and I suppressed a groan. "We're only a couple minutes away now."

He kept checking Simone's face, I noticed, and his hands seemed to be gripping the steering wheel more tightly than was strictly necessary. His nervousness was making me twitchy. It had increased noticeably in the last few miles. What was at the house that he didn't want Simone to see? Or what was going to happen once we got there?

I soon found out.

At first it looked like Lucas was taking us right to the ski slopes. We turned off the main street into a side road that quickly became residential. Big detached houses with the front driveways neatly cleared of snow, and basketball hoops above the garage doors. A number had American flags hanging limply from poles in their front gardens. Just about every house had a pickup truck or a big four-wheel drive in front of it. Still, the snow must have been a couple of feet thick in places, so you actually needed the extra traction.

99

We crossed a railway line and turned left onto a street called Kearsage, then right onto Snowmobile. I kept glancing out of the rear window so I'd recognise them again from the other direction. Never get yourself into anywhere you can't get out of. It was one of the first things I'd learned.

I examined my options. In theory, when it came to Simone's security I was in charge. Yes—technically—she was my employer, but if she was actively exposing herself to danger, I had the authority to override her decisions. It was a nice theory. Practice was another matter.

In practice, I couldn't physically restrain her. One of Sean's rules was that if a client constantly disregarded advice, we walked away from the job. Better that than put his team at risk doing something they knew was unnecessarily dangerous or taking the fall for their principal getting killed instead. Not, at this stage, that I felt there was any real danger involved here, and leaving Simone and Ella to cope on their own was not an option.

Besides anything else, the whole purpose of her visit to the US, as she'd pointed out, was to find and get to know her father. Even I had to admit that this trip to North Conway with him was a perfect opportunity for her to do that. The fact that I had reservations about him—albeit ones that I couldn't turn into anything concrete—counted for nothing. Simone dismissed my cautious approach as an overreaction like the one she believed I'd had on Boston Common.

We seemed nearly at the base of the mountain now. I could see the lines of the ski-lifts rising above us, dotted with people taking advantage of the sunshine. Just when it looked like we were heading right for the ski lodge at the bottom of the mountain and were going to have to complete our journey by sleigh, Lucas made another right turn, past the tubing park and the Fitness Center that even boasted its own climbing wall. Another quarter of a mile further on,

Lucas slowed and said in a tense voice to Simone, "Well, here we are."

The house was impressive, even by American standards. What I would have called a one-and-a-half-storey building, with huge gables in the roof to show rooms on an upper floor. Directly in front of us was a three-car garage, with the house itself set back slightly to the left. A raised deck ran right the way round the outside, and there were steps leading up to it and the glass-panelled front door. The walls were covered in green shingles and dark-stained clapboard. With the trees overhanging from all sides, it seemed a little dark and forbidding, but I suppose it was meant to blend.

Sitting behind her, I couldn't see Simone's face to judge her reaction, but she was leaning forwards slightly as we swung onto the cleared driveway, craning her neck to look at the place. I glanced at Ella, but she was still spark out, head lolling sideways against the bunched-up coat she was using as a pillow. It was only as Lucas pulled up in front of the garages and actually switched off the Range Rover's engine that she snuffled into wakefulness, squinting in the bright sunlight, her hair all flattened on one side. Lucas, Simone, and I all climbed out. The cold took your breath away.

"How're you doing, princess?" Lucas asked Ella. Mistake. Even on my limited acquaintance with Ella I knew she always woke grumpy. Now, she scowled furiously at him and, showing an early feminine awareness of her appearance, hid her face in her mother's shoulder as soon as she was unbuckled from her seat. Lucas seemed a little taken aback by the little girl's response.

"Don't worry," Simone said apologetically, smiling at him. "She's always like this." She seemed to have forgotten her earlier reservations.

"OK, well, let's get her inside and see about that food I promised," Lucas said, recovering.

We'd just reached the bottom of the steps when the front door opened and a woman came out onto the porch. She

101

was medium height, the stiffness of her spine making her seem taller, with iron grey hair pulled into a tight French pleat at the back of her head. She was wearing khaki trousers and a rust-coloured blouse with a kind of big floppy collar that might have been trying to soften down her rather severe features but only served to emphasise them. Nevertheless, she was smiling in welcome.

My first reaction was that she was Lucas's housekeeper. She seemed older than he did and slightly out of step in both appearance and manner. It was Lucas himself who dispelled this myth, bounding lightly up the steps and planting a chaste kiss on the woman's cheek before taking her arm and turning to face the three of us.

"Simone, honey, I'd like you to meet Rosalind ... my wife."

I felt rather than saw Simone's jaw sag. For a moment she said nothing at all, just stared blankly. Eventually, it was Rosalind who disentangled herself from her husband and came down the stairs to meet us. She stopped in front of Simone and smiled with every appearance of real affection at Ella.

"I can see that Greg's kind of dropped this on you," Rosalind said, flicking Lucas a reproachful glance. Her voice was low and husky, like she was a heavy smoker, although I smelt no tobacco on her clothes. "But it's a pleasure to finally meet you," she said. She shrugged, the sudden uncertainty of the gesture at odds with her competent appearance. "I guess ... well, I guess this makes me your stepmom."

***

"So how well did that go down?" Sean asked.

"Like a lead balloon," I said wryly. "Simone's only just found Daddy—I think the idea of having to share him with anyone other than Ella came as a bit of a shock to her."

I was closeted in the guest room I'd been allocated and had taken advantage of the momentary solitude to check in with Sean. I sat on the bed alongside the giant teddy bear that Simone had bought for Ella in Boston.

I'd been right about the bear's ominous demeanour. Ella had been so unsettled by its presence that, after the first night, she'd refused to sleep in the same room. Now she was sharing with Simone, that meant the bear was rooming with me. I'd privately named him Hannibal and already decided that he was spending the night in the closet so I wouldn't wake up and find him looming over me.

Sean listened to my brief report on the situation without interruption, then said, "I can see why you're not happy, but Simone is the client. Unless there's a direct threat you can't insist she pulls out of there, and a dodgy sense of humour doesn't really count. Just watch for signs of that temper, though."

"I will. I just don't think Simone's asking nearly enough questions about this guy, and she doesn't like it when I try and get straight answers out of him," I said. "There's something that doesn't quite ring true about him for me. And we still don't really know how he managed to find us in Boston."

"Mm, that is a bit of a worrying one, I admit. I'll check with the hotel, but I'd be very surprised if they'd given out any information. Madeleine stressed the need for discretion when she booked with them."

"Have you managed to find out anything more about him?"

"Just that he had a mean streak and he liked to fight— on or off the battlefield. I get the feeling there's a lot more they're not saying about that, but I'll keep digging."

"If he was a brawler, he was either very good or very lucky," I said, "because he's picked up very little by way of scarring and if his nose was ever broken, he's had it very well fixed."

"That's not so unusual these days," Sean said. "Just as many men go in for cosmetic surgery as women."

"Maybe," I said. "But a photo would be good, so we've got visual confirmation that he is who we think he is, at least. I think this new phone's got picture messaging, hasn't it?" I'd been slow to catch on to the technological age, but I suppose I was making up for lost time now.

"I'll see what I can do. In the meantime, you need to push Simone to ask more awkward questions about her father, see how he reacts. What do you make of the new wife?"

I shrugged. "She seems OK," I said, cautious. "Businesslike and no-nonsense, though. If you don't dig your heels in she rides right on over you."

She'd tried it with me over the matter of which room I was due to sleep in. After the initial awkwardness of the introductions, Rosalind Lucas quickly regained her composure. Lucas might have been the army man, but his second wife had command of the home and he seemed happy to leave the domestic decisions to her in the same way officers casually deferred to their NCOs in the matter of day-to-day logistics. Rosalind gave us a tour of the house with brisk efficiency, automatically assuming that we'd fall in with her arrangements.

The house had four bedrooms in total, which would have worked out fine apart from the fact that three of them, including the master suite, were on the upper floor, and the fourth was in the basement.

Fitted-out basements are not a common thing in the UK. The only things that are normally kept in the cellar—apart from wine—are old tins of paint, mildew, and an inordinate number of spiders. In the Lucases' case 'basement' was a bit of a misnomer. The guest suite had its own windows to the outside, courtesy of the fact that at the rear of the house the land dropped down towards the ski slope a hundred metres or so away through the trees.

The whole of the lower floor was luxuriously appointed, with a fully equipped exercise room, a home cinema, and several locked doorways to rooms that were just described as "storage'. I eyed the heavy-duty padlocks and assumed that was where Lucas kept his gun collection. If Simone came to the same conclusion, she didn't mention it.

Rosalind had put Simone and Ella in the two spare rooms upstairs, leaving me in the dungeon, and looked very put out when I objected, ostensibly on the grounds that I ought to be nearer Ella, just in case she woke in the night.

"But surely ... is that likely?" Rosalind had asked, looking baffled. She'd glanced across to where Ella had been sitting on the sofa alongside the man who claimed to be her grandfather, proudly showing him the motheaten Eeyore and, from the slightly bemused look on his face, giving him the stuffed animal's life history and quirks of character.

Simone had hesitated, not wanting to be awkward with her hosts, but then she saw the way my eyebrows had come down meaningfully.

"Well, it *is* Charlie's job," she said then, with an apologetic smile. Rosalind had done her best to make friends with her stepdaughter, but I don't think Simone would have been fighting my corner quite so hard if it had been Lucas himself who'd raised the query.

Eventually, they found a roll-out bed for Ella to use in Simone's room, while I was given the smaller of the guest rooms on the upper floor nearby. Rosalind was clearly mystified at my insistent disruption of her plans, but she accepted it with some measure of grace. When she showed me up to my room she even apologised profusely for the fact that it didn't have its own en suite bathroom.

Now, I finished my quick call to Sean and left the room, pulling the door closed behind me. As I did so, Rosalind stepped out of a doorway across the landing, leading from the master suite. I wondered briefly if she'd been able to eavesdrop on my conversation, then dismissed the thought. I'd never been in the habit of shouting into a mobile phone, and the house seemed well-built enough to be reasonably soundproof.

"So, how long have you been Simone's au pair?" Rosalind asked as she led the way back down the polished wooden staircase.

"Oh no, I'm paid to work for her," I said cheerfully, deliberately obtuse.

"Excuse me?"

"Au pairs are traditionally young girls who work for families for pocket money, in order to learn English," I said, smiling. "I'm a little old for that, and my English is fine."

"Er, yes, I see," Rosalind said, frowning.

We reached the ground floor. It was mostly open-plan, the through-kitchen and breakfast nook leading to the great room, which was a huge living area with a fireplace built of rounded fieldstone up the end wall. The furniture was dark wood, heavy and rather staid in design, at odds with the light airy feel of the house. Most of one side of the great room was glass, looking out over the deck through the trees and onto the lower part of the ski slopes.

There were elaborate drapes but they didn't look like they were ever closed, which was going to be tricky from a security point of view. Lovely to be able to enjoy the view, but anyone with a lift pass could see into the house and they had a perfect right to do as many runs past the Lucases' place as they felt like.

Simone was standing looking out of the window, cradling Ella. Lucas was standing beside them, his hand on Simone's shoulder as he pointed out the line of the ski run, their heads tilted close together. When Rosalind saw them she stopped abruptly and I caught the unguarded expression on her face before she had a chance to mask it. But was it hurt I saw? Or anger?

Lucas heard our footsteps and turned, letting his hand drop away a little too quickly.

Interesting ...

"Ah, there you are, Charlie," he said, overly hearty. "All settled in?"

"Yes, thank you," I said.

"You all must be hungry after your journey," Rosalind said, her features schooled back into a cool politeness once more. "I have a Brunswick stew in the crockpot. We can eat whenever you're ready."

***

The conversation over our late lunch was somewhat stilted. Lucas was doing his best to play genial host, but the tension in Rosalind communicated itself to Simone, and then on to Ella, like they were connected by wires. Apparently oblivious, Lucas appeared quite happy to chat about his first wife in front of his second. He seemed to be going out of his way to drop into little reminiscences about Simone's childhood—a well-loved toy, the wallpaper in her nursery, her favourite picture book.

To begin with, Simone seemed reluctant to join in this game of 'do you remember?' but as Lucas kept coming up with snatches of her infancy that she clearly *did* remember, she found herself inexorably drawn in. And, as the conversation began to flow more freely, so the whole atmosphere relaxed a little. When I glanced at Rosalind, even she no longer seemed quite so stiff in her upright dining chair.

The Brunswick stew turned out to be mainly chicken and vegetables, served up with mashed potatoes. Although Ella picked her way around the carrots with some caution, she was hungry enough to clear her plate and accept a second helping. Even if she did seem to end up wearing more of the gravy than she was managing to spoon into her mouth.

I, too, kept my mouth occupied with eating rather than joining in the talk, content to observe rather than take part, despite Lucas's occasional attempts to involve me in the proceedings.

"So, did you always want to work with children, Charlie?"

That question, from Rosalind, had me glancing up from my food in surprise. It had sounded so pointed, as if she knew I was either more—or less—than I was pretending to be. I wondered again if she'd been listening in on my conversation with Sean.

"Not really," I said, offering as much of the truth as I was able to, "but I suppose I like the idea of looking after people." Besides, during the previous summer I'd finally come to terms with the fact that I was capable of behaviour that took me to the extremes of social acceptability, and the more I was able to channel those traits into something useful—and legal—so much the better.

Rosalind frowned, something she seemed to do a lot if you gave an answer she didn't like or wasn't expecting.

"And how did you meet Simone?"

"She was recommended by a friend of the family." It was Simone herself who answered, shooting me a quick smile as she did so.

"I thought you didn't have any family—apart from the fact that you now have us, of course," Rosalind said, raising a small smile of her own in the direction of her husband, who answered it cheerfully enough.

"Yes, and it's wonderful to suddenly discover I have two of you where I only ever expected—dreamed, really—to find one," Simone said. She paused, picking her next words with care. "And I can't wait until Greg and I have the tests done and we can make it all official."

Simone delivered this news with such artful casualness, beaming at the pair of them and carrying on eating, apparently oblivious to the fact that they'd both frozen in their chairs.

"Tests?" Rosalind echoed.

"DNA," Simone said. "I'm assuming we can get them done locally, can we?"

I scanned their faces quickly, suppressing a cheer and the desire to jump up and hug Simone for her sudden display of level-headedness. Lucas and his wife exchanged glances, too fast for me to catch the message that flashed between them.

"Surely there's no need to go that far, is there?" Rosalind said with a breathless kind of a laugh. "After everything Greg's told you ...?"

"Oh, it's a formality, of course," Simone said breezily. "I mean, *I'm* absolutely convinced, but my solicitor will skin me if I don't come back with undisputed proof—especially when there's Ella to consider."

"Yes, but—"

That was as far as Rosalind got when, suddenly, the doorbell rang.

Rosalind's eyes flew to her husband's, startled. Lucas almost ducked sideways slightly in his seat, as if to hide. The dining area wasn't quite in direct line of sight to the glazed front door, but it was pretty close.

"I'll go," he said, but the smile he gave Rosalind was a strained one. He wiped his mouth on his napkin and dropped it onto the table as he got to his feet.

Unconsciously, we listened to his footsteps on the polished wooden floor of the hallway, could imagine the blast of cold air washing towards us as he opened the front door, heard the murmur of voices. Only Ella seemed unconcerned—both by the interruption and the turn the conversation had taken before it. She was totally absorbed with making a sandcastle of sorts out of her second helping of mashed potato and trying to create a moat for the gravy round the outside of it.

The voices continued by the front door. Lucas and another man's, deeper and somewhat colder for it. I couldn't make out the words but thought I detected a note of strain in Lucas's. His tone went sharp, then stopped abruptly, like it had snapped off.

I glanced at Rosalind and found her apparently placid expression belied by the fact that she was gripping her fork so tightly her knuckles had turned white. I pushed my chair back slightly from the table and found myself automatically measuring the distance between us and the nearest doorway to the outside, which was behind where Ella and Simone were sitting. A pair of double doors led out onto part of the external decking that seemed to surround the house on three sides, with steps down into the woods.

There was another door leading to a screened porch by the fireplace in the great room, which was behind me and over to my left. I hadn't initially liked the number of different access points to the house, but now I was glad of the options they provided.

Lucas came back into view at the end of the hallway with another man beside him. There was a study off to the right and as they passed it Lucas tried to shepherd the visitor into it, saying firmly, "Come into the den and we can talk," but the man kept walking towards us, as though Lucas hadn't spoken, almost brushing straight past Lucas's outstretched arm. As they reached the dining area, Rosalind pushed back her chair and stood, defensive, allowing the man to kiss her pale cheek. An act of submission rather than affection.

The man was of a similar age to Lucas himself, perhaps a little older—into his early sixties—but this was clearly no pensioner. He had iron grey hair, cut short enough to see his scalp through it, and there was an altogether harder edge to him.

"Rosalind, my dear," he said smoothly as he advanced. He had a craggy face with a strong nose and a full-lipped mouth, and his eyes were pale, a faded green or grey. "A pleasure, as always." His eyes skimmed over the three of us as he spoke, and he made a convincingly rueful face. "My timing is impeccable, I see."

"You know you're always welcome, Felix. Why don't you join us?" Rosalind said, contriving to keep her voice pleasant, even though her face was frigid.

"I wouldn't dream of it," he said, but making no moves to leave. His gaze swung to Lucas. "I saw your car was out front, but I didn't realise you had people visiting."

"Yes," Lucas said bluntly. There was a long pause. The man, Felix, raised his eyebrows slightly and craned his neck forwards, as if straining to hear. Eventually, he said softly, "So, aren't you going to introduce me to these lovely ladies."

Lucas flushed as his lack of manners was rammed down his throat. I saw his eyes flick to Simone and realised she was the one whose good opinion he wanted to maintain.

"Of course," he said. "This is, er, my daughter, Simone, and her friend Charlie Fox."

The stranger's eyebrows, if anything, climbed a little higher at this news. He directed a piercing stare first in Simone's direction, then in mine. And finally he looked at Ella, who was gazing at him without apparent concern and chewing artlessly with her mouth open. "Well, well," he murmured. "Is it really?"

"And this is Felix Vaughan," Lucas said, with obvious reluctance. "A business colleague of mine."

"Oh, but surely we know each other better than that, Lucas?" Felix Vaughan said in that soft deep voice of his. "Charmed, my dear," he added, shaking Simone's reluctantly proffered hand, although his eyes still seemed fixed on Ella. He held on to Simone for just a little too long. I saw the way Simone's shoulder flexed as she tried to withdraw and was unable to, and rose from my seat.

"Pleased to meet you, Mr Vaughan," I said, offering him my hand instead.

Vaughan's eyes glittered as they flickered over me very deliberately, insulting in their calculation. Eventually, he released Simone's hand in such a way that he managed to make it look like she'd been the one who'd been prolonging the contact. Simone winced and massaged her crushed fingers.

Vaughan liked that. He was smiling as he reached for me, but as our hands came together I jammed mine forwards, so the fleshy vee between my thumb and forefinger was hard up against Vaughan's before he had the

111

chance to close his fingers around my knuckles. I'd dealt with too many macho squaddies whose first instinct was to prove how weak and feeble female soldiers really were. The bone-crushing handshake was usually their opening salvo, in my experience, and I'd learned a long time ago how to counteract it.

As it was, I saw Vaughan's eyes widen slightly, then narrow as he tried to apply pressure and found himself outmanoeuvred. I offered him a bland smile and said nothing. After a few moments he got bored with the game and let my hand drop.

"So, what's your story, Miss Fox?" he asked, casually taking Lucas's chair at the head of the table. Lucas, I noticed, had moved to stand behind his wife and was gripping the back of her chair with both hands.

"I look after Simone," I said, level, letting Vaughan know that if he was determined to cause trouble for her, he'd have to go through me.

"She's the nanny, Felix," Rosalind put in quickly.

"Ah yes, of course—the child," Vaughan said, turning his attention back to Ella. The way he said it made all the hairs come up on the back of my neck. "So you're Ella, are you, my dear?"

Ella, completely unafraid, shovelled in another mouthful of mashed potato and said, through it, "Yes, and I'm four."

"Are you really? And is this your mommy, Ella?" Vaughan asked, inclining his head towards Simone. He moved with a kind of controlled violence, as if his instinct was to lash out and he had to make a conscious effort to keep himself in check at all times.

Ella chewed thoughtfully for a long moment, then nodded vigorously, and I could have sworn I heard the hiss of collected breath escaping from Lucas. Simone edged her chair closer to her daughter's and glared at Vaughan. I saw her flick a reproachful little glance in Lucas's direction, as though she couldn't understand why her father was letting this man torment her. Come to that, I couldn't understand it, either, but I was prepared to let it ride a little longer, just to find out.

"It's strange that you've never mentioned having children before," Vaughan said directly to Rosalind, and a faint edge of colour crept along her pale cheekbones.

"We made the decision not to have any children," she said stiffly. "Simone is Greg's daughter from his first marriage. This is the first time I've met her."

"Ah, I see," Vaughan said carefully, his pale eyes ranging over Rosalind and Lucas. "How fortuitous that she should decide to reacquaint herself with her father now, don't you think?"

"I live in England," Simone put in, her voice puzzled but growing more defensive by the minute.

"Really?" The raised eyebrow and the faintly sardonic tone sent a flush across her cheeks. "He's never mentioned you."

"We lost touch after my parents divorced," Simone snapped. "I've been looking for him for years."

"Is that so?" Vaughan said, his voice entirely neutral. "And can you be quite sure that you've found him now?"

I heard a gasp that might have come from Rosalind, but I didn't want to take my eyes off Vaughan long enough to make sure. Simone's flush went into instant decline, leaving her pale. Her lips thinned. "We'll be having DNA tests to confirm it," she said, "*If* it's any business of yours."

For a moment Vaughan said nothing. Then he nodded once, almost to himself, and smiled. "Excellent," he said. "And—always assuming the tests turn out to everyone's satisfaction, of course—how long do you plan to stay?"

I'd had enough of this interrogation. "We haven't made any definite plans," I put in before she had time to answer.

Simone frowned. "Is it any surprise that, having found him again, I want to spend a little time and get to know him?" she said, smiling hesitantly in Lucas's direction. Lucas returned the smile, little more than a twitch of his lips.

"Of course not," Vaughan said. He rose, started to button his jacket and then stilled, adding weight to his words even though they were delivered in a chillingly pleasant tone. "But you've come at a busy time for your father, my dear. Perhaps it might be best if you didn't plan to stay long."

OK, that's enough.

I got to my feet, much the same way Vaughan had done. Slowly, deliberately. Vaughan had the best part of a foot on me and he utilised all of it now, craning his neck, making a big thing out of just how far he had to look down to meet my eyes.

"With respect, Mr Vaughan," I said, always a nice phrase to use when you intend to speak without any, "the decision on just how long Simone remains a guest here is down to Mr and Mrs Lucas, not you. And her own choice, of course." I kept my voice light and my face carefully blank. "I would hate to think she feels under any kind of pressure to leave before she's ready."

Vaughan blinked, just once, and a muscle twitched in his cheek. The silence stretched one second into another.

"Yes," he murmured at last, inclining his head. "Yes, I guess you would."

He nodded to Simone, more of a bow. "Ladies," he said, coldly polite. His eyes slid across to mine. "I'm sure we'll be seeing more of each other." He turned to the couple stationed tensely at the other end of the table and his face tightened almost imperceptibly. "Don't trouble yourselves," he said. "I can see myself out."

Nevertheless, despite his words both Rosalind and Lucas followed Vaughan to the door, as if to make sure he really was leaving. While they were out of earshot Simone leaned across to me, her face fearful.

"Who *was* that guy?" she asked. "He gave me the creeps."

"I'm not surprised," I said, grim. "He did the same to me."

Simone raised her eyebrows. "You think?" she said quietly. "I'd say it was the other way around."

I glanced at her in surprise, but before I could question her last remark the couple returned. Lucas suddenly looked his age. He sank into his chair with a brief smile to Simone that was supposed to be reassuring but didn't quite make it far enough. "I'm sorry about that," he said, running a restless hand through his short beard. "I guess Felix's manner can be a little abrasive if you aren't used to the way of him."

"Abrasive' is putting it mildly," I agreed, not inclined to let either of them off the hook too easily. It was the way they'd stood by and let Simone and her daughter be intimidated that I took issue with, more than anything Vaughan himself had done.

"He didn't seem to faze you, though, Charlie," Rosalind said, and I realised she'd been giving me a coolly appraising stare from the other end of the table.

"Maybe I just don't like being bullied," I said, matching my tone to hers.

"Well, Felix certainly didn't manage that with you," Lucas said. "I don't think I've ever seen him back down quite like that before. You must have a knack with people, huh?"

"Oh, Greg, for heaven's sake!" Rosalind bit out. "Can't you tell that Charlie isn't simply Ella's nanny?"

Lucas stared between the two of us, taking in Simone's shocked and ever so slightly guilty expression on the way. "She isn't?"

"Of course not," Rosalind snapped. Her eyes swung to me and there was a strange mixture of anger and something else that could even have been desperation there. "Isn't it obvious? She's Simone's bodyguard."

Lucas's gaze rounded on me. "A bodyguard?" he repeated blankly. He made a noise that might have been intended as a laugh, strangled at birth when his wife showed no signs

115

of matching his amusement. "I mean, she's just ... are you sure?"

"Oh yes, quite sure," Rosalind said, more quietly now, her voice almost silky. "Let me guess—are you an ex-cop? Or army?" She must have seen something in my face. "Army then," she said, with a certain satisfaction at her own accuracy. Her eyes narrowed. "Not an easy job for a woman to get into. You must be pretty good, to have picked up that kinda work."

"Yes," I said, returning her stare with icy calm. "I am."

TEN

I'm beginning to have some serious doubts about Greg Lucas," I said.

It was the morning after Vaughan's visit and I was sitting in my room, on the bed, watching the icicles hanging from the guttering outside the window, melting gently like they were weeping. Simone and Ella were downstairs and, much as I didn't like to leave them unaccompanied with Rosalind and Lucas, I felt I needed to bring Sean up to speed.

"Why?" Sean's question was put in that calm, neutral voice of his.

I gave it a moment's further consideration. "He just doesn't give off the right vibes," I said at last, knowing he wouldn't dismiss my answer out of hand. "The training he had, the amount of time he spent in the Regiment ..." I let my voice trail off, shook my head even though I knew he couldn't see me do it. "I don't know. He just doesn't move right, doesn't have the right instincts. I know he's been out for a long time, but I don't think you ever really lose that."

"You could be right," Sean said. "And I don't think the Lucas we've been finding out about would stand there and let this guy Vaughan walk all over him, like you said."

"No," I agreed. I twisted away from the window, back towards the room's interior, which was almost gloomy by comparison. Hannibal the psycho teddy bear watched me with a glassy stare from the chair across the other side of the room. I switched my gaze back to the window again.

"Funny, isn't it?" I said. "From the information that Neagley gave me, and what you've found out since, Felix Vaughan fits the role of Simone's missing father much better than Lucas does."

"Now there's a thought."

"I know, but Vaughan's certainly got that nasty streak in him, and I should imagine there's quite a temper lurking beneath the surface. And although he didn't say anything, he made me for what I was, almost as soon as we met."

"Whereas Lucas didn't."

"No," I said. "And I'm not that good an actress. He should have cottoned on. Maybe not in Boston, but when he nearly left me behind on the way up here I thought I gave myself away big-time then."

"He could just have been playing with you," Sean said. "Apparently he was noted for playing mind games with trainees, and they pulled him out of any involvement with Selection after he blindfolded and handcuffed two guys and pushed them out of a helicopter during a Resistance-to-Interrogation exercise."

"He did *what*?"

"Yeah, well, they'd stopped us doing that by the time you were on the course," Sean said with a hint of a smile in his voice. "And in Lucas's case they were only about six feet off the ground, but one of them landed badly and broke his collarbone. Even back then, when there was less of a stink about training methods than there is these days, there was hell to pay."

"So," I said, my voice tinged with sourness, "should the opportunity arise to get into a helicopter with him, remind me not to sit next to the door."

"The other things that came up were that he was very good at hand-to-hand, and an excellent shot with a pistol."

"Oh great," I said. "What am I supposed to do to find out for definite if he is who he says he is, then—pick a fight with him?"

Sean laughed softly. "I know who I'd put my money on," he said.

***

When I walked down the staircase I heard the quiet murmur of voices behind the door to the study. Simone and Lucas. I thought briefly about knocking but couldn't think of a good excuse to do so other than nosiness. For a moment I was tempted to use that one anyway, but I didn't.

So far, Lucas and his wife had been somewhat nonplussed by the news of my real role in Simone's life. Simone had explained my presence by telling them about her problems with an ex-boyfriend—being careful not to name Matt, or admit he was Ella's father. She also left out all mention of the fact that most of her problems had started the moment she became a millionairess.

Even I have to admit the way she put it, it sounded reasonably convincing. She'd been stalked, she'd said, and Ella had been scared by the whole thing. The promising reports from the private eye, O'Halloran, had convinced Simone to fly out to Boston and I'd come along to make sure the boyfriend didn't follow her over here and cause more trouble.

Yes, there were holes in the story if you looked closely enough, but fortunately neither of them seemed inclined to do that. Interestingly, they *had* asked if she had any hopes for a reconciliation with her ex. When she said a categorical no—even going so far as to hint he was into drugs—they'd lost a lot of the stiffness in their attitude, become friendly again. I thought I'd even caught a hint of relief in them, but I could have been wrong about that.

Now, I followed the sound of chattering voices to the open-plan kitchen, where Rosalind and Ella were baking cookies. At least, Rosalind was baking the cookies and Ella just seemed to be making a mess over as wide an area as possible. At Rosalind's invitation, I helped myself to coffee

119

from the pot and stayed well back, strictly in an observational role.

Ella was in her element. Rosalind had given her a flattened piece of cookie dough and a plastic cutter in the shape of a star and she was busily stamping out as many ragged shapes from the dough as she could manage. Her little face wore a frown of utter concentration and a liberal coating of flour. Flour was also down the front of most of her dress, in her hair, and spread across an ever-increasing area of the kitchen tiles.

To my surprise, Rosalind didn't seem at all disturbed by this sudden intrusion of chaos into her well-ordered domain. In fact, she was supervising the operation so skilfully that I'm sure even Ella didn't realise the level of her intervention. Not enough to frustrate the child, but sufficient that the end results were likely to be edible, at least.

Rosalind arranged Ella's misshapen cookies on a baking tray alongside the perfect examples she'd already cut, and whisked them into the oven.

"Now then, Ella," she said, "if we can get this all cleared up by the time those cookies are done, we might be able to have some while they're still hot. What do you say?"

Ella nodded enthusiastically.

"OK, well, I think a big girl like you can wash her hands all by herself, can't she?"

Ella quickly clambered down off the chair she'd been using to bring her up to tabletop height and skipped off towards the downstairs cloakroom near the front door, eager to prove how grown up she was without quite realising how well she'd been conned.

"You're very good with her," I said as Rosalind began wiping down the work surfaces.

She gave me a sad little smile. "Yes, well, I always wanted a family."

"But you and Greg never had children," I said, remembering her comment to Vaughan the day before. *We*

120

made the decision not to have any children. Not exactly a free choice, by the sound of it.

She paused a moment and flicked her eyes over me and there was a touch of defiance in them, as though I was deliberately goading her. I kept my face neutral, friendly. "No," she said at last. "We married late and, well—" she shrugged, '—it was never to be."

"Have you two been married long?"

She paused again, as if looking for the catch in every question. "Coming up on fifteen years," she said, almost reluctantly, as though I was probably going to use the information against her in some way. "I hired Greg to work for me," she added, grudgingly.

That surprised me. "At the military surplus store?"

"That's right," she said, pride lifting her chin. She wiped a pile of spilt flour into her cupped hand and dropped it into the sink. "My daddy built the store up from nothing, right after he got home from Korea."

For want of a better reaction I raised my eyebrows and nodded, looking suitably impressed.

Rosalind's shoulders came down a fraction. "Daddy was a quartermaster sergeant."

"He and Greg must have got on well," I said. It was a throwaway comment but she tensed.

"Why do you say that?"

Damn, the woman was touchy. I shrugged. "Well, Greg was a sergeant, too, wasn't he?" I said carefully. "I understood Simone's father was in the SAS."

"Daddy died before I met Greg," Rosalind said, and some fleeting emotion passed across her face, too fast for me to fully identify it. "And anyways, Greg doesn't like to talk too much about those days."

I nodded again. "The genuine ones never do," I said. "For every one real SAS trooper there must be a dozen who claim they've been in the Regiment."

She gave me a smile that seemed almost grateful, that she didn't have to explain it, that I understood.

"And now Greg's taken over the store," I said.

The smile blinked out. "We both run it," she said stiffly.

"Of course," I said, with what I hoped was an ingratiating smile of my own. "I look forward to seeing it." That earned me another quick frown. Whatever I said seemed to make Rosalind uneasy.

"So where does the charming Mr Vaughan fit in to all this?" I asked. *Hell, if I was going to make her uncomfortable, I might as well go the whole hog.* Besides, the pair of them had neatly sidestepped any previous questions about the man.

She came upright and practically glared at me. "Greg felt we needed some additional investment to expand and Felix was generous enough to provide it," she said, terse. "I know he can seem a little abrupt, but military men can be straight talkers if you're not accustomed to them."

I thought of Vaughan's deliberate rudeness, and the Lucases' own discomfort with it, but wisely kept my opinion to myself.

Ella reappeared at that moment. Her hands were wet and largely free of flour, but where she'd splashed the front of her dress it now looked like she was wearing a pastry vest. Rosalind took charge of her, wiping her down and dusting her off as she quickly returned the kitchen to its former pristine state. If I hadn't known better I would have said the woman was glad of the excuse not to have to answer any more of my questions.

Ella seemed to have really taken to the bony woman, and I wasn't quite sure whether to be insulted or relieved by the little girl's sudden shift in allegiance. Maybe Ella found Rosalind's rather reserved manner refreshing after all the anxiously smiling faces that adults usually present when faced with a small child.

Now, Ella had turned coy and giggly. When I glanced in their direction, she was whispering to Rosalind, hiding her lips behind her hand. Rosalind's eyes were on me, coolly appraising. Suddenly irritated, I turned my back on the pair of them.

It was then I heard Ella's voice pipe up, "And Charlie hurt her neck, but I kissed it all better for her."

I gritted my teeth for a moment, then forced my face to relax and turned back. "That's right, Ella," I said brightly. "All better now."

"Really?" Rosalind said and I could see her eyes flicking busily over the high collar of my sweater, but I was damned if I was about to give her a demonstration.

Fortunately, I was saved by the bell—or rather, the timer for the cookies, which bleeped to announce they were ready to come out of the oven. Just as Rosalind retrieved a perfectly browned set of odd-shaped cookies and left them on a wire rack to cool, Lucas and Simone strolled in.

They'd disappeared into Lucas's den when Rosalind had first suggested baking as a way of keeping Ella occupied without her usual array of toys. It was only now, when they surfaced again, that I realised how long they'd been in there together.

"Ah, perfect timing," Lucas said, smiling as he moved to put an arm round his wife's shoulders and give her a squeeze.

Rosalind glanced sharply at him and stepped away from his embrace. For a moment he looked offended, but he shrugged it off with the air of someone trying just a little too hard to promote his innocence. Simone looked flushed, almost excited. *What the hell had they been up to?*

"So, what have you been up to?" I said, keeping my tone mild.

She frowned at me in much the same way Rosalind had been doing all morning.

"Oh, you know, just catching up on old times," she said, making too much of an effort to be casual about it.

Behind Rosalind's back, Lucas flashed Simone a quick smile, conspiratorial. Simone saw that I'd caught the gesture and that I was about to dig deeper. She glared at me. I raised my eyebrows but said nothing.

Ella filled the awkward gap by insisting they admire her cookies.

"Wow, those look just wonderful," Simone said. "You *have* been busy, sweetie. Did you make all these yourself?"

Ella paused, torn between taking the credit and sharing the glory. "Well, Grandma helped," she admitted at last, her face grave. "A little bit," she added, just in case we got the wrong idea of her own contribution.

Grandma.

I heard an intake of breath, but I couldn't swear whose. All eyes were suddenly fixed on Rosalind. Her face had frozen and—just for a moment—I thought she might actually break and cry. Then the corner of her mouth trembled, fluttered, and gradually curved upwards into a shaky smile.

She reached out, almost tentative, and stroked a hand over Ella's silky curls. Ella dimpled into a heartbreaking smile and I felt some small relaxation of the muscles across the top of my shoulders, that I hadn't realised had been tense until then.

If you have to protect a child, I thought, *it always helps to have the people closest on your side ...*

***

I must admit, I thought I'd got away without having to explain any further about what had happened to my neck. I should have known that Rosalind's distraction was only temporary.

After lunch we all climbed into the Range Rover and headed into town. Simone had apparently expressed an interest in seeing the military surplus store the Lucases ran, and I must admit I was curious about the place myself.

We piled into the luxury four-by-four, with Ella sitting between Simone and Rosalind in the back, and me up front with Lucas.

"Ella was telling me how she has the gift of healing," Rosalind said to Simone, and recounted her earlier conversation with Ella. I was aware of Lucas snatching little sideways glances at me as he drove, but I stared rigidly out of the front windscreen and pretended to a bout of deafness.

"Oh, er, yes," Simone said, and I could hear the tension in her voice. She gave a nervous laugh. "Ella noticed that Charlie had a bit of a scar on her neck and so—"

"It was when those nasty men frightened me," Ella told Rosalind in a loud whisper.

"What nasty men, honey?" Rosalind said, frowning.

"They came to our house and banged on the windows and shouted and took pictures," Ella said solemnly.

"And you cut your neck during all this, Charlie?" Rosalind asked, getting hold of the wrong end of the stick— deliberately, I'm sure.

"No," I said, twisting in my seat so I could answer her directly. "It's an old scar—from years ago. That just happened to be the first time Ella had seen it."

"But—"

"How about a milkshake?" Simone interrupted quickly. "Would you like that, Ella?"

Ella nodded vigorously and treated her mother to a dazzling smile, all mention of scars and paparazzi instantly forgotten.

"OK, sweetie. And what flavour would you like?"

Ella gave her a cunning little sideways look.

"Goo'berry," she said.

***

In the end, in the absence of gooseberry, Ella settled for a strawberry milkshake at the Friendly's on the main street. It arrived in a huge glass, with at least as much again still in the stainless-steel mixer. I had visions of her being heartily sick, but Simone helped her out, and we carried at least half of it away with us for later. I could see Rosalind eyeing the lidded container with concern for the Range Rover's immaculate upholstery.

Lucas gave us the guided tour of the town, which was much larger than I'd suspected when we'd driven in the day before. We ended up with a visit to his surplus store in Intervale, about five miles west of North Conway on Route 302. Mind you, sometimes it was hard to tell where one town stopped and another began. New construction was happening all the way along. I think the way buildings were spread out was the most surprising thing to me. There was none of the crammed-in feeling of home. Every business had a huge car park with the snow hunched up at the edges of it. I'd already seen half a dozen pickup trucks with snowploughs attached to the front, and Lucas told us that you weren't allowed to park overnight on the streets so they could keep them clear.

The surplus business was housed in a long blockwork building, timbered along the front with a covered veranda and a railing for tying up your horse. A World War II military Jeep was parked on the snow-covered pitched roof at a jaunty angle, just in case you missed the signs. By the double entrance doors was an ashtray made out of a hollowed-out artillery shell and a full-size mannequin dressed as a World War II paratrooper.

Lucas drove round to the side of the building, past great piles of dirty snow, where I assumed the staff normally parked. There were a couple of hulking full-size pickups there, but they were dwarfed by a Hummer H1, the civilian version of the US military vehicle, in metallic sand like it had just been transported there from the deserts of the Middle East. Loaded with extras, the H1 must have cost at least a hundred and fifty thousand dollars. I didn't need to hear the hiss of Lucas's indrawn breath to guess who the vehicle belonged to.

"Damn," he muttered, braking to a halt in the middle of the cracked concrete. "I didn't think Felix would be here today." He glanced at Simone's white face in the rear-view mirror. "Sorry, honey. I know you and he didn't hit it off yesterday. We can come back another time or—"

"No, no, I'm fine," Simone said quickly. "And I'd like to see the store."

I twisted in my seat. "Are you sure about this?"

She nodded. "I can't keep running away from the guy, can I?" she said. "Not while he's a sort of partner. We've got to see him again sometime."

Lucas stretched a hand out behind him and Simone reached for it, giving his fingers a quick squeeze. I checked Rosalind's face, but she was determinedly fussing with the collar of Ella's coat.

"OK," I said, "but if he makes any threatening moves towards you, or Ella, we're leaving. OK?" I stared at Rosalind until she shifted uncomfortably and was forced to meet my eyes. "I know he's involved in your business, and I don't want to interfere with that. Don't put me in a position where I might have to."

"Felix isn't a bad guy once you get to know him," Lucas said.

"Yes, I was telling Charlie earlier that he can be a little abrupt," Rosalind said quickly, "but we owe him because he helped us out by making such an investment in the store."

For a moment Lucas was silent before he smiled to Simone's reflection in the rear-view mirror again and nodded. "That's right," he said. "But hopefully not for much longer."

Despite the Lucases' attempts at reassurance, I went through the little entrance lobby and into the store as though it was a semi-hostile environment, keeping close to Simone, who was carrying Ella.

Inside, the building—like North Conway itself—was far bigger than the exterior suggested. It was laid out like a small department store, with equipment round the outside edges and clothing on long racks in the centre. I've spent some time around army kit, at one time or another, and even I had to admit Lucas's stock looked good-quality gear, the whole place smart and well organised.

He introduced Simone to the two staff members, Jay and Kevin, who were behind the long counter. They both had the air of college kids—alert and respectful—and they called everybody sir and ma'am like their lives depended on it.

I was half-surprised that Vaughan didn't appear as soon as we arrived, but no doubt he was lurking somewhere in the background. Out of habit, I noted the location and the number of security cameras and guessed that he was probably well aware of our arrival. And if he was watching us, there was no point in giving him the satisfaction of looking on edge.

Rosalind murmured her excuses and disappeared into one of the offices behind the counter, leaving her husband to show Simone their inventory with a bullish pride. They certainly seemed to be doing well out of army boots, tents, camping equipment, camouflage sleeping bags, flying suits, and mess tins. I strolled in their wake, casually running my fingers over the occasional item, some more familiar than others. It all even had its own distinctive smell that stirred a lot of memories—not many of them good.

The display area only took up part of the footprint of the building, and it was no surprise when Lucas led us through a doorway marked "Staff Only: No Unauthorized Entry' at the back and into a large racked-out stockroom.

The room was lit by fluorescent tubes strung across the steel rafters above, which left darkened alleyways between the high racks. Ella, not at her bravest in the dark, gave a little whimper and buried her face in Simone's chest.

Lined up along one wall were rows of heavy-duty gun safes. Simone eyed them with distrust as we walked through, and I noticed she kept Ella's head turned the other way.

What had they talked about this morning, I wondered, that had changed Simone's mind about bringing Ella into contact with firearms? True, you couldn't see any, but they were practically close enough to touch. I could smell the gun oil, a sharp, pervasive odour. And there was something more. Burnt powder.

"You have a range here?" I said, making a question of it, even though I hardly needed an answer.

Lucas paused and nodded. "Just two-lane—twenty-five yards," he said. "Handguns only. If we want to fire anything bigger, we have to go elsewhere."

"I thought you said you didn't deal in guns," I said.

"It's not the main thrust of my business," Lucas said, sidestepping.

"But it is a part of it," said a new voice—a deep cold tone that I recognised instantly. "Didn't you tell the ladies that, Lucas?"

Vaughan stepped into view from between two of the racks just ahead of us, making an entrance. He smiled at Simone's shocked face. I checked no-one was coming up on our rear, then moved alongside her. Vaughan watched me do it and nodded, as though he'd been expecting that.

Lucas hadn't replied to Vaughan's taunt. He seemed to have coiled back in on himself, like he'd done the day before when Vaughan had sat in his house and made his not-so-veiled threats towards Simone. Now, in the gloom of the stockroom, I thought I saw Lucas's hands clench just briefly by his sides and realised that maybe his feelings towards the other man weren't quite as ambivalent as first impressions had suggested.

Lucas cleared his throat. "I didn't expect to see you here today, Felix," he said at last, and there was nothing more than polite inquiry in his voice.

Vaughan eyed him for a moment, as if making sure. "No, I thought I'd come and put in some practice on the range. Care to join me?" he said lightly. "The British SAS versus the US Marines. We could put a little money on it—make things more interesting."

Lucas looked uncomfortable now. Sean had told me the man had been a first-class shot, but that was twenty-five years ago. Was he still up to the same standard? I supposed that he wouldn't have let himself slide too far. Not if he was part owner of a business that dealt in firearms regularly enough to have its own range—despite his denials to Simone. Vanity alone would have kept him sharp. So why the hesitation?

Then I glanced at Simone and found her gaze fixed on him, her mouth a thin flattened line. She didn't like guns—had made that fact pretty plain to Lucas. Maybe Vaughan knew that, too, or maybe he was guessing. Maybe he'd decided there were ways other than subtle threats of getting Simone to pack up and go home.

Vaughan's washed-out gaze drifted in my direction.

"What about you, Miss Fox?" he said, his voice a slow taunt. "Ever held a weapon?"

I gave him a vague smile and didn't answer. There wasn't one he couldn't distort with innuendo.

"Personally," he went on, "I never approved of women in the military being given firearms training. Waste of time and money." He stared at me again. "Oh, I suppose they have their place in the modern military machine—medics, drivers, cooks, even mechanics—but why waste time giving them a gun and teaching them how to use it when they just don't have the guts for it."

"You're not a fan of Kipling, Mr Vaughan?" I said quietly. "That the female of the species is more deadly than the male?"

He laughed. "That has not been my experience," he said flatly. "And trust me, Miss Fox, I've had plenty of experience. Women are too flighty, too easily distracted, and generally just not disciplined enough to make good troops under battlefield conditions."

"Is that so?"

"That is so," he said softly, eyes locked on mine. "And besides anything else—if you'll excuse my language—they can't shoot for shit."

"I'd be careful what you say to Charlie," Lucas broke in. "She happens to be ex-army herself."

Vaughan eyed me for a moment, as if working out how much of that he believed, even though I knew he'd already worked out exactly what I was. He laughed again, a short exhalation of amusement, quickly past, that had my teeth grinding, nevertheless.

"Is she really?" he murmured. "Well, my comments still stand."

"Perhaps, in that case, you might like to give her the opportunity to prove you wrong?" Lucas said, a little defiance creeping in now. "Not quite the Marine Corps against the Special Air Service, but how about the Women's Royal Army Corps? We could even put a little money on it, make things interesting."

I thought I caught the faintest trace of a flush across Vaughan's cheekbones. "That's hardly fair," he said.

"I know," I said gravely, "but I could give you a head start if you like."

Simone's laugh was quickly smothered, but it earned her a searing glance from Vaughan. Even Ella, picking up on her mother's amusement, was smiling, and that seemed to irritate Vaughan all the more. He took a step forwards. Simone stopped laughing and I moved in front of her. Something of the glint disappeared from his eye.

"Very well," he said. "I'm sure Lucas will find you something you can handle." And he turned on his heel and stalked away.

Lucas watched him go and I saw him roll his shoulders like a cat with its fur up, dying to get its claws into something. He turned to me, speculation in his eyes. "What *can* you handle?" he said.

I shrugged. "A SIG P226 would be my preference," I said, "but any 9mm automatic will probably do. I don't have to beat him, do I? I just have to not disgrace myself."

"Oh no," Simone said, and the bitter note in her voice surprised me. "I think you have to beat him."

***

The range itself ran along the back of the building, a long narrow tunnel of a room with a sand berm at the far end and pockmarked blockwork walls. Lucas switched on the lights and I heard the whirr of the extraction fans kicking in at the same time. It was cold back there, away from the heated interior of the store, and there was the faint smell of mildew in the air.

Simone was torn between wanting to watch, and wanting to keep Ella out of the way. In the end Simone stayed just outside the range, behind the thick glass panel that separated it from the stockroom. I slipped out of my bulky jacket and gave that to her for safekeeping.

Lucas quickly gathered up targets and ear defenders for all of us—especially for Ella, even though the range was soundproofed inside. He unlocked one of the gun safes and pulled out a small canvas holster containing the familiar shape of the SIG. I slid the gun out and automatically dropped the magazine and racked back the slide to check the chamber was empty. It seemed in reasonable condition, well-oiled and free moving.

"So, are you any sort of a shot, Charlie?" he asked.

"I'm reasonable," I said.

He nodded. "If you are, take his money," he said quickly. "I don't get the opportunity."

I would have asked him more about that, but Vaughan strode back in, an aluminium gun case in his hand. He set it down on the workbench under the window and opened it up.

Inside was a beautifully kept .45-calibre Heckler & Koch Mark 23, the civilian version of the SOCOM military pistol.

An expensive piece, designed for covert work, to take out sentries. The end of the barrel was threaded to take a suppressor and the weapon had the option to prevent the slide coming back to eject the spent shell after each shot, to maintain the silence of the kill. The sight of that gun made me more wary of Vaughan than almost anything else about him.

He loaded it quickly, feeding in twelve rounds of Federal jacketed hollowpoints. I fed in the same number of plain old military ball ammo from the box Lucas had given me. I kept my face blank as I did so, concentrated on regulating my heart rate and breathing, slowing my systems down so, when I faced the target and it mattered, I'd be calm and relaxed.

Vaughan finished his task, palmed the magazine back into the pistol and pinched back the slide to chamber the first round. Lucas clipped two paper targets to the pulley system and ran them out to the twenty-yard mark, side by side. Plenty far enough with a gun I'd never fired before.

"So," Vaughan said, raising an eyebrow in my direction, "are you prepared to put money on who's the finer shot?"

"How much?"

He pursed his lips. "Shall we say a straight hundred?"

I nodded shortly and pulled my ear defenders into place. The loudest thing in my world was suddenly the sound of my own blood beating inside my head.

I half-expected Vaughan to insist I went first, but he shifted into a stance, legs braced and the Mark 23 held out in front of him in a double-handed grip, and commenced firing without ceremony. The first round out of the big .45 made me flinch, even though I'd been expecting it. The others were just background noise.

The targets were reduced-size B27s, a black head and torso silhouette on a white background, with a series of rings numbered 7 to 9 as the size decreased closer to the body's centre. The last two rings were unnumbered apart from an X dead centre.

Vaughan took his time, finished firing, and lowered his gun, letting out a long breath. A lazy trail of smoke wafted up towards the extraction system. He'd put all twelve inside the two inner circles, just breaking the line to the 9 ring with the first two. They were low and left, which told me he was jerking the trigger just a little until he settled. He turned to me with challenge in his face. I returned his look without emotion, then picked up the SIG.

I'd already made up my mind to do whatever Vaughan hadn't. He'd fired slow so I knew I had to fire fast. I waited to see where the first cold shot landed, and as soon as I realised the gun hadn't been abused, that it was accurate, I put the next seven rounds straight into the centre of the target with hardly a pause, obliterating the centre X.

Four left.

I deliberately shifted my aim. Two high in the 8 ring, exactly where the target's heart would be.

The last two rounds I placed outside the numbered circles altogether. They went into the head. Not dead centre, but slightly low and within ten mil of each other. Through the mouth, if the target had had one. Killing shots.

As the twelfth shot fired, the working parts slid back and locked on an empty magazine. I put the SIG down on the bench and pulled off my ear defenders. The blurred sounds of the outside world sharpened instantly.

I turned and found Vaughan watching me as the door opened and Lucas came in, together with Simone and Ella, who'd taken charge of my jacket. Rosalind had also joined them, and she didn't look happy to find us here.

"Looks like you win, Mr Vaughan," I said as Lucas winched the targets back in.

Vaughan studied the targets for a moment. Despite the cold there was a trickle of sweat at his temple and he was slightly pale. I reached into my back pocket and pulled out my wallet, started to count out the dollar bills inside, but he waved them away.

"You have a talent, Miss Fox," he said, recovering his poise. "What a shame to waste it."

At that moment the mobile phone in my jacket pocket started making the horrible tweedling noise that indicated I had a new text message. Ella dropped the coat on the floor and dived for the appropriate pocket. Before I could stop her she'd seized the phone and, like any four-year-old worth her salt in this technological age, she'd pressed the button.

"Ella," I said quickly, "can I see that, please?"

Ella ducked under my reaching arm and darted away, giggling. She avoided Simone and in the end it was Rosalind who managed to pluck the phone from the child's grasp. Rosalind moved to hand it over and then, as the screen caught her eye, she stilled.

"What is it?" Simone asked, crowding round to look. "Are you getting dirty pictures from your boyfriend, Charlie?" Even Vaughan craned his neck at that.

I reached over and snatched the phone, but by that time it seemed that everyone except me had seen what the message contained. When I looked at it myself, I cursed silently and wished that they hadn't.

On the screen was a small, grainy digitised image, obviously scanned in from an old colour photograph. It showed a man in his forties, wearing Army uniform and smiling into the camera.

"But who is that?" Simone asked, but I saw the rising fear in her eyes and knew she didn't really need an answer.

I scrolled down. Underneath the picture Sean had sent was a line of text. It said: *Greg Lucas?*

ELEVEN

Simone waited until we were on our own outside before she ripped into me. I suppose I should be thankful for that, at least. She got all of three strides past the outer doorway, then whirled to face me, shoulders hunched like a boxer about to strike.

"What the hell's going on, Charlie?"

"I'm doing my job," I said, keeping my voice quiet.

"Oh yeah? Your job is to keep us safe," she said, stabbing a finger in my direction. "Not to go digging around and upsetting my father by making it obvious that you don't trust him."

I sighed. "It's not a question of that," I said, even though I knew it probably was. I dragged out my phone again, flipped it open. "Look at the picture, Simone. No, *look* at it! Can you honestly say you can see the resemblance?"

"From a picture like that?" she said, without hesitation. "Could you recognise *your* father from a blurry snapshot that's less than two inches square, taken probably thirty years ago, before he grew a goddamn beard?"

Damn. I hated it when she was right ...

Her breath huffed out into a cloud around her head in the frozen air. I glanced back at the entrance to the store, just in case our voices were carrying. Rosalind was standing a little way back behind the glass doors, holding Ella's hand. Ella was chewing her hair and rocking from one foot to the other. Rosalind was watching the pair of us argue with narrowed eyes but it was difficult to tell if she could hear us or not. Maybe she didn't need to.

136

"Simone," I said, "calm down before you upset your daughter any more than she is already."

"She—"

"Just listen for a moment! Remember, there's a lot at stake here. Not just your happiness," I said, not wanting to mention the money out loud. "You're already convinced this guy is Greg Lucas, that he *is* your father, but until we get that DNA test to confirm it, we have to keep checking him out. And even you have to admit that he doesn't seem in any hurry to get that test done, does he?"

Simone stared at the snow beneath her booted feet and took a deep breath, even though she was still humming with anger. "It's already done," she muttered.

I stilled. "It's what?"

She looked up at me and the defiance was back in all its glory. "We took the swabs and labelled them and sent them off this morning."

I rubbed a hand across my eyes. "You took the swabs—yourself," I repeated flatly. "So—no doctors, no witnesses, no legal standing whatsoever."

She had the grace to flush. "I don't give a damn about legal standing! As long as I know he's my father. Why would he be so keen to have the tests done if he had something to hide?"

Why indeed? This changed things. In fact, it changed them a lot.

"So why the secrecy?" I countered, a little blankly. "Why hide it from me, what you were up to?"

"We weren't hiding it from *you*, Charlie," she said. "It's just, well, Greg didn't want Rosalind to find out."

"Rosalind? Why on earth not?"

She shrugged uncomfortably, shoving her hands into her pockets and kicking her feet through the slush, like a naughty kid. The windchill was making my cheeks numb. "He said it's always been a bit of a sore point—his first marriage. He said he never told her about me, and finding out—when that private eye, Mr O'Halloran, came to see

137

him—has been one hell of a shock for her. I guess he didn't want to upset her more than he had done already, so he suggested we didn't tell her about the test. But we've done it—doesn't that tell you something about him?"

That he's sneaky and underhand—even with his own wife? I didn't think voicing that opinion would win her over, so I didn't bother. "When will you know the results?"

"A few days apparently. Greg says the lab he got the testing kit from promised a fast turnaround."

"When did he get it—the kit, I mean?"

Simone opened her mouth, frowned and closed it again. "I don't know," she said. "When we went into the den this morning, he had it in his desk. I didn't ask. Surely the important thing is that we've taken the test, isn't it?"

I shook my head. "I don't know," I said. When Simone had first brought the subject up—only yesterday—Lucas had seemed reluctant, or was that just Rosalind's reaction? Either way, he must have had the kit sitting ready to be used. It spoke of a certain amount of premeditation, of planning. He could be genuine, trying to reassure his daughter. Or he could be just buying time.

For what?

After all, who was to say that the address of the lab wasn't just that of some crony, waiting to send back a sheaf of official-looking paperwork. I wouldn't be able to tell the difference between a genuine result and a clever fake, and I was betting Simone wouldn't, either.

The door was pushed open and Ella came running out, leaving Rosalind inside. The little girl flew over to Simone, who bent to scoop her up. Ella put both arms round her mother's neck and held on tight to the collar of her coat.

"What is it, sweetie?"

"Are you being cross with Charlie?"

Simone sighed. "No, sweetie, we just needed to talk about a few things, out here in the quiet."

Ella turned, fingers clamped into fists, and threw me a curve ball. "You're not angry with Grandpa and Grandma,

138

are you, Charlie?" She pinned me with that clear violet gaze. It lanced straight through my chest and slid into my heart, sly and brutal as a blade. A revelation.

Damn. When did this child manage to climb under my skin so deeply?

I reached out a hand and brushed Ella's curls back from her face, even managed to dredge up a reasonable facsimile of a smile from somewhere.

"No," I said, my voice soft. "Of course not."

She smiled at me, full, open, and without guile and stretched out both arms, reaching for me. I hesitated for a second, then let Simone hand her over to me. Ella cuddled on tight, burying her face into the collar of my shirt, her hair tickling the underside of my chin. I held her very close, breathing in the soft smells of the baby shampoo Simone used to bathe her, and strawberries. For some unaccountable reason, I felt my eyes dampen and I determinedly put it down to the rawness of the wind. But right at that moment I would have killed or died for her, without a second thought.

And that's when it really hit me. If Lucas and Rosalind *did* turn out to be trying to pull a fast one, it wasn't just Simone's heart they were going to break.

I looked back through the doors to where Rosalind was still watching us. For a second I allowed everything that was running through my mind to channel into that one hard stare. After only a moment, she turned away. I felt the rage lose its colour until it was dirty grey like the snow, and just as cold.

If this was no more than a cruel hoax, how would Simone even begin to explain it to her daughter? *They didn't really love you, Ella—they were just pretending ...*

My mind snapped back to the target I'd just fired at on Lucas's range. The last four shots. Two in the heart. Two in the head. And if anybody threatened my principals, I knew I had the guts to shoot like that for real. I'd already proved it.

Am I angry with them, Ella? No. But if they hurt you, that's when you'll see me really *angry ...*

***

For the next two days, everything was calm. Rosalind and Lucas were perfect hosts. They played the role of doting grandparents with aplomb and spoiled Ella rotten. Felix Vaughan was notable by his absence. No more information arrived about Lucas from Sean—good or bad. Knowing there was nothing further I could do until the DNA test results came back, I'd just have to stay close to Simone and Ella, and wait for the first sign of trouble.

It came at four in the morning, when no doubt they expected that everyone would be asleep and at a low physical ebb. It was the textbook time for a grab raid. Ask any policeman—state or secret—and he'll tell you the same thing.

Unfortunately for them, I hadn't been in the US long enough for my body clock to fully reset to local time. Four A.M. in North Conway was 9:00 A.M. at home. I'd been awake for an hour and a half by then and figured I'd slept late as it was. I'd got up, silently, in the dark, pulled on my sweatpants and a T-shirt, and quietly eased through some stretching exercises and a few isometrics.

I normally ran when I was at home, and if I wasn't on a job I spent four mornings a week in the gym, usually with Sean pushing me through a tougher workout than I would manage if I'd been doing it alone. The days I'd spent with Simone and Ella hadn't allowed for more than some hurried callisthenics first thing each morning, just to stop me seizing up.

I didn't need a light on to see what I was doing, so I worked in the dark, and I found myself thinking about Simone. And about Ella.

I'd always accepted that part of the job description of close protection was that I might have to lay down my life for my principal, and I'd been willing to do that. Not eager, perhaps, but willing, nevertheless.

The proof of that willingness was tucked away in a fold of cloth at the bottom of my bag. Two stopped 9mm rounds I'd deliberately put myself in the path of. I carried them as a kind of talisman. The only difference was, the person I'd been protecting then had been Sean. At the time, I would have died for him. And now, I realised I felt the same way about Ella.

Sean had warned me against making decisions based on emotion. But now I didn't have a choice. Did that make me better at my job, or worse?

I was just finishing up the last of my hamstring stretches when I heard the noise from downstairs.

It was only a tiny ripple of sound, the scrape of a chair leg on the wooden floor, perhaps, quickly stilled. Not enough to have woken me if I hadn't already been alert. I froze with my chin an inch from touching my left knee and straightened up very slowly, trying not to let my clothing rustle. The waning moon was still high and bright above the trees outside the bedroom window, but I squeezed my eyes tight shut as though that would divert auxiliary power to my hearing instead. Then I stood absolutely still for five seconds. Ten.

Nothing.

I shifted over to the bed, moving as softly as I could, and groped for the pair of trainers I'd left alongside it. I knew it was wasting time to put them on, but if I was going to have to do a full intruder search that meant going outside and it was around eleven degrees below freezing out there.

A pair of beady eyes stared at me from across the room. Hannibal, Ella's sinister giant teddy bear. On impulse, I lifted him off his chair and slid him under the quilt on the bed. From the doorway, in the half-light, he would just about pass for me. If you happened to think I was a rotund dwarf with both ears on the top of my head and a severe facial hair problem.

I was already well aware that the doors in the Lucases' house operated on well-oiled hinges. Even so, I opened the door from my room onto the landing with extreme caution, gripping the knob hard so it didn't rattle. The moonlight reflected harshly off the snow outside and sliced through the gloomy proximity of the trees, plenty strong enough to cast exaggerated shadows from the nearest window frame.

I took half a dozen noiseless steps across the landing, ducked and peered down through the spindles towards the living and dining area. For a moment I saw nothing untoward. Then a creepily elongated shadow flitted across the polished wooden floor below, a momentary blip at the corner of my field of vision, that quickly disappeared.

When we'd arrived at the Lucases' house I'd automatically checked out their security alarm system and been surprised to note it was an older type, not particularly sophisticated and lacking any additional triggers other than door and window sensors. Even I could have bypassed it, and I was far from an expert. Sean would have been in there in seconds.

I edged back from the stairwell and paused to steady my breath. We had at least one intruder, who might or might not be armed. All Lucas's guns, as far as I knew, were in the strong-rooms in the basement and I dismissed them without any real consideration. Even if I knew where he kept his keys, getting to a weapon would mean leaving the bad guys with uncontended access to my principals, and that was a nonstarter. Especially without knowing their objective here.

I wondered briefly if Lucas had a safe in the den, but even as the thought formed I somehow knew that robbery wasn't the motive for this incursion. And if they weren't here for financial gain, there weren't many palatable alternatives. I didn't have the manpower—not to mention the firepower—for a counter-offensive. That left stealth, and guile.

I glanced along the landing to the door to Simone and Ella's room. Sense told me to attempt an evac, but I couldn't risk going in and startling them. Ella had a tendency to get very loud when she was frightened and the last thing I wanted was to tip off the men below that we were on to them, or push them into extreme action. After all, I still didn't know what their intentions were. Criminal, almost certainly, but if they didn't pose a real and immediate threat to my principals, it wasn't my fight. What I needed was a hiding place where I could keep out of sight, but be close enough to intercept anyone who tried to get to Simone and her daughter.

I crawled further back from the stairwell. Halfway along the landing was a walk-in storage cupboard with a louvred door. It was largely filled with shelves containing spare bedding, but there was still enough room for me to squeeze in at the front as well and get the door shut, although I had to hold it closed.

Then I simply had to wait, like a spider, for them to come to me.

It didn't take long. There were two of them, dressed in dark clothing and moving with smooth efficiency. All I could see through the downward-facing slats of the door was their legs to mid-thigh. They both put their feet down with an almost excessive care, keeping their knees soft. Professionals. Taking either of them by surprise was going to be damned difficult, but taking both of them was going to be well-nigh impossible.

They halted, seemingly right outside the cupboard doorway, as though they could hear my breathing, the rush of my blood. Then one pair of feet continued on towards Simone's room. The other turned back, heading for the door to my own room, and the one to the master suite.

Divide and conquer. There wasn't going to be a better chance than this.

I closed my eyes briefly, released a little spurt of anger, feeling the tingle as the flame of it took hold and began to burn. I reminded myself that these people had made the choice to step inside my circle in the dust. They'd crossed the line and whatever happened to them now was because their own actions had brought them to this point.

I opened my eyes, let my breath out slowly and opened the cupboard door a crack, just enough to peer out. The man who'd been headed for my room had disappeared around the corner of the corridor. I slipped out of the cupboard altogether. The second man was stooped at Simone's door, his left hand on the knob, trying to ease it open without a sound. His head was covered with a close-fitting hood and he was big without being bulky. I was suddenly glad he was crouching there with his back towards me to give me a little advantage. There was something that was probably a gun in his gloved right hand. If I didn't get this right the first time, things were going to get nasty very quickly.

I took a run at him, two strides and up onto his back. I stamped hard into the back of the calf muscle of his right leg as I went. At the same time I landed a short vicious blow into his left kidney. As his back arched from the impact, I hooked my right hand around his neck, grabbing his Adam's apple through the thin material of the hood and jerking his head back.

My weight came down, one foot landing heavily on the back of the man's knee. He let out a low grunt as it folded and he twisted instinctively, trying to bring the weapon to bear, but he was too slow. I stayed on him as he dropped hard to his knees, riding him down, then stepped to the side to swing him away from the door. I released my hold, only for a second, to wrap my right arm around his throat and lock it in place with my other hand just behind the nape of his neck, making sure I kept my head well to the side in case he tried to reverse-head-butt me.

He was expert enough at hand-to-hand to know I'd got a killing grip on him. He started to panic then, scrabbling at my arm, letting the gun drop. The weapon hit the polished wood floor with a crashing thud that was desperately loud in the darkness.

He thrashed under me. I took up whatever slack remained and jerked him still, knowing that I could cut off the blood supply to his brain any time I wanted to. Or worse.

By the time the other man darted back into view at the far end of the landing, the one I'd grabbed was rigid and motionless. I could smell the fear and the anger rising off him like cheap scent.

The second man was smaller, almost slender. He froze in mid-step when he saw the two of us and he was cool enough to pause and consider his options. The nearest window was behind him and to his left, but all I could see of his face was the matte material of the ski mask he wore. I had time to register, despite the mask, that he was wearing glasses. I could tell from the set of his shoulders that he, too, was carrying something in his right hand.

"Put it down," I said, gruff, "or I'll break his neck."

The man with the glasses didn't move, just continued to stand and stare me out. We were only three metres or so apart and he was armed. At that distance, even in semi-darkness with me using my captive for partial cover, he would have had to be a very mediocre shot to have missed.

"Harder than you think," the man with the glasses said calmly, "to break a man's neck in cold blood."

"Easier than you think," I returned, "to do it while your blood's up." I left it a beat, then hardened my voice, knowing it was unlikely he would believe me, even so. "And this won't be my first time."

I sensed rather than saw his eyes flick to the face of his larger friend. I bunched the muscles in my arms and an involuntary muffled hiccup of sound escaped my prisoner. I could feel him trembling, little more than a mild vibration, and knew he, at least, was convinced.

The man with the glasses let the muzzle of the gun drop slightly. He seemed about to speak when suddenly we heard muffled voices coming from the Lucases' room behind him. Rosalind's sharper tones overlaying her husband's deeper mumble.

The man with the glasses glanced over his shoulder. Clearly he didn't want to be the filling in a hostile sandwich. I saw him lift his shoulders slightly in a shrug that could have signified either defeat or apology. Then he was moving for the stairs.

As he made a fast but somehow unhurried descent, he swung through the full glare of the moonlight, lighting him fully for the first time. In that split-second I mentally photographed the shape of his body and head, the way he moved. I wouldn't be able to pick him out of a police line-up, but I was damned sure I'd know him if I ever saw him again on the street. Then he'd dropped from view, his footsteps suddenly heavy now the need for stealth was gone.

As his comrade abandoned him and withdrew, the big man erupted, a last-ditch attempt to effect his own release before my reinforcements arrived. Just for a second I tightened my grip, felt the creak of sinews under tension as I considered the wisdom of finishing him and going after the slim man.

Then the door behind me was yanked open and I heard Simone gasp, then Ella's voice.

"Mummy, what—?"

"For God's sake, Simone," I snapped, back over my shoulder, "don't let her see this!"

"See what?" I heard Simone take a step out onto the landing. Her voice was low with shock. "Charlie, what the hell d'you think you're you doing?"

"What you pay me for," I said. "Now get Ella back into your room and lock the door."

For once, she didn't argue. I heard the door close behind her and realised sweat was dribbling past my left eyebrow. I leaned close to where I judged the man's masked ear to be, and whispered, "You'll never know how lucky you just were, sunshine."

He made a strangled grunt that sounded a lot like, "Fuck you!"

With a sigh, I let go my choke hold and kneed him roughly between his shoulder blades, punting him down onto his face. He landed hard, the air gusting out of his lungs so that it was easy enough to haul both his wrists as far up his back as the tendons would allow.

At that moment, the bedroom door at the far end of the landing was yanked open and Greg Lucas came stumbling out, dressed in pyjama trousers and a towelling robe. Rosalind was right behind him and before I could stop her she'd reached out to flick on the landing lights.

I flinched under the harsh bulb, momentarily blinded. The man tried to use the distraction to break my restraint, but I had leverage on my side and I used it, piling on top of him so my weight helped hold him down.

"There's another guy," I threw at Lucas. "He headed downstairs, and he's got a gun."

If I was expecting the ex-SAS man to give chase, however, I was disappointed. When my eyesight recovered enough for me to glance up at the pair of them, they hadn't moved, both staring wide-eyed at the man I had pinned on the ground in front of them.

"Lucas!" I snapped, and he finally seemed to register the urgency in my voice. He looked up, a little dazed, and shook his head as if to clear his ears but made no moves to check out the lower floor.

"Get me something I can tie him with," I said to Rosalind.

"Like what?"

I jerked my head towards Lucas's robe. "His belt will do."

They unthreaded the thin cord belt from its hoops and handed it over without a word. I tied the man's hands together behind his back as tightly as I could manage, not caring about whether he still had circulation or not. The belt was on the thick side to be totally secure, but at least it was long enough for me to tie his ankles as well, cinching them up and back towards his wrists so his spine was bowed awkwardly. I hoped it hurt.

When it was done I patted him down quickly, just in case he was hiding another weapon. Nothing. I reached over and picked up the gun he'd dropped when I'd first grabbed him.

The gun was a Beretta M9, a 9mm standard-issue US Army pistol, but with an extended barrel to take a quick-detach Advanced Armament suppressor. I thumbed the release just behind the trigger and dropped the fifteen-round magazine out, just to check, but it seemed our boy had come prepared. I shoved the full mag home again with the flat of my hand.

Before I got to my feet, I reached down for the man I'd caught, yanking the mask roughly off and tossing it aside. I rolled him over slightly—as much as I was able to with his hands and feet bound together—so his face was in the light. It gave me my first proper look at him.

And as soon as I did so, I realised I'd seen him before. It was the man from the Aquarium. The one who'd lured Simone out of the sea lion display and charmed her enough for her to call him and set up the scene of their next encounter on Boston Common. Or what would have been, if I hadn't got in the way of it. *How the hell had he followed our trail up here—unless Simone had called him?* I let go of him and swore under my breath. Rosalind glanced at me sharply.

"You know him?"

"Unfortunately," I said, my voice grim.

I watched the guy's face while I spoke. He was utterly calm, almost relaxed. If anything, there was the hint of a smile pulling up the corner of his mouth, as though he found something about this whole situation faintly amusing. As if he knew something I most definitely didn't. It made my spine itch.

"Who is he?" Lucas said, anger beginning to override his inertia. "What the hell was he trying to do?"

I bit back the snappy retort I'd been about to make and eyed them both.

"I need to check downstairs," I said. "Can you watch him?"

Lucas nodded, his lips thinning, and picked up a lamp from the side table near the cupboard where I'd hidden. As a lamp it was ugly, with a heavy twisted brass stem, but as a temporary cudgel it had a beauty all of its own. He whipped the plug out of the wall socket, coiled the wire like a lasso, and nodded to me.

"Oh, I'll watch him."

"I'll stay with Simone," Rosalind said, her face very white. She edged past me and the man on the floor, seemingly unable to take her eyes off the Beretta. Simone opened her door immediately in response to Rosalind's quiet knock. "Is it safe?" she asked, opening the door a little wider to admit the older woman.

"No," I said shortly. "Stay inside."

The door closed again quickly behind them. I turned to Lucas.

"Anything comes up that stairway that isn't me," I said, "hit it."

"Got it," he said, flexing his fingers around the lamp.

I edged carefully down the staircase, holding the gun with my arms outstretched. The man with the glasses would not, I knew, have waited around in the house. If he had any sense he would be long gone by now, but I still had to make sure. I did a slow, careful survey of the ground floor, finding the double doors from the dining area out onto the deck slightly ajar.

There was no sign of a forced entry, which meant either our visitors had acquired a key, or the doors had been left unlocked. I closed them and slid the bolts home, as sure as I could be that they'd been bolted up tight when I'd checked them before we'd turned in the night before. Lucas and

Rosalind had still been moving around, I remembered, and I berated myself for not coming down and doing another check after I'd heard them come upstairs. I had taken it for granted that for anyone with his kind of military background, securing your location would be a habit ingrained so deep you'd never lose it.

Or maybe it was. Which left all kinds of other unanswered questions, most of which I didn't want to examine too carefully right then.

I did a quiet pass around the ground floor, then eased down into the basement as well, just in case, but there was nothing amiss down there. Lucas's storage looked untouched. *Not a robbery then.* But I already knew that.

Just as I reached the ground floor again, I heard a muffled cry and a tremendous crash from somewhere above me. Then the endless falling splinter sound of glass breaking. I almost didn't need to scan the stairwell as I ducked past it to know that someone had just taken a dive out of the landing window.

The window looked out onto the half roof that covered the deck surrounding the house. From there it was a relatively short drop to the ground. I pelted for the front door, cursing as I fumbled with the locks and threw the door open.

The darkened figure of a man dropped into view from the roof. He rolled easily through the fall and then lurched away across the drive, running hard.

Even though I knew I shouldn't, I gave chase. I was barely halfway across the driveway when I heard the roar of an engine in the road, the scrabble of tyres on the loose shoulder, and the protesting whine of an overstressed transmission.

My stride faltered. No point in continuing a hopeless pursuit when my principal was still not secure. I ran back to the house, slamming home the locks on the front door as I went. I jogged back up the stairs, trying to avoid the worst of the shards of glass that now littered the treads.

The window at the top of the stairs was gone completely, the drapes flapping listlessly in the faint breeze. The frigid air came tumbling into the house like water into a torpedoed ship, rolling down the stairwell as it sought to flood the place from the ground up.

I found Lucas sitting with his back to the stairwell, legs splayed. Rosalind was on her knees in front of him, dabbing at her husband's bleeding forehead with a hand towel.

"What happened?"

She shot me a dark look. "He got loose," she gritted out, her voice brimming with a suppressed fury that eventually vented into shrillness. "Greg could have been killed!"

Lucas ducked away from her ministrations the way a horse avoids flies. "I'm OK. Don't fuss," he said, blurry, gesturing vaguely to the looped coils of Aquarium man's erstwhile bonds. "I guess I wasn't quite watching him as close as I should have been, huh?"

"I'm sorry," I said, remembering the smug little smile Aquarium man had given me. "I should have made sure it was tight enough to cut his damn circulation off."

Simone's door opened and she put her head out again. *Why couldn't the woman just do as she was told ...?*

"Daddy!" Simone cried when she caught sight of Lucas's injury. She ran out and knelt in front of him, grasping for his hand.

"I'm fine, honey. Don't you worry," he said, giving her a reassuring squeeze. "It's just a scratch. I guess I'm not quite as quick on my feet as I used to be, huh?"

Simone gave him a tremulous smile.

I felt something brush against me and found that Ella had sidled out onto the landing, sucking her thumb, and had ducked under the muzzle of the Beretta to attach herself to my right leg. She was wearing white pyjamas with pink ponies on the front and clutching the battered Eeyore so tightly his glass eyes were bulging. I transferred the gun into my other hand and stroked the side of her face.

Her skin was warm and very soft. She snuggled harder against me, not speaking.

"What did they want?" Simone asked in a subdued voice.

My hand stilled in Ella's hair.

"Isn't it obvious?" I said. I held up the Beretta so she could see the suppressor on the end of the barrel, keeping it away from Ella's view. "You don't bring this kind of thing to a burglary, Simone. This was a snatch." She paled and started to shake but I couldn't leave it there. "And guess *who* brought this with him?" I added.

If anything, Simone grew paler still. "Who?" she demanded.

"Your friend from the Aquarium," I said. "The one who *you* called and set up that meeting with that day on Boston Common. I don't suppose you also told him we were coming up here and—"

"No!" she cried. "How could you think I'd put Ella in danger after—?" And then it was her turn to break off, aware she'd nearly said more than she was willing to, more than was wise, in front of the Lucases. "How could you think that?" she muttered, more quietly.

I felt my shoulders weight. This was getting us nowhere. I turned to Rosalind and Lucas. "I think we should call the police," I said. "Do you need a medic as well?"

"No," he said. "It looks worse than it is. I'm fine."

"Do we really need to involve the police?" Simone asked quickly.

I stared at her. "You can't be serious," I said. "Two armed men break in here in the middle of the night and you're asking me if we really need the police? Get real, Simone! I should insist we pack up right now and get you both on the first flight out of here."

"I'm not leaving, Charlie," she said. Her voice had deepened the way some people's do when they're losing their balance on the edge of breaking down. I'd pushed her about as far as I could tonight and I hadn't the heart, or the energy, to make a stand over it now.

152

I sighed. "Look, let's talk about this later, OK?" I said. "Let me just do a quick check up here. You and Ella ought to go back to bed for a few hours, see if you can get some sleep."

She nodded and reached for Ella, but the little girl clung all the harder to my thigh. I had a sudden flashback to the hallway of the house in London, when the paparazzi had struck.

"It's OK, Ella," I said. "You go with your mummy. I won't be far away—I promise."

She looked up at me with those luminous eyes. "Are you going downstairs again?"

I thought of the shadows, and of the fear that would build in a child's mind from such a night.

"Yes," I said gently, trying to slay the monsters I could see forming. "I'll be going downstairs again."

"We-ell, if you are ... can I please have a cookie?"

I heard Simone's quiet gasp of disbelief.

"You are the cheekiest little madam I've ever come across," she said, but her voice was choked. "You can wait for breakfast like everybody else."

Ella allowed herself to be parted from me, still arguing the case for pre-meal cookies with her mother. My leg felt surprisingly cold without Ella around it.

I checked their room first, particularly the window locks, but it was clear. I did the master suite next, the first time I'd been in there, but it was also secure. I ducked my head into my own room expecting it to be the same, but as soon as I opened the door I knew there was something wrong, something in the air.

I flicked the light on. Hannibal the giant teddy bear was still lying under the bedclothes where I'd left him, but in the short space of time between separating from his friend on the landing, and reappearing after I'd tackled Aquarium man outside Simone's door, I found that the slim man with the glasses had definitely been into my room.

153

Oh, not all the way in, perhaps. He probably hadn't taken much more than a couple of steps over the threshold, sliding the door quietly closed behind him. I'd certainly never heard a thing, but now, when I peeled back the blankets, I discovered that poor old Hannibal had proved a convincing substitute for me.

Convincing enough for the slim man to have put three bullets into him, at any rate.

I couldn't feel any particular anger about that. It was line 1, page 1, for just about any kind of rules of engagement against a protected principal.

First job—kill the bodyguard.

TWELVE

By ten thirty that morning, I'd moved Simone and Ella into the Presidential Suite on the top floor of the elegant White Mountain Hotel on West Side Road. The suite was spacious and had a connecting door to the room next to it, which I'd taken.

I'd called Sean and brought him up to speed on the night's events, keeping my report cool and impersonal, particularly the part about the shooting of the teddy bear. Sean had responded in kind. There would be a time for emotional reaction, but we both knew this wasn't it.

At Sean's suggestion, I'd also called the private investigator Frances Neagley in Boston and given her as much information as I could about Aquarium man. She'd listened gravely, superhumanly restrained herself from saying, "I told you so," and promised to find out what she could. She asked if I was bringing in additional security and, when I said Sean was arranging it, she offered me the temporary loan of her guy from the New York agency, Armstrong's, until they arrived.

"Well, I could certainly do with some back-up, but what about you?"

"Right now," she'd said, "I think your need is greater than mine."

I'd removed the suppressor from the Beretta to make it easier to conceal, and was carrying it in the right-hand outside pocket of my jacket. I knew I'd be in deep trouble if I was caught with it, but if it was a choice between that and facing another attempt on Simone and Ella unarmed, I thought it was worth the risk. Just the weight of it there was a comfort.

The only thing I *hadn't* done—at Simone's absolute insistence—was call in the police. Instinct told me it was a bad idea to try to keep them out of it but, at the end of the day, no harm had been done beyond a broken window and the loss of some stuffing from an oversize bear. I could appreciate Simone's viewpoint that explanations would have been long and, bearing in mind the Lucases' ignorance of her financial situation, possibly embarrassing.

Not only that, but she swore she wasn't going to risk putting Ella through the same kind of press uproar she'd experienced at home. I tried to convince Simone otherwise, but it ended in a clenched-teeth argument with her telling me in no uncertain terms that if I didn't like it I could go home and leave her to it. I gave in at that point. How could I abandon them now? Besides, it wasn't the first time people had tried to kill me.

And it certainly wouldn't be the last.

Nevertheless, when there was a knock on my door shortly before eleven, I answered it with caution. I took great care when I looked through the Judas glass to ensure whoever was out in the hallway would not be able to tell when my eye was in line with the peephole.

Outside was Greg Lucas. He was rocking a little on his feet, obviously uneasy, the distortion of the fisheye lens making the movement more apparent. The dressing taped to his forehead seemed much bigger than I remembered the size of the injury demanding.

I waited a beat. I deliberately hadn't told him our room number. Had Simone called him? I glanced back at the connecting door to Simone's room. She was trying to settle Ella down for a nap after her disturbed night and the door was closed. I transferred the Beretta from my jacket to the back of my jeans, under the tails of my shirt, and slipped the security chain.

"Hi, Charlie," Lucas said. "Can we talk?" He gave me a weary smile, one that attempted to bond us through a shared struggle, one soldier to another at the end of a bloody engagement.

I didn't want that kind of connection with him. I jerked my head and said, "You'd better come in."

As soon as he was through the door I shouldered his face up against the wall to the bathroom, regardless of his recent injury, and patted him down. He seemed neither surprised by my action nor offended by it.

"Right-hand side," he said mildly.

"Good job you pointed that out. I might never have thought to look there."

"Just trying not to make you nervous," he said. "We all had a difficult night."

He was carrying a short-barrel Smith & Wesson .38 revolver in a belt rig on his right hip. I tugged the gun free and stepped back, not taking my eyes off him as I dropped the cylinder and emptied the chambered rounds out onto the coverlet of the bed.

"Simone's with Ella," I said. "I'd rather she wasn't disturbed."

"That's OK," he said. "It's you I've come to see."

"In that case, make yourself at home," I said. "Coffee?"

He nodded again. I left the partially dismembered gun on the bed and went to pour two cups from the little coffeemaker on the desk. It was surprisingly drinkable coffee and I was on my third lot since we'd checked in.

When I came back the gun was still where I'd left it and Lucas was over by the window, staring out at the picturesque view of the Echo Lake forest and the mountains beyond.

I joined him, handing over his coffee cup and sipping my own while I waited for him to try to find a way into what he wanted to say. By his silence, I gathered it wasn't easy.

And, somewhat childishly, I didn't feel inclined to help him out. Instead, I concentrated on admiring the winter wonderland scene outside the glass. It should have been idyllic. In any other circumstances, it probably would have been.

Lucas had aged under stress. The dressing on his forehead was universal skin tone, but his waxy skin was almost white by comparison. He raised his coffee with both hands, as though thankful for something to occupy them.

"You don't make this easy," he said at last with a brief smile in my direction.

I sighed, admitting defeat or we'd be here all day. "What is it you want to say to me, Greg?"

He took a breath, as if gathering all the loose ends back into himself. "They could have killed her last night, couldn't they?" he said. "Simone and Ella, I mean. They could have killed them both."

I shrugged. "But they didn't," I said. "And you and I both know that wasn't their plan, don't we?"

He stiffened, made a conscious effort to relax, then saw I'd noticed both reactions and gave up on trying to hide either. "Do we?"

"Oh, come on, Lucas!" I said, allowing some bite to show through without letting my voice rise because the last thing I wanted was Simone hearing us. "Think about it for a minute—the masks, the suppressors on the guns, the fact they didn't even bother getting close enough to my bed to find out I wasn't in it before they wiped me out. It was a kidnapping attempt, pure and simple."

He stuck his nose back into his coffee cup, almost gloomy, as though hearing it out loud somehow made it more real for him. Eventually, he looked up, looked right at me, and said, "I want you to take Simone and Ella home."

I took a moment to drain the last of my coffee, then put the empty cup down on the desk behind me, using the time it gave me to consider.

"Why?"

He blinked. "*Why*?" he repeated. "Charlie, as you've just pointed out so correctly, someone tried to kidnap my

158

daughter last night." He leaned forwards slightly, lowered his voice. "Right out of my house."

"So you're afraid for your safety," I said, a deliberate taunt delivered in a bland tone, maybe a small payback for that car park stunt the day we'd driven up here.

His lips thinned. "No, but I'm certainly afraid for *their* safety," he shot back. "Aren't you?"

"Of course," I said evenly. "And I did my best to ensure it this morning. I've already taken steps to make sure any further attempts won't succeed, either."

He seemed suddenly uncertain how to proceed. "Well ... good," he said. He gave a rueful smile. "She was a lovely kid. I can't tell you how much I've missed her, but I'd rather send her away now than lose her again for good."

I turned slightly, so I was facing him, and saw ... something. Something that flitted in and out of his eyes, quick as a fish, then was gone.

Guilt. Not big guilt. Not weigh-you-down-and-crush-you-with-the-sheer-bone -numbing-size-of-it guilt, but guilt, nevertheless.

"How long have you known?" I said.

"Excuse me?"

"Neither you nor Rosalind has asked the right questions about all this, Lucas—like 'why?' for a start," I said. "That should have been the first thing you wanted to know. Armed men break into your house in the middle of the night and make a damned serious attempt to snatch your daughter and granddaughter from under your nose, and you just don't seem surprised about it. Where's the righteous anger, the outrage?"

He kept his eyes resolutely on his cup, even though it was as empty as my own had been. I lifted it out of his fingers and put it down on the desk. It landed with more of a rattle than I'd been intending.

"Look, there are things going on here—I can't explain," he added when he saw I was about to speak. "You'll just have to take my word for it. I thought I could keep Simone

159

separate from it all, but I can't. There's a chance," he went on, flicking his eyes to my face as if to check how I was taking all this. "There's a chance that last night was aimed as much at me as at Simone's—"

He broke off and I gave him a thin smile. "Her money?" I finished for him.

He nodded, folding his arms so that his shoulders were hunched, as if he were cold.

"Yes, OK, we know about the money," he admitted, sounding every one of his years. "Ever since Barry O'Halloran came to see me."

"He told you?" I said, surprised.

"He didn't have to. He told me my daughter was looking for me and as soon as I realised how much effort had been put into finding me, I ran her name through a search engine on the Web. There were any number of hits from the tabloid newspapers back in England."

Ah, of course ...

"So you discovered your daughter was a millionairess and lo and behold you suddenly decided you *did* want to be found after all."

"I'd already made that decision," he said with dignity. "I would just rather have waited until the business we're involved in here was over and done with."

"Which is?"

"That's got nothing to do with you, Charlie."

"It is if you want me to persuade Simone to go home," I said mildly. "I'm guessing Felix Vaughan is an integral part of whatever's going on."

"You're right. And, I admit, when I first heard about it, I thought that some of that money would sure help get us out of the hole we've got into with him, but not if it's going to put her in danger. Nothing's worth that. So, do what you have to, Charlie, but persuade her to go home."

"I'm not leaving."

We both swung round to find Simone in the connecting doorway between the two rooms, one hand on the frame.

160

She came in and closed the door quietly behind her, watching through the diminishing gap, presumably that Ella didn't wake. Simone gave the Smith & Wesson on the bed a single almost incurious glance as she passed it.

"Look, Simone, honey—"

"No, Daddy, I want to stay," she said, touching his arm, her use of the word "Daddy' more confident than the first time she'd tried it, whatever doubts might have been raised in the meantime. "I can help. All this money—what good has it done me so far?" She lifted her shoulders, suddenly looking very young and almost gauche. "If it will help you— you and Rosalind—tell me how much you need, and take it."

To his credit, Lucas only hesitated for a moment.

"No," he said, and there was a quiet finality to his voice, so that I perhaps caught a glimpse of what must have been the old Lucas, of the SAS sergeant who'd terrorised new recruits to the point of insensibility, and I was just a fraction more inclined to believe in him. "Simone, I want you and Ella out of here as soon as possible. Listen to Charlie. It's not safe for you here."

"But—"

"Don't argue, princess." He touched her cheek and the tender gesture silenced her better than a slap.

He crossed to the bed, picked up the Smith & Wesson and refilled it with short, efficient movements, before slipping it back into his holster.

"I know I haven't been much of a father to you," he said, straightening his jacket to cover the gun, "but I won't put you in harm's way now if I can help it. Do what's sensible. Go home."

As he reached the doorway, Simone made a noise alongside me that could almost have been a whimper. When I looked, I saw tears beginning to form along her lower eyelids. Lucas sighed.

"You know it's breaking my heart to do this, but I have to think of what's best for my daughter, not for me," he said gently as he pulled open the door and stepped through it. "See that you do the same for yours."

The man whom I'd seen guarding Frances Neagley that day in the bar of the Boston Harbor Hotel, arrived at the White Mountain just before three in the afternoon. He was big and quiet to the point of seeming shy around women, but his eyes were constantly on the move and he carried a 9mm Glock in a shoulder rig under his left arm. His name was Jakes, he told me in his soft-spoken Deep South accent. He had orders from his boss, Parker Armstrong, that he was to stay with us until they could send more people up from New York. I was glad to have him.

I'd spent most of the afternoon trying to persuade Simone to call it a day. She had taken some convincing, but she finally agreed to a tactical retreat. My biggest card was Aquarium man. The way he'd engineered his meeting with her in Boston and then led the attack on her up here in Conway had certainly unnerved her. It gave me a crack and I drove a wedge into it for all I was worth. By the time Jakes arrived, she'd caved.

I'd called Sean and within half an hour he'd called back to say we were booked on flights out of Logan the day after tomorrow, giving us time to get back down to Boston without breaking our necks in the snow. As I'd ended the call I'd checked the time. Less than forty-eight hours and we'd be in the air.

As soon as we'd checked in to the White Mountain, I'd asked the front desk to organise us a rental car. Without Lucas on hand, we were stranded without transport, and I didn't think Charlie the limo driver would be prepared to slog all the way up to North Conway just to collect us.

The hotel had arranged for a four-wheel drive of some description on a one-way hire and said they'd drop it off that afternoon. At about five thirty, the front desk rang to say the rental company's representative was in the lobby and would I go down to deal with the paperwork?

I picked up my jacket from the bed. Simone was watching my TV while Jakes read to Ella out of one of her storybooks in the other room. Something about a little princess and a frog, if the snatches I heard were anything to go by. Jakes showed no sign of embarrassment as he read out the appropriate sections in his version of a frog accent, which seemed, bizarrely enough, to be distinctly Scottish. Ella was sucking her thumb as she listened to him, captivated.

I ducked my head into the room and he looked up, flashing me a quick grin without breaking off the tale.

"I won't be long," I told him. "Put the chain on behind me."

There was only one person obviously waiting in the lobby when I got down there, a moustachioed man with a dark complexion, wearing a peaked cap with earflaps that stuck out from the sides of his head like a semi-alert hound. He was wrapped up in a thick ski jacket that he hadn't bothered to unzip despite the roaring open fire at the back of the lobby, and he was carrying a clipboard.

"Miss Fox?" he said, thrusting a gloved hand out. "How ya doing? Say, you wanna go check over the vehicle first, then we can come back inside and get you all signed up?"

"No problem," I said, glad I'd brought my jacket. "What have we ended up with?"

He held the door and followed me through it out into the sudden drenching cold. "Excuse me?"

"What kind of vehicle?" I expanded as he strode away towards the parking area at the side of the hotel. I had to hurry to keep up, shivering inside my jacket. The wind had picked up a little and it knifed straight through to my bones the moment we stepped out of the door.

"Oh, the vehicle?" he said, suddenly sounding vague. "Well, it's right over there, so you can see for yourself."

He pointed and, like a fool, I let my gaze drift in the direction he indicated. When I looked back, he'd taken his hand out of his right pocket and, this time, there was a gun in it. A black semiautomatic, maybe a Colt, but in this light it was hard to tell. The Beretta was in my own pocket, but I knew I didn't stand a chance of getting to it in time. I let my breath out slowly and forced myself to relax.

"Nicely done," I murmured.

The moustachioed man gave a tight little smile in acknowledgement of the praise and jerked his head to the side.

"Keep walking," he said.

"What's the point?" I said, eyes tracking his every movement for sign of a way in. The barrel of the gun was disappointingly steady in that regard. "If you're going to drop me, then drop me here. Why do I need to die tired?"

"I ain't gonna drop you unless I have to," the man said. "Someone wants to talk to you, is all. But you give me any trouble, ma'am, and you better believe I'll do what I got to."

"And if I don't feel like talking?"

The man smiled again, almost. "All you really got to do is listen," he said. "And trust me, you'll do it a whole lot better if you ain't in pain. So, we gonna do this the hard way, or the easy way?"

I paused, considering for a moment. As I did so I heard the long scrape of the side door of a van opening, away to our left. Any hopes I had of the noise causing a distraction were instantly dashed, however. Moustache never even flinched. I glanced sideways myself and found out why.

Another man had emerged from a dark-coloured van. He was medium height, neither small nor bulky, and his close-cropped hair gleamed slightly red in the lights from the hotel. He was also carrying a semiautomatic. My chances of escape had just halved.

"Quit messing with her and get her in the van," he said easily to Moustache.

Moustache still hadn't taken his eyes off me. Both of them had the look of pros, relaxed, confident, and unlikely to make any slips I could take immediate advantage of. I cursed under my breath for walking so lamb-like to the slaughter and shrugged my compliance, allowing the red-haired man to pat me down with rough efficiency. He took my mobile phone, then quickly found and confiscated the Beretta.

"Tsk, Charlie," Moustache said, and I couldn't suppress a twinge of unease at his use of my first name. "Now I'm betting you ain't got a licence for that."

"Why?" I said. "Do you?"

He didn't answer, just giving me a shove in the small of my back towards the still-open sliding door. I climbed in, aware of a sense of deep foreboding. After I'd left the army I'd made a living for a while teaching self-defence classes to women. One of the most important points I'd stressed was not to allow yourself to be taken to a place of your assailant's choosing. Yet, as I waited for an opportunity to grab for the gun that never quite arose here I was, breaking all my own rules.

Moustache climbed in after me, threw his clipboard into the back, and slammed the door shut. The red-haired man got into the driver's seat, reversed out of the parking space and stuck the gearshift into drive. The whole thing had taken no more than a couple of minutes from us walking out of the hotel lobby. There had been no witnesses.

As we began to move forwards I caught a glimpse of the hotel's lights glittering through the darkened back windows of the van, and wondered what the hell I'd just got myself into.

***

The two men drove me down into North Conway and almost all the way through the town until we finally pulled off next to a little seafood restaurant called Jonathon's. They stopped the van and the red-haired man twisted to face me, laying his arm along the back of the seat. He was wearing an ornate ring on the little finger of his right hand. The light was behind his head and I couldn't see his face clearly.

"Now, you been a good girl so far," he said. "Are you going to behave, or do we need to go through the whole threat business again?"

"That depends," I said, keeping my voice steady, "on what happens next."

The redhead smiled enough for me to see his teeth in the gloom. "Someone inside wants to speak to you," he said. "We go in, you talk, you come out, we give you a ride back to the hotel."

"O-K," I said slowly. "And the threat business?"

"Oh, we don't need to go into that, but just let me say that sure is a cute kid you're looking after."

I felt my face freeze over. "I think I've been pretty patient so far in allowing you two to drag me down here, but that, my friend," I said softly, "was a big mistake."

"Hey, now who needs to quit fooling around with her?" Moustache said. "She's said she'll do it, so she'll do it. Don't make trouble for yourself."

As my two escorts walked me towards the restaurant, one on either side, I asked, "As a matter of interest, how did you engineer that grab raid back there?"

The redhead merely looked smug, but Moustache was prepared to be more talkative. "I was hanging around in the lobby, keeping an eye out for you, and I heard them at the desk calling up the rental company. Soon as she mentioned your name, I went out and got myself a clipboard and some official-looking papers." He shrugged. "Reckoned it was a whole lot easier than trying to deliver you pizza you ain't ordered."

You reckoned right.

They'd put their guns away but had a tight grip on my upper arms instead, just above the elbow. The redhead did the talking to the waitress who offered to seat us, nodding to an occupied corner table. It was too early for it to be busy. In fact, when I glanced around I saw that the man I'd been brought to meet was the only diner. It came as little surprise to recognise Felix Vaughan.

I did a fast visual sweep of the place as I was walked across towards him. Formica-topped tables, plain wooden chairs, rough plaster, and simple clapboard walls, painted white like a beach house. The look was completed by mooring buoys and other nautical items strung along the walls, including an old harpoon gun.

Vaughan was sitting eating a large portion of what I would have called king prawns, but I'd learned were classified as shrimp over here, from a paper plate. They'd obviously arrived still fully dressed and he had sticky fingers and a stack of empty shells to one side of him. He looked up as we approached and carefully wiped his hands.

"Miss Fox," he said, nodding to the chair opposite. "Please, won't you join me?"

His voice was polite, but the men on either side of me forced my obedience, dragging me into a seat and then making sure I stayed there with a heavy hand on my shoulder.

"Mr Vaughan," I said, pleasantly. "Would you mind informing your minions that the next one who touches me will be feeding through a tube for the foreseeable future?"

It was gratifying that the hand lifted sharply, without any need for the scowl that Vaughan levelled in their direction.

"Thank you," Vaughan said, his voice dismissive and chillingly polite. "You can wait outside."

He waited until they'd gone before he spoke again, sliding his thumb up the exoskeleton of another shrimp and twisting its head from its body.

"Would you like some?" he said. He gestured to the paper plates. "Don't be fooled by the modest décor. This place does the best seafood for miles."

I sighed, looked away a moment as if to catch my breath, or my temper, but in reality just so I didn't have to watch him eat. Then I looked back. "You never quite got the hang of dating, did you, Felix?"

For a moment he frowned before a sly smile overtook it. "You're a cool one. I'll give you that," he said, shaking his head. He wiped his hands again, picking up a bundle of extra paper napkins. I leaned forwards, folding my arms onto the Formica surface and carefully palming a table knife in my right hand as I did so, just in case.

"Don't be foolish, Miss Fox," Vaughan said without looking at me directly. "I've been a fighting man since before you were born. I'd kill you before you got that blunt blade anywhere near me."

I sat back again, leaving the knife on the tabletop and he nodded as he reached for another shrimp.

"That's better. If I wanted you dead, you'd be dead by now, believe me. I hear you had a lucky escape last night."

How did you hear? Because you were involved, or because Lucas told you?

His patronising tone goaded me into bravado. "Luck didn't come into it."

He grunted. "You say you were a soldier?" he said. I gave the faintest nod. "Well then, you should know that luck always comes into it, one way or another."

"Would you like to get to the point?"

"Of course," he said. "The point's simple. I've tried to get it across to you as painlessly as possible, but it hasn't sunk in, so now I'm going to tell it to you straight. Go home. Take the girl and the kid and go home."

I sat and looked at him. *As painlessly as possible.* Had he had a hand in last night's failed kidnapping attempt, or did he have some other motive?

"Why?" I said.

He shook his head. "Not your problem," he said. "Your problem is that I want you to go. That's the start and finish of your problem. You do the right thing and your problem ends."

"My problem is my client," I said. "If she wants to stay, she stays, but," I added, raising a hand when he would have cut in, "fortunately—for all of us—she's already decided she's leaving."

"When?"

I paused, but reason told me that it wouldn't gain me anything not to tell Vaughan the truth. And it could even save a lot of hassle, so I said, "We'll be heading down to Boston first thing tomorrow."

"That's very wise," he said, nodding, giving me a tight smile. He ripped open a couple of packets of moist towelets and wiped his hands more thoroughly, fastidious about his nails. The scent of lemon cut across the fishy smell of the table, sharp and acidic. "So, your task is nearly over."

I shook my head. "I'll stay with Simone as long as she needs me," I said. "As long as there's a threat."

"And then?"

I shrugged. "Move on to the next job."

He reached for his glass, took a drink and stared at me. "I could use someone with your particular skills," he said. "I think I could work something out that would make it very worth your while for you to consider relocating."

"I'm flattered," I said blandly. "But it would have to be a very cold day in hell."

"Well, that's the beauty of New England—the weather's always just about to change," he said. "You don't like it, you wait five minutes."

"The answer's no."

It was his turn to shrug. "A shame," he said.

I pushed back my chair and stood. He let me take one step away from him before he spoke again.

"So tell me—has she found out the truth about him?"

"The truth?" I turned back, a flash image of that old ID photo of Lucas in front of me. "You mean he's not her father?"

Vaughan laughed, little more than a chuckle under his breath. "That would be much too easy, wouldn't it?"

For a moment I just stared, so tempted to ask but afraid he was just teasing to get me to beg. "And how would you know anything about that?"

"I make a point of finding out all about the people I do business with," he said. He sat back and smiled again, more smugly this time. "So, she doesn't know."

"The jury's still out," I said shortly, losing patience. "We leave tomorrow. By the time we come back, she'll know one way or the other."

THIRTEEN

Vaughan's boys dropped me off at the bottom of the steep driveway leading up to the White Mountain, tossing my mobile phone out into the snow after me. They did not return the Beretta, more's the pity.

I waited until they'd turned round, avoiding the spray of slush from their wheels, and their dirty rear lights were bumping away before I stooped to retrieve the phone, drying it on my shirttail. They'd switched the phone off and I turned it back on again as I trudged back towards the hotel entrance. It rang almost immediately with a voicemail message.

"Charlie? It's Jakes. Where are you?" said a man's voice, anxiety threading clearly through it. "Erm, look, Miss Kerse wants to go to her father's place. She got a call, about ten minutes ago, and she says she wants to go over there right away. I kinda told her we ought to wait for you to get back first, but she's getting kinda angry and she won't wait any longer. So, I'm gonna go over there with her and, when you get this, that's where we are, OK?" There was a pause, as though he expected me to speak, or offer some kind of advice or approval. "Call me when you get this, OK?" Then the bleep of the call being ended.

I tried to get the phone to show me what time the message had been recorded but fumbled with the technology. As I redialled, I was cursing under my breath.

The driveway curved round behind the hotel, but the shortest route was up a steep, snow-covered bank to the front entrance. I took it without hesitation, plunging into soft powder.

The cold scoured my throat as I struggled up the incline past the huge veranda that housed the heated outdoor swimming pool, listening to Jakes's phone ringing out without reply. Inside the lobby, the blast of warmth from the central heating and the blazing log fire hit me like a wall. I staggered, coughing. The woman on the reception desk stared at me like I'd just beamed down from the *Starship Enterprise*.

"Miss Fox! Are you OK? Did you have trouble with your car?"

I stared at her, uncomprehending, then realised that my jeans were wet past the knees and I was shaking.

"I need a phone," I managed. She flicked her eyes at the mobile I clearly had clutched in my hand but thrust the desk phone at me, the way you shove a toy into a dog's mouth to try to stop it jumping up at your clothing. I punched in the number of Simone's room and waited, impatient and in vain, for it to be answered.

When I knew for sure that it wasn't going to be, I swore under my breath again—or not so under my breath, if the sudden paling of the woman on the other side of the desk was anything to go by.

"Listen, I need some transport."

"Well, I can call you a cab—"

"I don't have time to wait for a cab," I said, aware of the panic scrabbling at the inside of my chest, causing my heart to pound. I was sweating with the heat and the fear.

So tell me, Vaughan had said with that patronising smile of his, *has she found out the truth about him?*

Oh God. Simone ... Ella ...

"Don't you have a rental car out there on the lot?" the woman asked.

"That guy ... it wasn't them," I said.

"Well, wait a minute now." She frowned, dug around under the desk and came back up with a set of car keys.

172

"There you go. The boy came and dropped it off not more than a half hour ago. Said if you could swing by the office first thing tomorrow, they'd deal with the paperwork and such then."

A half hour ago ... We must have almost passed each other on the driveway. I grabbed the keys with hardly a word of thanks and sprinted for the door again. She called something after me, but I didn't hear it.

The cold bit me as soon as I was out of the door, like it had always been waiting just below the surface, like I'd never really been warm. I didn't care.

As I jogged through the parking area, I fumbled for the button on the key fob, stopping short as the hazard lights flashed on a white Buick SUV to my right.

I jumped in, fumbling with the unfamiliar controls, and cranked the engine. I knew I headed down the driveway faster than it was wise to do, but the way the Buick slipped and slithered despite its four-wheel drive only served to make me angry, like it was trying to slow me down.

I don't remember getting between the hotel and the main road. The only reason the junction registered was because the traffic light was on red, but I suppose I would have hesitated there anyway. *Miss Kerse wants to go to her father's place,* Jakes had said. Did that mean the surplus store, or the house? Left for Intervale, or right for the centre of North Conway? I stabbed my thumb on the button to redial and listened to the empty ringing until the lights dropped onto green overhead and the driver behind me blew his horn.

Her father's place.

The house. I turned right, not knowing why I'd made that decision, or if it was the right choice. I gunned the Buick down the main street, not seeing the prettiness of the lights wrapped round the trees outside the Eastern Slope Inn, until I reached the turn off on the left for Mechanic Street, towards Mount Cranmore. The family houses I'd noticed the first time Lucas had taken us to his home looked very different in the dark, all lit up along the eaves like storefronts. The lights were deceiving and I almost missed the turn for Snowmobile, jamming the brakes on at the last moment.

I drove past the Fitness Center and plunged into darkness on the other side of the lights. Maybe it was the illuminated ski runs further up the mountain that made things look so shadowy at ground level, but people apparently didn't go for excessive outside lighting here. Maybe they liked to be able to see the stars, which were scattered starkly across the inky blue-black sky above the trees.

I stopped the Buick just short of the driveway and shut off the engine. I was close enough to be able to see that Jakes's nondescript Ford Taurus was parked in front of the steps leading up to the front door. The two lamps on either side of the doorway were lit, but otherwise the place was in darkness. I wished wholeheartedly that Vaughan's men had given me back the Beretta.

I slid out onto the road, staying low behind the front end of the Buick while I waited for my eyes to adjust and tried to take stock. There was nothing for it—I was going to have to get closer.

I left the cover of the Buick and ran across, doubled over, to duck behind the Ford. There was no response from the house. I waited a moment longer, took a couple of deep breaths, then pelted for the door.

The door itself was closed but not locked. I eased it open and stepped through into the hallway. There was a little light bleeding through from the two lamps outside on the deck, but it was dark enough so that I didn't see the body until I almost fell over it.

I stumbled back, biting off a gasp. A man, lying on his back at the foot of the stairs with his right leg twisted awkwardly underneath him. It was too dark to see his face clearly. I forced myself to kneel alongside him, feel for an arm and work along to the wrist so I could check for a pulse. Nothing. I ran my hands up over his torso, looking for obvious injury. As my hands reached his left side, I found the holster and identified the familiar blunt shape of a Glock semiautomatic.

Jakes.

I swallowed, pulling the gun free. Whatever had happened here, he hadn't seen it coming. Not enough to have got his gun out, at any rate. I ran my hands up to his head, gently, waiting for the fatal wound, but there didn't seem to be one. There was no blood. He didn't even smell dead. So what the hell had happened? Unfairly, maybe even unjustly, I cursed Jakes for allowing himself to die without even drawing his gun.

I pulled out my mobile phone and dialled 911. I gave them the address and the fact that there was a man dead and a child in danger, but I didn't stay on the line to give further details.

I picked up the gun and got to my feet without a sound. I knew Jakes wouldn't have carried it without one in the chamber, but I eased the slide back a fraction anyway, enough to see the indented nose of the hollowpoint round through the eject port. There was no conventional safety. It was ready to go. Point and shoot.

Over to my left, from the kitchen, I heard a faint noise, muffled almost to the point of silence. I turned slowly, as if that would help me get a better directional fix, but there was no repeat. I moved across towards the kitchen, holding the Glock out in front of me, double-handed. It wasn't quite so dark there, thanks to the windows that lined that side of the house. I could see the lights from the ski run a little way off through the trees.

I came round the corner of the first kitchen cabinet fast, leading with the gun, and found myself taking aim at a small figure huddled down in front of the oven.

Ella's eyes were huge in the half-light and awash with tears. She had her knees bent up and clutched to her chest, as if by making herself smaller she might succeed in disappearing altogether.

"Ella," I whispered, lowering the muzzle of the Glock so it was pointing away from her. "It's OK, sweetheart. It's me—Charlie." The words seemed to have no effect. I tried: "Where's your mummy?" but that didn't seem to work, either.

I eased closer and crouched next to her, putting a hand out to stroke her head. She flinched at my touch. She was trembling all over and, when I inhaled, I realised that she'd had a bit of an accident as well. Shame she was too old to still be in nappies. Still, I suppose I couldn't blame her, poor kid. God alone knew what she'd seen here.

"It's OK, Ella," I said quietly, trying to be soothing but aware that I only succeeded in coming out with a horribly fake brittle tone. "I need you to stay here and keep very quiet—like you were doing. Can you do that for me?" No response. "I'll be back very soon. I promise."

But as I started to rise, it must have penetrated that I, too, was going to abandon her. She pounced for my leg, fastening her little arms round my calf and holding on for grim death.

"Sweetheart, I've got to find your mummy," I said, trying to prise her hands loose. Damn, she had a grip a pit bull would give its canines for.

"Don't leave me alone," she wailed, her voice like a siren. "I want to come, too. I want my mummy."

I shushed her, alarmed, and found myself saying, "OK, OK, you can come. But you have to be very, very quiet."

She nodded furiously, unlocked her stranglehold on my leg and held her arms up to me. I stared at her for a moment, her eyes and nose streaming delightfully and a distinct sogginess around her bottom.

"Oh, you have to be kidding," I muttered.

Her lower lip had firmed, but as I hesitated it started to wobble and I could almost see her gather in her breath for a burst of raucous weeping. Before she could get into her stride I swept her up onto my left hip. She grabbed hold of my jacket collar in both hands and dug her bony knees into my ribs. I gave her what I hoped was a reassuring smile that was blankly met, then tried to ignore her.

Not easy to carry out a full search with a small damp child clamped to the side of you, but I did my best. First we went up, checking the bedrooms on the upper floor. I made sure I spun Ella round as we went upstairs so that as I stepped over Jakes's body she didn't get a clear look at him. The window on the landing had been reglazed, but the brass-stemmed lamp Lucas had used to threaten Aquarium man with was lying on its side on the floor, with the shade torn, and the rug was half turned back.

A struggle, I wondered, *then a fall? Was that what had happened to Jakes?* Coming down the stairs was worse. There was nothing much I could do to block Ella's view of him lying in the hallway.

"Is he sleeping?" she whispered in my ear, and I heard the hopeful note in her voice.

"Yes, Ella," I lied. "He's sleeping."

There was something unholy about the thick darkness as I felt my way down the stairs to the basement. The door at the bottom was shut and I opened it very carefully, only to find the lights were on down here. I shoved the door wide and went through it fast, ducking to the side, moving like an ape cradling my young with Ella attached to my side. To my right were the storerooms where I'd suspected that Lucas kept his guns. It did my nerves no good at all to see one of the doors standing open.

To my left was the door to the home cinema room. At first I couldn't tell if it was occupied or not, but as I edged closer I heard the sharp staccato sound of voices inside.

Simone's voice, in particular.

My first reaction was relief that she was alive. But crowding in on top of that came the realisation that Simone was screaming at someone, the sound disguised by the soundproofing of the room. I glanced at Ella. She'd stiffened in my arms at the sound of her mother's voice, still at an age where she picked up more by tone and vibration than by the words themselves. I wished that I didn't have to take her in there with me, but I knew she wouldn't let me leave her out here any more than she would have let me leave her upstairs.

Ah well, this is what they pay you for ...

I turned the handle and pushed open the door.

Inside, the occupants of the room swung to face me. Simone, Rosalind, and Lucas. Simone was holding a SIG 9mm that looked very like the one I'd fired on the range at Lucas's store. Tears streaked her face and her eyes were wild.

For a split-second, time slowed. I took in the scene like a freeze-frame in a movie, seeing everything and nothing in the blink of an eye.

The room was laid out with a blank wall for the home cinema screen at the far end, flanked by two tall loudspeakers. A projector was suspended from the ceiling and four huge recliner chairs, two at each side, faced the screen. Other than that, there was no furniture.

Lucas was standing to my left, near the chairs. He still had the dressing on his forehead from his tussle with Aquarium man, and was now leaking from a new wound somewhere high up in his hairline, but he didn't seem to notice the blood sliding down his temple and cheek. His back was very straight like he was awaiting execution. Next to him, his wife was slumped in her seat, her normally tidy hairstyle awry. She was staring at a spot on the far wall, away from Simone, and I would have thought she was in shock until she suddenly focused on my arrival.

Simone herself was bent forwards as though she was in pain, and shaking so hard she could hardly hold the gun. She gripped it in both hands, holding it away from her body like she was afraid of it, of what it might do, her hands much too tense. Perhaps that was why, as I entered and she turned, automatically bringing the gun round towards me, her finger tightened on the trigger.

The SIG discharged, twice in quick succession, almost slam-firing as the recoil took Simone by surprise and caused her to loose off a second shot.

The first round hit the wall high to my left, splintering chips of blockwork. The second went into the ceiling.

The noise of the gun discharging was enormous. Ella gave a single high-pitched squeal of terror, right in my ear, deafening me almost as much as the shot had done. I dived sideways and down, twisting my head away, rolling so I landed on my back, cradling the child.

As I went I could have sworn I heard Simone yell, "You bastard. You bastard!" but I had no idea at whom the words were aimed. If her shooting was anything to go by, it could have been anyone.

"Simone," I shouted. "For God's sake put the gun down before you kill somebody!"

"It's too late," she yelled back, the edge of hysteria in her voice. "It's all too late now." She gulped, her breath catching in her throat as though a sorrow too great to bear had suddenly overwhelmed her.

Too late. I remembered Jakes, lying dead in the hallway.

"Simone, what the hell is going on?"

"He killed him!" She was weeping openly now, great raw sobs that were wrenched out of her. "I saw him do it. I loved you!" she shouted at Lucas. "I trusted you! You bastard. You utter *fucking* bastard!"

Ella went rigid, then started to struggle violently against me, crying for her mother. It was like trying to hold onto a feral cat. She squirmed out of my grasp and scrambled away from me, terror lending her a speed and agility I didn't think she possessed. I half-rose and grabbed at her, but she zipped out of reach, moving into full view between the seats and the doorway.

"Ella!" Simone cried, as if realising for the first time she was there. Simone must have realised, too, that in firing at me she'd also risked her daughter. She gave a howl of outrage, barely human.

Ella froze at the unfamiliar sound. I stretched for her again, my fingers just brushing her sleeve as I sought a better grip.

Lucas, sensing what might have been his only chance, suddenly broke out of his immobility and lunged for Ella himself, whisking her out of my tenuous grasp. He scooped the child up, swinging her legs clear of the ground, and went for the doorway with her shrieking in his arms. I threw myself forwards, trying to hook a hand under his ankle, to slow or trip him, but he lashed out, catching me across the cheek with the back of his fist. For a second all I saw was instant static, jagged patches of lightning, a jumble of confused images. I let go and went crashing backwards.

By the time the world righted itself, Lucas was through the door, still clutching Ella. Simone hurled herself after them, throwing the door open and disappearing through it. I vaguely heard the muffled sound of feet pounding up the stairs, lessening into near silence as the door closed almost quietly behind her. I turned and found Rosalind still crouched in her chair, seeming too dazed to react.

"Rosalind, what the fuck is going on?" I lurched to my feet, staggering as the room tilted for a moment before it steadied and I could go for the door myself.

"I don't know," she said. "She just went crazy, screaming at Greg over and over. Oh my God," she spluttered, choking up. She got a grip, then said, more calmly, "You can shoot." I glanced back, took in her white face. "Will you …?"

Shoot Simone? Or Lucas?

"If I have to," I said, answering both questions. As I went through the doorway I threw a last parting shot over my shoulder: "Jakes is dead—the cops are on their way."

I wanted to ask Rosalind what the hell had happened, who had killed Jakes, and what on earth Simone had found out about Lucas that had suddenly turned her into a gun-wielding homicidal maniac. Ask? No, I wanted to scream and shout at the woman, to shake the answers loose.

I jammed my temper back in its box. There'd be time for that when the final body count was in. My job now was to make sure it stayed at one.

I went up the basement steps fast and through the ground floor of the house trying to pick up the trail. Lucas was running, apparently unarmed, carrying fifty-odd pounds of struggling four-year-old child to weigh him down. Logic said he should have made for the front of the house, for a vehicle and a means of escape, but in that brief snapshot I'd had of him in the basement, I'd seen fear written all over him. People who are afraid do not behave the way you expect them to. Yes, he'd been trained, and according to his record he'd seen action in some of the nastiest theatres of war in the world. But confronted by his daughter, with a gun, he'd reacted not like a soldier but ... how?

Like a criminal? By taking a hostage, something to trade his own life for.

Or like a coward?

I turned away from the front of the house and moved towards one of the doors out onto the rear deck, that led down into the woods. If Lucas was looking for somewhere to run, somewhere to hide, instinct told me he would have chosen this direction.

I stepped out onto the deck and stopped, pressed up against the outside wall of the house and holding my breath to listen for some sign that I was right. It only took a moment before I heard it—the snap of breaking branches, a bitten-off cry, the sound of a child wailing.

I moved to the steps and jumped down into the fresh snow at their foot. The moon had risen now, shining strong enough to produce eerie shadows from the trunks of the trees. It was enough to light the ground and I could see that two sets of footprints led away from the house and into the trees. Wide-spaced prints with the deepened heel impression of people running. Lucas and Simone. I headed in the same direction, but it was impossible to follow the trail for long and I lost it within a few metres of getting into the tangle of close-knit trees.

"For God's sake, give it up!" I shouted, to Lucas as much as to Simone, my voice stark and loud in the gathering gloom. "The cops will be here any moment." And I hoped that they'd taken me seriously enough that it was true.

Nobody responded. I closed my eyes for a second, tried to get a lock onto the sounds of flight through the debris of fallen trees across the shrouded ground.

There!

My eyes snapped open and I started to run, heading away from the house on a diagonal course, heading up the slope with the ski run to my left. The trees turned into a forest very quickly, closing ranks as though to defy an easy trail.

Suddenly, up ahead, I saw the fleeting movement of shadow flitting between the narrow trunks. Adrenaline injected into my system, giving me a burst of speed. I closed the gap and saw that the figure was Lucas, still clinging to Ella. She'd stopped screaming now and I just prayed that was of her own accord. The thought that this man had hurt her brought a cold hard flame of fury into my chest.

"Lucas!" I snapped, bringing the Glock up straight and level. "Hold it right there or I swear I'll shoot you in the spine."

For a moment I thought he was going to ignore me but then he faltered, his coordination deserting him as the fear-induced strength dissipated, leaving him almost spent. I crabbed nearer, dusting through the snow at my feet, keeping the gun up, and could hear him sobbing for breath. He had no coat and it was desperately cold. He must have been almost done. But not quite.

"What are you going to do, Charlie?" he said. He turned to face me, hefting Ella higher so that she was shielding most of his upper body. He ducked his head close to hers, so they were together, touching. "You really think you'd risk trying to shoot me, without even knowing why?"

"I don't need to know why," I said. I edged closer. Lucas was above me, on the higher ground. Between us was a ditch. I stopped on the rim of it, only a few metres away from them. "You're a threat to my principal. That's good enough."

He gave a hollow laugh. "Am I? Don't you think it's Simone who's a threat to me? And what about you? She fired at you, too. And at her own daughter! You both could have been killed."

"You know as well as I do she didn't mean to do that."

"Didn't she? Dead is still dead, meant or not," he said flatly. "And how do you know she didn't mean it? You saw Jakes, didn't you?"

I stilled. "You're not trying to tell me she killed Jakes," I said. "Get real, Lucas."

But when I heard a noise off to our right I tensed, just the same as he did.

"Right now," I said, "I just want to get Ella to safety. Give her to me, Lucas. Whatever's going on between you and Simone, for God's sake leave Ella out of it."

If anything, he gripped the little girl tighter. "No way," he said. "She's my insurance. My guarantee. Let's face it, Charlie, are you going to risk taking a shot?"

I hadn't lowered the Glock a fraction, still had it out in front of me. Lucas was less than four metres away, uphill and slightly to my right, keeping his face pressed against the side of the child's head as though the touch of her alone would keep him safe, like a protective force field.

Ella had given up her struggles now and was passive in his arms. She might even have been clinging on around his neck. After all, though she could well have been terrified, this was the man she'd learned to call Grandpa. You couldn't just undo that in an instant. I couldn't see her face, couldn't judge how aware she was of exactly what was going on around her.

I mentally calculated the amount of Lucas's head visible alongside hers and knew that, technically, I could take him out. One round, straight through the mouth. If I was quick I could probably reach Ella before he finished falling.

But I wouldn't be able to stop her seeing what I'd done. Wouldn't be able to stop her witnessing a bloody death. A sight no child should ever have to see. She was only four. How much would she forget in time? And how much would haunt her forever?

Slowly, gradually, I let the muzzle of the Glock rise, uncurled my finger from the trigger and laid it along the outside of the guard instead.

"OK, Lucas," I said. "You're right. I'm not going to—"

That was as far as I got.

The first shot ripped hot through my left thigh, jerking me off balance. For a few long seconds the only thing I felt was the jolt and the shock of it. Then the pain came rushing in. My nervous system overloaded and shut down, leaving my mind screaming for action. I started to turn, sluggish and clumsy, and that's when something hit me in the back like an express train.

I watched with a kind of horrified fascination as the Glock went tumbling into the snow from fingers that didn't seem to be mine any longer. I caught the briefest flash of movement above me, saw Lucas already twisting away, already fleeing without hesitation. I could see Ella's face staring back at me over his shoulder as he ran with her into the trees. I've never seen such terror on the face of a child.

I'd promised her she'd be safe with me, that I wouldn't leave her. I'd promised her mother that I'd look after the pair of them, come what may.

I tried to take a step after Lucas's rapidly disappearing figure but it was all so heavy, nothing quite worked anymore.

Oh, so this is what it's like ...

I stumbled and went down.

FOURTEEN

I can't pinpoint the exact moment of my waking. It wasn't like just flicking a switch between oblivion and reality. Instead, I made the transition slowly, merging the edges of one into the other, until it was all just a slurred emulsion of violent dreams and pain and darkness and hazy memories and odd moments of utter peace.

Then, finally, I opened my eyes and found that they were prepared to stay open without dragging me downwards again like a doomed submariner. Everything crowded in on me in a thunderous rush, too much information to take in, arriving much too fast.

I squinted in the harsh light and found I was lying on my back in what could only be a hospital bed. Hospitals look the same and feel the same and smell the same, the industrialised world over.

There was a foul taste on my tongue and an oxygen mask covering my nose and mouth. I had the strange feeling of being one stage disconnected from the rest of my body. But at least I had a body to feel disconnected from. So, I'd definitely imagined my own death.

But I hadn't imagined Simone's.

I squeezed my eyes shut, blocked it out, shied away from it. I wasn't ready to face that. Not yet.

I tried a few small experimental wriggles of my extremities. Both feet checked in, although flexing my toes on the left side caused someone to start burning a hole through my thigh with a blowtorch.

The fingers of my left hand came online as normal, but my right hand seemed to be having some difficulty complying with the simplest of commands.

I stilled, trying not to panic, then tried again, telling myself there was a perfectly reasonable explanation. Maybe I'd been lying on my arm in my sleep. Hell, I could have been like that for days—weeks, for all I knew. No wonder the damn thing was numb.

Because that's all it was, just asleep. I was not—*was not*—paralysed. I shut my eyes and focused all my will on moving my right arm. How the hell do you do that consciously? I'd never had to think about it before. The idea of reaching out for something had always just formed in my mind and, before I knew it, my hand was already acting on that impulse, in every sense.

Only now it wasn't.

Eventually, with a sluggish reluctance, my arm began to obey me. Movement, however small, sent a rippling ache up through my shoulder into my back. There was a blunted feel to the discomfort—the effects of the morphine most likely.

I took a deep breath and let it out slowly, taking a perverse pleasure in the fiery stab in my ribs that it caused. Pain meant feeling, at least, and for that I welcomed it. It felt like someone had got me on the ground and kicked me around a good deal while I was there. The drugs hadn't taken the pain away, just coated it with a sullen protective layer. It would account for the slight nausea as well. The thought of actually throwing up brought me out in a cold sweat.

From somewhere at the foot of the bed I heard the rustle of paper, then quiet steps, and a man walked round into my field of view. Good dark blue suit, impeccably cut, tailored shirt, silk tie.

"Ah, Charlotte," my father said, unsmiling. "You're back with us, I see."

186

I pulled the mask down away from my face, clumsily, with my left hand. There was a butterfly taped to the back of my hand, and an IV line disappeared off out of my field of view. I was careful that I didn't snag it.

"Shit, things must have been bad if you're here," I said, my voice clogged and my throat raw. "Where is here, by the way?"

My father frowned. He was holding what was probably my chart and he peered at me over the top of his thin gold-framed reading glasses, but whether his disapproval was at the profanity or the flippancy, it was hard to tell. I'd never been very good at reading him.

"You are at the Central Maine Medical Center in Lewiston, Maine," he told me. "How much do you remember?"

I swallowed, "I remember being hit," I said. *And seeing my principal die in front of me ...* but I wasn't going to admit to that.

"And after that?"

I concentrated hard, but any recall slipped away, elusive as smoke. The harder I chased it, the faster it escaped me.

"No ... nothing. How long have I been here?"

He hesitated, as if telling me might make a difference to something. "Four days," he said.

"Four days?" Instinct made my limbs start to paddle, like someone suddenly told their alarm clock had failed to go off and they'd slept in late for work. My brain was filled with cotton wool.

I was treated to that look over the glasses again and it was that, as much as the hand he'd placed on my shoulder, which stilled me.

"Charlotte," he said in that clipped, slightly acidic tone I knew so well. "Please bear in mind that you have been shot—twice. The first bullet missed the femoral artery in your leg by millimetres. If it hadn't, you would have undoubtedly bled out at the scene. The second bullet hit your scapula and deflected through your right lung. The fact that you have survived at all is a testament both to the skill of the emergency medical technicians who attended you at the scene, and that of the surgical team once you arrived here."

Of course, I should have realised that my continued presence on this earth would be due to members of his own profession and nothing to do with my own will.

He paused a moment, letting the import of that sink in before he hit me with the next volley. "Attempting to do anything without express medical approval could—and will—result in an increase in the severity of your injuries and delay your recovery. Do I make myself clear?"

"Yes," I muttered, battered and defenceless. I closed my eyes again so he wouldn't see the tears forming in them. "Perfectly."

***

I opened my eyes again after what seemed like no more than a slow blink, and found it was now dark outside, and my father's shirt had changed colour although his suit remained the same. The oxygen mask had gone, but the IV line had not. There was a bank of monitors to my left, turned away from me so I couldn't see the readouts.

"Have they told you when I *can* think about moving around?" I said, continuing the train of thought where I'd left off.

I thought I caught the barest flicker of a smile cross his thin lips.

"Not long," he said. "You'll know when you're ready, Charlotte. I wouldn't be in any hurry, if I were you."

He nodded towards my torso and I discovered, looking down, that I had a tube coming out of the side wall of my chest and disappearing over the edge of the bed. *My God, how much morphine was I on not to have noticed that before?*

"What the hell is that?" I said weakly.

"A thoracostomy tube," he said. "It's keeping your lung inflated and taking care of any residual bleeding. It will remain there until the lung's healed," he added, like a warning. *Until then, you're tethered to your bed.*

I took a shallow breath and channelled a lot of effort into keeping my voice casual enough to ask, "Is Mother here, also?"

I saw the uncharacteristic hesitation and didn't need his answer. *No, of course not.* "She didn't—"

"What's happened to Ella?"

He frowned at my interruption. "The child? She's with her grandparents."

Her grandparents … Lucas and Rosalind.

A picture of Lucas's face flashed into my head, holding Ella in front of his chest, using her for his own protection, and before I knew it my father had crossed to the bed in two short strides and was holding me down again.

"Calm yourself," he snapped, "or I'll have you sedated."

I abandoned my feeble struggles. "You don't have the authority," I said, gasping for breath, aware of the childishness of the comment even as I said it.

The doorway was slightly behind me on my left, and my view of it was partially blocked by one of the monitors. I'd tuned out the background noise of telephones and footsteps and the squeak of gurney wheels on the polished floor to the point where I didn't hear anyone come in until he spoke.

"Ah, the patient's showing signs of fighting spirit, is she?"

"Yes," my father said dryly. "A little too much of it for my taste."

There came a rich chuckle and a man moved round the foot of the bed into my line of sight. He was tall and wide without being overweight, with a distinguished head of short grey hair that contrasted with the dark mahogany of his skin. I could just see a yellow bow tie above the collar of his coat. He had the unmistakable ultimate self-confidence of a surgeon.

"You must be Richard Foxcroft," the man said, and I heard the respect in his voice as they shook hands, two equals weighing each other up. "Your work precedes you."

My father inclined his head graciously. "*Your* work," he said, with a nod in my direction, "speaks for itself."

The man laughed out loud, a deep belly laugh. "Yes, I suppose she does. Well now, young lady," he said to me, "and how are we feeling today?"

"Like we've been shot," I said.

"Well, nothing wrong with your recall, at least," he said, still smiling broadly. "You'll be pleased to hear that we successfully removed the bullet from your back."

"Can I see it?"

He raised his eyebrows. "Well now, I do believe the police had first claim on it."

I swallowed and said, "How far am I likely to be able to come back from this?" It wasn't the clearest wording, but he seemed to get the gist.

"Your injuries were serious," he said, letting the smile slide for the first time. "We nearly lost you on the flight over here. You were bleeding internally and we had to give you around four units of blood to get you stabilised. You suffered a hemopneumothorax—that is to say, you bled into your chest wall and your right lung collapsed. You're probably aware that you still have the chest tube in there, but so far there doesn't seem to be any infection. We should be able to remove the tube within the next few days."

He moved around the bed and lifted the sheet to inspect my misshapen thigh, his fingers cool against my skin. After a moment he gave a grunt of satisfaction. "The injury to your leg was more straightforward. We simply cleaned out the clothing debris and irrigated the wound with antibiotic solution. You had a drain tube in there for the first few days—which you possibly *won't* remember—but it's healing nicely now. All in all, you've been very lucky. That and the fact your treatment has been first-class, of course." He smiled again, magnificently. The man ought to have been advertising dental work. "There's no reason why, given time and hard work on your part, you shouldn't make a full recovery."

"I seem to be having some, ah, difficulty with my right arm," I said.

He nodded. "That's only to be expected," he said. "The bullet entered your back at an angle and gouged a nice lump out of your scapula before it headed off toward your lung. Along the way it did plenty of damage to the muscles in your shoulder. They're swollen and that's putting pressure on the nerves into your arm. And you've been through some tough surgery. Once the swelling subsides you should find things will improve."

"But, it *will* come back?" I tried to keep the pathetic note of hope out of my voice and failed miserably.

"Yes," he said, his expression kindly now, "we have every reason to think so."

I closed my eyes briefly. "Thank you."

"You are entirely welcome," he said. "So, are you going to take pity on that young man outside?"

I opened my eyes again, flicked them to my father's face and caught the faintest sliver of guilt about him.

"What young man?" I said sharply. At least, in my head I said it sharply, but I think by the time it reached my lips it was little more than a mumble.

The surgeon raised his eyebrows, glancing quickly between the two of us as if aware that he might have said the wrong thing. It only took a moment for his natural arrogance to step in and reassure him that wasn't a possibility. "Why, the young man from England," he said. "He's been sitting down the hall since the day after you were brought in here."

"Sean," I said and something broke inside me. I was suddenly filled with a relief so sharp it reduced me to tears. I felt them sliding sideways across my face, pooling

191

between my cheek and the pillow. And now they'd hit the surface, I couldn't seem to stem the flow. On and on I wept, trying to hold myself rigid through the sobbing and not succeeding, so the pain made me cry harder, and the crying caused only more pain.

"I take it, then, that you *do* wish to see him?"

I could only nod, unable even to voice the words of bitter recrimination towards my father that, once again, he'd conspired to keep Sean away from me when I needed him the most.

***

The next time I opened my eyes, it was daylight. I raised my head a little way off the pillow and saw Sean sitting back in the easy chair by the bed. His head was resting on his fist, elbow propped on the arm of the chair, and he was fast asleep.

Even sleeping, he looked dangerous. If it hadn't been for the expensive Breitling watch on his wrist—and someone with the obvious seniority of the surgeon granting him access—any member of the nursing staff who walked in and found him here would immediately call security.

For a moment I just lay there and watched him. He was wearing jeans and a plain white T-shirt and he hadn't shaved that morning. The haze of stubble lined his face, making his skin look almost pale above it and the dark eyelashes ridiculously long against his cheeks.

There had been a time, a long time before, when I'd been injured and frightened and ashamed, and I'd prayed every day that I'd wake in my bed in the military hospital and see this man waiting for me. But he'd never come. He hadn't even known what had happened to me, not until long afterwards, and by then it was much too late.

The involvement between us then had been clandestine, forbidden. He was one of my training instructors and any hint of a relationship between us would have been disastrous for both our careers. After the brutal assault on me but before the farce of the court-martial and my eventual disgrace—when I still thought, foolishly, that I had some kind of a future in the army—I hadn't dared ask for him.

I sometimes wondered what difference it would have made if I had.

It was strange, now, to lie there in circumstances so similar yet so different, to wake and find Sean sitting alongside me. I was profoundly grateful that he was here, without doubt. As soon as the doctor had spoken I'd been aware only of a lifting of the total weight of responsibility that had been pressing on my chest far more heavily than a collapsed lung could ever have done.

But on top of that alleviation, guilt had come chasing hard. Guilt that I had been trusted to do a job and I'd failed in the most basic way possible. Guilt that I was alive, and Simone was not. And as for Ella ...

No, best not to think about what Ella's going through.

My thoughts must have provoked some small change in my breathing because at that moment Sean's eyes twitched beneath his lids and then snapped open, instantly alert.

He saw me watching him and he smiled, without hesitation.

"Hi," I said.

"Hello, Charlie," he said softly. "How are you doing?"

"Oh, great," I said weakly. "But you'll forgive me if I don't come out dancing tonight."

He raised an eyebrow. "You dance?"

"Only when I'm very drunk."

"In that case," he said, igniting one of those slow-burn smiles, "remind me to ply you with cheap booze at the first available opportunity."

We both paused, our repertoire of inconsequential small-talk exhausted.

"So," he said, shifting so he was leaning forwards in his chair with his forearms resting on his knees, "do you feel up to a debrief?"

"I suppose so," I said, not bothering to hide my reluctance. "I daresay this has caused a real mess all round."

"We've had worse," he said with a tired smile. "The police have been clamouring to talk to you about what happened, by the way, but your father's been as good at keeping them away as he was with me."

"I didn't know you were here until the surgeon told me," I said, suddenly defensive.

"That's OK. I didn't think it was a good idea to punch out your dear papa in the corridor. At least this way they let me wait just down the hallway instead of in the car park."

"I'm sorry."

He shrugged. "Don't be," he said. "You and I both know there's no love lost there."

I went through a brief summary of events between my last phone conversation with Sean and the moment I was shot, keeping it as impersonal and objective as I was able to.

Sean interrupted rarely, preferring that I work through the story in my own way, gently pushing me when I faltered. Forcing my mind to concentrate and hold on to the thread of the story required an almost physical effort. I was aware of gaps and pauses where seconds and maybe even whole minutes slipped by before I could bring myself back on track. By the time I was done I was sweating and shivering and I had a bitch of a headache thumping away behind my left eye. The pain in the bottom of my right lung was like a stone, pulling down on it.

When I was spent he sat there for a time, eyes fixed on a point on the bed frame, frowning.

"Tell me again what Simone said, when you walked in on her at the house," he said.

"She said that he'd killed him and she'd seen him do it. That she'd loved him. Then she called him a fucking bastard and that's when Lucas did a runner."

"So, she—"

"What do you think you're doing?" My father's voice, from the doorway, was cold even for him. *Damn, I really must get them to shift some of this bloody equipment so people can't creep up on me like this.*

Sean got to his feet automatically. "We were talking," he said, in that blankly respectful voice he'd always used to disguise his intense dislike.

My father moved round to the side of the bed where I could see him, eyes sweeping over my face. He clearly didn't care for what he saw there.

"She needs rest and no emotional upset," he said tightly.

"Shame you didn't always feel that way," Sean murmured.

My father's face paled beneath his tan. They faced off, almost toe-to-toe. Sean was taller and wider and exuded the kind of menace that made people leave seats vacant next to him in crowded bars. But my father had been at the top of a tough profession for more than thirty years and along the way he'd acquired the ruthless superiority of a despot. Until someone threw the first punch, I would have said they were fairly evenly matched.

"Say, is this a private party, or can anybody join in?"

The new voice from behind me had what was by now a familiar New England twang to it, and the heavy cynicism that could only have belonged to a cop.

"The more the merrier," I said wearily, closing my eyes. "Did you bring a bottle?"

There was a grunt of laughter. "Round here, ma'am, the bottles seem to be mostly full of the kind of liquids you wouldn't want to drink."

"Charlotte, you're not up to this," my father said. I opened my eyes and found him watching me intently.

"Probably not," I said, mustering a shallow smile, "but I've got to talk to the police sometime."

He hesitated. "Just see that they don't over-tire you."

"If they do that, I'll just fall asleep on them," I said. "And I don't think they're allowed to beat up witnesses anymore."

"They won't bully her," Sean said, and the cold certainty in his tone earned him a sharp glance.

After a moment my father nodded slowly, as if reluctant to find himself in any kind of agreement with Sean. "No," he said with the wisp of a smile, "I daresay they won't." And with that he turned and left. He didn't even make it seem like a retreat—just that he simply had somewhere more important to be.

The cop who'd been doing the talking came round where I could see him. He was middle-aged and heavyset like he spent time in the gym rather than he'd gone to fat. At home I would have put him down as a rugby player, right down to the broken nose. Over here I assumed he played American football in some kind of offensive position. With him was a small, wiry, dark-haired woman with a face that didn't look as though it laughed easily. Partners, I assumed. Detectives, too, if their lack of uniforms was anything to go by.

They both dragged up chairs to the bedside and went through the rigmarole of introducing themselves and showing me their badges. The man's name was Bartholemew. The woman's was Young.

"We'd really like to speak to you alone, Miss Fox," Young said pointedly, taking the lead so we didn't mistake her for Bartholemew's junior.

My eyes slid over Sean. "If he leaves," I said, "so do you."

Sean showed them his teeth and they both took on a pained look, like they'd been told if they really didn't want the Rottweiler sleeping on the furniture, they'd have to physically remove it themselves.

"Er, we understand that you were acting as Miss Kerse's bodyguard, is that correct?" Young asked, and something about the unbridled scepticism in her voice made me regret the decision to talk to them right from the start.

"Yes," I said.

She raised a single eyebrow, mocking, and let her eyes travel over me, lingering over the tubes and lines I was hooked up to.

"Been doing the job long?"

"Long enough." It was Sean who answered for me, staring out the two detectives. They'd been doing their own jobs for a while and they must have interviewed their share of murderers and gangsters, but neither of them liked being the subject of Sean's dead-eyed stare.

"We assume, from the fact that you got it in the back, that you didn't see who shot you?" Bartholemew took up the baton.

"No, I didn't," I said.

"But you have an idea, right?"

I took a breath in, too deep, and had to wait a moment for the stabbing in my chest to subside. "I don't know," I said, stubborn. "As you so gallantly pointed out, I was shot in the back. I didn't see who pulled the trigger."

Bartholemew sighed, a noisy careless gush of breath that made me instantly jealous. "We have a preliminary ballistics match between the bullet removed from you and the gun found with Miss Simone Kerse," he said flatly. He let that one settle on me for a while. "I don't suppose you'd like to hazard a guess as to why Miss Kerse would take it into her head to shoot her own bodyguard, now would you?"

"I don't know," I said. I paused. "Is there any possible doubt that she actually fired the shots?"

"Well, her prints were on the weapon and she tested positive for gunshot residue. That's normally good enough for the jury," Bartholemew said, laconic. "We would sure like to have some idea of a motive, though."

"You and me both," I said. But in my head I saw a slow-motion replay of the moments before I was hit. I saw once again Lucas's head square in my sights. Saw the way I'd let the gun rise, taken my finger off the trigger. Even in the moonlit darkness, it must have been clear that I wasn't about to take the shot.

Was that why Simone had done it? I remembered the sheer fury in her voice down in the basement, when she'd called Lucas a bastard, when she'd said she'd loved and trusted him and sounded so desperately betrayed. I didn't believe those first two shots she'd fired had been meant to hit me—or anyone else, for that matter. But out in the woods, well, that was a different story, despite Ella's close proximity.

And who had Simone seen Lucas kill? Jakes? Was he the subject of her anger? Why—when she'd known Jakes for less than a day?

"We understand from Mrs Rosalind Lucas that Simone arrived at the house with her daughter, Ella, and her other bodyguard, Mr Jakes, in a state of some agitation. Can you shed any light on why that might be?"

"No," I said. "I had a message on my mobile phone from Jakes. It should be about somewhere, if you want to check it. He said something along the lines that Simone had had a call from her father and wanted to go over to his place and that she was getting angry about having to wait. By the time I arrived there I found Jakes dead at the bottom of the stairs and Simone in the basement threatening Lucas and his wife with a gun."

"But you don't know why?"

"Not beyond what I've already told you, no," I said dully. My voice was starting to rasp in my throat now and I desperately wanted something to drink. Not just the ice cubes and minute sips of liquid the nurses seemed determined to tease me with, but a long endless glass of iced water. The urge for fluids I could actually swallow was fast becoming a fantasy.

Young frowned and studied the notebook that lay open on her lap. "We understand that Miss Kerse had spent some considerable time and money tracing her father. Can you suggest any reason why she might suddenly turn against him like this?"

"Maybe," I said. I glanced at Sean, as if for reassurance. We hadn't had time to discuss any theories and I was loath to voice them now, untried, but I didn't see much of a choice. "The reason we moved out of the Lucases' house was because there was a break-in the night before."

Young leafed through the pages of the notebook and glanced at her partner, making a brief I-have-no-record-of-that kind of gesture with her right hand. He responded with a slight dismissive roll of his eyes that instantly put my back up.

"It wasn't reported," I said. "But you must have noticed that there was a brand new window at the top of the stairs?"

Young checked her notebook again. "I don't recall there being any damage to the property apart from a couple of fresh bullet holes in the basement," she said carefully. "And Mr and Mrs Lucas didn't mention anything about a break-in."

"Simone didn't want anything getting into the papers. She'd had a rough time with the tabloids before she left home."

"Wait a minute," Bartholemew said, sitting more upright in his chair. "Are you telling us you failed to report a serious crime because Miss Kerse didn't want it getting into the newspapers?"

His voice had started to harden and Sean sliced across him instantly. "Simone had just come into money," he said. "Charlie felt the break-in was possibly a kidnap attempt on the child. Any kind of publicity would have only increased the danger to Ella."

"Money?" Bartholemew said. "What kind of money?"

"Several million," Sean said shortly, severely playing it down and still provoking a jerked reaction from the cop. "According to her banker, Simone made a will just before she left England. If anything happened to her, then everything went to Ella," he went on. His eyes flicked to me. "I spoke to Harrington yesterday about it. There are plenty of strings attached, but if they become her legal guardians, the money will probably end up under the control of Ella's grandparents."

I knew Lucas was aware of Simone's money—had been practically from the start. But if his motive in contacting her had been financial gain, why did he come to the hotel that day and almost beg me to take her back to England? Why did he refuse Simone's offer? Unless he knew things were about to turn nasty ...

I remembered Vaughan's words in the restaurant, just before I left. He'd asked if Simone had found out the truth about Greg Lucas. What truth? What had he done?

"We caught one of the guys who broke in, but he got away from Lucas," I said, trying to drag myself back on track. "Maybe if Simone found out—I've no idea how—that Lucas was in any way responsible, she would have flipped. What happened to Jakes, by the way?" I asked. My mind was starting to disconnect now, and coherent speech was becoming noticeably more difficult. I had to fight to stay with Bartholemew's answer.

"His neck was broken."

"Lucas is supposed to be ex-SAS," I managed. My eyes had drifted shut without my realising it and I forced them open. The effort made my vision quiver. "One of the first things they teach you is how to break someone's neck. Practically the first lesson, huh, Sean?"

The two cops exchanged a look I didn't catch the meaning of. "The pathologist seems of the opinion that his injuries were consistent with a fall," Young said at last, carefully.

"O-K," I said slowly, slurring badly now, "but what if Lucas wasn't her father? His partner knows something— Felix Vaughan. Have you spoken to him? Only—"

Young cut me short. "Mr Vaughan was polite but unhelpful," she said, and I remembered Vaughan laughing when I'd asked him the same question about Lucas.

It wasn't that simple, Vaughan had said. *Why?*

"If Lucas *wasn't* her father, that would be a pretty good reason for a massive falling-out between them. Simone was already pretty convinced, but they were supposed to have had a DNA test to settle it," I mumbled. "If she found out he wasn't who he said he was, she might well have reacted badly. I've never been entirely happy that he—"

"The tests came back," Bartholemew cut in. "They were positive—and our own lab has run their own independently, just to be sure." He paused, looking almost disappointed that I'd come up with such feeble reasons for Simone to turn psycho. "As close as the science can call it, Greg Lucas was definitely Simone's father."

FIFTEEN

I dreamed of Ella.

It was Simone who'd died, but it was her daughter who haunted my sleep. Constantly. A jumbled-up barrage of splintered reflections, always anchored in that frozen forest. So cold it woke me shivering, my fingers numb with the psychosomatic effect.

Sometimes it was Simone who was holding the child. Or Matt, dressed as I remembered him from that first day at the restaurant, with that damned stuffed rabbit he'd been clutching sitting on his shoulder, egging him on. Or Rosalind, her face and clothing dusted with flour. Or sometimes it was Lucas again, and the dream was more vivid for the ghosted image of reality overlaid on top of it.

It never made a difference to the outcome. Sometimes I took the shot and watched in slow motion as the mist beaded outwards from the exit wound in the skull, Ella's screams reverberating inside my own head.

And sometimes I stayed my hand but the mist splayed out anyway. I saw the body tumble, but I could never reach them before they both fell. Didn't know for certain who'd been hit. I kept trying to turn and look behind me, to see who had fired the shot when I knew it wasn't me, but the shooter always moved too fast for me to focus on them, slipping away like a shadow into the trees.

This time, it was Felix Vaughan who held Ella in my dream. He smiled as he slid his thumb under the skin of her soft belly and peeled it up and away from her body as easy as a boiled shrimp.

I woke with a gasp to find Frances Neagley sitting in the chair Sean had occupied beside my bed. It was two days since the visit from the two cops. Two long frustrating days and nights, punctuated by periods of fearful sleep. I'd got to know the patterns in the ceiling pretty well by then.

The private investigator had clearly been flicking through the pages of *Sports Illustrated* magazine when my gasp had alerted her. There was a can of Tab in her right hand. I vaguely remembered seeing Tab in the UK, years ago, but the clear stuff, whereas this looked more like regular cola. I locked onto it with envious eyes.

"Sorry," she said, catching the line of my stare and putting the can down by her chair, out of sight. "Last time I was in the hospital, having my appendix out, it drove me crazy that they wouldn't let me drink anything for a couple of days."

"I think I'm starting to obsess about it," I admitted. "Still, they gave me some real food for breakfast—if you count jelly."

"Jelly?" Neagley said blankly. "What—on toast?"

I dimly recalled that jelly had a different meaning in America. "Ah, I meant Jell-O."

Her careful gaze told me she probably knew I hadn't been dreaming about kittens tied up with string or whatever the hell else Julie Andrews had been singing about in that old film but, by some tacit agreement, she didn't bring it up. And neither did I.

Instead, she smiled ruefully. "So ... would it be stupid to ask how you're doing?"

"Better than I was yesterday. Not as good as last week," I said, easing my position slightly. "At least they took the chest drain out yesterday, which means my lung's on the mend. If sheer boredom doesn't get me first, it looks like I'll survive."

Her smile grew serious. "You were lucky," she said, and her face clouded. "I was sorry to hear about Jakes. He was a nice guy. Friendly, but didn't try anything, you know?"

I didn't answer, mainly because I realised that I didn't know. I'd hardly had time for much of a conversation with Jakes before he died. I'd no idea if he was married or single, even—couldn't remember if he'd worn a ring. I remembered him the last time I'd seen him alive, reading that stupid story to Ella, and before I knew it the tears had rushed up out of nowhere, prickling behind my eyes, leaking across my face.

"Aw, I'm sorry, Charlie," Neagley said, sounding mortified. "I didn't mean—"

"Don't worry about it," I managed, shaky. "I think while the surgeons were messing around in there they must have wired me up wrong. I can't seem to stop damn well crying at every available opportunity."

She handed me a couple of tissues from the box next to the bed. The nursing staff were obviously well prepared for the outpourings—emotional and otherwise—of their patients.

I mopped my face and after a minute or so I had myself more or less back under control. I tried a smile that seemed to alarm Neagley more than reassure her. She sat uncomfortably on the edge of her seat, like she expected to have to leave in a hurry at any moment.

"I suppose," I said, trying to be brisk and businesslike, "with Simone gone you're off the case."

"Not exactly," she said and paused, as though uncertain how much to tell me, brushing at some imaginary lint on her black trousers. "Mr Meyer's asked me to stay on it," she said at last. "There are a lot of things about this case he's not happy with—not least you getting shot. And besides, if Lucas is somehow mixed up in this, well, he might just have had something to do with my partner's accident after all." She looked up, her mouth thinning. "I want answers and so does your boss. Determined kind of a guy." There was respect in her voice.

"Yes, he is that." I closed my eyes for a moment, surprised but grateful. After the two cops had gone I'd thought Sean was going to tell me that was an end to it, to let it go. Simone was dead. Her prints were on the gun that had shot me. Lucas was proven as Ella's grandfather and had claimed his right to the child. My job was over.

Dismally, deficiently, definitely, over.

Or—as it now seemed—not quite.

I opened my eyes again to find Neagley watching me, speculative, and I had the feeling that she was drawing her own conclusions about my relationship with Sean. I wondered if I should let that bother me and decided I'd other things to worry about.

"So, have you made any progress?"

"I've been doing some digging on the guy you saw at the Aquarium," she said, reaching down by her chair and hauling a large brown leather shoulder bag onto her lap, pulling out a slim grey file. She opened it but hardly needed to refer to the pages of notes inside. "From the description you gave me, and a couple of other things, I think we might have one or two promising candidates. The guy you mentioned didn't seem like an amateur."

"He wasn't," I said.

She caught something in my voice, glanced up, frowning. "Well, I've got some photos, if you're up to looking through them?" she said, slipping some glossy prints out of the file.

I reached out my left hand for them. The IV line had twisted in among the bedsheets and I had to untangle myself first. It was awkward to straighten it, one-handed, but my right arm still did little more than flop, and forcing any more than that out of it caused sufficient pain and frustration to curtail further attempts. Not to mention the fear.

I saw Neagley eyeing me, unsure whether to let me struggle or risk offending me with an offer of help. She settled for pretending a sudden interest in the pictures in front of her, sorting them as though into order, and I was glad that was the path she'd chosen.

Once she'd handed them over, I leafed through the prints. Some were formal police mug shots, but others were more candid, taken in a hurry with a long lens and very fast film if the grain was anything to go by. I didn't ask where they'd come from.

Near the bottom of the pile was one of a couple of men talking to each other. They were on a street and the photographer had been on higher ground. One man had his back to the camera and was wearing a hat. The other was caught in mid-sentence, or possibly laughter. His mouth was open, slightly amused, and his hands were spread as though he was shrugging. Difficult to identify anyone from that. The hair looked similar, but he was taller than I was and I'd only seen him standing, so the view of his crown was unfamiliar. I looked again, and something about the pure self-confidence of him struck a cord. That and the coat. He was wearing what looked very like the same tweed coat that Aquarium man had on when he'd approached us on Boston Common. I hesitated a moment longer, then set the shot aside, separate from the others. None of the remainder were even vague possibilities, and I came back to that one shot again.

"This one might be him," I said. "Might being the operative word."

She sighed. "I always hated relying on eyewitnesses when I was a cop," she said, pulling a face. "Give me good solid forensic evidence any day."

"Sorry," I said. "Who is this guy, by the way?"

She took the shot back and studied it, though I was sure she knew the details without needing the memory jog.

"A fine upstanding individual called Oliver Reynolds," she said. "Ex-military. Fancies himself as a bit of a ladies' man. Works freelance as a debt collector, hired muscle. According to my sources, his specialty is putting the squeeze on women—particularly if they've got kids. He's very good at worming his way in, then turning nasty, but he's never been arrested for it. Mostly people are too frightened to stand against him."

"Nice," I said.

"Yeah, well, by all accounts he's a man who enjoys his work."

Vividly, I remembered tackling the masked intruder on the landing of the Lucases' house, of having my forearms clamped around the man's neck and tightening my grip. That infinitesimal moment in time when we were balanced rocking on the blade edge of fate. If I was right and Aquarium man *was* this Reynolds character, and if I'd known his history then, would I have done it? Would I have finished him? Something shuddered down my spine.

Probably better that I hadn't known.

"Are you OK?" Neagley asked, and I realised that she'd stopped talking and was watching me again.

"Yeah," I said. "Sorry, my concentration is all shot to hell—if you'll excuse the pun."

She pulled a face again. "Anyway, if you think this might be our guy, I can dig a little deeper, see what I can find out about who he might be working for."

"That would be useful," I said. "He picked us up in Boston, before Lucas made contact, and I don't think it was chance. He knew who Simone was and that must mean he also knew about—" I broke off abruptly.

"It's OK, Charlie," she said, her voice wry. "Mr Meyer filled me in on the details. I know about Simone's fortune. To be honest, the amount of money she was spending on the search, we kind of had an idea she must have been pretty rich."

"Yes, but there's rich and then there's *rich*," I said. "When he and his oppo broke into the house the other night, I think he was after Ella."

She paused in the middle of sliding the grey file back into her bag. "A kidnap, you mean?"

I nodded. "And if that's the case, he's not going to let a little thing like Simone being dead stop him, is he?"

"You think he might make another try for the kid?"

"I don't know. I'd certainly be happier if she was somewhere safer than with Lucas, that's for sure. I don't trust him an inch—or the kind of people he chooses to do business with. And we still don't know what made Simone go after him the night—" I broke off again, couldn't even say it, improvised instead. "The night Jakes was killed."

Restless, I shifted my position again, rolling a little towards her. Mistake. When I kept still, the pain had been little more than a background ache and I'd grown hardened enough to it to forget the damage that lurked under the surface.

The pain the careless movement caused was a vicious spike in my chest, which was nasty in itself, but followed by a terrible feeling of something tearing inside. I pictured that bloody bullet again, rending its way through my internal organs with a dreadful inevitability about it. I thought of the careful repairwork to the damaged tissue that the surgeon with the beautiful teeth had put into saving me. For a moment I could only lie there, motionless, breathing fast and shallow, horribly afraid that in one thoughtless moment I'd just undone everything he'd tried to achieve.

The pain washed up over me and then, at last, began to recede. I refocused out into the room again and found Neagley was out of her chair and bending over me, frowning with concern. "Charlie, are you OK?" she demanded. "My God, I've never seen anybody lose colour like that. You want I should go fetch a doctor?"

I gave the slightest shake of my head, as small a gesture as I could get away with. "No," I said when I could speak again. I could feel the sweat in my hair between the back of my head and the pillow, the fire in my chest. "I'm fine. Sorry—catches up with me occasionally."

"No shit," she muttered, shaking her head slowly as she sat down. "You shouldn't be talking about this," she said with a flash of anger. "You shouldn't even be *thinking* about this. You should be sleeping and watching mindless TV and recovering."

"Yes, but try telling her that," said Sean's voice from the doorway.

Neagley's head snapped up and I saw her expression close in as she regarded him with a cool flat gaze. Maybe she was always wary when she was first introduced to people, or maybe the part of her—the instinct—that was still a cop recognised the inherently lawless element in Sean's make-up.

"You must be Mr Meyer," she said at last, and waited for Sean to cross the room before she offered a handshake. "Frances Neagley—we've spoken on the phone."

"Ms Neagley," Sean said, matching his tone to hers. After a moment she gave a flicker of a smile, as though acknowledging she'd been subjected to the same careful scrutiny.

He came round and sat in one of the chairs by the bed and I saw his eyes narrow as they swept over me.

"Any news?" I asked quickly, heading off any queries about my state of health.

"We've been digging around some more on Greg Lucas," he said. "Lucas had a nasty reputation in the army, as we already know. He had a temper on him— used to go out and pick fights with the locals wherever he was posted. He was also one hell of a jealous husband. Made his wife's life hell and after Simone was born he got a whole lot worse."

"Worse?" I said, frowning. "No wonder Simone's mother didn't want her to contact him."

"That's not the whole story," Sean said. "It seems that not only did he not trust his wife to behave herself while he was overseas, more often than not he took his anger out on the child."

"On Simone?" It was Neagley who broke in this time.

Sean nodded. "It seems that she made a lot of trips to the hospital as a baby—bumps, bruises, a broken wrist," he said. I thought of his own childhood, what I knew of it, and could understand the faint trace of bitterness in his voice.

"And nobody noticed?" Neagley said. "Nobody picked up on any of this?"

"Overworked staff and a convincingly concerned mother." Sean shrugged. "It happens."

"But if he beat her as a kid, why was Simone so desperate to track him down again?" Neagley asked. She glanced at me. "Did she have some kind of score to settle?"

I shook my head slowly. "No, I don't think so," I said. "Before we left London she said she couldn't really remember anything about him and I believed her. Could have blocked it out, I suppose."

I was starting to slur my words a little, I noted. It was catching up with me again. Every breath scraped my lungs, my mouth was arid, and my thigh was throbbing so hard it was making the whole of my lower leg ache. I wondered what time I was due some extra pain medication and hoped fervently that it was soon.

I heard the murmur of Sean's voice and Neagley say something in reply, but they seemed to be coming from a long way away, hazy and indistinct. *Stay with it, Fox. Come on ...*

***

I don't remember closing my eyes, but I must have fallen into a doze. Next thing I knew, I woke to hear my father's voice, quietly furious, at the end of the bed. I opened my eyes a fraction and found that Neagley's chair was empty, but I had no idea how long she'd been gone.

"I thought you were supposed to be concerned for my daughter's welfare," my father bit out. His voice was uncharacteristically harsh, as though there might be some danger of cracks appearing in that famously unemotional façade. "She nearly died, for God's sake! It's bad enough

210

that she's chosen to throw in her lot with you, Meyer, but I will not have you jeopardising her recovery by exhausting her like this—do you understand me?"

"Yes sir," Sean said. I could hear the tension in his voice, the holding himself in check, and I wondered if my father really comprehended what was likely to happen if that control broke.

"I still can hardly believe she would willingly come back to America again—not after what happened the last time."

"It was supposed to be a low-risk job, or I wouldn't have sent her," Sean said with an attempt at patience. "We thought—"

"Did you?" my father snapped. "Did you really *think* about what you were doing? She went through months of therapy to try and get over what she went through in Florida. Wasn't that supposed to be a low-risk job, too, hm? *Months* of therapy," he repeated, "to try and salvage my daughter out of the psychopath you helped create! And now what?"

For a moment Sean was silent. I felt sure the pair of them must be able to hear the sudden acceleration of my heartbeat and I was glad I wasn't still wired up to the heart rate monitors, or my pulse would have been setting sprint records. I wasn't sure what was worse—listening to them bickering over me, or the prospect of being caught eavesdropping on the conversation.

"Maybe that's the cause of the trouble," Sean said. "Charlie was a damned good soldier. And it wasn't just that she had enormous natural talent—it had to do with mindset. She had the right mind-set for the job. Her ability to kill—which scares the shit out of you so much—was always there. You may have hated it, but she was perfect for Special Forces."

"So perfect that the army allowed four of her colleagues to rape her and halfway beat her to death before she'd even finished her training, and then conspired against her to ruin her reputation," my father said, his voice so contorted with anger that I hardly recognised it. "But she came back from that. It took years, but she came back from it. And yes, I know we were wrong, her mother and I, to keep you away from her afterwards, but we felt she needed a clean break from the past. You were still in the army, part of the machine that had let her down so badly. Besides, what future did she have as some kind of camp follower?"

"Is that how you think of her?" Sean said with a deadly softness drawling through his tone. "How very flattering."

I heard rather than saw my father make a gesture of impatience. "We were making progress with her," he said. "And then you arrive back in her life and suddenly all that careful work is destroyed."

"Have you ever thought," Sean said, still ominously quiet, "that your interference might have brought her to this?"

"Oh no, don't try to lay the blame for this on me, Meyer! We both know who's responsible."

"Do we?" Sean said. He paused, as if picking his next words with great care. "She hesitated. She *had* the guy ... and she hesitated."

"You're talking about taking a life, for heaven's sake. Any normal person would hesitate."

"But Charlie's not a *normal person*. She's a bodyguard. And in this job you can't afford to let your emotions take over. Losing a principal is bad enough under any circumstances. Trust me, I know. But as soon as you begin to doubt yourself—or others begin to doubt you—you're finished."

"And you doubt her because of this?" My father's voice was suddenly very serious, very intent and almost hopeful.

"I think Charlie doubts herself," Sean said at last, "and the worst thing is that I think she started doing so long before she was shot."

SIXTEEN

The next day they got me out of bed and tried to work out some kind of a system so that I could move about under my own steam. My right arm had finally started to show some signs of life, which was a good thing. The downside was that it showed these signs of life in the form of a buzzing in my fingertips, extreme sensitivity that meant I couldn't bear anything to touch my skin, and spasms like cramp in every muscle from my elbow downwards.

The wound to the back of my shoulder was such that I had very little control over my trapezius muscles. Gripping anything in my right hand was dubious, and raising my arm in any kind of lateral movement was out altogether.

My back around the site of the wound was stretched and tender, although the skin itself was numb. It made me fearful to overstress any of it, in case it all pulled apart. There was an odd feeling of tension and restriction under the surface, like a shirt that hasn't quite been buttoned up in the right holes. The thought of having to use my back muscles to operate a pair of crutches actually made me feel faint.

But I also couldn't put any weight through my left leg. The bullet had entered through my hamstring muscle at the back and exited through the quadriceps at the front. The fact that it had bypassed bone, arteries, and major nerves on its way was a miracle but, even so, I had all the strength of a runt chicken in my lower limb.

In the end, the physiotherapist gave me one crutch for the left side and walked slowly alongside me as I staggered half a dozen paces down the corridor getting the hang of leaning on it. All the way, I dragged my left foot and damned near bit through my bottom lip in an effort not to break down and weep with the sheer bloody effort it entailed for apparently such small reward.

One of the nurses found me a chair to collapse onto and the physio held my hand while I shook and gasped like a marathon runner at the end of the home stretch and contemplated the vast distance back to the sanctuary of my bed again.

"It's going to be a long road back, Charlie," he told me, disgustingly cheerful, "but you're lucky to be here at all, and it *will* come, if you're prepared to work hard."

Work.

I'd spent a lot of time thinking about work—about my job—since I'd lain there and listened to Sean and my father discussing me so cold-bloodedly. In the absence of anything better to occupy my mind, I'd picked apart every sentence, second-guessed every nuance, and come to a couple of conclusions that were more painful to contemplate than any physical injury I might have suffered.

As soon as you begin to doubt yourself—or others begin to doubt you—you're finished.

Those words, more than any others, haunted me. What was the point of coming back, if there was nothing to come back to?

It had nothing to do with me having let my emotions dictate my actions out there in the forest. I'd tried over and over to analyse those final few minutes, but however I looked at it, I couldn't have justified shooting Lucas as he stood there holding Ella. Whichever way I dissected the facts, he hadn't been threatening her life—he'd merely been trying to save his own.

If I'd taken the shot, I wouldn't just have traumatised the child, I would have been guilty of murder. If it had been

214

the first time I'd used lethal force, a good legal team might have swung some kind of a plea.

But it wasn't.

I tried to work out how many lives I'd taken and found, to my horror, that I couldn't precisely remember. And that made it so much worse.

Or others begin to doubt you ...

What if Sean had lost his faith in me? And who could blame him? I'd failed to protect a principal. Not only that, but I'd allowed a principal to be killed, not by a lone assassin or a known threat, but by the very people who should have been coming to our aid.

The more I thought about it, the more I realised that as far as Sean was concerned—as far as the reputation of his company was concerned—it was a disaster. I knew that if it got out that he and I had anything other than a professional relationship, that would make things ten times worse. Sean was known to be a high flier. His staff were well paid because they were the best, and proud of it. But in truth that also meant there were plenty out there just waiting for him to crash and burn. Above all else, I hated the idea that I might be the cause of his downfall.

Suddenly it was like being back in the army, just after my attack. I wasn't just physically at a low ebb but mentally bruised and emotionally battered as well. I needed Sean more now than I'd ever done, but I knew I could not—would not—drag him down again.

***

When Sean walked in that afternoon, my unsettled thoughts must have made my greeting wary in some way. He studied me for a moment before responding, as though he could read my mind. No surprises there. He'd always been too sharp for comfort.

They'd propped me more upright in the bed, so I was able to watch the easy way he moved round the room. He didn't take the chair next to the bed, choosing instead to lean on the wall near the window, tilting his shoulder against it and folding his arms. I desperately wanted him to touch me but knew I'd chew my own tongue off rather than ask.

"The nurse said they got you up today," he said.

"I went for a stroll along the corridor," I agreed lightly.

He nodded. "I wondered how long you were going to just lie there and loaf."

That was all it took. My eyes started to burn, the lower lids filling so that I daren't blink or he would have seen the tears. He saw them anyway.

Now he approached me, stroked gentle fingers down my cheek, thumbed away the wetness. *Damn, and I was going to play it so cool ...*

"Hey, come on, Charlie," he said softly. "Fight it, or it will ride you all the way to the bottom."

"Fight it?" I said, almost a snort. "At the moment I can't fight sleep. I let you down—I'm a total, utter waste of space!"

He sighed and gathered me up close, careful where he put his hands. I laid my head against his shoulder and let him rock me. We stayed like that for what seemed like a long time, until the crying had worn itself out and left me. Then he eased back and looked down and there was no softness to his gaze.

"So, you were awake," he said.

I could only nod silently. He sighed again.

"I won't lie to you, Charlie," he said. "Losing a client the way we lost Simone is always bad."

"The company's going to suffer," I said dully. "Your reputation, everything you've worked for—"

"No, it won't—not if I can help it," he cut in. "And that means finding out what the hell went on out there. It's worth the cost of staying out here a little longer. We need to know what made Simone try and kill you. The good new is that Simone's banker has just retained us to look into his client's safety."

"Who—Simone?" I said roughly. "Isn't it a bit late for that?"

He shook his head. "Ella," he said. "With Simone gone, Harrington's just acquired his youngest client." He let that one penetrate for a moment, then added, more briskly, "Plus, Parker Armstrong's prepared to chip in to find out what really happened to Jakes. Right now the explanation the police have given us is just too convenient." He moved back a little further, giving me space. "Where did Simone get her hands on the gun, for a start?"

"Out of Lucas's storeroom, probably," I said. "The lock was off and the door was open when I got down there."

"Why, though? Why would he give her a gun? Had Simone ever expressed an interest?"

"No," I said, swallowing, trying to focus on being matter-of-fact. "If anything she was very anti about them. Definitely didn't like them around Ella."

"Right, so how did she end up with one? And if she was so anti that she'd never fired one before, how did she manage to shoot you so accurately—twice, in the dark?"

"She could have been aiming for Lucas and missed, but I can't believe she would have risked hitting Ella," I said. I shook my head. "I didn't see her coming at me. Didn't hear her, either, for that matter, until afterwards. Maybe she wasn't aiming for me at all. Maybe she just let off a couple of wild shots and I got in the way. She could have been aiming for anything."

Another brief freeze-frame of memory flipped out in front of me. The way Simone had appeared over the edge of that ditch with the gun held rigidly out in front of her. And I remembered, too, the anger in her eyes, anger that I could have sworn had turned to shock when she'd seen me lying there ...

"So you think it might have been unintentional?" Sean asked, as though he'd read my mind.

"I don't know," I said. I scrubbed at my eyes with my left hand, forgetting that although they'd unplugged my IV line, they'd left in the butterfly. I nearly took my eye out in the process.

"You're using it more," Sean said.

I looked down and found I'd been absently smoothing down the tape holding the butterfly in place into a vein in the back of my left hand, using the fingers of my right. For a moment I just stared at them. The nerves were still fizzing and every hair on my forearm felt wired to the mains, but at least the arm seemed prepared to be part of my body again, however distant, rather than some disengaged piece of meat.

"You *can* get past this, Charlie," he said with quiet vehemence, and I knew he wasn't just talking physically. "It *will* get better."

"Yeah, well, it better had," I said, dragging up a smile from somewhere. "The loafing in this place isn't all it's cracked up to be."

He might have said more, but we both heard the footsteps in the corridor outside my room, and when a tall thin figure in a sombre three-piece pinstripe suit appeared in the doorway, he didn't take me by surprise.

"Miss Fox," Rupert Harrington greeted me gravely. "How are you feeling?"

"On the mend, sir," I said, forcing a determined brightness into my voice that hadn't been there only a few seconds before.

Simone's banker eyed me doubtfully for a moment but didn't call me on it.

"Ah, good," he said at last, nodding. "That's good."

He still hadn't advanced from the doorway and seemed almost hesitant about doing so. I was almost on the point of telling him that gunshot injuries were not generally contagious, when he spoke again.

"Look, I have somebody with me whom I'd rather like you to have a chat with, but I'm not sure how you're going to react to him and—"

"Mr Harrington," I said, stopping him dead, "I'm hardly in any state to bite, am I? Not at the moment. Bring him in, whoever he is." *Some kind of detective, perhaps—taking over looking after Ella's welfare?* I ignored the spike of jealousy. *After all, I didn't make such a hot job of it myself, did I?*

Harrington stepped sideways slightly and made ushering motions to someone standing further out in the corridor, out of my sight. There was a pause before a bearded young man shuffled into view, hands in his pockets and shoulders hunched as though he would rather have been anywhere but here. Well, that made two of us.

"Er, hello ... again," he said.

Simone's ex-boyfriend—Ella's father—Matt.

Possibly the last person I would have expected to see in the company of the immaculate banker. Matt was, after all, the very reason that Harrington had originally hired us.

Sean moved round the bed so he was between me and the doorway, and for some reason the action irritated me.

"Oh, for heaven's sake," I said. "What are you expecting him to do?"

Sean's answering glance was hooded, but he didn't stand down.

Harrington stood looking awkward. "As I said, I realise this may seem somewhat irregular—"

"You could say that," Sean murmured, not taking his eyes off Matt.

'—but I'd appreciate it if you would hear what this young man has to say before you make any judgements," the banker finished with a little more snap to his tone.

"I'm sorry. I know this isn't a good time," Matt said, eyes flitting nervously from one of us to the other. He looked older, his gaunt face haggard, and a suspicion of red around his eyes and nose. Whatever his problems with Simone, I recalled belatedly, they'd lived together for five years and shared a daughter. The violent abruptness of Simone's death was always going to hit him hard.

219

The thought that he'd come to hear the grim details firsthand brought on an icy tightness in my chest.

"Come on in, Matt," I said, giving him a weary smile. "And I'm the one who's sorry—for everything. I was supposed to be keeping her safe."

I saw his shoulders drop a fraction. "But, according to the police, *she's* the one who shot *you*," he said, and his tone revealed bewilderment as much as bitterness. "What *happened?*"

"I wish I knew," I said.

Matt nodded as though that was the answer he'd been expecting. He'd developed a sudden interest in the toes of his old basketball boots, unable to meet anyone's eyes.

"So," Sean said. "What is it you have to say to us?"

Matt swallowed. He had a prominent Adam's apple and it bobbed nervously in and out of the vee presented by the open collar of his shirt.

"Look, I know you don't have any reason to trust me—or to think I'm telling the truth for that matter," he said. "But whatever you may have thought of me, I genuinely loved Simone. We had our troubles, yeah. She was insanely jealous—" He broke off, realising that any mention of insanity in the woman who'd been shot dead by the police was probably unfortunate.

"And I love my daughter," he muttered, earnest now, his voice low and shaking with sincerity. "You people just have no clue how much I love my daughter."

I said nothing. Matt was wrong. I had a very good idea of what he felt for Ella, even though I was no blood relation to her. Unless you counted the stuff I'd spilt trying to keep her from harm.

Matt had paused, trying to collect his thoughts, find the right place to start his story. Eventually, he said, almost tiredly, "A couple of years ago, when Simone's mum was very ill, we came over to Chicago to see her. She'd been too ill to travel for a while and she'd never seen Ella and we thought it was probably her last chance," he went on. He smiled a little sadly. "Pam was a nice lady. I liked her, you know? She was obviously in a lot of pain but she never made a big thing out of it, and she was just so happy to finally get to see Ella."

Matt wore a Russian wedding ring on the thumb of his right hand, three intertwining bands of gold. He played with them absently, rolling the narrow bands over and over one another, up and down his thumb. A habit, something to occupy his hands.

"Anyway, we ended up talking quite a bit, her and me, because even then Simone was starting to talk about finding her father, and while we were over here she was quizzing Pam about him a lot. I suppose she realised how serious things were with her mum's health and if she didn't ask her questions now, she'd never get the chance. But her mum wouldn't talk about him."

"Nothing?" I asked.

Matt shook his head. "Not to Simone—she just stalled her. Then she took me on one side one day when Simone had taken Ella out, and she told me that Greg Lucas was a right miserable bastard who made her life hell and she hoped to God that Simone never got to meet him again. She made me promise," he went on with a shaky smile, "to do whatever I could to stop her tracking him down."

He cast a reproachful glance at Harrington, who had taken a seat by the window and was picking imaginary lint from the knee of his wool trousers, pretending not to hear.

"She must have told you more than that," I said, remembering the air of sheer desperation when I'd tackled him in the restaurant.

He swallowed again and nodded.

"She had this boyfriend—John," he said.

"Who did?" Sean asked. "Simone?"

"No—Pam," Matt said, frowning at the interruption to his train of thought. "She said she met John a while before she and Greg split, and eventually John was the one who gave her the courage to leave her husband. She got a divorce and they moved away, made a fresh start, but Greg kept tracking them down, threatening them, hounding them. They were constantly on the move. Then, when they'd been living in one place for about six months, she came home one day and found John had just disappeared."

"Disappeared?"

Matt nodded. "She said she'd only been out for a couple of hours—left him looking after Simone. When she came back the place had been broken up a bit—couple of things smashed like there'd been a fight. Simone was all alone in the house, hiding under her bed, crying her eyes out, and John had vanished."

His eyes flicked between Sean and me, as if checking to see how the story had been received. Harrington's face was shuttered. This was clearly not the first time he'd heard it. I shifted a little, carefully, in the bed.

"Were the police involved?" I asked.

"She told me they weren't very interested," he said. "He was an adult whose girlfriend's ex was cutting up rough. They thought he'd just done a runner and she reckons they didn't put much effort into finding him."

"And what about Lucas?"

"Pam said that was the weird thing. Having been practically stalking her, he never bothered her again. When she made some enquiries of her own, she was told he'd left the army a month or so before John went missing. And he left the country the day afterwards." He paused, face sombre. "Pam swore John wouldn't have just upped and left her and Simone. She was absolutely convinced Greg Lucas had murdered him."

A brief silence fell into the void created by Matt's words. All I could think of was that Ella had been left in the care of such a man. And that I hadn't taken him down when I'd had the chance. The memory of Lucas using her as a shield, hiding behind her body, came roaring through my mind like a monster, licking at the back of my eyeballs with the flames of its tongue.

"Surely you must have told Simone what her mother said?" Sean demanded. "If not at the time, then later?"

Matt's head sagged. "Pam made me promise I wouldn't ever say anything," he said. He must have been aware how lame that sounded because his head swung up again, stared pleadingly between us, as though begging for understanding. "I gave her my word that I wouldn't tell. And then, when I did finally break my promise, it was too late," he added dully. "Simone and I had already split by then." His eyes skated over Harrington and the accusation sharpened the glance into barbs. "People had been telling her I was just after her money. She didn't believe me."

Harrington cleared his throat. "This information only came to *our* attention since Miss Kerse's tragic and untimely demise," he said with a little sideways glance at Matt. "Naturally, we are concerned for Ella's welfare."

And suddenly the reason the banker was here, with Matt, became clear. If Lucas wasn't fit to have charge of Simone's millions, Harrington had allied himself with the next in line to the throne.

"Naturally," Sean said, and the cynical note in his voice told me he'd drawn the same inference.

Harrington coloured slightly and ploughed on. "Part of the reason I'm here," he said, "is that I've spoken with my board and we feel we'd like to retain your services."

I gave a short laugh. "What as?"

Everyone frowned at me, briefly united in their disapproval.

"When we flew into Boston yesterday I drove straight up to see Greg and Rosalind Lucas," Matt said flatly. "They refused to let me in." He went back to his miserable study of the floor. "I just wanted to know my little girl was all right and they wouldn't even let me see her."

"On what grounds?" I asked. "You're her father—you should have automatic rights over her."

"They said Simone had told them I was a junkie," he said, and now the bitterness was loud and clear. "They said

223

they didn't want someone like me to have any contact with their granddaughter, and that the courts over here would back them up."

I raised an eyebrow at Sean, who shrugged. "If that's the case, then they're probably right," he said calmly. "They'd have to present some pretty compelling evidence, though."

"Of course it's not the bloody case," Matt said, his voice rising. "So what if I've done the occasional bit of weed on a weekend? Who hasn't? But the way they were saying it, I'd be shooting up in alleyways and dragging Ella into crack dens." He broke off, took a breath, glanced at Harrington. "They seem pretty well-off people, and I know you told me the DNA test came back a match—so it looks like he really is Ella's granddad. I don't stand a chance of getting her back, do I?"

"Not when there's so much at stake," the banker said. He coughed, as if forcing himself to regurgitate what he considered to be confidential information. "Whoever has charge of Ella also has, at today's exchange rate, around twenty-five million dollars to play with."

Matt eyed him glumly. "Looks like I've got a fight on my hands, then."

"Not quite, old chap," Harrington said, and I thought I caught just the faintest glimmer of a smile slide across his thin lips. "I'd say *we've* got a fight on *our* hands, hm?"

SEVENTEEN

Ten days after I was shot, I signed the necessary papers and discharged myself from hospital, much to the disgust of most of the staff there, although my departure fell just short of being totally Against Medical Advice.

My father definitely disapproved of my actions—but what else is new? In fact, my decision caused what I suspected was another flaming row between him and Sean, but neither would admit as much and—this time at least—they conducted it well out of my earshot.

By the time I made my escape I'd more or less mastered the art of staggering along on one crutch, although stairs were something to be avoided at all costs. I was beginning to be able to bear a little weight through my left leg, but walking unaided still seemed a distant dream rather than a reality. I remembered once having been able to run with a kind of wonder.

They'd unplugged me from all the machinery and declared the danger of infection in my wounds was probably past. I'd regained partial strength in my right hand and could just about raise it to my mouth, but not if it was attempting to lift a cup of coffee that was more than half-full. I couldn't dress myself without help, could barely cut my own food up, and doing anything at all for more than about five minutes at a time brought on pain in the bottom of my right lung like a hot blade, and exhaustion so extreme it made my hands shake.

They gave me pills for every occasion, announced they couldn't be held responsible if I keeled over, and provided an orderly and a wheelchair to take me down to the Ford Explorer Sean had waiting. I would have loved to have scorned their transport and gone on my own two feet, but the truth was I just didn't feel up to it. I thanked everyone who'd helped get me this far, trying to gloss over their hurt responses, like leaving before I was ready was a personal insult.

Some of the staff came down to see me off—or maybe they were just waiting to see me collapse before I made it that far. To my surprise, the surgeon with the perfect smile who'd operated on me was one of those who stood in the pale sunshine by the Discharges exit and watched me struggle the short distance between wheelchair and passenger seat. He shook my hand, frowning at the limp grip that was all I could manage to offer.

"Well, good luck, Charlie," he said in that grave tone they must teach them in surgical college. "If all my patients had your determination, their recovery rates would be even higher than they already are. Just remember that your body needs rest. You need to be gentle on yourself sometimes, you know."

"Yeah," I said with a touch of bitterness that surprised me as I settled back gingerly into my seat while Sean strapped me in. "Tell that to Simone."

I sensed Sean's sharp glance, but I was watching the doctor's face. He nodded, a little sadly, and stepped back.

My father hadn't joined the little farewell party. He'd said his piece earlier that morning and announced he would be spending the next few days visiting one of his old colleagues who was now based in New England. "Just in case you have need of me," he'd added cryptically.

Now, Sean slammed the door and moved round to the driver's seat. I gave the staff a final wave and a smile and then the engine was fired up and we were rolling the short distance towards the exit.

I let my breath out slowly and leaned back against the headrest, shutting my eyes.

"You can drop the act now, Charlie," Sean said quietly.

I opened my eyes again, reluctantly, and turned my head towards him. He was in his shirtsleeves, despite the freezing temperatures and the snow outside, and his eyes were hidden behind dark glasses. I wished they weren't. It made him even harder than usual to read.

"What act?" I tried.

He'd been leaning forwards slightly, looking for a gap to pull out into the traffic rolling down the hill past the hospital, and he didn't answer for a moment. Then he turned and stared right at me. I fought the urge to squirm. Even without being able to see his eyes, his gaze was cold enough to make me shiver.

"The act that pretends you're not injured, that you're not hurting. I've been there—remember?" he said at last and there was something compressed into his voice. It took me a moment to recognise it as anger. "The act that says you've just had a bit of a scratch and you'll be good as new in a couple of days." He jerked his head at the hospital, which was to the right of us as we moved off. The collection of buildings that made up the CMMC was huge and sprawling. "Your father gave me a right bollocking this morning for allowing you to leave that place today and I had to stand there and take it because, just for once, I completely agreed with him. You shouldn't be out."

"I'm fine," I said. "I can cope." *Besides, if I hadn't got out today, you and Neagley and Matt would have gone back to North Conway and started planning against Lucas without me ...*

We stopped again at the light just before we reached the bridge over the impressive Androscoggin River, and Sean regarded me for a moment longer, suddenly a stranger, someone I was trying to keep secrets from. Then the lights changed and he turned his attention back to his driving.

"Where are we going?" I asked as we crossed a railway line, heading for the 202. I had no recollection of the journey from Conway to Lewiston. The city outside the hospital, which seemed to be made up mainly of huge abandoned warehouse buildings, was all new to me.

"Back to Conway," Sean said shortly. "We're just swinging by the hotel to pick up Neagley and Matt. They're going to follow us over in Neagley's car. That way we'll have two different vehicles."

For surveillance. Surveillance was good, I told myself. Sitting in a car and watching I could do, if nothing else.

"We should be able to manage OK with the four of us," I said.

"And what exactly do you think you're going to be able to do?"

"Come on, Sean, I want to help," I said, hearing the stubbornness in my voice as a direct result of the coolness in his. "I *need* to help." *Damn, when did that note of pleading creep in?* I looked down at my hands and found them tightly clasped, left over right, in my lap. "Don't shut me out. Please."

He sighed. "In a war situation," he said, conversational, "it's better, tactically, to wound the enemy than to kill them. You know why?"

Of course I did. He just wanted to hear me say it. "Because it ties up able-bodied men, getting them away from the battlefield and treating them. And it's bad for morale for those going to fight to see the wounded."

"You're here because we couldn't leave you behind," he said bluntly. "I know you, and you'd have walked to bloody North Conway if we'd tried it. But looking after you once we get there is going to mean more work for everyone else."

"I won't be—"

"Face it, Charlie, you can't even go to the loo by yourself."

My face heated. "Give me a couple more days and I'm sure I'll have got the hang of that one," I bit out. "And if

228

we're using your battlefield analogy, aren't you forgetting something?"

He didn't respond other than to raise an eyebrow in query.

"If it comes down to it," I said with a certainty I didn't altogether feel, "one way or another, I can still fight."

***

Sean had arranged to rent one of the time-share apartments that bordered the eastern slopes of Mount Cranmore, which was further up the mountain from the Lucases' house and had a couple of alternative approach roads. Harrington was bankrolling us on this one—at least until he'd satisfied himself that Ella was in no immediate danger.

And then?

I didn't want to think about what happened then.

As it was, the dreams of Ella had lessened in their frequency, if not their intensity. I missed her with a ferocious anger that still took me by surprise, reaching out to claw at me unexpectedly when I was least prepared.

Every car we passed on the journey across into New Hampshire seemed to have a small curly-headed child in the rear seat.

It was dark by the time we arrived back in North Conway and pulled up in one of the designated parking spaces outside the apartment block. Neagley slotted her Saturn SUV in next to us and Matt climbed out of the passenger seat. He only seemed to have brought lightweight clothing, and the cold was biting. His teeth instantly began to chatter while he waited for Sean to help me out of the Explorer. I tried to hurry and that only seemed to make me more clumsy.

Neagley took the keys and unlocked, flicking on the lights and looking around the place. By the time I'd hobbled along the icy path to the front door, she'd done a full inspection.

"Only two bedrooms," she said. "One double, one twin. Do we draw lots?"

"I can take the sofa," I said quickly.

"You're in the double," Sean said, no arguments. "And so am I. I won't have you sleeping alone."

I felt Neagley's eyes on me, curious, but wouldn't answer her gaze.

Matt gave the private detective a strangely appealing, boyish grin. "I don't suppose that argument would work with you, would it?" he asked.

Neagley gave him a straight stare in return. "Not unless you want to need crutches, too," she said, but there was the suspicion of a smile twitching at the corner of her mouth.

Matt, I'd discovered, had an easygoing charm that included constant mild flirting, but I didn't get the impression it was a serious attempt. Simone, though, hadn't taken it so lightly.

Matt's trouble was that he's a man, Simone had said, back in the restaurant. *He didn't always think with his head—if you know what I mean.*

Now, watching the way he joked with Neagley, I didn't think Simone had quite understood him. *Insanely jealous,* Matt had called her and, unwillingly, I could almost believe that about her. And that made the whole business of their break-up, of Simone's focus on the search for her father and her death, even more of a tragedy than it already was.

The apartment was reasonably spacious and certainly well-appointed, with a large-screen TV and a huge leather sofa, and a whirlpool bath in the master en suite. Any other time, I might have enjoyed staying there.

I turned in early and lay listening to the murmur of voices in the living area for a long time, too tired to sleep. I'd grown accustomed to the incessant noise of a big hospital and the apartment seemed too quiet, too dark, by comparison.

I didn't hear Sean come to bed. He must have undressed in the dark because I woke to find him alongside me under the blankets. I didn't know how long he'd been there, but I could tell by his breathing that he wasn't yet asleep.

"Everything OK?" I murmured, drowsy.

"Fine," he said softly. His fingers stroked my hair back from my face, their touch a whisper. "I'm sorry I was tough on you today, Charlie," he said. "But Christ Jesus you gave me a scare." And, for the first time since I'd woken in the hospital and found him there, his voice shook.

Automatically I rolled in towards him in the darkness, moving carefully, seeking the warmth and the strength of his body against mine. And it occurred to me, vaguely, that perhaps I was giving as much comfort as I was taking by the gesture.

***

When I woke the next morning, the bed was empty. A glass of water and the first of the day's selection of medication was waiting for me on the bedside table. Sean, it seemed, was taking his nursing duties seriously, however much he'd claimed reluctance.

I struggled into a half-sitting position and swallowed the tablets and then sat for a moment relishing my freedom from captivity. I may have been feeling like shit and wouldn't have lasted one round in the ring with a medium-sized paper bag, but at least I was out.

There was a tentative knock on the door and Neagley stuck her head round.

"Hi, Charlie," she said. "We wondered when you were going to surface."

I looked round but there was no clock in the room. "Why? What time is it?"

"Nearly ten," she said.

I gave a guilty start and threw back the covers, only for various parts of my body to bring me up short. By the time I'd finished gasping and my vision had cleared, I found Neagley was crouched alongside the bed, a guarded expression on her face.

231

"Well, I'm guessing *that* wasn't a good move," she murmured.

"No, I'm fine," I said, forcing myself up slowly. "Just pass me my crutch, would you?"

"Do you want me to give you a hand to the bathroom?"

"I'm fine," I said again, through gritted teeth.

"O-K," she said, drawing it out, dubious. She got to her feet, an easy swift movement I envied instantly. "I'll leave you to it, then. We got Detective Young coming over in about a half hour. Sean wants Matt to tell her his story and see if we can't get her fighting in our corner."

"I'll be ready," I said, and hoped it was true.

In the end, I made it out with about five minutes to spare. I'd managed to dress myself only because Sean had been out and bought me a couple of pairs of sweatpants with elastic in the waistband that I could pull on with one hand, unlike my jeans.

The entry and exit wounds in the skin of my thigh had closed up without any apparent problems, leaving deep indentations where part of the muscle had been destroyed by the path of the bullet. With time, the physio had told me, I could build the bulk up again, but I was always going to have an interesting set of scars. At the moment, where it wasn't wasted it was swollen. It looked and felt like a deformity.

When I hobbled out into the living room, the conversation paused while they watched my halting progress from the bedroom door to the sofa.

"Feel free to break into spontaneous applause at any time," I said, narked.

"Hell, Charlie, you probably deserve that just for standing up," Neagley said, her voice neutral. "You want coffee?

"Oh yes," I said, grateful, easing myself down onto the sofa. Matt had clearly been the one who'd slept there last night, and now he piled his blankets and pillows to one side for me to sit, shifting over himself into one of the other chairs.

I saw Sean watching Matt carefully moving out of my way and realised that he was not entirely comfortable around me. And who could blame him? The first time we'd met I'd humiliated him, in public. But, worse than that, I'd humiliated him in front of Simone and Ella. And then I'd been responsible, one way or another, for their safety. Strike-out on both counts.

Neagley handed me my coffee and turned to Sean, obviously picking up the conversation exactly where it had broken off at my arrival.

"The answer's no, Sean," she said. "If you were caught with it—never mind firing it—I'd lose my licence. Besides, since Barry died, I've had it on me at all times."

"Really?" Matt said. "You're actually carrying a gun right now?"

For an answer, Neagley picked up her shoulder bag and pulled out a .357 Smith & Wesson Model 340 PD Centennial revolver.

"Only five shots," Sean murmured.

"Yeah, but with Magnum loads—if it doesn't go down with five, it ain't going down at all," she said, tucking it away again. "Damn thing kicks like the proverbial mule, but it's light and easy to conceal."

"You must have a back-up piece," Sean persisted. He had that dogged, head-down, nothing's-getting-in-my-way air about him.

"Yeah, I have a Glock nine," Neagley said, starting to bristle, "but there is no way in hell you're getting your hands on it, so back off."

They'd just dug in for a full-scale glaring match when there was a knock on the front door. Sean put his coffee cup down and went to answer it. When he came back, the stringy, dark-haired detective who'd interviewed me in the hospital was with him, and she didn't exactly look happy to be here.

233

Today she was wearing black trousers and a polo-necked jumper, with a rust-coloured tweed jacket over the top. Her gaze went round the mismatched group, resting briefly on Neagley as if recognising the cop in her.

Sean introduced her, and let Matt repeat the story he'd told us about Lucas. Young sat and listened without any emotion showing on her thin face. She didn't fidget in her chair and she didn't make notes. When Matt was done she was silent for a moment before she looked at the assembled faces.

"So," she said, "let me get this straight. You're talking about the possible disappearance of an adult, more than twenty years ago, in another country, that Mr Lucas *might just* have had something to do with, but no charges were ever filed? Heck, you don't even know for sure there was a crime committed. Am I understanding this right?"

"That about sums it up, Detective," Sean said evenly.

"And just what is it that you want me to do about it now, Mr Meyer?"

Matt glanced at Sean, as if for courage, before butting in. "I'm worried about my daughter," he said. "I just want her to be safe and how can I be sure of that when she's with a man who could be a murderer?"

Young made a gesture of impatience with her left hand. "Sir, you can't possibly know that Mr Lucas is guilty of any crime. If anything, he was an intended victim in all this. Now, he and Mrs Lucas have a perfect legal right to care for his granddaughter and unless you can provide a good reason—and I mean a *good* reason—we're happy to leave her in their care until the courts have come to their decision about her future."

Matt started to object but she cut him off with nothing more than a stare. "Mrs Lucas has already made us aware that you have tried to gain entry to their property and that you made certain threats against them. She is in the process of filing an official complaint, and I should warn you, *sir*, that any further attempts to see your daughter would be inadvisable at this time."

Matt's face went from angry disbelief to anguish in one turn. Young rose, straightening her jacket so that I caught a flash of the gun on her hip, and regarded him with a flicker of something that might even have been sympathy.

"If I can offer some advice, sir, if you want to see your daughter again soon, you need to get yourself a fancy lawyer," she said, looking down at him. "We're still investigating the events leading up to the death of Simone Kerse, but at the present time all the evidence shows that she entered the property and attacked Mr Lucas, during which time Mr Jakes fell and died from his injuries. Mr Lucas, fearing for his life, went to his gun store in the basement to arm himself. But during the argument that followed, it was Miss Kerse who got hold of a gun—we're still not entirely clear how—and attempted to use it to shoot Miss Fox when she arrived."

"But why?" Matt burst out. "Why would she do any of that? It just doesn't make any sense."

"When people get killed it rarely has a whole lot to do with sense," Young said shortly. "I'll be in touch." She nodded sharply to us in dismissal. "In the meantime, stay away from the Lucases. If there's anything going on here, we'll take care of it. We do not need some goddamn vigilantes stepping in, you hear me?"

Sean rose, effortlessly, his face carefully expressionless. "Loud and clear, Detective."

He showed her out and the rest of us sat and listened as the front door slammed behind her.

"Simone must have remembered something," Matt said, almost to himself. He lifted his head, focused intently on me. "You told us she said that he'd killed him—but killed who? Her mum's boyfriend?"

I shut my eyes briefly and brought back Simone's bitter flood of words like they were permanently written to the hard drive in my head. "She said, 'He killed him. I saw him do it. I loved you. I trusted you. You bastard. You utter fucking bastard.'" I repeated the words devoid of emotion and opened my eyes again. "That was it. At the time I thought that when she said, 'He killed him,' she was talking about Jakes."

"But how come she said that she loved and trusted Lucas when we know he was such a bastard to her when she was a child?" Matt said. He had his hands in his lap, fingers locked together until his skin had turned white.

"If we now assume that she was furious because she remembered her father killing her mother's boyfriend, why did she shoot you and not Lucas?" Neagley asked.

"Look, as far as we know, Simone had never picked up a gun before that night," Sean said, moving over to the open-plan kitchen area and pouring himself another cup of coffee from the pot. "Maybe she knew she wasn't good enough to hit him and not Ella at that distance and she couldn't risk getting it wrong."

"But that doesn't explain why she shot Charlie instead," Neagley persisted.

Sean looked at me over the rim of his cup. "Charlie had the chance for a shot at Lucas and didn't take it," he said. "We've already established that Simone was beside herself with rage. Perhaps she saw him getting away—literally with murder—and she just ... snapped."

***

We lunched on takeaway pizza. I managed half a segment before the rich greasiness of the food dawned on my stomach and I had to leave the rest. While we ate we kicked around some theories on what might be going on, although without seeming to advance very far in the process.

Felix Vaughan's role bothered me. I'd already told Sean about the enforced meeting I'd had with him at the restaurant the night Simone was killed. I kept going over his parting shot about Simone finding out the truth about Lucas. What did that mean?

236

"After the way Lucas acted—like a bloody coward—and the fact that the photo message you sent me just didn't seem to compare all that well, I would have bet almost anything that the DNA test was going to come back a total mismatch," I said, watching the three of them fighting over the last piece of pizza.

Sean shrugged. "Well, it didn't," he said. "And from what Young and Bartholemew told us at the hospital, they've had it verified by their own lab, so there's no doubt."

"But all the stuff about his behaviour in the army," I said, still frowning, "and what Simone's mother told you, Matt, doesn't seem to fit the guy."

"People change I suppose," Matt said dubiously. "But he was an SAS thug, wasn't he? No changing a warped personality like that." He missed the slight eyebrow quirk that Sean fired in my direction. "But he's been out a long time, and maybe Rosalind had a settling influence on him, though she seemed a bit of a dragon to me."

"She can't have been that good an influence on him—not if he was behind my partner's car crash," Neagley said, wiping her hands on one of the paper napkins and taking a swig of Tab. She'd laid in a private supply in the fridge.

I shrugged, carefully. "It just doesn't fit somehow. I wish I knew what Vaughan was hinting at that night. And why he was so anxious to get us out of the way."

"Well, I've put out some queries about him with my contacts," Neagley said. "We know he's ex-military, which gave me a good place to start looking. Soon as they get back to me, we might have a better idea of what we're dealing with."

I sat back against the sofa. *What were the Lucases mixed up in with him that made them so scared of him?* Why had he been so against Simone staying in North Conway in the first place, and so keen on me taking her away? It couldn't have been a coincidence that he'd had me picked up on the very night Simone had gone rushing to confront her father.

So did that mean Vaughan was involved in some way in the shooting? I couldn't see how.

Jakes had been a good man, but I wished I'd been the one who'd gone with her. If I had … *Yeah, right,* said the sarcastic voice in my head, *because you managed things so well after you did finally get there.*

I mentally shook myself out of that downward spiral. The police were convinced it was an open-and-shut case as far as the "who' was concerned. What was driving me mad was trying to work out the "why."

"Have you got any further with tracking down this guy Oliver Reynolds?" I asked.

Neagley shook her head. "Not yet," she said. "Maybe you scared him off when you grabbed him. Or maybe he injured himself getting away. He did have to jump through a window, after all." She glanced at her watch, then at Sean. "We ought to get going," she said.

Sean nodded and rose, gathering the empty pizza box and folding it in half. "Neagley and I are going to go and do some digging around," he said.

Matt jumped to his feet. "What do you want me to do?" he said, eager.

Sean's eyes drifted over me. "You two just stay put here," he said, like I'd been contemplating going out jogging. When Matt opened his mouth to object, Sean added, "Why don't you make some calls—see if you can find yourself a decent legal man. Won't Harrington help out?"

Matt looked crestfallen. "I asked. He said he couldn't be seen to be taking sides and if it came out—," he began.

Sean took a business card out of his pocket and handed it over. "Call Parker Armstrong," he said. "He was Jakes's boss. He and I know each other—we've worked together in the past. He's a good guy and he's offered to help us get to the bottom of this."

Matt stood there for a moment, fingering the card in his hands. "I don't know what to say," he ventured at last. "I don't know how to thank you for—"

"There's no need," Sean cut in, lifting his jacket from the back of a chair and shrugging his way into it while Neagley grabbed her own coat and picked the car keys out of her pocket. They'd almost reached the door before he stopped and glanced back. "Besides, we're not doing it for you."

After Sean and Neagley had gone out, Matt got straight on the phone to Armstrong in New York, who in turn put him onto a firm of lawyers specialising in child custody cases who worked out of Manchester, New Hampshire.

There wasn't much I could do to help other than sit and listen to one side of the conversation. Besides, I soon realised that without the others to act as a buffer Matt was still uneasy around me. Eventually, I clambered to my feet, picked up my crutch, and mouthed, *I'll be in my room,* to him. He clamped his hand over the phone mouthpiece and nodded distractedly at me.

I hobbled back into the bedroom and shut the door behind me. I'd only been out of bed for a couple of hours but it was looking decidedly welcoming. I switched the TV on low, picked a news channel, and lay down on top of the covers to watch. I think I'd nodded off before the end of the first item.

I woke up with a start that sent my breath out on a hiss. The news anchor still seemed to be rattling on about the same story, but the clock in the corner of the screen showed I'd been out of it for about three-quarters of an hour.

My mouth felt terrible after the coffee and pizza, but the glass of water Sean had put out for me earlier was empty and I was damned if I was going to shout Matt and ask him to bring me another. I struggled up off the bed and limped slowly across the room, realising that I was finding it a little easier to use the crutch now, if nothing else.

Out in the living area, I looked around but didn't immediately see Matt or call out to him. Hell, he was probably jet-lagged to all hell and back and sleeping himself. It was only when I was almost in the kitchen area that I glanced across and spotted him sprawled on the floor between the sofa and the coffee table. Not where anyone would have chosen to take a nap.

"Matt?" I said, alarmed. I hurried—as much as I could hurry—across and eased myself down onto the floor alongside him, ungainly. "Matt! Are you OK?"

He had a trickle of blood running down behind his left ear from a small wound at the back of his head. I pressed two fingers into the hollow beneath his ear and felt what seemed to be a strong pulse. I hadn't heard anything, but I remembered the silenced Berettas that the men had used when they'd broken into the Lucases' house. When I parted Matt's bloodied hair and realised there was no bullet hole hiding underneath it, the relief was great.

But not that great. Assuming Matt hadn't fainted and hit his head on the coffee table on the way down, that still meant ...

I caught a soft noise from behind me and started to twist instinctively. The pain brought me up short before I'd turned halfway.

"Not so good at looking after people, are you, Charlie?" said a voice, soft and familiar. I turned just my head, although I hardly needed to in order to recognise him. The guy I'd dubbed Aquarium man was standing behind the sofa with his arms folded. He was smiling.

"I can't tell you," he said, "how much I've been looking forward to meeting you again."

EIGHTEEN

The fear hit hard, fast, deep.

"Mr Reynolds," I said flatly. "The pleasure is all yours, I assure you." As snappy comebacks went, I didn't think it was too bad. Not exactly James Bond, but the best I could manage under the circumstances.

"Oh-*ho*," he murmured at my use of his name. "We *have* been doing our homework, haven't we?" He came round the sofa, moving easily, in no hurry. I considered rising but knew I couldn't do it in time, never mind in style.

Reynolds stopped, too close to me. I had to tilt my head back to look at him. He was dressed in jeans and tan boots and a high-tech designer fleece jacket over a T-shirt. "I've been doing my homework, too. You've got quite a reputation, Charlie." He smiled. "From what I saw of you in action the other night, you might even have lived up to it—once."

He was on my left, which I tried to tell myself was good. My left arm had maintained more or less its full strength. His groin was well within striking distance. I was just going to have to be smooth in the delivery—otherwise the resultant shock of the blow was going to do me as much damage as it would him ...

And, just as I was contemplating making the first move, Reynolds lifted his foot and, almost casual, nudged my left leg with his boot.

At least, to him it must have seemed no more than a nudge. To me he'd just inserted a molten bayonet into my thigh and twisted it. Blind, I grabbed my leg with both

241

hands, gripping hard as though pressure alone would cut off the nerve impulses that were currently screaming a rampant distress call along my neural pathways. I bit back a cry, knowing that was what he wanted above all, and sat there, panting until the worst of the crisis was over.

Reynolds had moved back a little way, more than an arm's length, and squatted down on his haunches so he could better study my reaction.

"Through-and-throughs are a doozy, aren't they?" he said, conversational.

"Remind me to make sure you can speak from personal experience some time soon," I said, keeping my teeth clenched.

"Well, you see, Charlie, for that you'd need a gun, which I happen to know you don't have," Reynolds said, still cheerful. "And, unfortunately for you, *I* do."

He reached under his jacket and pulled out a semiautomatic from a shoulder rig. Another Beretta M9, minus the suppressor this time. A replacement for the one I'd taken away from him at the Lucases' house—and which Vaughan's men had then taken away from me. Or the same gun?

Reynolds was too much of a pro to be carrying the Beretta without a round in the chamber and he casually flicked off the safety as he brought the weapon to bear. He hadn't thumbed back the hammer, so the double-action would give it a long initial trigger pull, but I knew I couldn't count on that to slow him down by much.

He smiled. The action crinkled the skin around his eyes, which were very cold and very blue. A handsome face. One that lent itself easily to charm. Simone had certainly been taken in by it, had not seen past the attractive collection of features to what lay beneath.

"So tell me, were you planning on snatching Simone before we left Boston?" I asked. Anything to distract him.

"That would have been the easiest solution," Reynolds agreed. "I would have gotten her at the Aquarium if you'd been thirty seconds slower."

"What?" I said. "You think she would have walked out of there with you and left her daughter behind willingly?"

"Willing or not, she would have walked out of there with me," he said, supremely confident. "Make no mistake about that."

"And that would have achieved what, exactly?" I said.

He laughed and shook his head. "No, no, Charlie," he said, wagging a disapproving finger. "This is not one of those corny old movies where I tell you my whole evil plan and then let you escape moments from death. Let's face facts—if I wanted you dead, lady, you'd be dead already."

I glanced at Matt, still lying still as a corpse on the floor next to me. I took reassurance from the fact that I'd verified his pulse myself, and that the wound to his head was still bleeding. Just a trickle, but at least that meant his heart was still pumping blood round his system.

"So why are you here?"

"To pass on a message," he said. "A warning, if you like."

"Which is?"

"Go home," Reynolds said. "Simple enough, isn't it? You and the rest of your crew just pack up and go home. No harm, no foul."

The same message Vaughan had tried to deliver, right before Simone was killed. *But I'd told him we were going. Wasn't that enough?*

"Or ... what?"

He laughed. "Quite apart from the obvious threat, here and now, you mean?" he said. "Well, just remember that Ella's a sweet kid. How old is she now—four? You leave, today, and maybe she'll get to be five."

The fear was a sudden starburst rising from my belly, bunched up tight under my ribs, a bright, leaking coldness that froze my heart to the inside of my chest. A cold flame ignited at the base of my right lung

"That's it?" I said.

He considered for a moment. "Yup, that's it," he said. "That's the message, from my boss to yours, in full."

"So you're nothing more than the messenger boy, is that it?"

He smiled again, almost a grin this time. "Well, it was left to my own judgement how best to deliver the message— how to give it maximum impact, you might say."

He stretched out the Beretta and touched the barrel of the gun to my left leg. It was barely a brush against the fabric of my sweatpants, but I couldn't control a flinch that had nothing to do with the physical contact.

Almost lazily, like a caress, Reynolds used the gun to trace the indentation where the bullet had exited at the front of my thigh. I compelled myself to sit motionless, to show no response.

"I wonder what will happen," he said softly, "if I put another round through your leg in just the same place as the last. Will it hurt more or less than the first time?"

"Your message wouldn't get delivered," I said with a calm that came from somewhere else, somewhere outside of me.

"No?" He raised an eyebrow.

"No," I said, firm but matter-of-fact. "Last time, I was lucky. A millimetre or two either way and you'll hit an artery and I'll bleed out before the others get back." The tightness in my chest was making it difficult to get a whole sentence out in one breath. "And if that happens, Sean Meyer *will* find you and kill you, if he has to go to the ends of the earth to do it." The utter conviction in my voice didn't have to be forced.

Reynolds sat back a moment, as if considering. "Your death would be an inconvenience we could do without," he allowed. "But I still have to persuade you and your boss— and anyone else who's hanging around—that letting this drop would be in all your best interests. And if I can't shoot you—" he shrugged, regretful, slid the safety back on and put the Beretta back into its holster, '—I guess I'll just have to do this the old-fashioned way."

I tried to brace myself, brought my arms up to cover as much of my torso as I could, but it didn't do much good. He hit me a low relatively lightweight punch, almost experimental, somewhere around my kidney on the left side. An incendiary burst of pain exploded inwards and upwards, the shock wave buffeting through my body, robbing me of sight and breath and sanity. I screamed.

And then I fainted.

***

A moment later, or so it seemed, I opened my eyes and found I was sprawled face down on the sofa with a pulsating white-hot burn going on in my back that lanced straight through to my chest and pinned me there.

For a moment I thought that maybe it was all over, that Reynolds had delivered his message and gone. I should have known I wasn't that lucky.

"You're obviously not a party girl, Charlie," he said, shattering that fragile hope. "Here was I hoping we'd be up all night dancing, and you pass out on me at the first sign of a little trouble."

I lifted my head—very, very carefully—and turned it so I could see across the room. Reynolds was sitting in one of the chairs on the other side of the coffee table.

"I was shot, Reynolds. What did you expect?" I said, my voice thick. I had the hollow bitter taste of bile in the back of my throat and I had to swallow it before I could speak. "I thought your orders weren't to kill me."

A mistake to use the word "orders," I realised, but not until I'd already used it and it was too late to pull it back. Something even colder flashed through his eyes.

"Kill you, no," he said, getting to his feet with that deadly smile back in place. "Nobody said anything about what else I could do to you, though." And he reached for the fly of his jeans.

245

I panicked instantly, flapping like a landed fish. I tried to push myself up off the sofa, but my right arm wouldn't support my bodyweight and folded under me, so I nearly rolled over the edge and fell. Reynolds grabbed hold of my shoulders and hoisted me back onto the sofa, shoving my face down hard into the cushion so now I was suffocating as well. The spike of pain was such that I barely felt him tug at the waistband of my sweatpants.

In desperation, I reached my left hand back, clawed at him. My fingers brushed against something leather and he jerked back out of reach so fast that at first I thought I might somehow have hurt him, and then I realised that by chance I'd touched the holstered Beretta.

His weight shifted. Then came the sound of something heavy dropping onto glass. He'd put the gun down over on the coffee table, only a metre or so away. It might as well have been in Düsseldorf.

While he was leaning over I bucked under him, but it was a feeble attempt with no muscle behind it and he regained his balance easily.

"Oh no, you don't," he muttered, his voice tight and breathless, and he deliberately shoved one fist into the back of my right shoulder blade and leaned his weight onto it.

The pain was instant, inescapable. Deep inside, I swear I heard my own flesh tearing. I managed half a cry that shrank into a gasp and then I went utterly still. I think my mind detached from my body at that point and began to float. There was no other explanation for the fact that I could see his face clearly, the feral focus in his eyes, the dark primeval glitter. Except for the fact, of course, that it wasn't the first time I'd seen that look.

You can survive this. You have survived it before ...

Reynolds gave a satisfied grunt at my sudden capitulation. I felt him shift his weight again, positioning himself. I shut my eyes.

I felt the impact, second-hand, and the jerk as his body absorbed the blow and then collapsed sideways, dropping hard onto the floor alongside the sofa.

"Get off her, you bastard, or I will blow your fucking head off!"

I'd forgotten Matt, lying on the floor with a bleeding lump on the back of his head. So had Reynolds, clearly. He remembered him now, mainly because Matt had staggered upright, unnoticed until he snatched up the Beretta from the coffee table and smacked Reynolds round the back of his skull with the butt.

As he fell, the pressure lifted off the wound in my back as suddenly as it had landed. On the whole, I'd say it didn't immediately make things any better. I wanted to shout at Matt that he'd got a gun, not a bloody club, and to pull the trigger and keep pulling it, but I found Reynolds had stolen my voice along with half my self-respect.

Reynolds half-dragged himself upright, dazed from the blow, stumbled and went down again as far as his knees. I rolled onto my side, hauling my sweatpants back up with all the strength I could manage, and kicked him in the groin with my right foot. It wasn't hard enough to do him any lasting damage, and the resultant jar nearly made me black out, but it was definitely worth it.

Matt was on his feet, blinking, with the gun held stiffly in front of him in both hands now. He was trembling. I had a sudden flash reminder of the way Simone had held a gun, like it had been a living beast that might escape at any moment and devour her.

Matt clearly didn't know anything about firearms, either, and I noticed that fact at exactly the same time Reynolds did.

He lunged for Matt, making a grab for the gun. I saw Matt's hands clench as reflex made him jerk at the trigger. The barrel oscillated wildly as he took up the pressure and nothing happened.

"Safety!" I shouted at Matt. "Take the bloody safety off!"

I pivoted onto my side and lashed out at Reynolds again with my foot, catching him on the cheek, just under his eye. He half-fell onto the coffee table, which was made of glass. It should have been safety glass but he hit it hard. It splintered under his weight and he pitched through, tangling himself in the wrought-iron frame.

Matt stared at the gun in alarm. "How?"

"Give it to me!"

Reynolds was fighting out of the wreckage of the table, eyes burning intently into Matt. Matt saw the shark approaching with its mouth open and its teeth exposed, and threw the Beretta in my direction, like that was going to stop him getting his legs bitten off.

The gun landed on the sofa, almost hitting me in the stomach. I snatched it up and flicked the safety off just as Reynolds rolled clear of the debris. I aimed for the centre of his body mass and pulled the trigger without a second's hesitation.

And missed.

The bullet smacked into the body of the chair to his left. My right arm was still so weak that I could barely keep the gun up, never mind hold it steady under fire. The kick of it up through my arm and across my shoulders seemed immense. I jammed my left hand against my right and fired again.

Closer, but no hit.

Reynolds threw himself across the room and dived on Matt, who'd been crouched down with his fingers in his ears from the moment I'd fired the first shot.

He squealed as Reynolds yanked him upright and dragged him backwards towards the door. All the way, Reynolds kept Matt pinioned in front of him as a shield. I could just see Reynolds's head to one side of Matt's, one very blue eye watching my every move. As he reached the edge of the living room, I knew Reynolds was smiling through the faint drift of gunsmoke that hung between us.

"Not going to take the shot, Charlie?" he said, jeering. "Looks like that's getting to be one of your specialties, huh?"

I managed to get the Beretta to point a fraction higher, but the effort made my right arm shake so badly I couldn't sustain any sort of aim. I lowered the gun until the pistol grip was resting on the sofa.

"Lost another gun, Reynolds?" I said, tiredly. "Looks like that's getting to be one of yours."

For a moment I thought he was going to come back and have a go, but he thrust Matt away from him and ran for the door instead. To be honest, if Reynolds had decided on a counterattack, I'm not sure I could have done much about it.

Matt tottered back across the living room and collapsed into one of the armchairs. He dabbed a hand at the back of his head and looked blankly at the blood he found on his fingers.

"Are you OK?" he said. "I mean, did he ...?"

"No," I said. "He didn't—thanks to you."

"Thank God for that," Matt said. "I thought, when I saw—"

"You didn't see anything, Matt," I said, fighting to keep my eyes open, fighting to hold back the nausea and the sorrow. The pain was coming in waves on an incoming tide, each one crashing a little further up the beach. "Reynolds broke in. He beat the pair of us up. We got rid of him. Other than that there was nothing to see. Nothing you need to tell the others about, OK?"

He frowned. "Yes, but—"

"No buts. And if you tell Sean about this I'll kill you myself," I said, fierce, then added, with as much dignity as I could muster, "Now do me a favour and find me a bucket or something, would you? I think I'm going to throw up."

***

I still hadn't found the strength to move from the sofa by the time Sean and Neagley returned, two hours later. Matt had brought me the plastic liner from the pedal bin in the kitchen in place of a bucket and covered me with a blanket. He'd also found a dustpan and brush from somewhere and had gathered up most of the glass from the coffee table when I heard the key in the front door lock.

I'd been half-dozing, but I snapped awake and brought the Beretta up from under cover, slow and clumsy. I'd got my left hand clamped hard round my right, but if the way the front sights were circling wildly was anything to go by, I don't think I could have hit an elephant at half a dozen paces. Hell, for that matter, I don't think I could have hit an elephant if I'd been sitting on its back.

Sean did a fast assessment of the damage and was by my side almost instantly. He took the Beretta out of my hands, very gently and carefully. My palms had left clammy marks on either side of the grip.

"What happened?" Neagley demanded, looking at Matt. When I glanced across I saw that she had the short little Smith & Wesson out of her bag and in her hands, pointed low, and that she was moving through the living room quiet and careful, like a cop.

"Reynolds," I said, possessor of a fat tongue. "He came to deliver a message."

"And stayed to smash the place up," Sean murmured. "Well, there goes my security deposit."

Neagley shot him a fast disapproving glance, missing the wry twist of his lips. Sean didn't take his eyes off my face.

"Well, that was mainly me," I admitted, not aware until now how much it had been costing me to hold it together while we waited for them to come back. "Can't shoot for shit at the moment."

"You should be in bed," Sean said. "And I think I should call your father."

"No."

Sean silenced me with a single hard stare. "It's either that or we go back to the hospital in Lewiston," he said. "Your choice."

I shut my eyes. "Don't bully me," I said weakly. "I've had a bad day."

"Get used to it," Sean threw back at me. "Can you get up?"

I tried a couple of times, but both legs trembled too violently to be much use, and there was no way I could have leaned on a crutch, in any case.

With a sigh, Sean leaned down and scooped me up off the sofa. He was gentle, but it hurt nevertheless and I didn't hide that fact well. He carried me through to the bedroom and laid me very carefully on the bed, then pulled the covers over me and sat alongside.

"So, are you going to tell me exactly what happened?"

"Reynolds played rough," I said. "Maybe I should have broken his neck while I had the chance."

Sean's hand feathered in my hair. "No, you shouldn't," he said.

I eyed him, a man who'd killed without compunction for lesser reasons than dire necessity. "That's rich," I said, "coming from you."

"Ah, well, I see the right way and I approve it, but I do the opposite."

"Who said that?"

"Me, just now," he said. "Actually, I believe it was Ovid."

"God save us from philosopher squaddies," I said, aware that I was starting to slur again. "It's still rich, coming from you."

"Well how about, don't do as I do, do as I say?" he murmured. "I want you to be with me, Charlie. But I don't want you to try and *be* me ..."

NINETEEN

My father arrived later that evening and stalked straight into the bedroom, ordering Sean outside when he would have stayed with me. They had a brief stare-out competition, which my father won. He examined me without a word other than curt instructions for me to move or bend or breathe deeply, most of which hurt to perform.

When he was done he rose and said crisply, "Well, Charlotte, you've certainly managed to knock yourself about and have almost undoubtedly delayed your recovery, but by some miracle you don't appear to have done anything permanent. Next time you might not be so lucky."

"Thank you," I said.

For a moment he was silent as he folded his stethoscope neatly into his bag, his movements very deliberate and precise, as always. "This cannot continue," he said, without looking at me directly. "You can barely stand. I fail to see what purpose is served by your continued presence here, other than to lay yourself open to further attack, or as a burden to your colleagues."

Neither can I. "I'm staying," I said.

He closed the bag, snapping it shut with a briskness that could almost have been mistaken for temper in someone more human. "Well, I regret that I am not," he said.

There was a slight tap on the door and Neagley stuck her head round without waiting for an invitation. "Can I offer you coffee, Dr Fox?" she asked.

My father stiffened. "Thank you, but no," he said with icy politeness. "And my name is Foxcroft—Mr, not Dr."

He ignored her puzzled frown. At the doorway, he turned to fire one last salvo. "I shall be taking a flight out of Boston tomorrow, and if you had any sense you would do the same," he said. "I cannot keep doing this, Charlotte. I've done my best to help you, but if you won't heed my advice … well, there has to come a time when one calls a halt, don't you agree?"

"Yes," I said, and he paused, surprised. "But I'd call it making a stand."

Something tightened in the side of his jaw. He strode out past Neagley and I heard Sean intercept him in the hallway to get him to check Matt's head wound.

There was a long pause and something that sounded suspiciously like a sigh. Then my father's voice said, brusque, "Show me."

Neagley came further into the room and shut the door behind her.

"He really *is* a doctor, right?" she said.

I raised a smile. "He's a consultant orthopedic surgeon— they look down on mere doctors from a very exalted height."

"Ah," she said, understanding. "I thought for a moment he meant he was an ex-doctor—like he might have had his licence revoked or something."

My smile fleshed out. "Oh, how I *wish* you'd asked him that …"

She smiled with me for a moment before her face sobered. "So, does he think you're OK?"

"Oh, just peachy," I said. *Of course, he's probably disowned me, but what else is new?*

"What really happened this afternoon?" she said. "Matt was being kind of vague."

"I'm not surprised. He got quite a belt round the head."

Neagley came forwards and sat on the foot of the bed, regarding me with that serious cop's face.

253

"When I gave you the rundown on Oliver Reynolds the other day at the hospital, I didn't go into a lot of detail," she said. "I told you he was good at putting the frighteners on women, but I didn't tell you how."

She flicked her eyes in my direction, but I was concentrating on straightening out the bedclothes, smoothing the rumpled sheet.

"He threatens to rape them," she said flatly. "And if they have young daughters, so much the better."

"He threatened the kids?" I said sharply, remembering Reynolds's mention of Ella.

Neagley grimaced. "Only that he'd make them watch."

I looked her straight in the eye. "Good job we were able to get the better of him before that thought crossed his mind, then," I said levelly. "Have you said anything about this to Sean?"

"No, I—"

"Well, don't," I said. "Please." And when she still looked dubious, I added, "Believe me, you don't want to be responsible for what he'll do if he finds out."

Surprise crossed her face first, followed by a grim understanding. She nodded, got to her feet. "You know where I am when you want to talk," she said gravely.

"Yes—and thank you," I said, but I knew I'd never take her up on the offer.

If the look she gave me as she went out was anything to go by, she knew it, too.

***

"You're very quiet," Sean said. "Penny for your thoughts?"

"We're in the US," I said. "Shouldn't that be a cent?"

"No, it still works with a penny, I think," he said. "And you're hedging."

It was four days after my father's final visit and we were sitting in the Explorer in the car park at the Shaw's supermarket in North Conway. Inside the store itself,

Lucas and Rosalind had taken Ella with them to do their weekly grocery shop.

It was the first time I'd laid eyes on her since the night I was shot, and I was shocked by how clearly I remembered every little nuance of behaviour or movement. I could almost tell what she was thinking, feeling—even saying— just from watching her at that distance. As she trotted away from us towards the entrance, a tiny figure between the two adults, I was aware of having something vital stripped from me.

I would have liked to tail them into the store, but I had to admit it wasn't practical. I still wasn't moving anything like freely enough for covert surveillance. I would be needing a crutch to walk for a while, although my right arm was improving every day. Sean had brought me coffee in a polystyrene cup when we'd stopped for fuel, and I was able to hold it in my right hand while I drank, even if I'd had to get him to remove the plastic lid for me first.

And, besides anything else, there was always the fact that Ella would instantly recognise me—at least, I hoped she would. I'd now been away from her almost as long as I'd been with her. Children forget easily, I knew, but still I hoped that I hadn't disappeared entirely from her consciousness. She certainly hadn't disappeared from mine.

So, Sean and I sat in the car and waited for the three of them to come out. There was only one entrance and one exit, at opposite ends of the building, but Sean had positioned us so we could keep an eye on both of them. I knew from my own experience with Ella that she had opinions of her own about shopping that were likely to slow the proceedings down. We were prepared for a long wait.

At the moment, we still weren't quite sure what we were waiting for, but people tend to fall into a routine in their daily lives and it didn't do any harm to learn it. It beat sitting around in the apartment all day, that's for sure.

Now, I shrugged. "I was thinking about work," I said, half-truthfully answering his original question. "How long can you afford to be away from London?"

Sean gave me a shrug of his own, sipping his coffee. "As long as Harrington continues to pay me to be here instead," he said. His eyes were on the flow of people and cars coming and going, constantly checking. "By the sounds of it, Madeleine's coping without me with embarrassing ease."

"But is that because she's being her usual wildly efficient self, or because we're just not picking up the business at the moment?" I persisted.

He pulled a face. "Well, we're not quite down to pawning the family silver yet," he said. He sighed and turned to face me. "We're surviving, Charlie. Madeleine's been chasing electronic security work and it's starting to pay off, to the point where I feel I'm almost superfluous. But business has dropped off since we lost Simone—and Jakes—I won't lie to you about that."

"Does his boss, this guy Armstrong, blame ... us?" I wasn't sure if I'd been about to say "you' or "me'—'us' was a compromise.

"Parker Armstrong knows the risks of the game as well as anyone. If he blamed us he'd hardly be helping Matt with the legal side of things. Besides," Sean added with another shrug, "it certainly won't do any harm if we can make some sense of what happened. Help quash the rumours."

"What rumours—?" I began, stopping abruptly when Sean came upright fast in his seat, eyes narrowing. "What? What is it?"

"The dark blue Ford Taurus that's just pulled in at the end of the next row," he said. "Two guys just got out who don't look like they're here just for a bag of cookies."

I followed his gaze and saw two big men, their bulk accentuated by their heavy winter clothing. The sun was bright today, but the wind was cutting. Both wore hats, pulled down low over their ears, and gloves. Nothing unusual about that. It was the way they did such a studiously casual appraisal of the car park, that had nothing casual about it, on their way into the store. It was the kind of action I'd seen Sean carry out a hundred times. Only I suspect he would have died rather than have been quite so obvious about it.

The men had their backs turned as they walked towards the giant building, but halfway there one of them turned to do another counter-surveillance sweep and I saw his face clearly for the first time.

"That's one of Vaughan's men," I said. "In the green jacket. With the moustache. He's one of the pair that grabbed me that night and took me for my nice little chat with Felix."

"I'll go in and keep an eye on them," Sean said. He leaned over and unobtrusively slipped the reclaimed Beretta out of the glove compartment, then reached for his jacket from the back seat. "Stay here."

I hadn't been contemplating trying to join in on this one, but the fact that he felt he had to order me to sit and stay put like a disobedient puppy put my back up. "Yes, *sir!*" I muttered.

He just paused, halfway through shouldering his way into his jacket. "Charlie, we don't have time for this. I'm not trying to treat you like a child, but please, just stay put."

"OK," I said, with ill grace.

"Attagirl," he said. "And if you're very good I'll buy you a Happy Meal on the way home."

"Try it," I said sweetly, "and I'll throw up in my car seat before we get there."

He slid the gun into his pocket and gave me a quick bright smile as he climbed easily out of the Explorer, shutting the door behind him and hurrying after the two men. As he went, he pulled a scrap of paper from his pocket and stared at it with what appeared to be his full concentration. He was frowning heavily, just some harrassed guy who knew he'd left something off his shopping list and was trying to remember what it was before he got inside. The performance was so convincing that neither of Vaughan's men made him.

I was suddenly aware of being very alone inside the confines of the vehicle. Reynolds's face loomed in my mind's eye and I experienced a momentary wish, entirely selfish, that Sean had left the gun behind. Then it passed. If either of these two was a threat to Ella, then I'd much rather Sean was armed. He would, I knew, use the Beretta without a qualm if he had to, to protect the child. Regardless of the consequences.

It was hard to realise just how much I missed Ella. Her inventive food combinations, her occasionally sage pronouncements, her comical grumpiness first thing in the morning. I missed them all with a sharpness that surprised me.

I remembered Sean's report on Lucas's behaviour towards his daughter as a baby, the injuries Simone had received before her mother had divorced him and run. He'd been a bully, pure and simple. Would he return to that now?

You didn't just stop abusing. Lucas might not always have had the opportunity to indulge himself—certainly not since he left the army—but now he had another child to take his temper out on, over time he would surely revert to type. It was human nature.

And it was up to me and Sean to stop him before he hurt her.

The Explorer had started to mist up a little and the cold had a sullen dampness to it. Sean had left the keys in the ignition and I leaned across and flipped the engine on, just to run some heat through the car. The front screen demisted slowly.

It was another twenty minutes before I saw the Lucases emerge. Greg Lucas was carrying three bags of shopping in each hand, and his wife had Ella balanced on her hip.

They were some distance away and I craned forwards, trying to read Ella's body language. Was there anything about her that seemed scared or anxious? She was wearing a pink jacket with a fake-fur-trimmed hood that was up around her face, and she had one hand to her mouth, probably chewing her hair. I could almost hear Simone's voice telling her daughter to stop it.

While Lucas sorted his car keys and put the bags away, Rosalind stood happily holding Ella, rocking with her and talking, their heads very close together. Ella reached out and touched Rosalind's hair and she smiled. Whatever Lucas's feelings towards his granddaughter, I saw, Rosalind was forming quite a bond. I wondered why that fact hurt me quite so much.

Now, Lucas fumbled a little with the keys and it was Rosalind who put Ella down long enough to open the tailgate of the Range Rover. Ella stood, a couple of paces away, fiddling with the buttons on her coat, in a world of her own while people hurried past to their cars.

I skimmed the sparse crowd for signs of danger, but could see nothing immediate. I couldn't see Vaughan's men, either—or Sean. Not seeing them and knowing they were there was worse by far. I shifted in my seat, only too frustratingly aware of my physical limitations. They could be planning just about anything and I wouldn't be able to stop them.

Then the bags were inside the back of the Range Rover and Rosalind was fussing with the order of them, leaving Lucas to turn his full attention to Ella. I tensed as he crouched in front of her. I was watching them through the side window with Ella three-quarters facing me and Lucas almost dead side on. I could see both their faces, blurred slightly by the distance between us. Ella's showed a trace of wariness and her eyes kept darting over Lucas's shoulder— then back over her own—as though she was expecting something major to come and take her away. Or she was waiting for someone.

Lucas stroked a gentle hand down her flushed cheek. And it *was* gentle. There was no hidden message in the gesture. It was affection and nothing more.

The driver's door of the Explorer swung open and my head whipped round so fast I nearly ricked my neck.

"Sean!" I said. "Damn, you put the wind up me."

"Nice to know you're getting something out of it," he said as he climbed in, throwing a small bag of groceries onto the back seat—a decoy to allow him to linger at the checkout. "My God, it's like an oven in here."

"Sorry, being so inactive makes me feel the cold like crazy," I said. "So, what happened in there?"

He shrugged his way out of his coat. "They came. They shopped. They went," he said. "The two guys we saw didn't do much beyond hang around trying to attract the attention of security—or that's what it seemed like, anyway. They followed Lucas around, flexing their muscles, then left at the same time as we did."

"But they didn't try anything?"

"No, why?"

"I just thought Ella was looking a bit uneasy, that's all," I said, turning back to watch the Range Rover. Lucas had the rear door open now and was strapping Ella into her seat.

Sean looked a little discomfited. "Ah, well, she spotted me," he said.

I said nothing, just turned back and raised my eyebrows. He gave me a wry smile.

"She didn't say anything, I don't think, but that doesn't mean she won't at some point."

We were both silent for a moment. The Range Rover's brake lights flicked on as they climbed in and Lucas started the engine.

"What are we hoping for here, Sean?" I asked. "That we'll catch them mistreating her? That we'll stumble across some reason why they shouldn't be allowed to keep her?"

"I don't know," he said quietly, "but at least we're watching her—watching out for her. And it's not just the Lucases we have to worry about, is it?"

As he spoke, the blue Ford we'd seen Vaughan's men arrive in turned up the row where the Range Rover was parked. The Taurus accelerated hard towards them, then braked to an abrupt halt, blocking Lucas in. I tensed in my seat, waiting for the attack.

"Sean!"

He already had the Beretta out of his pocket, but there was no clear shot. And, besides, nobody had emerged from either car. Stand-off. The Taurus sat there for half a minute, ticking over, the men inside staring at Lucas, who was staring right back at them through layers of glass and mirrors.

As abruptly as it had arrived, the Taurus pulled away, rearing back on its suspension as the driver planted the pedal, engine and transmission protesting hard enough to turn heads. A warning, then. Nothing more. But a warning about what?

There was a brief pause. Then the Range Rover swung out of its space, lurching a little to show that Lucas had been as unsettled by the whole thing as, no doubt, he was supposed to be.

We followed them out onto the main road, keeping three cars between us. Lucas had been through all the same training Sean had and in some ways it was a surprise he hadn't spotted us tailing him before, but now he would definitely be on his guard.

"What are we going to do about this, Sean?" I demanded. "We can't follow them around forever. What good are we doing?"

"Parker's legal man is making progress," Sean said. "He seems to think Matt's claim for Ella is stronger, bearing in mind she's lived with him all her life. He thinks Matt would get custody if it came to a fight."

"Which Matt can't afford to fund," I put in. "Is Harrington prepared to back him?"

Sean shrugged, braking for traffic lights. "Well, we'll just—" he began, then broke off as his mobile phone started to ring. He checked the incoming number and handed the phone to me. "It's Neagley," he said.

I answered the phone. "Sean's driving," I told the private eye. "What's up?"

"I think you'd better get back here," she said, and there was something in her voice that hooked me. Was that excitement? "Matt's found something and it could be important."

"Like what?"

"We don't think Greg Lucas was Simone's father."

I frowned. Whatever I'd been expecting—or hoping for— that wasn't it. "But the DNA tests were a match," I said, nonplussed. "And the police double-checked."

"Yeah, but … it's complicated. We'll explain when you get here." And she rang off.

***

When we got back Matt had the apartment door open before the Explorer had even stopped rolling. He was almost hopping from one foot to the other like a little kid with a secret that's bursting to be let out. For the first time he allowed his impatience to show at my slow progress across the icy ground from car to doorway. Until Sean glared at him. Then he slunk indoors and waited for us to come to him at our own pace.

"OK, Matt," Sean said when I was back on the sofa. "Let's hear it."

Matt shuffled the papers spread out over the replacement coffee table in front of him. There was an uncertainty to his fingers as they leafed through, as though if he handled the information badly it might evaporate right in front of his very eyes.

"First of all, I need to know how good is your researcher—Madeleine, isn't it?"

"The best," Sean said without hesitation, and the bluntness of his tone would have flattened someone less buoyed up.

"So you're absolutely sure the dates she's given you about Lucas's army career stack up?" Matt said, wilting a little but still dogged in his persistence.

"Yes."

Matt swallowed. "OK, then," he said, picking up one particular sheet. "Simone's birthday was the sixteenth of September." His voice gave a tiny waver as he said her name, pricking my sympathy. He had not had time to grieve for Simone, I realised. And probably wouldn't until their daughter's fate was settled. I hoped that then he would just have one loss to mourn, not two.

Neagley came to sit down, bringing fresh coffee for Sean and me. As she passed Matt she put her free hand on his shoulder, giving it a slight squeeze of support. He threw her a wan smile.

"Er, yeah, anyway, according to the reports you have, Lucas was at the height of his bad-boy phase in the eighteen months before she was born. It was around that time that he chucked two trainees out of a helicopter and one of them broke his shoulder."

"Collarbone," Sean said absently, sipping his coffee. "And we know all this. How does it relate to him not being Simone's father?"

"Well, just stick with me on this. At the end of the previous November he got into an argument in a pub in Hereford and ended up making one bloke eat the cue ball off the pool table."

"Eat it?" I queried.

"Yeah, he forced it into the bloke's mouth and apparently they had to surgically dislocate his jaw to get it out again. Caused a real ruckus at the time. It seems that the bloke he injured had connections—his uncle was the local chief constable or something. The end result was that top brass came down hard on Lucas. They didn't just kick him out of the SAS—they stuck him in clink for it."

Sean had gone very still, like a dog on the scent of prey. "Go on," he said.

"Sergeant Greg Lucas was a guest of Her Majesty in the glasshouse in Colchester for a couple of months over Christmas and the New Year while they sorted out what they were going to do with him." He singled out a sheet of paper and handed it across. "From the third of December until halfway through February, actually."

Sean took the sheet and stared at it. "The dates don't line up," he said slowly.

Matt nodded, eyes suddenly very bright like someone in the grip of religious fervour. "I've seen Simone's birth certificate. She was just short of nine pounds in weight when she was born. And bang on time—not premature, not overdue. There's no way on this earth that Lucas could have been her father."

"But he is," I said blankly, looking up. "The DNA test proved it."

"That DNA test," Neagley said, breaking in for the first time, "just proved that the two of them were father and daughter. It didn't prove that the man who was Simone's father was Greg Lucas."

"In other words," Matt chipped in, "just because Greg Lucas happened to be married to Pam—Simone's mother—it doesn't automatically mean that he was Simone's father."

"But that's ... impossible," I said, and even as I spoke I knew it wasn't impossible at all. In fact, it made a lot more sense than anything else I could think of.

Neagley smiled at my obvious confusion. "Trust me, Charlie," she said. "We've done nothing but tear this thing apart all morning. There's no other conclusion that's feasible."

"But he's a match, so if he isn't Greg Lucas, he must be—"

"John Ashworth," Matt supplied, nodding. "Her mother's boyfriend. The boyfriend who magically disappeared at exactly the same time Greg Lucas upped sticks and moved over here. The boyfriend who everyone thought was dead but no-one could find a body for."

"The boyfriend," Neagley said, producing another sheet of paper from the pile, "whose middle name just happens to be Simon—which you have to admit kinda adds weight to the he's-her-real-father argument."

"If the DNA test is correct—and we can only assume it is—," Matt said, his voice tight, "then the only possible explanation is that the man who's been posing as Greg Lucas for the last twenty years is, in fact, John Ashworth."

"We thought the DNA test would prove Greg Lucas was who he claimed to be," Sean said, looking at me. "Whereas in fact, it's proved him to be the one man he couldn't possibly be."

"And he knew," I said. "Otherwise he wouldn't have agreed to take it. He knew he really was her father."

"Just as the real Greg Lucas must have known that *he* wasn't," Matt said, suddenly more subdued. "Maybe that was why he was so bloody cruel to her when she was a baby."

The more I thought about it, the more it made sense. The personality change from vicious psychopath to doting grandfather, the fact that I just hadn't got that professional soldier vibe from the man—and he hadn't picked anything up, in return, from me.

So what the hell happened to the real *Greg Lucas?* And even as the question formed, the answer bloomed over the top of it.

"Ashworth killed him," I said suddenly. I snapped out of my reverie and found everyone looking at me. "And Simone knew. The night she was shot," I said, aware of Matt's flinch at the words, "she went ballistic at Lucas. 'I saw him do it. I loved you. I trusted you.' That was what she shouted at him. She was only a child at the time, but I think

265

somehow she must have remembered back to the night Lucas and Ashworth both vanished. Think about it—Lucas was ex-SAS and a natural killer. He'd been stalking them for months. If Ashworth ended up with Lucas's identity, he must have had to kill Lucas to get it. You've seen his record. There's no other way the guy would ever have given in unless he was dead. I don't know what set Simone off, but what if she remembered seeing Ashworth kill Greg Lucas?"

"So," Matt said grimly, "he may not be quite the psychopathic killer we thought he was, but he's still a psychopathic killer, just the same."

Sean frowned. "Wait a minute. If I remember right, this Ashworth guy was a salesman. He wasn't even in the army. How did he manage to kill a fully trained SAS soldier?"

"He could always have shot him," Neagley suggested. "Guns are a great leveller."

Sean shook his head. "Guns just aren't that common in the UK—and certainly not twenty-odd years ago," he said. "And besides, the police searched the house pretty thoroughly, according to the reports. If he'd been shot it would have left a trace. They didn't find anything."

"What about Rosalind—do you think she knows that Lucas isn't really Lucas?" Neagley asked.

"How can you keep that kind of a secret from someone you're living with for all that time?" I said.

Sean shot me a sly glance. "Some people are very good at keeping secrets."

I ignored the gibe and reached for my crutch, struggling to my feet. "Well, there's one way to find out."

"How?"

"I'll ask her," I said.

TWENTY

Frances Neagley drove me over to the Lucases' house just before three that afternoon and walked slowly beside me across the slippery driveway. She was the one who rang the front doorbell when my courage might otherwise have deserted me.

The timing was deliberate. We knew that Lucas would be at the surplus store taking care of business for another couple of hours, giving us initial time with Rosalind alone. Mind you, there was always the chance she wouldn't let me through the door to begin with.

It seemed to take a long time for her to answer the summons of the bell. By then I'd got thoroughly cold feet in every sense of the words. I think I was actually shivering when she opened the door and stared blankly at the pair of us. Perhaps that was what made her take pity on me. Her gaze flickered over Neagley, standing close alongside me like she expected me to fall at any moment.

There was a long pause while the three of us stood there immobile. Then Rosalind stepped back and held the door further open. "You'd best come in and sit before you collapse," she said, her voice giving no clues on warmth.

"Thank you," I said, limping past her into the hallway. Neagley looked around the interior with professional interest, smiling at Rosalind's assessing stare.

"This is Frances," I said by way of introduction. "She very kindly brought me over—there's no way I can drive yet."

Rosalind nodded at that, accepting it on one level, questioning it on another. She gestured for us to follow her through into the living room area. I looked round, hopeful, but it was empty.

"How's Ella?" I asked.

A brief smile escaped across the corner of Rosalind's thin lips. "She's still very upset, naturally," she said, "but we're making progress with her."

"Where is she?"

"Upstairs, probably watching a little TV in her room." Rosalind paused, frowning.

Probably? You mean you don't know?

"I'd take it as a favour if you didn't ask to see her, Charlie," she went on. "I think it might … unsettle her too much."

Something reached into my chest and squeezed at my heart with very cold fingers. "I understand," I said, expressionless.

"Thank you," she said with another small smile. "Can I offer you and your … friend some coffee?"

"Thank you, Mrs Lucas, that would be great," Neagley said, her voice coolly polite. "You have a lovely home."

"Thank you, we like to think so," Rosalind replied, but her eyes had narrowed slightly, as though she was still trying to get a handle on Neagley's exact role.

Rosalind was still frowning as she moved across to fuss with the coffee machine in the kitchen area. I sat, taking the soft leather armchair near the fireplace, so I was sideways on to Rosalind and facing the window, laying the crutch down beside the chair. Neagley remained standing.

"So, I understand Ella's father has been in touch with you since the accident," Rosalind said smoothly, making it sound like Simone had died in a car crash. "Would he have anything to do with your visit? Because if you're here on his behalf, I have to tell you that we don't feel that young man would make a suitable parent for Ella." Her voice was prim.

"Matt *has* been in touch," I said with classic understatement, "but the main reason we're here is about your husband."

"My husband?" Rosalind said. She was measuring coffee grounds into the top of the machine and that might have been why she sounded distracted, but I didn't think so. Her hand faltered slightly. "What about Greg?"

"You told me you'd been married for fifteen years," I said, watching her pour in cold water and close the lid. "How long had you actually known him before that?"

She frowned. "A year or so," she said at last, cautious, as though I was out to trip her but she was unable to see how that answer might do it. "Why?"

"You remember that day at the store when Mr Vaughan issued his little challenge to me, and afterwards I got that photo message on my phone?"

"Yes, it was an old picture of Greg," she said. Her shoulders were too tense, I noticed. She saw me watching her and dropped them abruptly. "Funny how people change," she said, sounding almost breathless. "I almost didn't recognise him."

"No, Rosalind," I said gently, "the reason you didn't recognise him was because the man in the picture wasn't your husband."

She went very still. "So who was it then?"

"Greg Lucas."

"But—"

"Has your husband ever been violent towards you, Mrs Lucas?" Neagley cut in smoothly.

"What?" Rosalind shook off her confusion and flushed, outraged. "No, of course he hasn't! What kind of a question is that?"

"Back when he was in the military in England, Greg Lucas was a violent man," I ploughed on, taking up the thread, relentless. "Not just as a part of his career, but in his personal life. He beat his first wife and regularly put her infant daughter—Simone—in the hospital."

"I-I don't believe you," Rosalind said stiffly, but she was white-faced and tense enough to splinter if you'd dropped her.

"No? Well, the facts bear me out," I said. Neagley opened her shoulder bag—the one with that short-barrelled revolver inside—and pulled out a sheaf of paperwork. We'd detoured to get it copied at the Bob Duncan Photoshop on Main Street on the way over. She held the papers up for Rosalind to see and, when the other woman made no move towards her, put them down on the coffee table.

"Eventually," I went on, "Simone's mother decided she'd had enough. She got out from under. But Lucas wasn't giving up that easily. He tracked her down. She'd made a new life for herself, taken up with a new man. A guy called John Ashworth." I paused, let that one sink in on Rosalind, saw the merest twitch in the muscle of her cheek. "The thing was, he wasn't really a *new* man. You see, she'd been having a relationship with him since before Simone was born. We don't know how long for, but it had to be at least nine months, because John Ashworth—John *Simon* Ashworth, I should say—not Greg Lucas, was Simone's real father."

"Don't be ridiculous," Rosalind said, but she had to put a steadying hand out for the kitchen worktop. "Greg passed the DNA test. The police confirmed it—he's definitely Simone's father. And Ella's grandfather."

"Oh yes," I said. "But at the time of her conception Greg Lucas was in prison for assault. There's no possibility of mistake—we've checked," I added, when she opened her mouth to pursue that line. "It's documented fact."

Rosalind didn't speak right away. She moved slowly round from the kitchen, walking like an automaton, her eyes fixed on the paperwork Neagley had placed on the table. Unable to resist its lure any longer, she snatched up the pages and scanned down them quickly, taking it all in. When she'd finished, her hands were shaking.

"What does this mean?" she asked, almost a whisper.

"It means," I said, "your husband may not be quite the man you thought you married."

"It also means that sooner or later the cops in England are going to ask for him to be sent back over there," Neagley put in helpfully.

Rosalind's head came up sharply. "What for?"

"Well, Greg Lucas was not the type to happily let another man assume his identity," I said, "so, what do you think happened to the original?"

"And when that private investigator from Boston, Barry O'Halloran, first came looking for him, your husband must have thought the game was up," Neagley said, her voice flinty. "Is that why Barry had his 'accident'?"

Rosalind's mouth opened, gaped rather like a drowning fish, then closed into a thin hard line. "Get out," she said, her voice low and harsh. "Get out now."

I glanced at Neagley, who shrugged. Time for a tactical retreat. Perhaps later, when Rosalind had had a chance to read through the damning evidence again, and reflect, she might come round. But not now.

Now she was hurt and angry and liable to lash out at the nearest thing that could feel pain. Neagley must have sensed that in her, too, because she moved in close to me.

I reached for the crutch I'd laid next to my chair and struggled to my feet, feeling Rosalind's eyes on me very keenly while I battled with balance and damaged muscles.

"I don't stand to gain anything in this, Rosalind," I said once I was upright, a last-ditch effort to win her over. "But I do care what happens to Ella."

"Like hell you do," Rosalind bit out. "You're after the money, you greedy little—"

I saw the blow coming but couldn't do much to counter it. The palm of Rosalind's hand struck me flat across the cheekbone with surprising force. The power of it knocked me back so that I stumbled into the chair I'd just vacated, and overbalanced. Neagley made a grab for me and managed to slow my descent, but not prevent it. I fell backwards across the arm of the chair, landing on the seat. I jolted my back, but the fear of falling did more damage than the actual event. For a moment I just lay there gasping.

"Charlie!"

I heard the sound of my own name without initially registering the voice that cried it. Ella must have come downstairs unnoticed while we were arguing. Before I knew it, the tiny figure had threaded her way between Neagley and Rosalind and launched herself on top of me. I gave a grunt of pain and pushed her away weakly. Rosalind hoisted the little girl off. Any other time I would have been heartbroken, but I felt only relief.

"Charlie's hurt, Ella," Rosalind said. She looked straight at me. *Payback time.* "Your mummy hurt her. That's why your mummy got hurt, and the angels came and took her up to heaven."

You bitch! You utter, utter, bitch ...

Ella's confusion was writ large across her features. She turned a gaze on me that was suddenly wary and close to accusing as the connections formed and hardened. No doubt this wasn't the first time Rosalind had fed her this line. Ella took a minute step back, sneaking her hand into that of the woman she'd learned to call Grandma, looking to her for reassurance.

"Is that why you hurt Charlie?" Ella asked, wide-eyed, frowning.

For a moment Rosalind just gaped at her before she turned and glared at me, defiance and anger and guilt all written there, as though it were all my fault for pushing her too far and letting the child see me do it.

"She didn't hurt me, Ella," I said, managing to produce a rough facsimile of a reassuring smile even though one side of my face was stiff and smarting. "I slipped and fell, that's all. Don't worry."

"I want you both to leave now," Rosalind said with dignity. In the kitchen the coffee machine was still making gurgling noises, but I didn't think we were going to get that drink, after all.

"All right," I said quietly. "But think about what we've told you, Rosalind. You can't make a fight of this. Better to give in with good grace, don't you think?"

Rosalind stiffened her shoulders. "And what would you know about that?"

She followed us to the door, but keeping her distance, Ella clinging to her hand as though her life depended on it and chewing a strand of her hair. On the front step I turned and smiled down at her.

"'Bye, Ella," I said, a part of me still hoping for some sign of remembrance, of the affection she'd previously shown me.

Ella just stared, confused and uncomprehending, until the closing door cut her off from my view. And that, I realised, stung far more than a slap to the face could ever do.

***

"They're on the run," Matt said, sounding confident for the first time. "With what Mr Armstrong's told me, it's only a matter of time before I get Ella back." The underlying relief bubbled up through his voice, struggling to be contained. He was almost jubilant.

We were sitting in the bar at the White Mountain Hotel, having just had dinner at the Ledges Dining Room there. A young woman was playing a mix of soft jazz on the grand piano that stood on a raised platform between the two rooms and a sports channel was showing highlights of last season's baseball on the flat-screen TV behind the bar. One of the teams was the San Francisco Giants and Neagley's eyes kept sliding to the action. I remembered her saying she was from California and guessed that she hadn't switched her allegiance when she moved east.

We made an odd party in such elegant surroundings. I was still in the sweatpants that were all I could comfortably manage, and Matt always had that slightly untidy air about him. The kind that seems to make otherwise quite sensible women want to smooth his hair and do his laundry. Only Sean and Neagley looked as though they'd dressed for the occasion.

"Don't get your hopes up, Matt," Sean warned now, reaching for his glass. He'd had wine with the meal, but now he'd moved on to mineral water. "This thing's a long way from over yet."

"Why—what are they going to do?" Matt asked, unwilling to have his celebration squashed entirely. He looked round at the three of us, who must have appeared pessimistically subdued by comparison.

Neagley shrugged. "Who knows?" she said quietly, swirling her Scotch round in the bottom of her own glass. "They've proved they're capable of plenty so far." And I knew she was thinking of her dead partner. We might never find out whether his death was an accident or not.

Matt gave her a rueful smile and squeezed her arm as though he read her thoughts. There was something intimate about the gesture that stopped short of invasive. He seemed to have a heightened female empathy. I could imagine he got more attention than his looks would have suggested. And Simone had been jealous, I remembered. Corrosively so.

Funny, when I'd first met Simone that day in another restaurant, some three thousand miles away, I'd thought of Matt as the enemy, someone from whom I had to protect my client and her daughter at all costs. Now he was the one we were all fighting for.

I glanced over and found, despite his apparent jubilation, Matt's eyes were misty. We'd had to tell him, again and again, every tiny thing we could remember about Ella's appearance today and he'd been storing it away ever since, hugging the memory close like a blanket. "My baby," he said and his voice wavered a little. He took a swig from the glass of Sam Adams in front of him. "My God, I miss her."

Into the silence that followed that statement came the trilling of my mobile. I rooted in my jacket pocket, ignoring the pointed stares from other diners at nearby tables. Irritation with the mobile phone, it seemed, was universal.

I fumbled the phone open awkwardly with my left hand. "Hello?"

"Charlie?" said a man's voice. "It's Greg Lucas."

"Is it really?" I said, sceptical, mouthing his name to the others. "That, it seems, is a matter of opinion."

I heard his annoyed expulsion of breath. "Can we put that matter aside for the moment?" he snapped. "This is serious."

More serious than what happened to the real Greg Lucas?

"Go on," I said.

"It's Ella," he said, his voice rising. He stopped, got control of it, and added, "She's gone."

"*What?*" Now it was my turn to snort. Then I was speaking fast and low. "I don't know what the hell game you're playing, Lucas—"

"For God's sake," he burst out, anger and anguish distorting his voice. "This is no game! I got back from the store and found Rosalind absolutely distraught. She said you'd been round to see her this afternoon. They came and took Ella, right from the house, just after you left."

"Who took her?" I demanded. The others had been listening to my side of the conversation and all three of them tensed at that. Matt started to speak but I waved him quiet. I waited, but Lucas still didn't respond. "Who took her?"

At last he said, reluctantly, "We think it's Felix Vaughan. From what Rosalind said, it sounded like a couple of his guys. They turned up while we were out shopping this morning, trying to scare us, I think. Looks like they got bored with that and went for the real deal."

275

"Have they said what they want?"

"What do you think?" Lucas said, acid now. "Money. Ten million dollars. They left a note when they took her. If we go to the cops, they mail her back in pieces."

"Are you at the house?" I said, struggling to fish my crutch out from under the table with my right hand. Sean was already on his feet. "We'll come now."

"No!" Lucas said sharply. "They might be watching the house. I-I can't risk that." I had to hand it to him, he sounded genuinely shaken. But then, whatever his identity, he *was* Ella's grandfather, after all. "We'll come to you."

"What if they try and call you?"

"They have my cell, and they said they'd call tomorrow, anyway. Where are you?"

I glanced at Sean. He seemed to understand my unspoken question and gave me a brief nod. "We're up at the White Mountain Hotel," I said.

"OK, we'll meet you up there," he said, then added with a bitter twist to his voice, "Personally, I'd rather meet you in hell, but Rosalind seems to think you may be our only chance of getting Ella back alive."

***

It was already dark outside. We waited in the car park with the lights of the hotel behind us. It was dazzlingly cold, with the monolithic slab of Cathedral Ledge looming up into the star-cast sky above. I'd picked out the constellation of Orion hanging high and bright above the trees as we came out. We sat in the Explorer with the engine running and the air con set to full heat, but I was shivering violently nevertheless.

Ella.

I recalled, starkly, her terror when the press photographers had ambushed her in her mother's kitchen. The brush of her lips against my neck afterwards. An urge to rampage against the men who'd taken her now was so strong I had to clasp my hands tight in my lap to keep them from acting. *So this must be part of what it's like—maternal instinct.* I'd thought that particular emotion had passed me by.

I had the front passenger seat purely because I needed the legroom. Sean was behind the wheel, leaving the back seat to the others. Neagley was sitting behind Sean.

As soon as we'd climbed in, Sean had reached over and taken the Beretta we'd won from Reynolds out of the glove box. Neagley had studiously looked in the other direction as he checked it over and slid the gun into the side pocket of his jacket. I noticed she pulled her handbag with the .357 Smith & Wesson a little closer towards her, bringing the gun out just far enough to confirm it was loaded and ready to go. Habit, more than necessity.

Sean twisted in his seat.

"Have you ever had cause to use that for real?" he asked, nodding to the revolver.

Neagley hesitated, then shook her head. "Not really," she admitted. "I don't even take it to the range much."

"So why have it?"

"Because it's great for concealed carry and because I thought that if I ever *did* have to use it, something this size would stop a truck."

Sean smiled at her. "If Vaughan's in that damned Humvee of his, we might be glad of it."

"Just who *is* this Vaughan bastard?" Matt demanded. He was sitting hunched up, arms wrapped round his body like he was about to be physically sick.

"He's another ex Special Ops man," Neagley supplied. "Spent the best part of four decades with the US military, but he left in an all-fired hurry a couple of years back. Something to do with army supplies for the Gulf disappearing and turning up on the civilian market. They couldn't prove anything, but there was enough suspicion to get him kicked out."

I moved carefully round in my seat so I could see her face. "These stolen supplies wouldn't have been turning up at surplus outlets not unlike the Lucases' place, would they?" I asked and she nodded. "Well, that explains their connection, I suppose."

"Fuck that," Matt said sourly. "What the hell's he doing kidnapping Ella?"

"It all boils down to money," Neagley said. "Vaughan wants it. Ella's the key."

Matt rubbed his hands slowly over his face. "How I wish Simone had never bought that bloody ticket," he said. "You think it's going to be the answer to all your prayers, don't you? But it's been a nightmare from start to finish."

"And it's going to get worse before it gets better—one way or another," Neagley said grimly.

"Heads-up," Sean murmured. "Those look like Range Rover headlights."

He was right. The Lucases drove the length of the car park towards us very slowly, like they were looking for indications that we were going to cause them trouble along the way. I suppose I couldn't blame either of them for being nervous, under the circumstances.

The Range Rover came to a halt about ten metres away and I saw vague movement beyond the lights as both front doors opened.

Sean put his hand on the door handle and glanced sideways at me.

"Don't bother saying it," I warned. "I'm coming, too."

He shrugged and climbed out without a word, leaving me to make my own way.

Both sides met on the middle ground, like some kind of Cold War exchange. It was starting to snow again, I saw, tiny butterfly flakes that swirled in the combined beams of the lights from both vehicles, and it was colder than the grave. I thought the period in the car had warmed me through, but I quickly discovered it was all superficial. As soon as I was outside again, I froze down to my bones almost instantly.

It's just like Christmas, Mummy, Ella had said in Boston.

Not like Christmas now, Ella ...

Lucas and Sean approached until they were only a metre or so apart and stopped to stare at each other in the sparkling glow from the light-wrapped trees. Lucas waited until I'd haltingly closed up to them before he asked, "So who's this?" without taking his eyes off Sean.

"Sean Meyer," I said, short. "My boss."

"Ah." Lucas nodded slightly, barely a twitch, as though he knew if he made any sudden moves he was likely to get bitten.

Sean watched him, shoulders apparently relaxed, completely expressionless. Lucas's eyes kept flicking nervously to Sean's hands, which were buried in his coat pockets, as though he could sense the Beretta hidden beneath the material.

"We're wasting time," Rosalind said, the sharpness in her voice not quite masking something I took to be fear that vibrated along under the surface. "We know Felix has got Ella, for God's sake! What are we waiting for?"

Lucas, galvanised by the urgency in his wife's voice, started to move, clearly expecting us to follow.

"Hold it," Sean said quietly. "We're not going anywhere until we've got a few things settled."

Lucas threw him a look of pure distaste. "You want to haggle over a price for my granddaughter's life, is that it?" he jeered.

Matt pushed his way forwards. "She's my daughter," he said. "D'you really think we don't care what happens to her?"

Lucas stared at him, then let his eyes skim across the rest of us. I don't know what he expected to see there, because he made a brief gesture of impatience. "I don't need your help anyway," he muttered, turning his back and taking a step towards the Range Rover.

"You do need us, or you wouldn't be here," Sean said. "Maybe the Greg Lucas who served at Goose Green and Port Stanley might not need our help, but a salesman like John Ashworth certainly does."

Lucas arched and froze like he'd been speared between the shoulder blades. I saw his head move slightly, making eye contact with Rosalind. Her mouth thinned and she dropped her gaze, almost an admission of defeat.

Slowly, he turned back, and the man who faced us now was not the one who'd turned away only moments ago. His shoulders weren't so square—much less like the old soldier whose skin he'd been animating for the last twenty-odd years. Like he could finally stop pretending and it was something of a relief to him. He tried to raise a smile, but it never quite developed.

"So ... my secret's out," he said, and even his voice didn't seem quite the same, rusty and wry. "At last."

"Where's the real Lucas?"

"Dead, of course," he said, matter-of-fact.

"You killed him," Sean said, and it wasn't a question.

Lucas—somehow I couldn't think of him yet as anyone else—nodded. "But it was self-defence," he added quickly.

"Of course," Sean said blandly. "That's why you hid the body, stole his identity, and skipped the country leaving your baby daughter behind."

Something skittered across Lucas's face that might have been irritation, or guilt. "What does it matter now?" he asked, sounding suddenly tired. "What matters is Ella. If you're not going to help us then, as Rosalind pointed out, we're wasting time we don't have."

"We didn't say we weren't going to help," Sean said. He glanced over his shoulder at Neagley. She nodded, her face serious, and I waited for him to look to me, too, but I wasn't altogether surprised when he didn't. "Where is he likely to have taken her?"

"Felix has a place out on the 302 toward Bretton Woods," Rosalind said, stepping forwards. "It's isolated—no close neighbours. I'd guess that's where they'll be."

"And even if *she* isn't," Lucas said, grim, "that's certainly where Vaughan will be. I'm sure we can find a way to persuade him to tell us where his guys have taken her."

"I wouldn't be so sure about that," I said, and felt their focus on me. I shrugged. "From what I've seen of him, Vaughan isn't the kind of bloke who gives in easily, however much you try to bully him."

Lucas gave a short, mirthless laugh. "If I threaten to turn state's evidence against him, he'll cave, believe me," he said, ignoring the shocked glance from his wife, like she didn't think he had it in him.

"Is that what's made him take her now?" Sean asked. "Why's he waited this long to make his move?"

Lucas hesitated and it was Rosalind who took a deep breath and said, "Because he realised—as we do—that we're not going to be able to keep hold of Ella for much longer."

"What?" It was Matt who uttered the surprised question.

Rosalind gave him an old-fashioned look. "Surely your legal people have told you by now that your claim is much stronger than ours is—or was?" she added sadly. "Even before you started digging up the dirt on Greg."

"And, just as surely, you must have known there was a chance the truth would surface sooner or later, regardless?" Sean said.

She shrugged. "It hadn't so far," she threw back with a hint of defiance. "What would change?"

"You found out about Simone's money, and you got greedy," Matt said, disgust in his voice.

Rosalind didn't reply to that one, just flicked a glance at her husband that I couldn't fully discern the meaning of.

"Whatever you may think of my motives," Lucas said tightly, "Ella's in danger. If you're going to help, then let's go. We can settle anything else later."

"We'll take our vehicle," Sean said. "It's less distinctive and Vaughan won't recognise it." And he spoke to me directly for the first time since the Lucases had shown up. "You're not coming with us on this, Charlie," he murmured, putting his hands on my upper arms. Despite the softness of his voice, it was an order, not a suggestion. And when I would have argued anyway he said, brutal, "You're no use to me like this. We can't afford to carry anyone."

I swallowed, knowing he had a point and bitterly resenting that fact. "Yes, sir," I said, jerking myself out of his grasp. He let me go, or I never would have achieved it.

"Matt," Sean said. "I want you to take Charlie back to the apartment."

"But—"

"I need you to stay with her, OK?" he said, cutting across the other man very deliberately. "Wait for us there. If anything goes wrong, we'll need someone on the outside to call in the cavalry."

Matt shut up abruptly and nodded. He looked both disappointed and relieved to be ordered out of the action, and guilty over both emotions.

Sean's gaze swung back to me and I saw an understanding in the dark depths of his eyes.

He knows, I thought, panicked. *He knows what Reynolds tried to do to me and he doesn't want to risk him trying it again, if we should fail.*

"Take the Range Rover," Lucas said to him, curt in his generosity to the man who would, ultimately, rob him of his granddaughter. He threw the keys over, aiming high, and Matt caught them with a flinch before they would have struck him in the face.

He turned them over in his hands. "I've never driven left-hand-drive," he admitted, subdued. "Or an automatic transmission."

Lucas sighed and turned to his wife. "Rosalind, honey," he said gently, "you better take them."

"Greg, let me come with you," she said, urgent. "I can help. I can be useful. We can still come out of this—"

"I know," Greg said, his voice soothing. He reached out a hesitant hand and stroked her pale cheek. "But it's too late for all that now. All that matters is Ella."

Rosalind's face hardened and she stepped back out from under his touch in much the same way, I thought, that I must have done from Sean's.

"Very well," she said, almost snatching the keys out of Matt's hands.

We stood, the three of us, and watched as Sean got behind the wheel of the Explorer. Neagley and Lucas climbed aboard, and they drove quickly away into the darkness and the softly falling snow. We none of us moved until the big Ford's taillights had reached the end of the hotel car park and disappeared completely from view.

Then Rosalind eyed the pair of us with much the same disfavour she'd shown towards me and Neagley earlier that day.

"Get in," she said, jerking her head towards the Range Rover, still standing in the middle of the car park with its lights on and its doors open and nobody at home. If the plain resentment in her voice was anything to go by, I wasn't the only one who was completely and utterly pissed off to be left behind.

TWENTY-ONE

So, I don't suppose you'd care to tell us the whole story now, would you?" I asked as we drove down the sloping driveway away from the White Mountain Hotel.

Rosalind paused as she reached a junction, pretending a preoccupation with checking for other cars when the darkness would have made it easy to spot them. She was a slow and cautious driver, and I didn't think that was just down to the conditions.

"What 'whole story' is that?" she said, noncommittal.

"You've been married to the guy for fifteen years," I said, "and you were an army brat. You've spent most of your life around soldiers. There's no way Lucas could have kept up the pretence of being ex-SAS for long, Rosalind. Not in front of you."

In the glow from the car's instrument lighting I saw her suppress a small smile. A compliment's a compliment, after all. I was sitting alongside her in the front, with Matt relegated to the rear seat.

"You're right," she said. "But I knew he wasn't who he said he was, long before I married him."

"So why did you?" It was Matt who asked the question, sounding baffled. "You loved him, right?"

"Love?" Rosalind almost scoffed. Then her voice turned bitter. "Do you have any idea how hard it is for a woman to be in the kind of business I'm in?" she demanded as she pulled away. "After my daddy died I couldn't get anyone to deal with me on any account. We were going under and there were plenty of my daddy's so-called friends who were just waiting for that to happen so they could step in and buy up the business for a rock-bottom price."

We were driving past individually designed houses set close to the shoulder of the road, home lights spilling out brightly across the crystallised snow.

"So he was a figurehead," I said, almost to myself. "Weren't you worried someone else might spot him for a fake?"

She shrugged. "The British SAS has a certain reputation and I coached him some," she said with just a hint of a sneer in her voice. "As long as he talked quiet, stared hard, and didn't blink, people believed he was what he said he was."

"And he was," I agreed. "Or the real Lucas was, at any rate, if anyone cared enough to check the records. Speaking of which, did Greg ever tell you what happened to the real Lucas?"

We stopped at a junction and turned left, the road twisting through the trees looming over us, over a small flat bridge with steel barriers at either side.

"He was in the house alone, just Greg and Simone," she said at last, her voice dull, almost monotone. It took me a moment to realise when she said "Greg' she wasn't talking about the original.

"Simone was in her room. It was a tiny cottage somewhere in Scotland, he told me, a cheap rental, but they moved around a lot and they couldn't afford to be fussy. Lucas was searching for them, threatening them, but they'd been there six months and heard nothing. They thought they might be safe. They weren't."

"He found them."

She nodded, slowing again as we reached another junction, each one connecting to a larger road. This one had houses set back further into the woods, with mailboxes lining the edges of the road.

"Greg said there was a phone call that afternoon, but when he answered there was nobody there, and he knew that they were going to have to run again, and the child was just starting nursery and she was old enough to be making friends and Pam had a job that she enjoyed. And he knew they couldn't keep doing this forever."

"So he killed him."

Rosalind shook her head. "It wasn't like that," she said, softly bitter. "He started to gather up a few essentials, waiting for Pam to get home. He heard something upstairs and, when he went up to see, he found Lucas coming out of Simone's bedroom, carrying the child. She was terrified."

Rosalind paused again as we made another turn, each junction bringing us onto a larger road, heading towards the middle of North Conway. It was snowing harder now, big flakes that rushed towards the beams of the headlights like distant stars. The luxury of the Range Rover closed out the elements, separating us. We crossed a series of bridges over frozen water, the ice showing a dull grey between the pale snow of the banks.

"So he killed him," I said again. "How?"

She flicked me a fast glance and the tail of it cracked like a whip. "Lucas attacked him," she said, dogged, her speech becoming jerky, staccato. "Greg just defended himself, as best he could. Lucas was a trained killer, for God's sake, and Greg didn't want Simone to get hurt. They struggled. It was a tiny cottage and there was hardly any room. Lucas tripped, fell down the stairs, and Simone fell with him. She was screaming, but she didn't have a mark on her. His neck was broken. It was an accident, but what could Greg do?"

"He could have called the police and taken the consequences—if indeed there were consequences," I said. Self-defence was a plea that was sometimes accepted by the courts, as I had cause to know only too well.

If it was genuine.

"He panicked," Rosalind said, as though she had a bad taste in her mouth. "He and Lucas were similar enough in looks to pass for each other. He told me he sometimes wondered if that was what Pam saw in him—almost the same face but without the brutality."

"What about the body?" I said. "What happened to that?"

"Apparently, the cottage was pretty isolated," Rosalind said. "Greg knew there were plenty of places in the Scotch countryside to hide a body where it wouldn't be found easily."

"So he buried the real Lucas, took the dead man's identity, and scarpered over here," I said flatly. "That takes some forethought and planning. That's not just something you can do on the spur of the moment."

"Lucas had already planned it," Rosalind said. "Greg said that he found Lucas's car nearby. In the trunk was a bag, all packed, with his passport and airline tickets already booked for a flight the next day. Greg said he knew that Lucas had come north solely to kill Simone and his ex-wife—his last act before he left the country."

"I don't know how he could just walk out and leave Simone—an infant—on her own in the house, after she'd just witnessed a murder," Matt said, his voice paled with shock.

"She was young," Rosalind dismissed, braking for the traffic lights onto the main road now. She indicated right and edged out of the junction, even though it was on red. I still couldn't get used to the idea that you were allowed to do that over here. "Young enough to forget what she'd seen."

Blanked it out, more like. The human mind has a way of blanketing trauma, like growing a scab over an open wound. But all it took was a careless nudge and suddenly the scab was off and the wound was bleeding afresh …

"She remembered, didn't she?" I said quietly. "When Jakes took a tumble down your staircase and broke *his* neck, Simone remembered."

We were on the main street now, heading east, passing the Eastern Slope Inn and the old-fashioned Zeb's General Store, draped with lights that spoke of Christmas celebrations overrunning. I'd never felt less like celebrating anything.

"It was all my fault," Rosalind said quietly then. "Greg didn't tell me about the DNA test. I didn't want them to take it. I thought it would ruin everything. Greg never told me Lucas's daughter really was his, after all," she muttered, almost to herself. "He should have told me!"

I glanced across and found her face was filled with sorrow. I remembered her words that day at the house when we'd talked about her childless marriage. *It was never to be*, she'd said, wistful. Her grief now was not caused by her husband's sins of omission, I realised, but by her own. It was not the fact that the man she'd called Greg Lucas really did turn out to have a child. It was the fact that she did not.

"So how did you find out they'd taken the test?" I asked.

"The results arrived back by courier. Greg was out. I didn't know what they were and I was curious, so I opened them ... and then I knew he'd lied to me, all these years."

You should have been expecting that, Rosalind. His whole life's been a lie since before he ever met you ...

"So you rang Simone at the hotel," I said. "Why? What was that going to achieve? If it was the money you were after, surely your best course would have been to keep quiet and say nothing. Simone was already convinced Greg was her father, and she turned out to be right. Why spill the beans?"

"I was jealous," she said simply. "And hurt, and angry. So, I told her to come to the house because the results were back ... and then I told her the truth."

I sucked in a breath. "Which part of it?"

"I told her that Greg wasn't really Greg Lucas," she said, a tremor in her voice. "And I also told her that he'd killed the man she thought of as her father."

"Does that mean," I said carefully, "that you neglected to tell her the part about Greg actually being her *real* father?"

There was a long pause while we drove on, Rosalind's eyes fixed so firmly on the taillights of the car ahead that she couldn't possibly actually be looking at them. Then she said, barely audible, "Yes."

My God, I thought. *That would have been enough to send anyone off at the deep end.* I was suddenly overwhelmed by tiredness that went bone-deep. *What a waste. What a bloody awful waste.*

"And how did she react to that?"

"She went crazy," Rosalind said, sounding not surprised exactly but maybe slightly awed at the force of Simone's reaction. "She went for me with her claws out. I ran upstairs to try and get to my bedroom—at least there's a lock on the door—but she caught up with me before I'd reached the top of the stairs and she was screaming because she was angry, and Ella was screaming because she was frightened. Then the bodyguard she had with her— Jakes—he came to try and break us up."

She paused again, took a deep shaky breath. "I don't think she meant to hit him, but somehow she did and he fell ... and I knew as soon as I saw him hit the floor that he was dead. And then Greg walked in and Simone looked at him, standing over Jakes's body in the hallway, and then she *really* lost it."

I thought back to the words I'd heard that night and even I had to admit that it all fitted. I glanced back over my shoulder. Matt was sitting behind Rosalind, leaning forwards so his head was almost between the front seats. He was listening with a mix of emotions playing round his thin features, from anger to disbelief to an all-engulfing grief. I could see the tears had finally broken cover and were running freely down his cheeks, but he didn't seem to be aware of them and made no moves to brush them away. I closed my heart to his pain and pressed on, regardless.

"So how did you all get from the upper floor to the basement?" I said.

Rosalind glanced at me. "I shouted to Greg that Simone had gone crazy, that she had killed her own bodyguard and I needed his help. He bolted for his gun safe in the basement but—"

"What about that Smith & Wesson revolver? Wasn't he still carrying it?"

She looked momentarily surprised. "No," she said slowly, frowning. "I suppose he can't have been. He doesn't always."

We'd turned off the main street now and were starting to thread through the quieter residential side roads leading towards Mount Cranmore. The lights for the ski runs were clearly visible, stretching above us.

"So he got to his gun safe and pulled a gun," I prompted. "What then?"

"He couldn't do it," Rosalind said, her voice barely audible. "It didn't matter than Simone could have killed me as well as Jakes. He let her walk right up to him and take the gun out of his hand." She glanced sideways again. "And then you arrived and, well, I guess you pretty much know the rest."

Not really ...

"I don't suppose," I said, "that you happened to mention any of this to Detective Young after Simone was killed?"

Rosalind shook her head. "How could I and still protect Greg's identity?" she said, mournful. "And what good would it have done? My duty was to the living."

"Including Ella?"

"Of course," Rosalind said, brusque. "She may not be mine—in any sense of the word," she added with a rueful little half smile, "but I've come to love her like she was my own. I'm sure we both do."

"So why let Greg take her? If he's so fond of his granddaughter, why did he use her like a human shield out there in the forest?"

Rosalind made the final turn into the car park and slotted the Range Rover into a parking space outside the apartment, right next to Neagley's Saturn, putting the gear lever into neutral.

"He's not a professional soldier, Charlie," she said, with just a hint of the patronising in her voice. "He was frightened and he genuinely thought that by taking the child he could get her to safety. After all, it was *you* who brought her down to the basement and put her into danger."

I sat for a moment without speaking, working through what she'd said and trying to get it straight in my own head. Matt was silent behind us. I unclipped my seatbelt and turned to face Rosalind.

"You're good," I said, reflective. "Very good, in fact."

"Excuse me?"

"Very convincing," I said. "You damned near had me convinced, that's for sure. I think claiming Simone was the one who hit Jakes was over-egging it a little, but otherwise you play the loyal wife and the doting grandmother almost to perfection. Academy Award stuff, really."

She tensed and her eyes narrowed. "What the hell are you talking about?" she said, almost a growl. "I've told you nothing but the truth."

I gave a short laugh devoid of mirth. "Oh there might be some truth mixed up in there, but it's been so watered down with the lies, it's difficult to tell."

Her mouth opened, closed again. "Frankly, Charlie, I don't really care much one way or the other what you think." She reached down to unclip her seatbelt. "What matters at the moment is Ella."

"Of course it does," I agreed. "And the ten million dollars you hope to get for her. This has nothing to do with Felix Vaughan, has it, Rosalind?" I raised an eyebrow but she didn't answer. "That's just a wild-goose chase."

"I—"

"Oliver Reynolds—it is *you* he's working for, isn't it?" I cut across her, my voice turning harsh. "Just remember one thing, Rosalind. If he hurts her, I will kill you myself."

Rosalind's face was blank for a moment longer before it twisted into a derisive smile. She brought her hand back up again—the one that had been fiddling with her seatbelt—only now there was a 9mm Beretta in it, and she was pointing it firmly in my direction.

"Oh yes?" she said silkily. "And just how do you propose to do that?"

I mentally cursed myself for not seeing that one coming and made sure I kept my hands very still.

"Give me a minute and I'm sure I'll think of something," I said, and she snorted.

"How did you know? I thought I'd covered all the bases."

I nodded towards the apartment building in front of us. "You never asked directions," I said. "But Reynolds knows where we are. He paid us a visit." I eyed the gun but she held it confidently, relaxed, like she was only too familiar with handling and firing a weapon. Hardly surprising when I thought about her background. Shame I hadn't thought about it earlier. "If you'd kept up the outraged innocence, you might even have got away with it."

A flicker of annoyance skimmed across her face. Then she shrugged. "Ah well," she said. "Too late for that now."

There was a moment of silence while the big, fat snowflakes floated down softly and lay on the windscreen and died in the residual warmth coming up through the glass.

I sat quiet in my seat with my right hand lying in my lap and felt the sharp throbbing in my back that had been there since the shooting, and the dull ache in my left leg that never quite seemed to go away.

Oh, I knew all the theories for dealing with armed opponents. I'd studied the methods and in the past I'd practised until the bruises wrote their own record, but it was always a last resort. Besides, any of the moves I knew

292

required outstanding speed and strength and agility, and at the moment I was severely lacking in all three.

I thought of Matt, frozen in shock or fear—or quite possibly both—in the rear seat, but I resisted the urge to glance at him and draw Rosalind's attention there. He'd come to my rescue with Reynolds, but Matt wasn't a fighter by either instinct or training. I couldn't—and didn't—expect him to butt in now.

I looked up.

"What is it that you want, Rosalind?"

She smiled, recognising my capitulation for what it was, and rooted in her coat pocket with her left hand, quickly pulling out her mobile phone. She keyed in a number without having to take her eyes off me. All the time the gun never wavered.

"Just in case you get any ideas," she said, tucking the phone up to her ear while the call rang out, "my daddy taught me well and I'm a very good shot. Not up to your standard, probably, but at this distance I hardly need to be. Of course, I'd rather not make any additional holes in this car, if I can help it, but if it comes down to it, well—" she shrugged, careless, '—the lease agreement's in Greg's name."

Tinnily, I heard the phone answered. Rosalind's face was tense now, but she never dropped her guard.

"Get me Felix Vaughan," she said, clipped. My heart started to canter at an uneven rhythm, accelerating. "Felix? ... It's Rosalind. Oh, let's dispense with the pleasantries, shall we? I have a proposition for you."

The voice at the other end—obviously Vaughan—gave some short indication of assent.

"I want my business back, Felix," Rosalind said, her voice ringing with conviction like struck steel. "No, that old threat won't work anymore," she interrupted when he began to speak again. "Greg's about to be unmasked anyway. That's right ... the bodyguard." She said the words looking right at me, contempt rich in her voice.

293

There was a long pause and I could picture Felix Vaughan taking the information in, sifting through it, analysing the content, looking for the angles.

"Yes, I know the agreement's watertight, Felix, believe me. What I'm proposing is a trade," Rosalind said when he began to speak again. My chest tightened. I knew where this was going. There could only be one outcome. "You sign the business back over to me and I'll give you something much more valuable in exchange—Ella."

Vaughan's derision was clear. Rosalind cut across him like a razor, so sharp he didn't feel the slice of the blade until it was already through his skin. "She's worth approximately twenty-five million dollars, Felix. The money was Simone's, but Ella is, after all, her only heir. I'll give you an hour to think about it. Then call me. Oh, and as a gesture of good faith, I think I should warn you that Greg is on his way over there now. He's got a couple of hired guns with him. Professionals." She gave a tight little smile. "Yes, I'm sure you will, Felix." And she ended the call without saying good-bye.

In the back seat, Matt began to hyperventilate like he was about to have an asthma attack.

"You bitch," he muttered. "How could you just—just *sell* her off like that? What kind of a monster are you?"

"The desperate kind," Rosalind said calmly.

Matt started to curse her then, getting louder and more fluent as he got into his stride. Rosalind sighed and twisted a little further round in her seat so her back was more against the window glass and she could keep both of us in view.

"Don't make me shoot you just to shut you up," she said to him, her dispassionate tone silencing him better than venom would ever have done.

She stiffened as another car turned into the parking area, its lights sweeping across us. For a moment I entertained a tiny glimmer of absurd hope that it was Sean and Neagley, who'd somehow seen through Lucas's story—

and Rosalind's trap—and come back to rescue us. The car drove past and disappeared round the end of the next apartment block.

"OK," Rosalind said. "Let's go inside. Who has the keys?"

For a moment neither of us spoke.

"You're not just making things worse for yourselves by being awkward," Rosalind said, holding the mobile phone up. "Perhaps you'd like to consider Ella's welfare."

"I've got the keys," Matt said, speaking fast and a little breathless. He fumbled in his pocket and brought them out, his hands shaking so badly that they jingled on their ring. "Just don't let him hurt her. Please."

Rosalind made no moves to take the keys. "We're all going to go inside—you first," she said. "We'll be right behind you."

Matt scrambled down out of the Range Rover's back seat, too frightened to get creative. As soon as he was out of the car, I said softly, "I meant what I said. If you hurt Ella, I *will* kill you. You do know that, don't you?"

Rosalind gave me an assessing glance, one hand on the door handle.

"If I was foolish enough to give you the opportunity?" she said. "Yes, I reckon you would."

I took my time about getting out of my side, exaggerating it, trying to give Matt time to do something. I'm not entirely sure what I expected of him, exactly. But he didn't do it, anyway.

Eventually, Rosalind tired of my tactics, moving in behind me and kicking into the back of my left knee. The leg buckled and I collapsed against the side of the Range Rover, gasping. I let go of the crutch, which bounced off the bodywork and clattered onto the icy ground.

"Pick it up," Rosalind said to Matt. "And quit stalling," she added to me. "Get inside before I lose my patience completely."

This time, the way I hobbled to the door to the apartment didn't have to be feigned. It was eight degrees below freezing that night, but by the time we reached the doorway I was sweating under my coat.

Rosalind stayed well back from the pair of us, keeping the gun steady. At some point during the walk from the car, she'd taken the time to screw a suppressor to the end of the Beretta's barrel, very like the one Reynolds had used when he'd made his abortive attempt to snatch Ella from the house. At least I now knew where he shopped for his weaponry. All those ex-military M9 Berettas. I hadn't given it a second thought.

She kept us standing in the hallway while she moved further into the lounge area, sweeping books off the coffee table and even the scatter cushions off the sofa before she motioned the pair of us to sit there. Not giving us anything we could throw, however lightweight, to distract her.

"What now?" Matt asked, trying to control the waver in his voice and not quite succeeding.

"We wait," Rosalind said. She sat in one of the chairs opposite and pulled the mobile phone out of her coat pocket again. She keyed in a different number rather than hitting redial, her eyes flicking to her wristwatch before she put the phone up to her ear.

"It's me," she said when the call was answered. "How's our little guest behaving?"

Reynolds.

I felt Matt stiffen alongside me, felt him draw breath and hold it, trying to hear what was being said even though he knew he didn't stand a chance.

"Good, let's hope she stays that way," Rosalind said now, giving the pair of us a cold straight look.

There was another burst of speech that might have been agitated, or it might just have been the quality of the speaker in the handset.

"Not much longer," Rosalind said in reply, soothing. "Listen, I may need you to arrange another nice little auto accident for me—Charlie and the child's father." A smile. "Yes, I thought you might. By all means make it look that

296

way. I'll bring them down to you shortly. Who?" The smile widened. "Oh, I've sent Sean Meyer and Greg off on a wild-goose chase. Divide and conquer. They won't be any trouble." The smile blinked out. "When *I'm* ready. Just you be ready to move the child. I've offered her to Felix Vaughan. Oh, you'll still get paid. Don't worry about that. Just make sure she's ready to go in an hour." And she ended the call. Clearly not one for long good-byes, Rosalind.

"Where is she?" The question fought its way past Matt's clenched teeth, as though he'd been trying to force himself not to beg.

"Somewhere safe, nearby," Rosalind said, putting the phone away, giving him a look that clearly said he wasn't going to get any more than that out of her.

"I assume from that," I said, "that you and the charming Mr Reynolds were behind Barry O'Halloran's crash."

She nodded.

Frances Neagley would be relieved to find out the truth behind her partner's death, I thought. If only I could be sure I was going to live long enough to tell her the news.

"What happened, Rosalind? You decided to get rid of him and then you found out about the money, was that it?"

"Something like that," she agreed. "I thought it was too risky for Greg to meet with her, but I let him talk me into it—of course, I didn't realise at the time why he was so keen on that." She shook her head, almost crossly. "I wanted just to let Reynolds get in there and snatch the child from the start, keep us out of it, but Greg hightailed it down to Boston with his tongue hanging out. Couldn't wait to bring her back up here and parade her in front of me." She let her breath out fast, annoyed. "Maybe it would have been simpler all round if I'd gotten Reynolds to arrange an accident for Greg instead."

"Very probably," I said. I paused and only kept my voice neutral by sheer force of will. "You're very patient, keeping Reynolds on when he bungled Ella's kidnap first in Boston, and then again at the house. Must have been quite a shock for you when I caught him."

"I told him to make sure he took care of you first," she said, shaking her head. "He was lucky I managed to help him get loose while you were downstairs. Good thing Greg *isn't* a soldier, or we'd never have gotten away with it right under his nose like that." She allowed herself a small smile. "Reynolds sure wasn't happy, though. You made yourself quite an enemy there."

I matched my tone to hers and there was no warmth in any of it. "If Reynolds has something special planned for us, it's going to be hard to make it look like just another accident."

"Oh, you'd be amazed what can be covered up by a good strong fire," she said.

"Sean will know."

She smiled with every indication of amusement. "What makes you think he won't be dead by then, too?"

TWENTY-TWO

A n hour goes by very slowly when you have nothing to do but sit and listen to every second of it pass, and wait for an opportunity that never comes. I tried to tell myself that there would be a better chance, somewhere along the line, but that didn't help Sean and Neagley now, on their way to Vaughan's place out towards Bretton Woods. And it didn't help Ella.

Rosalind was not a nervous waiter. She sat without impatience, without signs of anxiety, without apparent fatigue. She sat and watched us and kept the gun pointed in our direction firmly enough that there was no window.

Matt disintegrated visibly as time wore on. Somewhere around the thirty-minute mark he began to weep, quietly, into his hands. Whether for himself or his daughter I didn't ask, but I'd prefer to think his tears were for Ella.

"What will you do with your husband?" I asked Rosalind. "Providing, of course, that Vaughan doesn't kill him for you."

She shrugged. "The truth about him is bound to come out now, one way or another," she said. "If he had stayed away from Simone, well, who knows? But I assume you have people in England who've been digging out your information for you and I can't silence them all." Another shrug, indifferent. "He's brought this on himself."

I nodded. "So now his usefulness is over." I glanced at her impassive face. "You would have been happier, wouldn't you, if I'd shot him that night in the forest?"

"Yes," she said without hesitation. "And you were so close, Charlie. So *close*. I saw what you could do on the range that day and I couldn't believe it when you didn't take the shot." Her lips twisted. "Very disappointing. I really thought you had it in you."

"I wasn't about to blow anyone's brains out when he was so close to a child," I said sharply. "She—"

And my voice deserted me as my brain stopped driving it, suddenly entirely diverted onto another track like it had swerved off a highway and gone crashing into an ice-cold river. My eyes flew to Rosalind's and her smile widened.

"Well, well," she murmured. "You finally got it. I was beginning to think I was going to have to come right out and say it."

"It was you who shot me," I whispered.

"That's right," she said, pride overlapping. "Must have been at least forty yards, in poor light, moving target. One heck of a piece of shooting, even if I do say so myself."

"Not particularly," I said. "After all, I'm not dead yet."

Her satisfaction dimmed. "As good as," she said, gesturing with the barrel of the Beretta. "Look at you, Charlie, all crocked up. What use are you to anyone? Didn't the British Army teach you that old rule about it being better to wound an enemy soldier than to kill him?"

"Yes they did," I said, remembering Sean telling me much the same thing as we left the hospital. My reply to him still stood. *That only applies if the soldier can't fight, Rosalind. Give me half a chance and then see what I can still manage ...*

Matt had raised his blotchy face from his hands, confused. "But they said Simone shot you," he said unsteadily, his eyes streaked with red. "That's why the police killed her. She shot you." His insistence was almost childlike. *Say it isn't so.*

I shook my head, gently. "Rosalind did it," I said. I turned back to her. "How did you fool the ballistics people?

The police told me the gun they found with Simone was a match."

"She dropped it in the snow and they didn't find it right away—what with the EMTs scrambling around working on you," she said. "Did you know your heart stopped at the scene, by the way?"

I shook my head again. "No, I didn't." I gave her a tight little smile. "I suppose then, technically, you did kill me."

She pulled a face. "So anyway, what with all the confusion, it wasn't hard to get the gun I'd been using into Simone's hand. All it needed was for you not to make it, and the whole thing would have been neat and tidy. But, they called in the LifeFlight helicopter and flew you over to Lewiston and damn me if they didn't put you back together again."

I was silent. I thought of the shadowy figure I'd registered watching me as I lay bleeding into the bottom of that ditch, and of the doctor with the perfect smile. I thought of Simone, bursting through the trees with the wild look in her eyes and the gun held rigid out in front of her— of how it had looked and how it was. And I thought of Ella's terrified face when I'd been moments from killing her grandfather and, at some level, she'd known what I was contemplating.

Is that why you hurt Charlie? she'd asked when Neagley and I had gone back to see Rosalind. I'd thought Ella meant the slap in the face, but she must have seen who was behind me ...

And finally, I remembered Reynolds's words that day right here in this very room. *I wonder what will happen,* he'd said, *if I put another round through your leg in just the same place as the last ...*

At the time I'd had too many other things on my mind for that last piece of information to penetrate. How could he have known the details of exactly how I was shot, unless someone had told him? Someone who'd been there at the time and seen it happen.

When I looked up again I found Rosalind checking her watch. She got to her feet, smoothing down her clothes. As businesslike and no-nonsense as she'd been since our first meeting.

"OK," she said. "Time's up. Let's go."

I'd stiffened with sitting for so long and getting up off the sofa again was a struggle. Matt hooked his hand under my elbow and for once I didn't shrug off the assistance. Rosalind watched from across the room, her expression cynical as the pair of us staggered upright.

"She can manage—get the door," she said sharply, and Matt dropped my arm right away, obeying without hesitation. He looked beaten. His eyelashes were so wet they had clumped together, and the end of his nose had turned very red.

No help there, then.

As I made my way across the room behind him, limping heavily, my mind was turned inwards, and it was burning.

I needed a way out, and right now the prospects for that looked slim enough to qualify as anorexic.

***

Rosalind forced Matt to drive us back down to the main street and out on Route 302 towards Intervale. I sat in the front seat alongside him, with Rosalind in the back this time, where she could cover the pair of us with the Beretta.

Matt was an awful driver, slow and jerky even with the Range Rover's automatic transmission and cushioned ride. He had no idea how to judge the width of the vehicle or place it on the road, and he wandered alarmingly.

Eventually, Rosalind jammed the silenced end of the Beretta against the base of his skull and growled at him to quit messing around. I thought Matt was going to burst into tears again at any moment.

"Ease up on him," I snapped over my shoulder. "He's never driven on the wrong side of the road before."

"And if he carries on like this," Rosalind said grimly, "he never will again."

The snow had stopped coming down now and already people with pickup trucks that had snowploughs attached to the front of them were out clearing the streets. There was a quiet efficiency to it all, a kind of small-town neighbourliness that was totally at odds with the woman in the back seat. I wondered when her determination to succeed with her father's business had passed over into the kind of obsession that meant she was willing to shoot someone in the back and use a four-year-old child as a pawn in the game.

We didn't talk again until Rosalind instructed Matt to turn off the main road into the parking area for the surplus store. It was well past closing time, but there were still lights on inside the building, although there were no tyre tracks in the fresh coating of snow in front of it. Matt nosed the Range Rover gingerly into a space at the side and braked to a halt.

"What now?" he said, swallowing. "Where's Ella?"

"She's inside—being well looked after, don't you worry about that," Rosalind said, and something about the way she said it made my skin shimmy over my bones.

Reynolds. The images of what he might be doing to Ella twisted and writhed and shrieked through my subconscious.

I heard the muted bleep of a mobile phone dialling and knew without turning round that Rosalind was calling Vaughan again. She'd said she'd give him an hour to make his decision and that time was gone. It was so quiet inside the car I could hear the sound of the phone ringing out at the other end of the line.

"Felix? … It's me again," Rosalind said, and her voice had a rich quality to it, gloating, riding a crest of self-confidence. She chuckled. "Oh, I'm sorry—are you entertaining guests? I kinda thought you might be, by now."

I was aware of a leaden weight in my chest. Until then I'd clung to a slight conceited notion that Sean and Neagley and Lucas might somehow have avoided the trap Rosalind had engineered at Vaughan's place out near Bretton Woods. I'd become so used to Sean's abilities that I'd expected too much this time. They'd thought they were going in under cover of stealth and surprise, only to find they were thoroughly expected. Even so, I'd held out an unrelenting sliver of hope that Sean had sidestepped the trap and prevailed.

I heard Vaughan's muttered response, not clearly enough to discern the words, but I picked up a vibration in them nevertheless. I heard the quick hiss of Rosalind's indrawn breath, and when she spoke again her voice was harder and flatter than it had been before. "What do you mean, you've been having a nice little chat with them?" she demanded. "Felix, you can't possibly listen to—" and she was cut off abruptly as Felix Vaughan clearly told her what he thought of being given orders.

Matt kept his eyes fixed on the front windscreen, shoulders hunched and hands on the wheel, like he was still driving. I risked a glance back and found Rosalind sitting stiffly upright, her whole body practically trembling with rage.

"You'll regret this, Felix," she snapped. "Greg won't be around much longer anyway—did they tell you that? You think you're showing solidarity with your old comrade in arms and he wasn't even a soldier, just some goddamn salesman!"

My eyes dropped surreptitiously to the Beretta in her right hand, but she caught the gesture and brought the gun up, glaring at me. She looked agitated enough to shoot me out of sheer temper, just to let off steam. I quickly faced forwards again.

"Well, you can pass on a message to that worthless no-account husband of mine," she said now, low and bitter. "You tell him he's going home to England after all these years and he's going to jail for what he did, and his precious little granddaughter's going home with him—in a box."

She ended the call and sat for a moment, fighting for calm, breathing hard. I heard the hitch in it and realised that she was crying. Beside me, Matt's shoulders had begun to quiver.

"She's only four," he said brokenly. "For God's sake show some compassion ..."

"Oh, spare me the woe-is-me crap," Rosalind told him, harsh. "If you want to feel sorry for anyone, feel it for yourselves. I don't know what kind of a deal your boyfriend worked out with Felix, Charlie, but he's just ensured that the pair of you won't last the night."

"You were planning on having Reynolds kill us anyway," I pointed out.

"True," she said, and I heard the smile in her voice. "But now he doesn't have to make it look accidental, he can have some fun with you first."

She ordered us out of the Range Rover, Matt first and me after. The cold numbed me again as soon as I opened the car door. It was like I'd never been warm. I slid clumsily to the ground and fumbled with my crutch.

Rosalind began urging us towards the entrance to the store, to where Ella was stashed away and Reynolds awaited. Was he alone? Or did he have the same guy with him who'd been there in the Lucases' house the night they'd first tried to snatch Ella?

I knew to get out of this I needed speed and strength and right now I didn't have either. So, what did I have?

Motivation. Experience. Technique.

Motivation. If I didn't get out of this soon, I was going to die. Matt was going to die. I tried not to think about the method. And while Vaughan might have decided not to accept Rosalind's offer of a trade, that didn't mean he and Sean and Neagley were suddenly bosom pals.

As for Ella, the time when she might have been sold to the highest bidder was way past—if, indeed, it had ever been realistic in the first place. The chances of her surviving the ransom exchange had been poor. Even if Harrington and whoever else was in charge of Simone's money had agreed to pay. Harrington might have claimed to be concerned for Ella's welfare, but big organisations like his bank tended to have very strict rules about refusing to give in to kidnappers. I imagined them cold-bloodedly discussing the matter over a nice Merlot in a smart restaurant somewhere in Soho and I knew then I would die fighting before I let that happen to her. To any of us.

Matt reached the outer doorway to the store and opened it, looking back over his shoulder as if anxious to please. I shuffled forwards another step. Rosalind moved in behind me.

Experience. This wasn't the first time people had tried to kill me, up close and personal. I had the scars to prove it. And not just the one on my neck that Ella had been so curious about that day in her pink bedroom in London.

Rosalind nodded to Matt and he swung the inner door open. That one hinged outwards, into the lobby area. To open it he had to step back. I stopped abruptly and sensed Rosalind close up unintentionally at my back. Her focus was beyond me, on Matt, anxious that he didn't make any sudden moves once we got inside.

Technique. Rosalind was less than a metre behind me, holding the Beretta in her right hand. She kept herself in shape, but she was a sixty-year-old woman who'd put all her faith in the gun she was carrying and who had never been through the military machine in all its nasty glory.

She was also angry, and so close to home turf she'd already begun to relax. I gambled everything on the fact that while she might know how to shoot, she didn't know how to fight.

I dropped my crutch, letting it fall away sideways, shifted my weight onto my good leg and pivoted to face her. The shock that I would try something so stupid, when she had a gun and I didn't, froze her for a vital half a second.

Then she started to bring the Beretta up, knuckles whitening as her grip tightened.

I reached over the suppressor and grabbed hold of the top of the slide with my left hand and pushed back as hard as I could manage. Not very, all things considered, but I was counting on Rosalind's instinct and, sure enough, she immediately pushed against me.

Between the two of us shoving at it, the Beretta's slide moved back fractionally in relation to the frame, opening up the breech and breaking the positive lock. I could feel the bunching as Rosalind's finger clenched round the trigger, but as long as the breech is open, however minutely, most semiautomatic pistols will not fire. When nothing happened, she didn't understand enough about the mechanics to realise why. Her mouth sagged open.

Still with my hand on top of the slide, I forced the gun out sideways, twisting the end of the muzzle to my left, away from me. Her grip on the gun lessened very slightly. I was working against the natural flexion of her joints and her finger was still inside the trigger guard, trapped there.

Too late, she began to counter me, starting to turn to her right to ease the pressure I was putting on her hand in general, and her trigger finger in particular. I couldn't afford to let her get further than that. Couldn't afford a straight fair fight. Not with Ella's life at stake.

Motivation.

With a final jerk, I twisted the gun round so the steel trigger guard bit hard against her tethered finger. I held her there, teetering, just until I saw the realisation sink in, then completed the move.

Her right index finger fractured cleanly halfway between her knuckle and the first joint. By the time the real pain hit and she began to scream, I had the pistol grip firm in my own fist and the end of the extended barrel pointing square at the centre of her body mass.

307

Rosalind fell back, keening, cradling her injured right hand across her chest with her left. Disbelief that she'd been beaten, and fear of that defeat, amplified her distress.

I took a halting step after her and brought the Beretta up, swapping to a double-handed grip now. My right arm was already trembling with the weight of the gun and the effort of aiming it. The only way I could be sure of my shot was to jam the end of the suppressor against Rosalind's mouth, forcing her lips open, hearing the click of the steel against her teeth.

For the longest moment we stood like that, suspended almost. I felt every quivering muscle in my arm begin to tighten and felt no hesitation or regret. There was only a fierce roaring glory somewhere in the back of my mind.

"Charlie, for God's sake!" Matt yelped. "You can't!"

"I can," I said through my teeth. "She tried to kill me. She even succeeded, however briefly. She's responsible for Simone's death. Oh, I could kill her like swatting a fly, Matt, trust me."

Right at that second I was consumed by the enormous and almost irresistible desire to squeeze that trigger and watch her lifeless body fall. To hell with the legal system. To hell with the security cameras that I knew covered the inside of the store. I wanted justice. I wanted revenge. And I wanted it now …

And then cold, hard realities seeped in. Cold enough and hard enough to have me dropping the Beretta away from Rosalind's startled face and stumbling back away from her until I had the support of the nearest wall. I found I was in the far corner of the small lobby area, but I didn't remember getting there.

"Don't worry, Matt," I managed. "I said I *could* kill her, but I'm not going to." I shook my head. "She's an evil bitch and I hope they electrocute or poison her, or whatever the hell it is they do to people over here who've committed murder, but that doesn't mean I have to do their dirty work for them."

Rosalind sagged against the outer glass, cradling her injured hand. Her face was wet with tears but she didn't seem to be aware that she was crying again, from pain and shock this time, rather than frustration. I looked round, exhausted, and found my crutch was lying too far away for me to reach. Matt had to retrieve it for me. He helped Rosalind to her feet and the three of us finally made it into the store proper.

"Where's Ella, Rosalind?" I demanded, more quietly now. For a moment I thought she wasn't going to answer. Then she seemed to come out of her daze.

"In the back," she said. "In the stockroom. I don't know exactly. Reynolds didn't say."

"Matt," I said, "find me something we can tie her with, would you?"

"But she's got a broken finger," he pointed out.

"So? She was going to kill the pair of us."

"Oh … yeah. OK."

"And find me a swivel chair," I said. "Preferably one with castors on the bottom."

He disappeared behind the counter and was soon back with a roll of brown packing tape and a typist's chair with a high back and two sturdy-looking arms that came out from the underneath of the frame. One wheel squeaked slightly as he pushed it towards me.

I gave Rosalind a rough shove in the chest and she sat down heavily.

"Oh," Matt said, surprise in his voice, and when I glanced at him he gave an embarrassed shrug. "I thought the chair was for you."

I bit back a laugh, not sure if I'd be able to stop once I started, and kept the gun on her while Matt taped her in. The packing tape turned out not to be the no-noise type and every piece we ripped off the roll seemed horribly loud inside the empty store.

It only took a few minutes before we had Rosalind's wrists and ankles bound with enough tape to ensure that, if we'd mailed her, she would have arrived intact in just about any country, anywhere in the world.

"Now what do we do with her?"

"We leave her," I said. "We have to find Ella."

"And what will you do then, Charlie?" Rosalind threw at me, disdainful. "You might have gotten the jump on Reynolds once, but he won't make the same mistake twice. He's got someone with him—a professional—and he'll be ready for you this time."

"Like you were, you mean," I said with more bravado than I felt. "We'll take our chances." I glanced at Matt. "Tape her mouth."

Matt stuck a last piece of the packing tape across Rosalind's lips. I patted down her pockets, retrieving her mobile phone and a spare magazine for the Beretta out of her inside coat pocket.

"Do we leave her here?"

I jerked my head towards the entrance. "Outside. I don't want her causing any trouble."

"It's freezing out there," Matt protested.

I looked at him. "Good," I said. "It should slow her down a bit."

He grabbed Rosalind's shoulders without further comment, wheeling her out through the lobby into the snowy car park. After a few moments he returned.

"I stuck her round the side of the building so she won't be seen from the road so easily," he said, still looking uncomfortable. He took a deep shaky breath. "Look, Charlie, shouldn't we just call the police and let them handle this?"

He kept his voice low and his eyes skimmed nervously over me, the Beretta sagging by my side now. The gun itself weighed less than a kilo—thirty ounces, and the suppressor only another seven ounces. So why did they feel so heavy?

"Call them," I said, nodding to the phone by the till on the counter. "But by the time they get here Ella could be dead."

He looked at the phone for a moment, but made no moves towards it.

"What can we do?"

"We can find her and persuade Reynolds to hand her over," I said, matter-of-fact, calm, and with far more confidence than I could probably justify.

"OK," he said, his face very white. "What do you want me to do?"

The counter was glass topped and held an array of hunting knives with wicked-looking serrated blades. "Pick a weapon," I said. "You might need it."

Matt's eyes strayed along the collection, but he shook his head. "I-I don't think I could use one of those things," he said in a small voice. "I'm sorry."

"OK," I said. "Just stay close behind me and watch my back."

My jacket seemed soaked through with sweat and I shrugged out of it, letting it drop onto the floor. I thumbed the magazine out of the Beretta and checked it. The standard M9 magazine held fifteen rounds and the spare was filled to capacity, too. Well, at least I wasn't going to run out of ammunition. I shoved the spare magazine into the side pocket of my sweatpants.

The last thing I did was unscrew the suppressor from the end of the barrel and drop it onto the counter.

"Don't you need that?" Matt asked. "I mean, to keep things quieter or something?"

I glanced at him. "I can do without the extra weight," I said.

He nodded, like that made sense to him.

"OK," I said, dredging up a poor excuse for a smile. "Let's get this over with."

We moved towards the back of the store. Towards the doorway that led to the stockrooms and the gun range. Someone seemed to have moved it further away than it had been the last time I'd been there. My every step dragged and I could feel my breath rasping in my chest from the struggle with Rosalind. I was horribly out of shape, and I knew it.

Horribly vulnerable, and I knew that, too.

I'd told Matt that we could persuade Reynolds to hand over Ella, but that wasn't true. He had nothing to gain by giving up his last best bargaining tool. In reality, to get Ella back we were going to have to take her. And that could only mean a fight of some kind.

The first time Reynolds and I had clashed—at the Lucases' house—I'd had the element of surprise and I'd physically overpowered him. I experienced that same tingle of regret, that I'd had his life balanced in my hands, literally, and hadn't taken it.

The next time—in the apartment—he'd had all the advantages and the fact that I'd escaped relatively unscathed had been down to luck more than anything else.

This time I couldn't afford to let him get close to me. I couldn't afford to let *anyone* get close enough to tackle me, or I was going to go down and it was all going to be over. Not just for me, but for Ella as well.

Ella.

I'd killed before, but never in cold blood. The one time I'd set out to deliberately take a life, I'd faced my target and bottled out at the last moment, unable to complete what was, in effect, an execution. And somehow I'd clung to that very hesitation as though it were the final proof that I wasn't quite the psychopath my father feared I had become.

Ella.

I could only hope that the prospect of saving the child would be the spur I needed now.

I moved forward cautiously, trying not to let my left foot scuff against the thin carpeting. All the time, I was aware that my heart rate was still too high, the thump of my blood making my hands tremble alarmingly. My head was starting to buzz as my system overdosed on adrenaline.

Not good. Not good at all.

We reached the door marked "Staff Only: No Unauthorized Entry'. I pushed it open and we went through.

TWENTY-THREE

Only about half the lights in the front of the store had been on, and it was dimmer still in the stockroom, with the high storage racks looming off like narrow darkened alleyways to our left, and the row of solid gun safes to our right.

I was leaning heavily on the crutch to counterbalance the weight of the Beretta in my right hand. It was getting heavier all the time and the spare magazine in my pocket bumped annoyingly against my hip. I stopped and fished it out, handing it back to Matt.

He looked at it blankly for a moment. "Are you sure?" he asked in a low voice.

I nodded. I was putting all my energy into focusing on what was to come and I didn't have anything left over to formulate coherent words. Besides, how could I tell him that I doubted I'd have the strength to fire the rounds I'd got, never mind to reload?

I was going to have to make them count.

And then, from a doorway ahead of us, a man stepped out into view. He was dressed in a dark shirt with an open ski jacket over the top. He wasn't particularly tall, quite slim, wearing gold-framed glasses. I recognised the size and the shape of him, rather than the face—Reynolds's partner from the kidnap attempt at the Lucases' place. The man who'd seen Reynolds captured and who had calmly abandoned him.

Cool, calculating, and not to be underestimated.

He came out with purpose, head already turned in our direction, gun in his right hand but held loosely, down by his side. Rosalind had called ahead. He knew we were coming, so we were not a surprise to him.

I saw his eyes flick to the space behind us, to where Rosalind should have been, covering the pair of us, herding us forwards. His eyes flew back to me, startled. He saw the Beretta in my hand and he started to bring his own gun up to fire, diving for the cover of the nearest wall of racking.

I stayed planted lump-like in the middle of the space between the racking and the gun safes. It felt as though I had a bloody great target painted on my chest. I had to stand and fight because I couldn't run and hide. And I had to be totally ruthless because I couldn't afford to let him get a second shot.

I swung the Beretta up, using my whole shoulder. The crutch was trapped tight into my armpit. I daren't let go of it this time, but I released the handle to wrap my left hand round my weakened right, wedging my elbow hard into my ribs to stabilise my aim. As a shooter's stance went, it wasn't exactly pretty, but it was the best I could do.

I didn't wait for the man with the glasses to complete his move, or give him a chance to drop the weapon, or shout a warning. I didn't attempt to aim for an area of his body where I might wound rather than kill him, either. Most of the time, unless you're looking at your target through a sniper's scope, that's a fallacy anyway. You shoot to stop, and if the other guy dies, well, at least it wasn't you.

I was vaguely aware of a hot white flare from the end of the gun facing me, and some part of my brain registered the fact that he'd fired fractionally first. I was a stationary target, which was bad, but he was moving, which proved better.

The shot went wide to my left, close enough to my ear that I heard the high-pitched whine as it passed, but that could just have been the outrageous noise of the report, bruising my ears. I sensed Matt flinch down behind me, but I didn't have the mobility to duck myself.

As soon as I had the sights more or less levelled on the centre of my target's mass, I pulled the Beretta's trigger twice in quick succession, no finesse, feeling the vicious slap of the recoil through my palm. It exploded along my arm and up into my shoulder, a jolt that took my breath away. If I'd missed I wasn't certain I could go again so soon.

I hadn't missed. The man with the glasses stopped moving suddenly as the realisation that he'd been shot caught up with him. After the initial shock, the pain hit him hard and fast. He froze, as though by keeping quiet and still he could somehow evade it.

You can't, friend. Trust me on this ...

With a kind of disbelieving grunt, his fingers opened to let go the gun, and he folded both hands almost tenderly across his stomach.

He staggered backwards a pace. Then his knees gave out, twisting him so his back hit the gun safe nearest to him and he slid slowly down the face of it until his rump hit the floor. He was starting to gasp now. He sat there, legs splayed out in front of him, staring at nothing.

I didn't so much lower the Beretta as simply stop making the effort to keep it raised. Without the support of my left hand, I could barely maintain my hold on the gun. The pistol grip was greasy with sweat. I grabbed the handle of my crutch so I could edge forwards. Matt was behind me like a shadow.

The man with the glasses looked up with difficulty as I reached him, like his head was suddenly too heavy for him to lift his chin. He gave a breathless little laugh.

"Who'd have thought it?" he murmured, wonder in his voice. He let his hands flop to inspect the blood that coated his palms, as though he couldn't quite work out how it had got there. I saw that I'd managed to place both rounds into his stomach. One had just nicked the belt of his jeans so the leather had split and frayed. The other was slightly lower, and the blood that oozed from it was very dark, almost black. *Probably from his liver*, I noted with detached interest. Without a medic he didn't have long.

His gun had fallen next to him, less than half a metre away from his thigh. Another Beretta. He seemed to have lost interest in shooting us, but I nudged it further out of his reach with the rubber tip of my crutch, just in case.

"Where is she?" I said.

The man's face twisted. "Get me a doctor."

"Tell me where Ella is and you'll get one."

"I need one now!" His voice was scared but there was more to it than that. He had the air of ex-military about him, and I guessed that he'd been around firearms enough to know how badly he was hit. He swallowed, desperate not to plead with me but prepared to do it, all the same. "I-I can't feel my legs."

"Where's Ella?" I repeated, dogged, shutting down the emotion that was struggling to rise, the sharp empathy with what he was going through. Behind me I heard the quiet hiss of Matt's indrawn breath.

The man with the glasses held out a moment longer, his breathing quick and shallow, then caved. He indicated with a sideways flick of his eyes, further back into the stockroom. "Range," he said.

"How many of you are there?"

"Just me and Reynolds." He was panting now. He made a poor attempt at a smile, but there was a bitter edge to it. "She said that would be enough."

I didn't need to ask who "she' was. I straightened, stepping awkwardly over his legs.

"Hey," he said, wheezy. "What about that doctor?"

I glanced back at him without pity. "When we've got Ella, and she's OK, we'll call you one," I said. "And if she's not OK, you'll wish you were dead anyway."

He tried to laugh again, but he was crying at the same time. The pain brought him up short, cut him off. "She should have finished you while she had the chance."

I gave him a tight little smile of my own. *Had everybody known but me?*

"Yeah," I murmured. "It's a shame about that, isn't it?"

As I hobbled away I sensed Matt hesitate next to the wounded man, torn over whether to help him or follow me. Eventually, Matt's desire to find his daughter won out. He caught up with me within a couple of strides. I glanced at him as he reached me, just to see how he was holding up. He was staring.

"What?"

"How can you just leave him like that?" he demanded in a rough whisper, gesturing backwards. "How can you just ...?" He tailed off, unsure what it was exactly that he wanted to ask.

You think this is easy?

I turned away, limped on. "You want your daughter back? This is the only way I can do it," I said thickly. "You saw what Reynolds was like with me. What do you think he'll do to her?"

Matt didn't answer. We'd reached the door to the range. I paused outside it, swapped the Beretta to my other hand while I wiped my damp palm on my sweatpants. Never was a garment more aptly named. I touched Matt's arm. He almost flinched.

"If it all goes bad and you get the chance to grab Ella," I said, keeping my voice low even though I knew the range was soundproofed, "take her and get out—understand? Don't wait for me." *Because if Reynolds gets his hands on me again, I won't be getting out ...*

Matt nodded, eyes so wide I could see the white of them all the way round the iris. He was scared witless, but he was holding it together for the sake of his child. If she remembered nothing else about him as she grew up, I thought fiercely, she ought to remember this.

The outer door into the range was on a strong self-closer, so nobody could accidentally leave it open. The last time I was there, the day I'd matched against Vaughan, it had just

318

been part of the scenery. I hadn't even noticed it. Now I could barely get the door open against its mechanical opposition. Matt had to lean in close and lend a hand.

Reynolds was waiting for us inside. How could he not be? As we pushed the inner door open I took in the whole scene in an instant, like the flash of a strobe, a snapshot.

He was standing on the other side of the small room at one of the firing points—the same one, coincidentally, where Vaughan had stood. Blond, good-looking and supremely self-confident, he was dressed in the same three-quarter-length tweed coat he'd worn that day on Boston Common and he was smiling the same friendly, open smile he'd given Simone at the Aquarium.

He was holding Ella so she was straddling his left hip with her little hands gripped so tight onto his coat it was like she was making fists in the rough material. He had his left arm around her body, supporting her, keeping her close. The very sight of him with his hands on her threw up a burst of white noise behind my eyes.

As we'd opened the door, Reynolds began to shift his stance, drawing his right foot back to present his left side—the side with Ella—as the target. He, too, had a semiautomatic pistol in his right hand and his grip on it was firm and strong. The gun was aimed at Ella's head, the muzzle almost touching her downy cheek.

I lurched a full step into the room and fought my flagging muscles to bring the Beretta up. This time, as I brought my other hand up to grab it, I jettisoned the crutch. One chance, and one chance only. After this, it wouldn't matter much one way or the other.

I saw him take in my shambling gait, my sweat-stained clothing, the fact that I needed both hands to raise the Beretta at all, and the effort it was causing me to do so. I saw the smile start to widen. I could almost hear the thoughts that rushed through his brain. He held all the cards. No way would I risk a shot when he was holding Ella so close, when I could hardly stand and my aim was likely to be all to hell. He might not have to bargain his way out of this, after all. Might not have to leave witnesses behind ...

And he made a snap decision. He took the gun away from Ella's head and began straightening his arm to aim at me instead, and I knew this was no idle threat. You only bother to threaten someone with a gun if you're reluctant to actually use it. Reynolds had no such qualms.

I'd humiliated him at the Lucases' place, and Matt and I had outmanoeuvred him at the apartment. And now he had the opportunity to kill us both and make his escape with a hostage worth millions. There was no contest. His only disappointment would be that he didn't get to make me suffer first.

His mistake.

The muzzle of my Beretta continued to rise in front of me, slow and ponderous, like the nose of an overladen airliner coming off the runway. It seemed to take forever, but actually it all happened in the blink of an eye. The gun reached cruising altitude and I stared along the barrel at a target so small the sights practically obscured it.

I'm sorry, Ella. I'm so sorry ...

And I took the shot.

The noise in the confined space was monstrous. The round hit Reynolds smack in the centre of that smug, self-satisfied smile. It smashed through both his front teeth with hardly a pause, continued its slight upward path grazing across the roof of his mouth, ploughed on through the stem of his brain, and then removed a good chunk of the back of his skull on the way out. It glanced off the bare concrete ceiling of the range at about the ten-metre mark and must have eventually come to rest somewhere in the thick sand berm at the far end of the elongated room, along with thousands of other spent rounds.

Reynolds's body jerked as if on a wire. It might have been my imagination, but I could have sworn that he just had time for the shock and the anger to register. I saw it on his face and was triumphant. He fell back, cannoned off the firing point and started to rebound forwards, with Ella still clutched to his body as he went down.

Matt unfroze and darted past me to grab his daughter before she would have gone crashing into the floor, snatching her from Reynolds's dying grip.

Ella, who'd been quietly terrified to this point, broke her silence with a vengeance. She screamed and screamed, on and on so the world didn't seem a big enough place to contain her anguish. She'd seen too much and it had finally broken her. Matt threw me a single desperate accusing glance and hurried out with his blood-spattered daughter in his arms.

I could hear Ella still howling as he ran with her through the stockroom and out into the front of the store. The sound faded like a passing train, dropping another level as the outer door from the range swung slowly closed behind them.

Dazed, with the after-effects of the shots still sending up a muffled buzzing in my ears, I let my hands drop to my sides and stared dumbly at Reynolds's body in front of me.

At least he'd fallen half on his side with his face tilted away from me, so I didn't have to look at it. His heart had ceased to pump fluids round his system, but the damage to his skull was sufficient that gravity ensured they continued to leak out of the entry wound anyway. A dark pool was seeping into the concrete around his head.

It was suddenly very quiet in there, and very cold. My crutch had fallen too far away for me to reach and I found I couldn't move in any case. I'd over stressed just about everything to make this last effort for Ella. Now it was done there was nothing left inside. I could almost feel my mind begin to drift. I remembered her screams. We'd saved her life, yes, but at what cost?

Somewhere in the far distance, I heard voices and shouting, but I didn't call out. My only action was to relax the fingers of my right hand enough for the Beretta to fall to the floor next to my foot. If it was the police, I didn't want there to be any more misunderstandings. And if it was anyone else, well, I simply didn't have it in me to do any more. Not when the only person at risk now was myself.

The door to the range crashed open behind me, but everything had taken on a surreal, oneiric quality, nothing was quite true any more. I didn't jump, couldn't turn my head as a figure moved round in front of me from the right. I wasn't even surprised when I saw who it was.

Felix Vaughan was carrying his favourite .45 H&K pistol in a double-handed grip and this time he had the suppressor attached to the end of the barrel. He approached Reynolds with soft-footed caution until he saw the gaping head wound. He paused a moment, staring at the body without expression. Then he straightened, shrugged out of his soldier's skin and let some pretence of civility cloak him again.

"You?" he asked calmly.

"Yes," I said in a remote voice. Staying upright was becoming an effort now. My right leg had begun to shake from the strain of taking all my weight. My vision was tunnelling down, prickling at the edges. For the first time since I'd entered the range, I realised that every breath burned a dark molten hole in the bottom of my lung.

"I assume the one in the stockroom is yours, also?"

Ah. Too late to call that doctor now, then ...

I didn't answer, but he nodded as though I had. He looked at me for a moment longer, a hard penetrating stare that stripped away the outer layers and laid me bare. I slid my gaze away, ashamed, and he crouched to better inspect Reynolds's face.

"Good shot," he said at last, with quiet intensity. "Well done."

And getting praise from him brought the whole of my revulsion for the actions I'd just taken bubbling to the surface. My stomach heaved. I whirled away from him and put too much weight through my injured leg. It collapsed under me.

Vaughan caught me with surprising speed before I hit the floor. I should have been grateful but instead I fought against him, ineffectually and without technique, until I was utterly exhausted. It didn't cause him much difficulty, nor did it take long.

I leaned against the rough fabric of his coat and shut my eyes. He smelled of wood smoke and wintergreen. Anything was better than the dull coppery odour of Reynolds's blood.

In the periphery of my awareness, I heard more footsteps, running this time. Vaughan leaned back from me and called out to whoever was approaching. A second later the door crashed open again and then it was Sean who was in front of me, lifting me out of Vaughan's arms and up into his own as though I weighed nothing. I let him do it. The fight had gone out of me now and I doubt I could have made it out under my own steam.

As Sean turned away his gaze lingered on the corpse. "Reynolds?"

"Yes," I said through stiff lips. "He had Ella." It sounded plaintive, defensive.

Sean nodded, understanding more than I'd voiced.

"You did what you had to, Charlie," he said, and right at that moment I probably almost believed him.

He carried me back through the stockroom to the front of the store. Vaughan, no more anxious than anyone else to be alone with two dead men, was right behind us. He'd picked up my fallen crutch and was carrying it with him. The three of us followed the path Matt had taken with Ella. That meant we had to pass the slumped body of the man with the glasses, still sitting propped against one of the gun safes, hands now slack in his lap. He was still staring at nothing but, this time, nothing stared right back. I averted my eyes.

In the store I found the two men who'd grabbed me from outside the White Mountain Hotel—Vaughan's men—

hanging around with guns in their hands and looking nervous. Frances Neagley was crouched next to Ella, helping Matt to mop the blood off his daughter's face and clothing with wadded-up paper hand towel. The child had quietened to grizzling until she caught sight of me and then she started to yowl again, an almost knee-jerk response.

Matt threw me a look that was half angry, half apologetic as he swept her up and carried her through into one of the offices behind the counter, closing the door firmly behind the two of them. Out of sight and out of mind.

Neagley's gaze was coolly assessing as she got to her feet, as though she had pieced together what it was I must have done in front of Ella to cause this kind of a reaction, and had come pretty close to the mark.

Sean put me down next to a chair and I drooped into it, leaning forwards to rest my elbows on my knees, scrubbing wearily at my face. My hands smelled of gunpowder and sweat and blood. The right one reacted slower and more clumsily. I let them drop and looked up to find both Sean and Neagley studying me.

"You OK?" the private investigator asked carefully.

I shrugged. "More or less," I lied.

"The cops are on their way," Sean said. "Are you ready for this?"

"Would it make a difference if I said no?" I watched Vaughan lean my crutch against one of the displays and move across to speak with his boys in quiet murmurs. "What are they doing here?"

Sean followed my gaze. "When we got to Vaughan's place we found that he was expecting us—as you probably know," he said. "But, fortunately for us, he was prepared to listen to what we had to say before it got to any shooting." He pulled a rueful face. "Good job, too, or we'd be filling a number of little wooden boxes by now."

"And he convinced you he hadn't got Ella."

He nodded. "And that Rosalind had sold us a pup," he agreed. "And then when she called him and offered him a

324

trade, it actually convinced him that we were telling the truth—that we'd genuinely believed he'd got Ella. He knew Lucas wasn't Lucas almost from the start—it was what gave him his hold over the pair of them. The last thing Vaughan wanted was Simone exposing the deception, or he'd lose his leverage. He never wanted to involve her in any of this. That's why he tried to persuade you to get both Simone and Ella out of line of fire."

Vaughan finished his conversation and came over, sliding his pistol inside his jacket as he approached. He'd clearly caught Sean's last words, because he favoured me with the ghost of a smile.

"I may be guilty of many things, Charlie, but child kidnapping and murder are not among them," he said flatly. "Besides, I doubt dear Greg and Rosalind are going to get away with any of this and I found I had nothing to lose by hightailing it down here and helping your boss bring them down." He waved a hand around him at the store. "After all, if that happens, I take over this place."

"Aren't you worried the police might look into your own business dealings a little too closely for comfort?" Sean asked, a hint of a challenge in his cool tone.

Vaughan showed his teeth more fully. "I'm a careful man. They can look all they want," he said. "Now, if you don't mind, I think we'll leave you to explain things to the cops." He handed Sean a set of car keys that I recognised as belonging to the Explorer, and nodded to me. "Good-bye, Charlie. And good luck."

I didn't respond, waiting until the doors had closed behind Vaughan and his men before I glanced back at Sean.

"What *was* he up to with the Lucases?"

"He's been using them as a central distribution point for stolen military gear," Sean said, almost casually. "Mixing it in with genuine surplus stuff. Quite a lot of weaponry, from what Lucas was telling me. You must have noticed how everyone seems to be using US Army-issue Beretta M9s? All from Vaughan's contacts."

"And Rosalind wanted out," I said. "In fact, I got the impression she never wanted in in the first place."

"Vaughan contacted Lucas when he was looking for an outlet and Lucas was quite keen to strike a deal, but Vaughan spotted him for a fake almost right away," Sean said. "After that, I don't think Rosalind had much of a choice if she wanted to keep up the pretence."

Neagley looked round. "Where is she, by the way?"

I flushed as the realisation struck. "Oh hell—we left her outside," I said guiltily. "Gagged and tied to a chair round the side of the building."

"I'll go fetch her," Neagley said, heading for the door.

"She admitted that she used Reynolds to arrange your partner's accident," I said to her. "I'm very sorry."

Neagley just paused and nodded, her face shuttered as though this news was no real surprise to her.

After she'd gone, Sean retrieved my crutch from where Vaughan had left it and leaned it against the side of my chair. I was coming round, I recognised, to the point where I might actually be able to use it. I made the effort to keep my mind locked on the present.

"Where's Lucas?" I asked.

Sean glanced round, frowning. "I don't know," he said. "We left him in here while we searched the place."

"You don't think—"

The lobby door banged open again and Neagley stood in the gap, looking pale and tense.

"Sean, you'd better come," she said.

I grabbed the arm of my chair and the crutch and heaved myself upright, every muscle squealing at the effort.

"No, Charlie," Sean said. "Stay here."

"That's what you told me last time," I said, "and look what happened then."

His mouth flattened but he helped me struggle back into my jacket, which had been still lying in a heap on the floor from when Matt and I had gone after Ella. Even after a brief respite, walking was a battle. Sean had to lend me some support or it would have taken all night to follow Neagley outside.

The cold instantly highlighted the residual dampness in my coat, arrowing straight into my chest. I started shivering as soon as the door had swung shut behind me. Neagley led the way round the side of the building. As I rounded the corner I wasn't sure what I was going to see, but the sight of Rosalind—still taped to her swivel chair but with a dreadful familiar stillness about her—wasn't it.

For a second I thought she'd frozen to death, and then I saw the gunshot wound to the middle of her forehead. I stared at her blankly, aware of two sets of eyes suddenly turned in my direction.

"I didn't," I said, swaying as the shock buffeted me. "We'd disarmed her, tied her up. Why the hell would I kill her?"

"Because she's the one who shot you?" Neagley said calmly. Sean's head snapped towards her and she shrugged. "Matt told me."

"I didn't," I said again, like sheer repetition was going to make them believe me. I had to swallow back the tears. "I—"

"Wait!" Sean said. He spoke quietly but it was still enough to cut me off. I followed his gaze and saw nothing but the Lucases' Range Rover, parked where Rosalind had left it. It took a moment for me to realise that the interior light was on.

Sean nodded to Neagley, who pulled the short-barrelled little Smith & Wesson out of her jacket pocket. The two of them circled round behind the vehicle, leaving me to flounder along behind them, moving dreadfully slowly over the frozen ruts of snow underfoot.

By the time I reached the Range Rover they had both front doors open and Neagley was pointing her gun firmly at the figure of Lucas, who was sitting slumped in the passenger seat with his head in his hands. Sean had used a discarded glove to lift Lucas's S&W revolver out of his hands by the barrel, being very careful not to disturb any prints.

"What happened?" Sean said, his voice gentle.

Lucas lifted his head blindly, tears streaming from his eyes. "I loved her," he said. "It broke my heart to leave her behind."

For a moment I couldn't work out who he meant. Then it clicked in that he was talking about Simone, rather than his oh-so-recently-dead wife. Simone as a child after she'd watched him kill the man she'd believed was her father.

"I gave up everything," Lucas went on, sobbing now. "Everything I had, everything I was, to become *him*." For the first time the disgust and the self-loathing tore through the veneer of the life he'd created for himself. In the distance came the first yelp of sirens thrashing through the night air towards us, but he didn't seem to hear them.

I glanced at Sean. He shook his head.

"And it was never enough," Lucas went on bitterly, staring out through the dirty windscreen at his wife's body. "She took everything I had to give and wanted more. I tried so hard to be what she wanted. But it was never enough ..."

It had started to snow again, big fat flakes that floated down and laid themselves almost graciously on whatever they touched. They had already covered Rosalind's head and shoulders like a white lace shroud.

"Lucas—," Sean began, but the other man shook his head vigorously.

"No," he said. "Don't call me that anymore. I spent God knows how many years trying to *be* Greg Lucas, trying to be the kind of husband Rosalind wanted. And then she took away the last thing that meant anything to me and tonight I realised, she never really wanted me at all, did she?"

He pulled back his focus and looked at me directly. "I found her out here and took that tape off her mouth and do you know what her first words to me were?"

I didn't answer and his gaze swept me up and down. "She said that you were half-dead and a woman, and you were still twice the man I'd ever be." His face crumpled, consumed by bitterness and anger and regret. "So I finally decided to become exactly the kind of cold hard ruthless bastard she wanted me to be," he said, "and I shot her."

EPILOGUE

Three months after I was shot, Sean and I walked through an unfurnished apartment on the Upper East Side in New York City, listening to the echo of our own footsteps on the polished plank floors.

I no longer had to use a crutch, but I still favoured my left leg a little, especially if I was tired. Intensive physiotherapy and spending just about every morning in the gym meant I was approaching something like my former level of fitness, but it was—as the physio at CMMC had predicted—a long road back.

"What do you think?" Sean asked as I moved over to one of the tall windows. If you stood on a chair and squinted sideways, you could just about see Central Park from the spacious living room. That fact alone should have added at least another thousand dollars a month onto the rent.

"It's fabulous," I said. "But are you sure about this?"

He shrugged. He had on the same dark suit he'd worn when we'd met Harrington the banker and Simone, that day in London. It was June and the temperature outside was in the nineties, but Sean still managed to look crisp and unflustered. He put his hands on my upper arms and turned me to face him.

"Are *you* sure about it?" he asked softly. "This partnership offer from Parker Armstrong is too good to turn down, but I will turn it down without a second thought if you can't face the thought of coming with me. Of living over here. I couldn't do it without you, Charlie. I wouldn't want to."

I didn't answer immediately, but pulled away from him and turned back to the window. I still hadn't gained enough distance from the Lucas job to find true perspective. As far as the law was concerned, I was in the clear. Parker Armstrong's formidable legal team had seen to that.

After all, they'd argued, I was still barely recovered from my wounds. The doctor with the perfect smile had expressed his disbelief that I'd been capable of walking through a building and shooting two men dead at that stage of my recovery. It must have been an act of extreme determination, he said, for someone who had suffered such injuries to do what I had done. But there was something sad in his eyes as he said it, something disappointed. As though he hadn't expended so much of his energy and skill carefully repairing me, only for me to go out and kill people by way of a thank-you.

Sean and I had flown back into a rainy Heathrow and I'd tried to pick up the pieces of my former life. I worked hard on my rehabilitation, as though if people couldn't see the physical after-effects, they wouldn't see the freak I'd become. The stuff of children's nightmares, who sent a little girl I would cheerfully have died to protect into a fit of pure hysterics at the sight of me.

I hadn't seen Ella since that day at the surplus store when I'd killed the man who was threatening her as he'd held her in his arms. It was for the best, the child psychiatrists told me, if she never saw me again. My image was forever tainted with the kind of horrors no-one of Ella's age was ever supposed to witness. Just the mention of my name, they told me, caused her enormous distress. The very fact that it did so caused me enormous distress also, but I didn't tell them that.

Matt had taken her home to the house he and Simone had shared in north London, where the people who claim to be experts in this kind of trauma felt Ella might achieve some kind of stability. Harrington's bank had arranged a trust fund that, properly managed, would ensure she never wanted for anything in her life.

Apart, possibly, from a mother.

And I hope, when she's old enough to understand, that Matt will tell her the truth about what happened to Simone. Better for Ella to have the cold hard facts than to half-remember, and to wonder. And maybe to have history repeating itself in twenty years' time when she goes looking for her grandfather and finds him in a New Hampshire prison serving life for the murder of his wife.

After all, if Simone had been told the truth about the real Greg Lucas, would she have wanted so badly to track him down? Would six people now be dead?

"You did what you had to," Sean said now, as though he could read my thoughts. "Reynolds would have killed her."

"Would he?" I turned back to face him. "He knew what Ella was worth—and she wasn't worth anything dead. Maybe—"

Sean shook his head. "You couldn't let him take her," he said. "And you said as soon as he saw you—the state you were in—he went for a shot. You did what you had to," he repeated. "Let it go."

From the hallway we heard the apartment door open and a voice call an echoing hello.

"In here," Sean said, not taking his eyes away from my face.

Parker Armstrong ducked his head into the living room, smiling. A tall, slim man in his early forties, with artistically greying hair that seemed older than his face but not as old as his eyes. Sean's new partner. My new boss.

"Well?" he said, advancing when he saw us. "What d'you think?"

Sean raised his eyebrow at me. I hesitated just for a second, then plunged into a decision and felt a weight lift as I did so. I turned to Parker and smiled.

"It's perfect," I said, and thought I saw his shoulders ease a fraction.

He grinned. "So's the rent," he said, wry. "What use is it having family who own property in Manhattan, if you don't abuse your connections, right?"

"Right."

Parker held his hand out to Sean. "I guess this means we're in business," he said.

A slow smile spread across Sean's face as he took it. "I guess it does."

"Charlie," Parker said, offering me the same. "Good to have you with us." His grip was firm and dry without being overly macho. One of the things I'd liked about him from the outset. "Losing Jakes was a bad time for everyone. He was a good guy. I hope this will be a breath of fresh air for all of us."

"So do I," I said, and meant it.

"We'll get the lease signed for this place when we get back to the office. You guys hungry? You want to go get something to eat?"

We rode south on Sixth towards TriBeCa and the Financial District, in one of the ubiquitous yellow Crown Victoria taxicabs that had the suspension of a water bed. I sat behind the driver, next to the window, watching the vibrant sun-drenched New York streets as they flashed past. Manhattan Island was small enough that it seemed so much more concentrated than London, more intense, and I wondered if I craved that noise and bustle as a means to drown out other voices.

I thought about Ella and wondered how long it would be before the memory of her faded. Her smile, and her healing kiss, and her screams.

And ultimately I thought about Reynolds and I replayed, as I'd done so many times since that night, the way he'd made his decision to try to kill me. Sean was right, to a point, because the moment Reynolds had taken the gun away from Ella's head and started to turn it in my direction, there was only going to be one possible outcome. One of us was going to die.

But that didn't take into account the fact I'd gone into that room with the image of Reynolds attacking me at the apartment burning fiercely in my mind. I hadn't wanted his meek surrender. I'd wanted his blood.

So I'd gone in there ready to take him out, not face him down. I'd known he was a natural predator and he'd taken one look at me and he'd decided I was easy prey, as I'd suspected he might. But at the end of the day, it was purely luck that he'd reacted in such a way that justified my actions, fractionally after the event.

Matt had asked me why I'd removed the suppressor from the gun before we went into the stockroom and I'd told him it was purely to save those extra seven ounces, but that wasn't the whole story. It was entirely plausible and nobody had questioned it since, but I knew if I'd gone in there and shot Reynolds with the suppressor still attached, I would have had a much harder time convincing anyone it was self-defence, rather than assassination.

So, still I ask myself the question: Did I kill him because I had no choice? Or because I made one?

ACKNOWLEDGEMENTS

Writing this book would not have been possible but for the patience and understanding of a number of very special people, who allowed me to pick their brains without a murmur. They are, in no particular order, fellow mystery author D. P. Lyle, M.D. for his superb detailed medical information; other fellow mystery authors Fred Rea and James O. Born for gun stuff and for US law enforcement info; gunshot wound survivor Mick Botterill for his unique insights; fellow mystery author and lawyer Randall Hicks for legal info and for attempting to keep me straight on some of my accidental British-isms; and friend Lucette Nicol for filling in some of the bits of Boston I'd forgotten. As always, if it's wrong, it's probably my invention.

Other answers to probably stupid questions were given freely, and with grace, by Barbara Franchi, MaryEllen Stagliano, and Jann Briesacher, as well as a number of the enthusiastic contributors to the DorothyL website. Thank you all for your invaluable assistance.

My thanks, too, to the staff at The White Mountain Hotel, and Jonathon's Seafood Restaurant in North Conway NH, and the Boston Harbor Hotel in Boston MA, for generously allowing me to set parts of the action in these outstanding locations.

As always, my advance readers were ferocious and vigilant. Thanks go to Judy Bobalik, Andy Butler, Peter Doleman, Emma Dunford, Claire Duplock, Sarah Harrison and Tim Winfield for not flinching, even when I did. My grateful thanks, too, to fellow author Tony Walker, who spotted another of my deliberate mistakes, and of course to my superb cover designer, Jane Hudson of NuDesign.

Some extraordinarily talented and generous people deserve thanks for lending more than their share of support to this book when they didn't have to. Above and beyond. I'm speechless other than to list their names—masters of their art Ken Bruen and Lee Child, and the incomparable Jon and Ruth Jordan at Crimespree magazine.

Finally, a special mention goes to Frances L Neagley, who made the generous successful bid in the charity auction in support of the Youth Literacy Program run by Centro Romero—held at the Bouchercon mystery convention in Chicago, 2005—to have her name used as a character in this book. You are included with great pleasure.

Zoë Sharp opted out of mainstream education at the age of twelve and wrote her first novel at fifteen. She became a freelance photojournalist in 1988 and wrote the first of her highly acclaimed Charlie Fox crime thrillers after receiving death-threat letters in the course of her work. She has been nominated (sometimes more than once) for Edgar, Anthony, Barry, Benjamin Franklin, and Macavity Awards in the United States, as well as the CWA Short Story Dagger. The Charlie Fox series was optioned for TV by Twentieth Century Fox. Zoë blogs regularly on her own website, www.ZoeSharp.com, as well as wittering on Twitter (@AuthorZoeSharp) and fooling about on www.Facebook.com.

ROAD KILL
Charlie Fox book five
by Zoë Sharp

The fifth in Zoë Sharp's highly acclaimed Charlotte 'Charlie' Fox crime thriller series.

"If you stay involved with Sean Meyer you will end up killing again," my father said. "And next time, Charlotte, you might not get away with it."

Still bearing the emotional scars from her traumatic first bodyguarding job in the States, Charlie Fox returns home trying to work out both her personal and professional future.

Instead of the peace for which she's been hoping, Charlie is immediately caught up in the aftermath of a fatal bike crash involving one of her closest friends. The more she probes, the more she suspects that the accident was far from accidental – and the more she finds herself relying on the support of her troubled boss, Sean Meyer, despite her misgivings over the wisdom of resuming their relationship.

Charlie's got enough on her plate trying to work out who suddenly wants her dead. The only way to find out is to infiltrate a group of illegal road racers who appear hell-bent on living fast and dying young.

Taking risks is something that ex-Special Forces soldier Charlie knows all about, but doing it just for kicks seems like asking for trouble. By the time she finds out what's really at stake, she might be too late to stop them all becoming road kill.

"It's really quite impossible to put this book down, but what really makes this—and the whole series—shine is how Charlie's kickass skills are rooted in her own femininity and character." Sarah Weinman, **Confessions of an Idiosyncratic Mind**

THIRD STRIKE
Charlie Fox book seven
by Zoë Sharp

The seventh in Zoë Sharp's highly acclaimed Charlotte 'Charlie' Fox crime thriller series.

'I was running when I saw my father kill himself.'

The last person ex-Special Forces soldier turned bodyguard, Charlie Fox, ever expected to self-destruct was her consultant surgeon father. But she is shocked to see him throwing away his reputation on the New York news, and knows she can't stand by and watch him fall.

That's not easy when the emotionally distant Richard Foxcroft rejects her help at every turn. The good doctor has never approved of Charlie's career choice—or her boss, Sean Meyer. Now, just as Charlie and Sean settle into their new life in the States, Foxcroft seems bent on ruin, taking his daughter and everyone she cares about with him.

But those behind Foxcroft's downfall have not bargained on Charlie's own ruthless streak. A deadly professional who's always struggled to keep her killer instinct under control, this time she has very personal reasons for wanting to neutralize the threat to her reluctant principal.

When the conspiracy reaches deep into a global corporation with unlimited resources, the battle is going to be bitter and bloody ...

*"Ill-tempered, aggressive and borderline psychotic, Fox is also compassionate, introspective and highly principled: arguably one of the most enigmatic—and coolest—heroines in contemporary genre fiction. Male and female crime fiction fans alike will find Sharp's writing style addictively readable. Breakneck pacing and a surprising undercurrent of wry wit make this one of the very best crime fiction sagas out there." **Paul Goat Allen, Chicago Tribune***

If you've enjoyed SECOND SHOT, why not try this brand new standalone crime thriller from the highly acclaimed author of the bestselling Charlie Fox series?

THE BLOOD WHISPERER
by Zoë Sharp

They took everything she had,but not everything she was

The uncanny abilities of London crime-scene specialist Kelly Jacks to coax evidence from the most unpromising of crime scenes once earned her the nickname of the Blood Whisperer.

Then six years ago all that changed. Kelly woke next to the butchered body of a man with the knife in her hands and no memory of what happened.

She trusted the evidence would prove her innocent. It didn't.

Now released after serving her sentence for involuntary manslaughter, Kelly must try to piece her life back together. Shunned by former colleagues and friends, the only work she can get is with the crime-scene cleaning firm run by her old mentor.

But old habits die hard.

Dealing with the apparent suicide of Matthew Lytton's wife at the couple's country home should have been a routine cleaning job. But Kelly's instincts tell her things are not what they appear—even if the police seem satisfied. She wants to trust Matthew but is he out to find the truth or silence the one person who can expose a more deadly game?

Plunged into the nightmare of being branded a killer once again, Kelly is soon on the run from police, Russian thugs and a local gangster. Betrayed at every turn, she is fast running out of options.

But Kelly acquired a whole new set of skills on the inside. Now street-smart and wary, can she use everything she's learned to evade capture and stay alive long enough to clear her name?

"Zoë Sharp is at the top of her game"
New York Times bestselling author Harlan Coben